About the Author

Mike Gayle has contributed to a variety of magazines including FHM, Sunday Times Style and Cosmopolitan. His bestsellers, My Legendary Girlfriend, Mr Commitment, Turning Thirty, Dinner for Two, His 'n' Hers and Brand New Friend are available in Hodder paperback. To find out more about his novels, visit Mike's website at www.mikegayle.co.uk

Praise for *Wish You Were Here*

'As you'd expect from Gayle, the laughs flow thick and fast, making this a top match for your sunny holiday spirits. ' *Glamour*

'An observant offering' *Heat*

'This book explores the strength of friendship, getting older and settling down with forthright honesty and humour. Wise, witty and with endearing characters, this is a feel-good read with lots of laughs.' *Woman*

'The prolific Mike Gayle knows a thing or two about the male psyche, and how not even an extended adolescence will prevent the pain from catching up in the end.' *Herald*

'If we needed more proof that men don't think like women, then Wish You Were Here delivers it in extra strength doses . . . A fun story of three 30 somethings as they come to rueful – and thankful – realisation that they are no longer 18.' *Candis*

'This book makes great beach reading . . . A heartwarming and funny tale.' *Love It!*

'A delightfully witty tale' *Star*

'This is Mike Gayle's sixth novel and his appeal lies in his ability to give even the most banal detail a lurid resonance, and to spell out the bleeding obvious in more ways than one could have thought possible. Yet the whole thing becomes almost hypnotically relaxing.' *Sunday Telegraph*

Also by Mike Gayle

Brand New Friend
His 'n' Hers
My Legendary Girlfriend
Mr Commitment
Turning Thirty
Dinner for Two

WISH YOU WERE HERE

MIKE GAYLE

HODDER

First published in Great Britain in 2007 by Hodder & Stoughton
An Hachette Livre UK company

First published in paperback in 2008

9

A CIP catalogue record for this title is available from the British Library

ISBN 978 0 340 89566 5 (A format)
ISBN 978 0 340 82542 6 (B format)

Typeset in Benguiat by Hewer Text UK Ltd, Edinburgh
Printed and bound by Clays Ltd, St Ives plc

Hodder Headline's policy is to use papers that are natural, renewable and recyclable products and made from wood grown in sustainable forests. The logging and manufacturing processes are expected to conform to the environmental regulations of the country of origin.

Hodder & Stoughton Ltd
A division of Hodder Headline
338 Euston Road
London NW1 3BH

www.hodder.co.uk

'Whatever happens in Las Vegas stays in Las Vegas.'

– Well known maxim attributed to holidays in Las Vegas
aka 'The Entertainment capital of the world'

For Mr and Mrs O'Reilly (Jnr)
who met on holiday.

Beware your local travel agent's

When you're sitting at home flicking through the bunch of holiday brochures you picked up from your local high street travel agent, you never really think to yourself: 'This will be the holiday that will change my life', do you? Granted you might think: 'This will be the holiday that will leave me broke for the rest of the year.' Or: 'This will be the holiday that I finally learn to speak the local lingo.' Or even: 'This will be the holiday where I won't snog random strangers.' But I doubt very strongly that you'll be thinking: 'This will be the holiday that will change my life.'

But last year this was exactly what happened to me: a cheap last-minute seven-night package holiday changed my life in a way I never could have imagined. And I don't mean change like making the decision to re-decorate the hallway when you get back, or to give up smoking (again), or even changing careers. I'm talking about a big change. A life change. A change that might not seem huge if you're prime minister of England but if you're say, a thirty-five-year-old man working for Brighton and Hove city council, and you've just split up with your girlfriend after ten years together, it will seem huge.

I'm talking about a change that spins you round one-hundred-and-eighty degrees. I'm talking about a change that hits you like a bolt of lightning. I'm talking about the kind of change that lasts a lifetime. I can still barely believe it. But it's the truth: a cheap package holiday changed my life completely. So take it from me, if change isn't exactly what you're looking for in life just beware your local travel agent's.

In the beginning

It all started, as these things do, with the end of something big: me and Sarah. Ten years we were together. And then one day she just packed some of her stuff and left. It was difficult to work out how we'd managed to travel from the one state to the other but somehow we had. Then three weeks later on a warm and sunny August morning she called by to collect a few more things and tell me when she was going to move out the rest of her possessions.

'This time next week,' she said as we stood in the hallway. 'Is that okay?'

'Fine,' I replied choosing to stare intently at the pattern on the carpet by her feet rather than at her directly. 'Whatever you want – although I'm pretty sure that you're not going to get it all into the back of your Micra.'

I'd meant it as a joke not a dig. (Although in the time that had elapsed since she had left I had made many jokes that were actually digs, and many digs that were nowhere near to being jokes, and a few digs that were virtually indistinguishable from being verbal assaults, such was their subtlety.) Anyway, I could tell from her face that she had taken my joke about her car as a dig at her. For a few moments I thought about explaining to her that I was over her and that normal service had been resumed but I didn't of course because that would've shown that I was sensitive to her feelings. Being sensitive, at least in her presence, seemed a tad too close to being vulnerable, which was a definite no-no with a vampire like Sarah. So instead of doing the joke explanation thing, I just stood there like an idiot and carried on staring at the carpet.

'Oliver's brother's got a van,' she explained, mentioning the 'O' word to me for the first time that day. 'He's agreed to help me move the rest of my stuff to the new place.'

Oliver was Sarah's work friend. I'd never liked him and I'm pretty sure he'd never liked me either. Unlike him, however, I was justified in my feelings on the grounds that he had clearly always fancied Sarah. I could tell from the moment she first dropped him into a conversation when he started working with her (Sarah was a senior case worker for Brighton Social Services) that he was bad news. When she came home from work her conversation was always 'Oliver said this . . .' and 'Oliver said that . . .' and then it was only a matter of time before it became, 'Oliver was telling me over lunch . . .' I couldn't say anything, however, because it was supposedly obvious that Oliver wasn't interested in her because he had a girlfriend. She came round to ours for dinner once but I never saw her again, because soon after that they split because things weren't 'working'.

I saw plenty more of Oliver though. Sarah became his shoulder to cry on. He'd come round for dinner at least once a week, and when friends came round to see us she'd invite him too. I once made the mistake of pointing out to her that as she spent every single second with him at work there was a strong chance that he saw more of her than I did. She didn't like that at all. 'He's just come out of the biggest relationship of his life,' she said. 'Can't you show even a hint of sympathy?' I couldn't of course because I didn't like Oliver. I found him insufferable, and overly conscientious and a bit too pleased with himself but I didn't say any of that. Instead I said that I would try my best and give him a second chance.

'Nothing's going on with Oliver, you know,' said Sarah, now.

'Even if it was,' I replied, 'it's not exactly any of my business any more.'

'I know,' she said. 'I just wanted to make it clear, that's all.'

Sarah's 'I know' comment, rather than being bitter and twisted, was, I think, meant to be comforting. She wasn't having a go at me. Rather she was stating a simple fact of life. Still, I wasn't comforted in the least.

'What time do you want to come?' I asked.

'Around ten?'

'That's fine.'

'Will you be in?'

'Do you want me to be?'

Sarah didn't reply.

I sighed heavily. 'Don't worry, I won't be here.'

Sarah looked visibly relieved. 'I'll leave the keys in the hallway for you when I go.'

Another long silence signalled the end of business. This was going to be the last time we would ever see each other. Though Sarah had moved less than twenty minutes away she had managed to separate our lives so well that there was little chance of overlap. She had switched supermarkets so that we wouldn't accidentally bump into each other in the cereal aisle; she no longer took early evening walks in 'our' local park; our local pub, The George, was now (at least for Sarah) a no-go zone; and as for mutual friends they all knew the score so there was no chance of an embarrassing encounter at a dinner party.

'Well, that's everything then,' she said. She glanced at the front door and then back at me and pressed her lips tightly together. 'Take care of yourself, Charlie.'

'You too,' I replied and then I offered a half-smile to signal that I appreciated this moment of warmth. She smiled back and in that instant I took a snapshot of her in my head. Brown hair tied back in a ponytail. Pale grey/green eyes. Fresh-faced features. Small silver hoop earrings. Mint-coloured pinstriped jacket. Green vest top. Tight blue jeans with huge black belt with silver buckle. Flat black shoes that looked like ballet pumps. A summer outfit.

Sarah then reached down to the floor by her feet and picked up the H&M carrier bags crammed full with stuff plundered from what used to be our bedroom. Without saying another word she opened the door, stepped into the communal hallway and closed the door behind her. Though I hated myself for it I found myself staring at the front door long after she'd gone, hoping and praying that there might be a sudden rattle of the letterbox signalling a last-minute change of heart. But it never came. She had gone. For good. And probably for ever.

At a loss what to do next I retired to the living room, collapsed on the sofa and turned on the TV. As I randomly channel-hopped, the phone rang. I couldn't help it but once again the first thought that leapt into my head was, 'It's her. She's changed her mind and she's standing on the front door step ringing me from her mobile.'

'Charlie, mate,' said the male voice at the end of the phone. 'What are you doing a week next Sunday?'

'What?' I stammered, battling with my disappointment. 'What are you on about now, Andy?'

'I'm asking you what you're doing a week from Sunday. That's what I'm on about.'

I projected myself into the future. All I could see was a lot of moping around the flat trying to make myself feel even worse than I already felt.

'Nothing much,' I replied eventually. 'Why?'

'Because you . . .' he paused to give himself a silent drum roll '. . . are coming on holiday with me.'

'Holiday?'

'Yeah.'

'With you?'

'Yeah.'

I went completely silent. This was typical of Andy. And I knew that if I was going to prevent him from talking me into something I didn't want to be talked into I was going to have to be firm.

'I can't.'

'Why not?'

'Because . . . because I can't.'

Andy wasn't fazed for a second by my sub-standard debating skills. 'You do know that I'm doing this for you, don't you?' he began. 'I was sitting here at home thinking about you and . . . everything that's going on and it just came to me – what Charlie needs is a holiday. Think about it. You, me and a nice beach somewhere hot. We can chill out for a week, sink a few beers and have a laugh – it'll be great. And you won't have to do any of the legwork either, mate. I went to a travel agent this afternoon and checked it all out for you. All you need to do is write me a cheque for roughly four hundred quid and in exchange

I'll give you the holiday of a lifetime.' He paused as if waiting for a round of applause. 'So what do you say?'

I had many reservations about my old college friend's suggestion, but they had less to do with the idea of going on holiday than with the idea of going on holiday with him. Despite his long preamble, I knew Andy well enough to know that this holiday wasn't about him wanting to help me out at all. It was about him wanting to go on holiday without his fiancée and using me as an excuse. He'd probably told Lisa that he wanted to take me away to help me 'get over Sarah' and while there might be a modicum of truth in that statement I strongly suspected a far more self-interested motive. I could just feel in my bones that Andy was going to use this holiday as a week-long practice run for his eventual stag-night, meaning he would inevitably end up dragging me to a lot of places that I wouldn't want to go to, persuade me to do things that I wouldn't want to do and generally force me to act in a way that wasn't really me at all.

And yet he was right. I did need a holiday. I did need a break from my usual routine. Sarah's leaving had completely kicked the stuffing out of me. And other than the option of going solo (which given my state of mind wasn't really an option at all) Andy's was the only firm holiday offer on the table. Fortunately for me I had one last trick up my sleeve – the perfect way to ensure that should he persuade me to go with him the balance of power wouldn't always be in his favour.

'What about Tom?' I asked.

There was a brief but telling silence.

'What about Tom?' he replied, faking indifference.

'Well, aren't you going to ask him too?'

'Of course not. Why would I conceivably invite a born-again Christian on holiday? It's not like they're particularly renowned for being the life and soul of the party.'

'But he's our mate.'

Andy sighed. 'To be fair to Tom, mate, even at university he was always more your mate than mine.'

'Well I'm not going without him,' I replied. 'So if you want me to go you'd better get dialling now because you're really going to have your work cut out for you.'

After that I didn't expect to hear from Andy on the subject of holidays again because I was absolutely confident that Tom would turn him down before he even managed to finish his first sentence. As I was getting into bed, however, just before midnight, the phone rang.

'You'd better start packing,' said Andy, 'because bible-bashing Tom is coming on holiday with us.'

'Yeah right,' I replied laughing. 'Do you think I'm going to hand over a cheque just like that so by the time I realise Tom's not coming you'll have cashed it and it'll be too late to back out? Give me a little bit of credit, Andy, I'm not that stupid. There's no way that Tom's agreed to come on holiday with us. In fact given the sort of thing I suspect you've got in mind for this holiday I'd say that you'd have more chance of persuading the pope to come with us.'

'Oh-two-four—' began Andy.

'What are you doing?' I interrupted.

'Encouraging you to call him.'

'Do you think I won't do it?'

'I'm telling you to be my guest. But just so that you know, Tom was actually much less work than you. All I said was: "Do you fancy coming on holiday next week?" And straight away he replied that August is always pretty quiet in his office and that chances are it should be no problem for him to get the time off.'

'You're telling me he said, "Yes," just like that?'

'My powers of persuasion must work well on the God fearing.'

I paused and mulled over the situation. This didn't sound like Tom at all. There had to be something else going on. 'You know I will phone him, don't you?' I warned Andy. 'And I'll well and truly kick your arse if you're winding me up.'

'Like I said,' replied Andy boldly. 'Be my guest. And when you do, just remind him that we're going on holiday to have . . . fun.'

The following Monday, Andy called me at work to tell me he had booked the holiday. When I asked where we were going he refused to say, on the grounds that he wanted it to be a 'surprise'. The idea of being surprised by Andy made me feel very uncomfortable indeed: he was the sort of person whose surprises tended to be genuinely surprising. For example, once when we were at college Andy announced that he was nipping out to get a paper. Seventeen hours later, he called me from Belgium to ask if I could electronically wire him enough money to fly home. He's that sort of bloke.

Regardless of my concern, I was actually so relieved to have a date fixed when I would be free of the four walls of my flat that I actually didn't care where we went. All I knew was that once Sarah moved out of the flat for good my life would be as empty as my home. And so the idea of being somewhere in the sun – if only for a week – seemed tailor-made for the peculiarities of my situation. I could escape day-to-day reality and recharge my batteries at the same time. And whether Andy had booked us in for a week in the Canaries or at a Butlin's in Minehead, it didn't matter. All that mattered was being somewhere else.

During that week Andy set a plan of action in motion. Tom (who was based in Coventry) would get the train down to Brighton on the Saturday night before the flight and stay over at my flat. Andy (who lived with his girlfriend Lisa in Hove) would come round to mine on the Saturday evening and stay over too. Following a leisurely Sunday morning breakfast we would make our way to Gatwick and catch the plane to our mystery destination. It felt good having a plan. For the first time in a long while, it felt as though I was moving forwards.

SATURDAY

Born again

It was just after three o'clock on the Saturday afternoon and I was standing in my bedroom staring at the empty suitcase in front of me. In terms of symbolism (always useful when you're looking for new and inventive ways to make yourself feel that little bit more unhappy) it was hard to find an object more fitting than an empty suitcase because my heart was empty and the flat itself was pretty empty too. Sarah and Oliver had been and gone while I'd been last-minute shopping for holiday stuff in town. In the time that elapsed between the two events they had managed to remove everything she owned. Now, given that when I'd bought the flat twelve years ago my furniture had consisted of a decrepit wardrobe, a musty-smelling chest of drawers and a sofa that I'd rescued from a skip; and given that the deal when Sarah had moved in two years later was that she would (with my blessing) systematically eradicate the flat of every single item of furniture and replace it with things that worked and looked nice (and hadn't come from skips) the flat was now, inevitably, empty. Oh, she'd left a desk in the spare room (I'm guessing because the front of one of the drawers has come off), a bookshelf in the living room and a few other items as well but these were all things that, like me, either no longer worked or were no longer needed.

Back to the suitcase. I had always hated packing. Always. This was mainly because I don't understand how it all worked. How was a person supposed to guess what they might need for every single occasion that might come up when visiting a foreign land? For instance, I have a band T-shirt that I bought when I was at college that says 'Death To The Pixies' on the front of it. Back in my college days I used to wear it all the time but now I don't wear it that often. That said, however, there are still times when I wake up at the weekend and think to myself, 'I really want to wear my "Death To The Pixies" T-shirt,' and I'll rummage through all the clothes in the ironing pile until I find it. And even though it's now grey (where it once was black and is now much tighter than it used to be), frayed on the neck and with loose stitching underneath one armpit, I'll put it on and wear it all day. And I'll be happy. And at the end of the day when it has fulfilled its function, I'll take it off and throw it in the dirty laundry basket where it will slowly make its way through the decommissioning process (dark wash clothes pile on kitchen floor to washing machine to tumble dryer to ironing pile in spare bedroom – where it will remain unironed until the next time I need it). Now, multiply the problem I have with my 'Death To The Pixies' T-shirt with a pair of favoured jeans, a white shirt that I think I look good in, trainers that are good for walking in (but not necessarily all that good to look at) and various assorted other clothes and accessories for which I feel various degrees of attachment and it becomes easy to imagine the problems I had with packing to go on holiday.

So how did I manage in the past? The quick answer is Sarah. She always did it. She'd get sick of me standing there slack-jawed with a 'Death To The Pixies' T-shirt in one hand and a pair of threadbare-in-the-crotch faded Levi's in the other and she'd kick me out of the bedroom and sort it out herself. And the funny thing is, even though I hadn't had anything to do with the packing of my suitcase, once we'd reached our holiday destination I would always (without fail) find absolutely everything that I needed for every occasion. The right shoes for the right kind of bar. The right shirt for the right kind of restaurant. The right shorts for the right kind of beach. Everything. And on the one occasion (a holiday to Turkey in year five of our relationship) when I needed the right T-shirt for a day of wandering round a local market I opened the case and there it was: 'Death To The Pixies' in all its faded glory, neatly ironed and folded right in front of me. Right there and then I took off my hat to her (she had packed that too). No one could pack a suitcase like Sarah. No one. I can't really remember what I did about packing suitcases before Sarah came into my life. I suppose that back in those days I had a lot less stuff so it was an awful lot easier just to pile everything I owned into one suitcase and close the lid.

As the afternoon began to slip away from me and the suitcase remained empty I came to the conclusion that the best thing I could do would be to leave packing until later in the day. Retiring to my now sofa-less living room I sat down on one of two old dining chairs Sarah had left behind and turned on the TV. An old episode of *Murder She Wrote* was on one of the cable channels but despite being drawn into the plot I switched it off after ten minutes because I was unable to adopt my usual slouching position. As I debated in my head whether it was too late to drive into town and order a new sofa from Argos (possibly something in black leather?) the phone rang. It was Tom. He was at the station and needed me to pick him up. As I put down the phone, picked up my car keys, grabbed my coat and locked the front door I remember quite clearly feeling happy for the first time in a long while. Tom's arrival meant that my holiday plans were in motion. There was now an implied momentum to my life. I was no longer stationary. Instead I was hurtling towards the unknown.

At the station I spotted Tom instantly amongst the crowd of recently arrived travellers. Though we were roughly the same age, Tom had always looked a good few years older than me. It was his lack of hair that did it. Tom had begun losing his hair in his early twenties and now that he was in his thirties I barely registered his lack of hair. There's something about men whose hair loss comes earlier in life that makes them cooler than the rest of us. It's as if they've had an entire decade to come round to the idea that their hair has gone for good and so by the time they reach their third decade it's quite clear that they patently don't give a toss about what's going on on top of their skulls. Possessing a full head of hair is no longer linked to their masculine identity. It's just the way things are. And when women say that they find bald guys sexy (and there are quite a few out there) it's this lot that they're talking about and not the late arrivals who are always too panicked by their hair loss to do anything other than look mortified.

'How long do you think we're going for?' I asked, staring at Tom's hulking suitcase and marginally smaller rucksack as I helped him load his luggage into the back of my car. 'We're going for seven nights. Not seven years.'

'And I bet you haven't even packed yet,' laughed Tom.

'You know me too well. How are you, mate?'

'Good,' he replied. 'Really good. And you?'

'Me?' I paused and thought about it for a few moments. Tom didn't know that Sarah had gone because I hadn't told him, although I reasoned that the situation would be pretty much self-explanatory once he saw the absence of furniture in the flat. 'All the better for seeing you,' I concluded.

In the past few years I must have seen Tom only a handful of times at best. This had more to do with conflicting timetables than a lack of desire. As far as I was concerned, even if I didn't see him for an entire decade he would remain, along with Andy, one of my closest friends in the whole world.

One Saturday afternoon about six years ago, when we had both managed to get our schedules straightened out, we finally managed to set up a weekend to see each other. Sarah had gone away to see her parents in Norfolk so I'd driven up the M40 to Coventry to stay with Tom for the weekend. It had been a while since we'd had a proper chat on the phone and even longer since we'd seen each other in the flesh, so this trip was in a lot of ways long overdue. It was great to see him. We spent the afternoon visiting hi-fi shops because Tom was in the market for a new system and in the evening we'd gone for a drink at what I assumed was his local pub. Anyway, we'd been doing the catching-up thing over a couple of pints of bitter in front of a roaring log fire when Tom suddenly gave me this oddly solemn look and told me he had some important news.

'I've become a born-again Christian,' he told me sombrely. 'I just thought you ought to know.'

He then took a sip of his bitter and looked at me expectantly, as though this was my cue to tell him my reaction. And if I'm honest I really didn't know what to say. I couldn't help thinking that it would've been easier if he'd told me he was gay, because at least then I could've given him a great big hug and thanked him for confiding in me. I could've shown him how accepting I was of this new 'side' to his personality by conjuring up a list of men that I reasoned I might be attracted to if I were that way inclined and had fun gauging whether there was any common ground in our 'types'. But of course Tom wasn't gay. He was a Christian, which though I tried hard not to, I admit I found disappointing.

I'd always found born-again Christian types to be little more than a walking cliché. I didn't really much care about what they got up to in the privacy of their own churches but it bothered me greatly when it all came out into the open. I didn't like them in the news trying to affect the laws of what is essentially a secular nation; I didn't like them handing me leaflets proclaiming that the Kingdom of God was nigh; and I especially didn't like them knocking on my front door trying to palm off their literature on me. In short if I were going to choose a group of people with whom I would genuinely like to have no contact at all, it would be born-again Christians. And now, much to my dismay, Tom was one of them.

Part of my surprise at Tom's revelation was based on a key factor that I was sure excluded him from potential born-again Christianisation: at university he had been pretty much the king of casual sex and though I hadn't kept track with his private life of late I was reasonably confident that little had changed. Over the course of the evening Tom proceeded to tell me how it had all happened. One evening a few months earlier he'd been out with a bunch of work colleagues when he'd got chatting to a woman sitting with her friends at the next table. He told me that much of what happened next was a blur of alcohol and sexual tension but the next thing he recalled was waking up the next morning in this woman's bed. And although this sort of thing had been a semi-regular occurrence in his life what made this encounter distinct was that he didn't know this woman's name and never learned it. The guilt of the experience stayed with him for a long time. He told me that he realised that ever since his dad had died when he was nineteen, he'd felt he had a huge void in his life that he had desperately been trying to fill. A few weeks went by and then a chance conversation with a female colleague at work resulted in his accepting her invitation to attend an Easter service at her church. For the first time in his life, he'd found what he had been looking for.

My reaction was puzzlement. I was convinced that Tom was just going through a weird phase which he would eventually come out of. (Weird phases that had affected various college friends and associates in recent years had included interests in: militant veganism, druidism, Krishnaism, agoraphobia, burglary and suicide.) And so when he commented: 'You think I've gone a bit mental don't you?' my reply, I have to admit, was: 'Yes.'

Subsequently every time I saw Tom, I half expected him to have taken up dressing badly or I waited with bated breath for him to start trotting out stuff about God and Jesus in the middle of a conversation about transfer rumours at Chelsea. But he didn't do any of these things. Instead, he was just the same as ever, only he seemed less, well, . . . restless . . . I suppose. Definitely less restless than me . . . or Andy . . . or any of the people I knew my age. He seemed as though he knew where he was going and why. As if everything was going to always be all right for him. And he didn't start spouting bible verses, singing hymns or being weird. He was simply less agitated.

A few months later Tom and Anne (the woman who had taken him to the Easter service) got together. A year after that they got engaged and the year after their wedding, Callum, their first kid, arrived swiftly followed by Katie, sixteen months later. And although I found it difficult over the years to stop thinking of him as being the victim of some sort of brainwashing conspiracy, over time that sort of stuff seemed less and less important and eventually I just went back to thinking of him as my friend Tom.

Every single day

Back at the flat Tom followed me inside and I offered to make him coffee. He asked if he could sit down and I said, 'Yes, of course, make yourself at home,' which was missing the point because I think what he was actually saying was, 'Mate, why haven't you got a sofa any more?' I decided that it still wasn't the right time to go into the Sarah thing and so disappeared to make his coffee. He didn't follow me into the kitchen and instead sat down on one of the uncomfortable dining chairs to wait for me.

'So how are tricks?' I asked, handing over his coffee on my return to the living room. It was a repeat of my greeting at the station but I was hoping that this time it would elicit slightly deeper answers that might shed light on why he had agreed to come on holiday.

'Good, thanks,' replied Tom.

'And Anne and the kids?'

'Anne's great . . . and the kids . . . as always they're that odd combination of complete brilliance and nail-biting frustration. Katie's three now, and Callum's four and actually starts school in September – which really freaks me out. I mean, once they start school that's it, they're almost off your hands.' Tom paused and looked pointedly around the room. 'So is this what you trendy Brighton types call minimalist living?'

'Do you like it?' I replied. 'My interior designer did it. She's very good. I'd recommend her to anyone although I do think that living with her for ten years is part of the bargain.'

Tom sighed. 'Has she gone for good?'

I nodded.

'When did she go?'

'A while ago but she only took the last of her stuff this morning.'

Tom shook his head sadly. 'I'm sorry to hear that. I thought Sarah was really good for you.'

'Me too,' I replied.

'I suppose there's no way you two could sort your problems out?'

I shrugged half-heartedly. 'Not really. It's not like it was a mutual decision.'

'Oh.' He paused and then asked: 'But you're all right?'

'Me?' I replied. 'I'm a bit down obviously but it's nothing that can't be cured by a week in the sun.'

Tom nodded again and sighed as though drawing a line underneath the subject and then launched into a conversation about the flat which led to other conversations about mortgages, work promotions, getting older and getting fatter, old friends who seemed to have dropped off the face of the planet and policemen getting younger by the minute. The one thing we didn't talk about was the one thing I wanted to know most of all. So in the end, rather than wait for him to bring up the subject, I just came out with it.

'So, mate,' I began carefully. 'Not that I'm not glad you're here but what made you agree to this holiday jaunt of Andy's?'

'I can always go home if you don't want me cramping your style,' replied Tom mockingly.

'Of course I want you to come,' I replied. 'It's just that . . . well when Andy came up with the idea I was pretty sure that you wouldn't be into it, that's all.'

'Because?'

I shrugged awkwardly. 'Because . . . you know . . .'

Tom laughed. 'Ladies and gentlemen,' he said with a theatrical flourish, 'presenting for your delight and delectation that world-renowned born-again Christian stereotype.'

'Come on though,' I said trying to dig myself out of the hole I'd just dug, 'you must know what I mean – a week in wherever Andy has booked us – well it's not exactly going to be bible friendly is it? I mean, I was pretty wary the second Andy called and my moral standards are pretty lax. I'm just wondering how he talked you round?'

'He didn't,' replied Tom. 'I wanted to come. The week before I'd been thinking to myself that I could do with a bit of a break and then Andy called and I thought, "Right, well that's that sorted".'

'So you're saying that Andy's phone call was a message from God?'

Tom smiled. 'All I know is that thanks to you guys I get a kid-free week off work in the sun . . . which is exactly what I need right now . . .' He paused and looked around my empty living room, '. . . and I'm guessing it's probably what you need too.'

'You're not wrong there,' I conceded amiably. 'Well, it's good to have you on board because there's absolutely no way I'd go on this holiday with just Andy.'

'Nor me,' he replied. 'Although I'm guessing that it wasn't his idea to invite me.'

'That's not exactly true,' I replied, as I attempted to

fudge the truth. 'You and Andy are mates; it's just the whole religion thing he's not into.'

'Maybe,' replied Tom, 'but I wouldn't call us mates. I mean, even at college Andy was always more your friend than mine.' Tom paused and smiled. 'Is he still the same?'

'Could he ever be any different?'

'Hasn't he even mellowed a little bit with age?'

'I think getting older has actually made things worse,' I replied. 'Opportunities to let loose aren't quite as forthcoming as they used to be when we were younger. And now it's like he's constantly this huge ball of pent-up energy waiting for the chance to be released. Say he calls you for a drink, you can't just have one, it'll be six or seven and then he'll drag you to a club. Say you fancy some company while you watch a couple of DVDs. The DVDs won't get watched and your home will be turned over for an impromptu party. In between he's as right as rain, but I feel as though he's always looking for his next opportunity for excess.'

'Is he still doing the painting and decorating thing?'

'Yeah.'

'I wonder if the people who pay him to paint their houses realise that he's got a first in Applied Maths?'

'I shouldn't think even Andy remembers that sort of information. The good news though is that he and Lisa are finally going to get hitched.'

Tom raised his eyebrows in surprise. 'They're still together?'

'She's what you might call long suffering. You know, sometimes I look at Andy and I can't help but feel as if the whole of his life is really fragile . . . actually forget that. What am I talking about? The whole of all our lives is fragile. Like the only thing holding us together is Sellotape.'

'I think you're right,' said Tom. 'But with Andy it always seems more obviously so. But he's always been a bit like that hasn't he? Even at college.'

'But that's just it. We're not at college and we haven't been for a very long time. We've all moved on.'

'Apart from Andy.'

'Yeah. Apart from Andy.'

'Anyway,' said Tom finally. 'What about you?'

'What about me?'

'I know you probably don't want to talk about it. But, really, how are you coping? I mean with Sarah gone after ten years together you must find yourself really missing her.'

'Every day,' I replied. 'I miss her every single day.'

Milk, two cans of Boddingtons and half a tin of beans

When the doorbell rang at about a quarter past eight that evening I knew it would be Andy. So when I made my way downstairs to open the door I was somewhat surprised to see his girlfriend Lisa with him. There was an air about Lisa, not of someone dropping off her boyfriend and then immediately going, but rather of someone who was coming in, possibly having a cup of tea and a general nose around and maybe a chat too. Childish as it might seem, I had been in a bit of a 'no girls allowed' frame of mind for some time (they're all unhinged/don't know what they want/all on the same side – delete as inapplicable). Of course women had their place in the world but, I reasoned, at this particular point in time their place wasn't my flat, with my friends, spoiling our pre-holiday enjoyment.

There was no doubt that Andy had done very well in getting (and even more so in keeping) a woman like Lisa. Though he was reasonably good looking (slightly less so than Tom but slightly more so than me) there was no arguing that Lisa was in her own quiet way the more attractive of the two. Her long brown hair was so dark that in certain lights it looked black and it framed the delicate features of her face perfectly. In contrast Andy had light brown hair with flecks of grey at the temples. His features were dark and craggy, as though he had lived a hard life working in a coal mine and his eyebrows were so heavy that they cast a shadow over his entire face. But what lifted his looks were his eyes. They were an immediately striking shade of green mixed with grey.

Andy had met Lisa in a bar in Brighton one evening seven years ago when the two of us were out for a drink. Lisa was Canadian and had been working for a food marketing company for a year but had only just managed to get an extension on her visa. When she and Andy first got together I used to joke that Lisa was only after him for a British passport. What other reason could there be for someone that attractive to be with someone as useless as Andy? Actually I was well aware why someone like Lisa would be with someone like Andy. He had charm. By the bucket load. And not cheesy smarmy charm either. But the good type that makes girls fancy you and boys want to be your best friend.

I'd met Andy through Pippa, a girl I'd just started seeing in my first year at college. One night when Pippa and I were out drinking in Brighton, Pippa's friend Lara brought Andy along to join us. After the pub a whole gang of us walked back to Lara's house in Coombe Road and Andy and I ended up talking. It was friendship at first conversation . . . a few notches down from love at first sight. Andy told me about a party that was going on in Kemptown that we'd be mad to miss. Though I knew that Pippa would be upset if I went to the party without her, Andy presented such a persuasive argument ('There'll be girls, and loads of booze and really good music') and was so steadfast in his refusal to accept no for an answer that in the end it was easier to say yes. And though my actions resulted in me getting dumped by Pippa the following day, the demise of my relationship led me to later pulling Holly, a mind-blowingly beautiful third-year fashion student who'd been at the party.

The downside of being Andy's friend was that there were times when he was no more and no less than a right pain in the backside. Back in college if I had an essay to hand in for the following morning, I would literally have to hide myself away from Andy because I knew if he found me I'd end up at a bar or a club or a party and then I'd wake up the following morning with a raging hangover and the essay still not done. And it would be me that would have to face the consequences of the big night out. It would be me that would have to sort out all the trouble that he'd get the two of us in. It was always me that had to clean up after him. I think that at the heart of the problem back then was the fact that Andy didn't want to grow up and did everything he could to delay the inevitable arrival of full adulthood. Once he left college he didn't want a career (hence his chosen diversion into painting and decorating). He didn't want the responsibilities of a mortgage (preferring instead to pay long-suffering Lisa rent).

The fact that he had finally relented to Lisa's suggestion that they get engaged said less about any supposed change of heart on the subject of matrimony and far more about the fact that even he was coming to realise that he couldn't stay twenty-one for ever. This was why I was sure that this holiday was more about him than – as he'd pitched it – about me. With his own wedding less than a year away, I could see that the holiday represented an opportunity for him to be young and stupid again. And I got a huge feeling of discomfort in the pit of my stomach that he was going to go all out to enjoy it.

'All right you two?' I said breezily greeting Andy and Lisa in a bid to cover my initial surprise.

'Yeah fine,' replied Andy. 'Are you going to let us in then or what?'

I suddenly realised that I was standing on the doorstep as though I had no intention of letting either of them past the door and quickly ushered them upstairs. At the front door to the flat I stopped and issued a sort of catch-all world-weary disclaimer: 'Sarah's taken her stuff. Yes, it is difficult to watch TV when a dining room chair is your only comfort. Yes, I will be buying some more furniture when I get round to it. No, I'm not interested in any furniture that you're trying to get rid of but I do appreciate the thought.'

Andy laughed and patted me on the back while Lisa rolled her eyes, kissed me on the cheek and followed Andy into the flat.

'Oi, Bullock!' yelled Andy in Tom's direction. 'Are you still in the God squad?'

'Just ignore him, Tom,' countered Lisa, digging Andy sharply in the ribs with her fingers. 'My boyfriend is a pig and he knows it.'

Tom seemed more amused than upset by Andy and as he hugged Lisa she commented on how long it had been since she'd last seen him. (Two years to be precise when Tom, Anne and the kids had come to stay with Sarah and me.) As Lisa released him from her embrace he turned to face Andy and the two men stood staring at each other for an uncomfortably long time and then they both burst out laughing.

'It's good to see you again,' grinned Tom.

'You too,' replied Andy. 'You too.'

As the two men fell into conversation I asked Lisa if she fancied a drink; this was the most subtle way I could think of to find out how long she was staying for.

'What time are you guys going out?' she asked, gazing around my empty living room.

'There's no rush,' I lied. I doubted whether my honest answer: 'The second you leave,' would've been appreciated.

'I'll stay for a cup of tea then,' she replied, 'but you can stop with the cold sweats, Charlie, I only came round because Andy needed a lift. I think in his ideal world he would've hurled himself from the car and had me drive by without stopping.' She leaned forward and ruffled Andy's hair affectionately. 'Isn't that right, sweetie? I'm cramping your style aren't I?'

'Massively,' said Andy with his eyes still fixed on the TV. 'I'll have a coffee while you're up there, babe.'

'Hang on,' she replied, 'it was Charlie that—' she stopped and sighed, something which I guessed she did an awful lot living with Andy. She looked at Tom. 'Since I've been nominated designated maker-of-hot-drinks for the evening would you like one too?'

'I'm fine thanks,' said Tom warily.

'No really,' said Lisa, 'I don't mind.'

'Okay then,' he replied. 'I'll have a coffee too if that's okay. White, no sugar. Thanks.'

'Right, you,' said Lisa addressing me in a tone that didn't invite any form of debate. 'Come and help me in the kitchen.'

As I stood at the tap refilling the kettle, Lisa rummaged through the various jars and tins that lived on top of the microwave looking for the coffee and the tea.

'So, how are you keeping?' she asked as she located

the tin that held the tea bags and fished one out ready on the counter.

'I'm fine.'

'Really?'

'Yeah, really.'

Lisa opened the fridge door and peered inside. 'Milk, two cans of Boddingtons and half a tin of beans,' she said woefully. She closed the door and rested the open milk carton on the counter in front of me. 'You're not fine at all, Charlie. At least that's not what this fridge says.'

'Well it's wrong.'

'And it's not what Andy says either. He says that you're still really cut up about . . . well, you know.'

I picked up a dirty teaspoon off the counter and ran it underneath the tap for a few seconds. 'Have you seen her at all lately?' I asked, avoiding eye contact. 'I know you two still see each other.'

'I spoke to her on the phone at the beginning of this week,' said Lisa after a few moments. 'It was nothing special. Just a catch-up call. We've been trying to come up with a date to have a proper meet-up somewhere in town.'

'How did she seem?'

'All things considered, she seemed okay.'

'Did she ask about me?'

'Don't, Charlie,' sighed Lisa. 'Please.'

I shrugged and stared at the kettle as it heated up in front of me. 'I've got some post for her.' I nodded at a pile of letters jammed in next to the tea bags on the microwave. 'It's mostly junk mail. I should've left it out for her to take with the furniture. I don't know whether she's that desperate for another credit card but if you're seeing her . . .'

Lisa declined the offer with an awkward smile.

'Fine,' I replied. 'I'll just bang them back in the post then.'

As the kettle finally came to the boil and switched itself off, I reached across to the wall cupboard, pulled out the first mug I could find and handed it to Lisa. It was only when it was in her hand that I realised that emblazoned across it was the inscription: 'The World's Greatest Lover.' Lisa just laughed and rested it on the counter while I stood there squirming with embarrassment.

Whenever Lisa came to my flat, she always made a big deal about the fact that she was quite fussy about the way that she liked her tea made and so usually made her own. Today was no different, and for some reason I found myself carefully studying her tea-making process. It didn't seem any different from my own.

'I need a favour,' said Lisa as she stirred the milk into her tea.

'What?'

She paused and looked at me. 'It's to do with Andy. I want you to make sure that he doesn't cheat on me.'

How was I supposed to react to a request like that? My gut instinct was to laugh it off but there was a look in her eyes that made me realise that this was no laughing matter.

'I'm not stupid, Charlie,' continued Lisa. 'I don't believe for a second that Andy came up with the idea of this holiday just for your benefit.'

'Well actually—'

'You don't have to deny it. You can still have the brownie points for being loyal to your friend, if that's what you're after.'

'Look,' I began, 'Andy might be a lot of things but he's not that much of an idiot.'

'Maybe not,' said Lisa. 'But he's not above trying anything once is he? Look, Charlie, I've got three brothers back in Montreal. I know what guys are like when they go on vacation.'

'I think you're forgetting that he's going away with an emotional cripple and a born-again Christian,' I replied. 'He'll be lucky to get anywhere near a girl with me and Tom in tow.'

She didn't seem convinced.

'All I'm asking is that you at least try to stop him doing anything he might regret.' Lisa paused and took a sip of her tea. 'You know he's going to ask you to be his best man,' she continued.

'No, I didn't,' I replied. 'He hasn't mentioned it at all. What about his kid brother?'

Lisa shook her head. 'You're his first and only choice.'

'That's really nice to hear and . . . well . . . I appreciate you coming to me like this but you know . . . I'm probably not the best—'

'You're his friend,' she interrupted. 'Nothing else matters does it? Surely you want what's best for him? Because I'm telling you now that if he's unfaithful I'll leave him. And I will not change my mind. Ever.'

'Have you told him that?'

'Not in so many words.'

'Maybe you should spell it out.'

'I told him that I didn't want him to go on this holiday and he's still going. I know what he's like, Charlie. And I know what girls on vacation are like too. And it scares me. This whole thing feels like some sort of mid-life crisis come a decade too soon. I know he'll get over it and then he'll feel like he's ticked it off his list of things to do before he gets married but if I try to stop him he'll just resent me. You know as well as I do that he can't always be trusted to use his best judgement . . . at least not without some encouragement.'

'Fine, I'll try,' I conceded.

'Do you promise?'

'I don't need to. I'm sure he won't do anything, anyway.'

'I hope you're right. But at least this way I'll feel better if I know you're looking out for him.'

Putting down her tea, Lisa walked over to me, put her arms around me and hugged me tightly. I bristled immediately. Andy's girlfriend was putting her arms around me, and we were in the kitchen out of sight of the others and though there was nothing going on I didn't like the possibility of this situation being even slightly misinterpreted. At the same time I suddenly recognised in Lisa the same desperate loneliness that had dogged me during my last days with Sarah. I couldn't help myself. I put my arms round her.

'He loves you, you know,' I whispered in her ear as she clung to me.

'That's nice of you to say,' she said quietly. 'But I don't think it's true.'

He really must be having some sort of early mid-life crisis

'Right, then,' said Tom as Andy returned from the bar carrying three pints of Hoegaarden. 'I know you've been enjoying keeping us in the dark over this holiday but enough is enough. Where exactly is it we're supposed to be going to tomorrow?'

It was now just after nine and the three of us were sitting in my local pub, The George. The George was nothing special. Just another one of those light and airy refurbished pubs with stripped floors, overstuffed leather sofas, a food menu that leaned towards the Mediterranean and a bar that featured a larger selection of bottled wines and imported beers than most. Its chief selling point was its clientele. Too lacking in loud music to attract the needlessly young but too trendy to attract the needlessly old, The George was the kind of place where a man of thirty-five could still feel at ease.

'Drum roll please, maestro,' said Andy as he set the beers down on the table. 'Prepare yourself to be shocked and amazed as once again your favourite uncle Andy delivers the goods because tomorrow, my friends, we are flying to . . . Crete.'

I stared at Andy in horror.

'I know,' said Andy, presumably mistaking the look on my face for delight. 'Genius, isn't it?'

'You do remember we've been to Crete before don't you?' said Tom, barely able to hide his incredulity.

'Of course I do,' said Andy defensively.

'And so you do remember what happened there?'

'Of course,' he replied. 'Which is why we're not only going back to Crete but we're staying in the same resort.'

'Malia?' I spat in outraged disbelief. 'Malia? You're telling me that of all the places in the world you could have chosen you had to choose the one place you know I would least want to go?'

'Hair of the dog,' said Andy firmly. 'Take your poison and turn it into a cure.'

'Andy, mate,' I said as calmly as I could, 'apart from the obvious that I won't go into right now, you know as well as I do that we can't spend a week in Malia. Malia's the unofficial capital of the Club 18–30 world. And in case you haven't noticed, Andy, none of us is between the ages of eighteen and thirty.'

'Exactly,' replied Andy, 'which is why I had to lie about our ages. So if anyone asks if you're thirty, Tom's twenty-nine and I'm twenty-eight next birthday.'

I looked over at Tom to make sure that I wasn't alone in thinking that this was the worst kind of bad news we could be hearing. Rather than being shocked, however, Tom apparently found the whole thing amusing.

'You think this is funny?'

'No,' said Tom chuckling to himself as he looked at Andy. 'I think this is what happens when you let McCormack book a holiday for you.'

'Tom's right,' said Andy calmly. 'This *is* what happens when you let me book a holiday for you. I mix things up. I make things happen. Think about it, Charlie. You had the best holiday of your entire life in Malia when you were twenty-five. What better way could there be of getting over Sarah than going back there and meeting someone else?'

The ice cube game

It all happened two years after Tom, Andy and I graduated from Sussex University and were living in a shared house in the Bevandean area of Brighton. At the time Tom was back at the university doing a post-graduate course, Andy was on the dole and I had got my first job in the lower echelons of the council's Economic Development unit.

Up until this point I'd never been on holiday with the two of them together. In my first year I'd spent a month Interrailing around Europe with Tom as he wasn't a lying-on-a-beach-soaking-up-the-sun type; and in my second year I'd spent a week on Kos with Andy as he wasn't a-museum-and-monument type. And so, as far as the idea of the three of us going on holiday together went, it just never seemed likely to happen.

But one summer evening Andy put forward the suggestion. While I was into the idea straight away I was sure Tom wouldn't be. But I was wrong.

'Sounds like a great idea,' he said. 'A week in the sun will give me the chance to catch up with all the engineering text books I'm supposed to have read by September . . . and have a few beers too.' With that settled, we came up with a list of criteria for what we wanted from the holiday. The list, as far as I can remember, went something like this:

1) Girls.
2) Places to meet girls.
3) Cheap alcohol.

Andy volunteered to book the holiday because he had the most free time and the following day, over dinner, he pulled out a list of three resorts that he had managed – with the help of the girl he'd chatted up in Thomas Cook – to whittle down from a cast of thousands:

1) Faliraki, Rhodes.
2) San Antonio, Ibiza.
3) Malia, Crete.

Whether it was because of the girl in Thomas Cook or because of his desperate need to go on holiday, Andy knew his stuff. He gave us a detailed presentation of not only the pros and cons of each resort, but each hotel and apartment block, too. Casting aside Ibiza on the grounds that we suspected the type of girls who went there might possibly be a bit too trendy for guys like us, we narrowed our options down to Faliraki and Malia. We debated the issues as best we could. Tom pointed out that the flight and hotel package in Faliraki was a bit cheaper than the one in Malia. Andy countered by making the point that the girls on the Malia page of the holiday brochure seemed marginally more attractive. We put it to a vote and despite Tom's earlier defence of Faliraki decided unanimously that Malia would be our destination.

We were already having the best holiday on record when, after two days, I first noticed Sarah and her friends lying on sun-loungers by the side of the hotel swimming pool.

She was absolutely amazing to look at. Shockingly so. And I was well aware that none of my tried and tested cheesy chat-up lines would have worked on her in a million years. A girl like Sarah required a special kind of approach. A one-off that would get me noticed without making me look like the sort of bloke from whom she'd run a mile. And so began my campaign . . . of smiling. That was it. Nothing else. I smiled when I passed her table as she and her friends had lunch by the pool; I smiled when I passed by her in the hotel's reception; and if we were out for a drink in the evening and our two groups met in the street, I'd smile at her then too.

I always gave her the same kind of smile too. Short, friendly, and not in the least bit suggestive, as though we were work colleagues or vague acquaintances. After the smile, I'd follow up with a quick exchange of eye contact and then look away. Initially she didn't notice me but then gradually her friends picked up on what I was doing so she started to notice too. Soon it got to the stage where if I looked up to smile at her she'd be all ready to smile straight back at me. And that was when I knew I was right where I wanted to be: slap bang in the middle of her consciousness.

Of course being in her consciousness wasn't the ultimate aim of my campaign. What I needed was the opportunity to take things further. And it came in the form of a night out organised by the tour operators billed as: 'The Club Fun Big Night Out' – a gigantic pub crawl involving about forty of us from the hotel.

Halfway through the night, having already consumed more flavoured vodka shots and luminous-coloured jello shots than would normally be advisable on an empty stomach, we were herded by the tour rep into a bar called Flashdance. Over his loudhailer the rep informed us that once we had downed the bar's free strawberry-flavoured jello shots we would have a couple of rounds of The Ice Cube Game.

The rules were as simple as they were off-putting to the sober. Two teams had to form a line behind each other in a 'boy/girl' fashion. The two people at the front of the line would then be handed a beer glass filled to the brim with ice cubes and instructed to pass as many ice cubes down the line as quickly as possible without using their hands. On realising that this so-called game was just a huge excuse for a free-for-all snogging session a number of the more attractive girl members of the pub crawl bailed out immediately. Sarah was one of them. I was just about to drop out myself as a fearsome-looking Welsh girl sidled up in front of me and grinned suggestively in my direction. In desperation I looked across at Sarah and realised she was already looking at me. She smiled. But this was a different smile to the others we had exchanged. Without saying a word she came and stood at the front of my queue. And without saying a word I squeezed out from behind the Welsh girl and – much to the chagrin of a short guy in glasses – slotted in the queue right behind Sarah.

Once everybody was ready to begin the game the rep handed out the ice-cube-filled glasses, returned to the podium and blew furiously into the whistle around his neck. A commotion broke out. The whole bar was yelling, screaming and cheering. While the guy at the front of the queue next to us was already doing battle with the girl behind him, Sarah had yet to begin. Tipping the glass up to her glossed lips she slowly sucked a solitary ice cube into her mouth and then turned to face me with a wry grin on her face. I put my lips to hers and closed my eyes as the ice cube slid a cool trail from my mouth to hers. For a moment I wondered whether I had misread the situation but then her tongue darted quickly into my mouth after the ice cube and I knew that I wouldn't be sharing any frozen water with anybody else.

SUNDAY

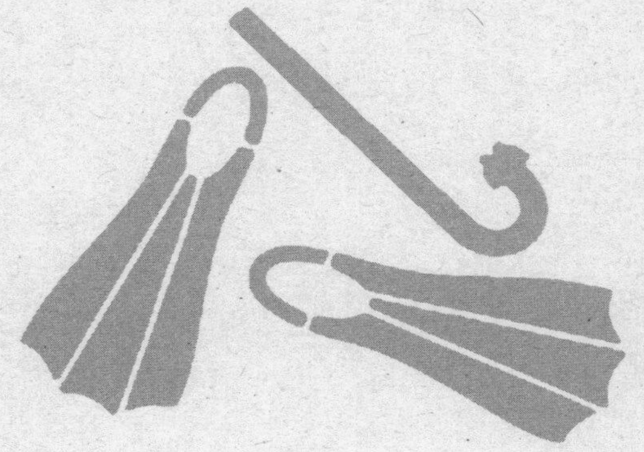

Long-stay car park blues

'Over there by that green Range Rover!' cried Andy.

'Forget the Range Rover,' said Tom. 'Head for that silver people wagon on the other side.'

'Sod it.' I slammed on my brakes. 'I'm just going to dump the car here and hope for the best. Because at this rate we really are going to miss the plane.'

It was now late in the afternoon on what had so far already been an extremely long day. Following Andy's revelation at The George that our holiday destination was to be Malia, he made things worse by badgering me into matching him drink for drink for the rest of the evening. Once we'd left the pub, he dragged me into an off-licence and bought yet more alcohol to finish off back at the flat. Anytime I looked even vaguely as though I was going to stop drinking he'd simply harangue me into having another. And though we did end up having a great time (I hadn't laughed so hard, sung so loudly or sworn quite so vociferously in a long time) I couldn't help but wish that sometimes he would turn his personality down a couple of notches.

At around three in the morning Tom declared that he was going to bed and although I wanted to go too, Andy held me captive for another hour until I could take no more and fell asleep on the carpet next to him. With no one to keep him company Andy allegedly did the only thing he could: he cracked open a few more beers, dug out a bunch of old *Fast Show* videos from a shelf in the hallway and stayed up by himself for another three hours until he finally succumbed to exhaustion.

Thanks to our late night, none of us stirred until well after midday. And when we did wake up, Andy insisted that we stick to our plan, the first part of which was breakfast at Stomboli's, a café in Bevandean that we used to frequent on a regular basis. It was comforting seeing the old place again with its fake wood-panelling wallpaper and cheery wipe-clean gingham table cloths. And even better to see that Georgiou the owner was still in charge. The only problem with our nostalgic late breakfast was that it dragged on far longer than the half an hour we had allotted for it. This wouldn't have been so bad if I'd already packed my suitcase but of course I hadn't. So once we got back to the flat I had no choice but to empty the contents of my wardrobe, chest of drawers and ironing pile into my suitcase and then randomly eject items of clothing until I could actually get the lid shut. Then I had just enough time to race around the flat making sure everything was safe and secure before finally squeezing all our cases into the back of my car and heading to the nearest petrol station. With a full tank of fuel I drove like the proverbial bat out of hell in the direction of the A23, thereby guaranteeing myself a sizeable number of points on my licence, if not a complete driving ban.

'You worry too much,' said Andy as we climbed out of the car and began unloading our luggage on to the tarmac. 'I promise you that speed-camera did not go off.'

'Of course it did,' I replied. 'I saw it flash.'

'You're wrong,' said Andy. 'Tom, tell him he's wrong, will you?'

'You're joking,' said Tom. 'It was a guaranteed licence-loser.'

Still arguing I locked up the car and then we made our way to the shuttle-bus stop. The warmer weather that had opened August had gradually faded away as the month progressed and as I looked up at the sky I could see that the sun was fighting a losing battle with the scattered cloud above. Regardless of the restrained sunshine all three of us donned our sunglasses without comment.

Just as I was beginning to believe that we might actually miss the flight, the shuttle-bus arrived. Even as we climbed on board, lodged our luggage in the space provided and took our seats my heart was racing. The thought of having to stay in England even one more day was bringing me out in cold sweats.

As we finally approached the front of the airport it was clear that pretty much everyone in the world was going on holiday. There were taxi drivers, family members, friends and lovers all parked in the bus's designated dropping-off zone. Right in front of us was a long white stretch limo that just screamed students with too much disposable income. Lo and behold a bunch of glamorous-looking types emerged from inside, spilling out on to the pavement. One of them pulled out a camera while the others congregated in front of the limo to have their photo taken. They all looked fresh-faced and energised, as though they were about to begin a new chapter of their lives. And despite myself I couldn't help but make the connection between them and my twenty-five-year-old self, recalling my own youth and eternal optimism. On the outside we didn't look all that much different; on the inside we couldn't have been more dissimilar. 'That's what a decade does to you,' I thought as I watched them laughing and joking. 'It changes water into oil.'

Strays

Standing in the entrance to the departure lounge with Andy and Tom ahead of me and the electronic doors hovering expectantly on either side I became gripped by the conviction that I had forgotten something important. I wracked my brain trying to work out what the missing item might be, but it was difficult to concentrate against the barrage of announcements over the Tannoy – delayed flights, opening check-in desks, heightened security – it was all putting me off. I double-checked my passport and tickets but they were safely tucked away in the back pocket of my jeans and I even opened up my suitcase and checked that I had my 'Death To the Pixies' T-shirt. When I closed the case I recalled what or rather who was missing – Sarah. It had always been Sarah's job to double-check that we had everything that we needed. That was why being here at the airport felt so odd. Without the safety-net of her presence, how could I be sure that I hadn't left anything important behind?

By the time I made my way over to the check-in desk there were only five minutes left until it closed but the queue was still some twenty to thirty people deep. Tom overheard something from the people in front of us about airport staff apologising over the late opening of the check-in desk that afternoon. We could finally relax. We'd been handed a reprieve.

The queue in front of us was made up of every sort of person. Old folk with luggage trolleys packed right up to the rafters; families over three generations who all seemed to be talking at once; well-groomed young couples clearly taking their first joint holidays abroad; preening young men with salon tans and highlighted hair pouting and posing to their hearts' content; scruffy-looking student types flirting with each other in a prelude to holiday foreplay; gangs of girls who looked as though they'd just stepped out of a nightclub; worried parents assisting their over-excited offspring with their luggage for their first holiday alone; rough-looking lads in baseball caps laughing and joking with each other; and then finally there was us: three relatively well-dressed but hardly stunning thirtysomething men suffering from varying degrees of hair loss. I'm sure we stood out a mile in our queue because we looked so incomplete – like stray dogs abandoned by their owners: grown men without their other halves.

Gradually the queue whittled down to us and a bunch of lads in their late teens who had attempted to push in ahead of us only to be set straight by Andy. The woman at the check-in handed the return tickets, boarding cards and passports to Andy, assuming in the way that everybody did that he was our leader.

'I'm going to get a paper,' said Andy. 'Anybody else want anything?'

'I'll come with you,' said Tom. 'I want to see if I can get a guide book to Crete.'

'What for?' asked Andy. 'All we're going to do is eat, drink, and lie on a beach. You don't need a guide book for that, do you?'

'If you think I'm going to spend all week staring at the

sun you've got another think coming, mate,' said Tom flatly. He turned to me and winked. 'You'll come with me on a few trips won't you, mate?'

'I'm easy,' I replied in a bid to keep the peace. 'I'll go anywhere with anyone.'

As Andy and Tom made their way to the newsagent's, I stood and watched a group of people who had obviously just returned from their holidays and had lost their way from the arrivals lounge. Some were wearing their market-stall-purchased straw hats as though they were still basking in the glow of the sun that they had long left behind. They looked relaxed and carefree, in stark contrast to the guys in the reflective yellow tops collecting the abandoned trolleys who looked miserable and hassled. Seeing these fresh-from-holiday people made me smile because what they had – their sunshine state of mind – was exactly what I wanted for myself. Maybe in seven days' time I too wouldn't feel quite so at odds with the world. Maybe I would return to Gatwick wearing clothing inappropriate for the non-existent British summer. Maybe I would come back changed somehow. Different.

In the pub the night before Andy had promised me that this holiday would turn my life around. He promised laughter and new experiences. New stories to tell and new women to tell them to. Though at the time I'd found myself thinking instinctively, 'Andy mate, that's asking a lot of a cheap last-minute package holiday,' but afterwards, as we walked home through the chilled Brighton night air I'd thought to myself, 'Maybe he's got a point after all. Everybody has expectations of holidays. We want them to restore us, entertain us and even find us new loves. So why should this holiday be any different?'

*

On Andy and Tom's return from the newsagent's we made our way through to passport control, now with only a security check between us and the departure lounge. When Andy stepped through the metal detector he set off the alarm, as did Tom – they had both neglected to empty out money from their pockets – so as I took my turn to walk through the detector I convinced myself that I too would somehow set it off even though my pockets were empty. It was with no small relief that I made it through without a single electronic beep or flash to the other side. I was through. I was safe. There could be no going back without a great deal of difficulty. Now I was standing in the kingdom of discounted perfume and aftershave; of multiple packs of fags and litre bottles of booze. This wasn't England any more. It was a shopper's paradise.

'Does anyone fancy a stroll around the shops?' I asked as Andy located a row of seats in the lounge to use as a base while we waited for our flight number to be called.

'No thanks,' replied Andy. 'I'm going to read my paper.'

I looked over at Tom. 'I'll give it a miss, mate. There are a few things I'm quite keen to check out in my guide book.'

Undeterred by my friends' lack of consumerist urges, I did the rounds of the various high street names inside the departure lounge alone. And although I didn't actually need anything at all I still managed to return from my sojourn with several packs of fruit pastilles, two bottles of mineral water and three books from Waterstone's.

'How long is the flight?' asked Andy looking up from his newspaper as I sat down next to him.

'Four and a half hours,' I replied. 'You're trying to work out if we'll have time to get to our hotel and then go and get slaughtered aren't you?'

'A wise man always knows how much drinking time is available to him.'

'Have you never heard of pacing yourself? I'm still feeling a bit rough from last night.'

'I would've been better off going on holiday with that lot,' chided Andy pointing to a group of girls featuring more peroxide highlights, spandex, gold rings, tattoos and naked flesh than any group of people had any right to. 'Do you think they're planning to go to bed as soon they reach Crete?'

'They're young,' I replied. 'They'll learn.'

'I doubt it,' said Andy. 'They might be young but I guarantee you they won't learn anything at all. Look, at me, I'm thirty-six next birthday and I'm proud to say that I haven't learned a single thing in my entire life.'

People to say goodbye to

We'd been discussing the phenomenon of how, when you've been away on holiday, someone famous always dies, when Andy was cut short by the announcement over the Tannoy of the departure gate for the flight to Heraklion. There was an instant flurry of activity in our corner of the departure lounge as people began to troop towards the gate.

'This is it then,' said Tom folding up his newspaper. 'Better give Anne a quick ring.'

'I suppose I'd better try Lisa too,' said Andy, pulling out his phone.

'Okay,' I said standing up. 'I'll see you guys at the gate.'

Tom and Andy both had people to say goodbye to but I had nobody and for a brief moment I felt as if the one thing I wanted most in the world was to have someone who wanted to hear from me. Someone who would miss the fact that I was no longer there. I considered calling Sarah and as I reached the queue for the gate I even pulled out my phone and scrolled through the address book for her number. But then I imagined her answering the call. And I imagined hearing the disappointment in her voice. And I imagined my reaction. And I knew I didn't want that feeling to be the last thing in my head as I got on the plane. So I turned off the phone before I could do any damage and slipped it into the carrier bag in my hand, next to my books and bottled water.

Even with the phone off, Sarah remained in my thoughts. She was there as we handed in our boarding cards and as we trooped aboard the shuttle-bus. She was there as we crossed the tarmac and climbed the stairs to the plane. She was there as we listened to instructions to turn off all mobile phones and electrical devices. And she was there as the emergency manoeuvres were drilled into us and the nearest emergency exits pointed out. She was even there as we prepared for take-off and taxied along the runway. But as the cabin began to shake and the roar of the jets filled our ears, her presence finally began to fade, so that by the time we had lifted up into the air and broken through the clouds above she was gone altogether.

Because when you go on holiday stuff like this happens

According to our pilot we would land at Heraklion airport at a quarter past eleven in the evening, local time. The flight had been fairly uneventful. With an initial burst of energy after take-off the three of us became quite talkative, taking great pleasure in unearthing a flurry of embarrassing anecdotes and memories from our student years, but as the journey progressed an oddly uniform lull spread across the plane and, with the exception of the odd screaming child, few passengers did anything other than eat, sleep, read or watch the in-flight entertainment: *Miss Congeniality 2*, an ancient episode of *Only Fools and Horses* and a documentary about clocks. I had entertained myself with the first of my three books: *Touching The Void* by Joe Simpson. A completely absorbing account of two friends who climbed the 21,000 ft Siula Grande Peake in the Andes only to get themselves in trouble on the way down. I'd seen the documentary they had made of the book a few years earlier at the cinema with Sarah. After the film Sarah had said to me that if it had been me and Andy on that mountain, Andy wouldn't have thought twice about cutting the rope and seemingly sending me to my doom. I'd told her she was wrong. Andy would never have cut the rope in a million years. It wasn't his style at all. But as I read the first few chapters of the book it dawned on me that I'd never really considered the situation the other way round. With Andy's life in my hand would I have cut the rope? I couldn't come to any kind of conclusion even after hours of internal debate. In the end I abandoned the book and distracted myself by watching *Miss Congeniality 2* without the aid of headphones.

With the sound of the electronic 'ding' the seat-belt safety sign switched off, plunging the entire plane into a flurry of frenzied activity. Passengers were frantically unbuckling, unloading the overhead storage lockers and squeezing into the aisles in a bid to be the first off the plane.

'What's the big rush?' said Andy a little too loudly. 'It's not like they're going to get to their hotels any quicker. They're still going to have to wait for everyone else.'

'I suppose,' I replied but the truth was, I was as eager to get off the plane as they were; like them I wanted to get my holiday started right away. Now I was on holiday my time was my own. I could go wherever I wanted to go and, more importantly, I could be whoever I wanted to be. I couldn't wait. And as our turn arrived to file into the narrow aisle and head towards the exit, it was all I could do not to run. As the cabin crew said goodbye I was too excited to reply, distracted by the exotic thrill of walking out of the air-conditioned cool of the plane straight into a thick fug of Mediterranean night air. The warmth was real. Almost palpable. Good things were going to happen to me in this country. I could feel it in my blood.

As soon as we passed through passport control Andy, Tom and I turned on our mobile phones and stared at them expectantly. But while Tom and Andy, despite their lack of messages, took great delight in comparing names and logos of the Greek mobile phone operators they had been assigned, I simply stared at my phone in disbelief. Unbeknownst to me, while we'd been in the air I'd received a text message from Sarah:

> **Message Sarah:** Charlie, I need to talk to you about something important. Please ring me when you've got a moment. S x

'What's up mate?' asked Tom, obviously reading the concern on my face.

'Nothing.' I shook my head as if waking from a dream. I quickly switched off. 'I'm fine. Just a missed call.'

Andy walked over to me and ruffled my hair as if I was a five-year-old. 'We're on holiday now, mate. Cheer up. Once we reach baggage claims me and Tom will get the luggage and you can go and get a trolley.'

Though I was already pretty sick of being organised by Andy, I didn't have the energy to protest. There were at least two flights that needed to be unloaded ahead of us and so it took quite a while for our luggage carousel to get started. And when it finally did get going, much to Andy's annoyance a good few of the passengers on our flight managed to get their luggage without a single sighting of our own. I however had my own problems to contend with. Sarah's text had sent my world into a spin. While I was curious about her message I was fearful of it too. I stared at my phone and silently cursed the progress of technology. A decade ago she wouldn't have been able to send me a guided missile via the airwaves. A decade ago I would have been blissfully ignorant of her desire to make contact. But it was now, not then. And despite my best intentions the message had been received. Loud and clear.

As I reached across with my thumb to switch off my phone I felt a tap on my arm. Standing in front of me was a girl wearing a straw cowboy hat. She had curly black hair, flawless mahogany skin and looked altogether amazing.

'You were on the flight from Gatwick weren't you?' said the girl-in-the-cowboy-hat in a bold south-London accent.

'Yeah,' I replied cautiously as I looked over her shoulder at a gang of girls in their mid-twenties who were trying their best to give the impression that they weren't watching us.

'I thought so,' said the girl-in-the-cowboy-hat. 'Which resort are you staying at?'

'Malia.'

'I knew it!' she exclaimed. 'Me and my friends are too. Have you been before?'

'Once, a while ago. How about yourself?'

'This is the third year in a row for me and the girls,' she replied.

'You must like it.'

'It's great. I guarantee you'll have the best time ever here.'

'That's good to know.'

She paused. 'Do you like clubbing?'

'Yeah,' I replied, mainly because I suspected that at least in her eyes this was the correct answer.

'Where do you go out in London?'

'I don't,' I replied. 'I'm from Brighton.'

'I know Brighton,' she replied. 'I've been clubbing there loads of times. I bet you're a regular at places like Purple Paradise and Computer Love.'

'Yeah, I know those,' I bluffed.

'Excellent,' said the girl-in-the-cowboy-hat. 'I don't suppose you know a bar in Malia called Pandemonium do you? It's on the main strip. You can't miss it. It's the one with the neon rabbit sign.'

'I could probably find it,' I replied.

'Well, I just thought you might like to know me and my friends will be in there around midnight tomorrow night if you want to join us.'

'That sounds great,' I said coolly. 'Midnight, tomorrow, Pandemonium.'

'Right then,' she smiled, 'I'd better go.'

'It was nice to meet you,' I said trying my best to hide my confusion.

'It was nice to meet you too,' she replied. She paused and then added: 'Oh, and bring your mates too. My friend Liz quite likes the one with the shaven head . . .' Tom. '. . . and my friend Luce quite likes the guy in the red top.' Andy. 'So, I might see you tomorrow night then?'

'Yeah,' I replied. 'Tomorrow night it is.'

Watching her walk away I was barely able to breathe as I considered what had just happened. It appeared as if an amazingly attractive young girl had just asked me out. I turned round to search out Andy and Tom to tell them my good news but they were standing right behind me wearing looks of pure bewilderment.

'Who was that?' asked Andy immediately.

'I don't know,' I replied. 'She didn't tell me her name.'

'She was spectacular,' continued Andy. 'What did she want?'

'I think she wanted to ask me out . . .'

'You're joking!'

'No, she invited me to join her and her friends in some bar in Malia around midnight tomorrow.'

'Now that is pretty amazing,' said Tom. He patted me on the back. 'Well done, fella.'

'You see?' said Andy. 'No offence, Charlie mate, but back in Brighton girls who look like that don't normally come up to blokes who look like you and say meet me in a bar around midnight, do they? The only place that things like that happen is right where we are now – on holiday.'

'This is too weird for words,' I said, still somewhat stunned. 'She even said that one of her mates fancied Tom.'

'Brilliant,' laughed Tom. 'It's always nice to know that you can still turn a few heads when you want to.'

'Just wait until they find out you're a married born-again Christian though,' teased Andy. 'So,' he continued, turning to me, 'which one of the girls fancied me?'

I opened my mouth to reply but stopped as I recalled my promise to Lisa. 'Sorry, mate,' I replied, 'she didn't mention anything about you at all.'

'Not a single word?'

'Nothing at all.'

'That's just because they've yet to feel the full force of my personality,' said Andy philosophically. 'You wait until tomorrow night when they finally meet me in the flesh. I guarantee you, my friend, the girls of Malia will be all over me like a rash.'

Steve-the-barman

With our luggage piled precariously high on a single trolley we made our way through customs and out the other side. It was easy to spot where we had to go next as waiting expectantly underneath an awning set up at the main exit were dozens of brightly jacketed holiday reps, clipboards and pens at the ready. Ours was a diminutive Glaswegian called Debbie who didn't bat an eyelid when we gave her our names and she pointed us in the direction of the coach that would transfer us to the hotel.

'Who'd have thought it would be this easy to shave five or six years off your age?' said Andy once we were out of earshot. 'There'll be no stopping us now.'

It took a good half hour for everyone assigned to our coach to arrive. Once we had our full contingent of passengers, however, our driver seemed determined to make up for lost time at all cost and drove with a recklessness that showed scant regard for his own or anyone else's safety. Despite the threat of impending doom, a combination of the constant growl of the diesel engine, the darkness outside and simple exhaustion sent me to sleep and I only woke up on hearing the driver bark in heavily accented English: 'Apollo Apartments! Quick! Quick!' from the front of the coach.

The three of us hurriedly gathered our things together and

launched ourselves off the coach. Leaving its air-conditioned cool we were once again plunged into the Cretan heat and within seconds were dripping with sweat.

'Home sweet home,' said Tom looking up at the lilac building in front of us; it had two floors and an outdoor terrace café that faced on to the road.

I was just about to ask Tom whether it was obligatory for all hotels to have some sort of reference to Greek mythology in their name when a male voice with a strong Welsh accent came from behind me.

'I see you've brought the weather with you then?'

I turned round to see a short, crumpled-looking middle-aged man with an overly red face. He was wearing a wide-brimmed straw hat tied underneath his chin to keep it in place, a bright pink T-shirt and Union Jack shorts.

'What an idiot,' he said taking into consideration our natural English sense of reserve as we stared at him blankly. 'It's all right, guys, I'm not just some random nutter. I'm Steve the bar man . . . but you lads can just call me Mr Barman if you like.'

Out of politeness we laughed and then watched as he introduced himself to our fellow residents (a group of six lads in their late teens and a couple of girls in their twenties). Along with the other new arrivals we followed Steve-the-Barman into the hotel lobby. Inside there was a small unmanned reception desk and standing next to it a large bright orange board with our tour operator's logo at the top. A cavalcade of leaflets was pinned to it, advertising a host of parties, barbecues and bar crawls. While Steve-the-barman took the group of lads and the two girls to their rooms the three of us remained in the lobby with our luggage momentarily lost in our own thoughts.

'I'm knackered,' said Tom eventually. 'It's two o'clock Monday morning back home. Normally I'd be in bed next to my Anne right now.'

'I'd probably be alone in bed right now,' I replied, 'which bizarrely doesn't seem like such a bad prospect at all.'

Andy sighed. 'What's wrong with you two? You're like a couple of old women. We're on holiday. There's no work tomorrow. If you want to sleep late you can. If you want to get up early and just stare out of the window you can do that too. This is what being on holiday is all about – getting the chance to do what you want when you want.'

'But it's two o'clock in the—' Tom stopped as Steve-the-barman returned.

'Right then, lads,' he said cheerily. 'I'll give you the guided tour shall I?' We all nodded. 'That over there,' he said, pointing to the gigantic wide screen TV which was showing an old Robert Wagner film, 'is fifty inches of top-class satellite televisual entertainment. It's got the lot. All the films. All the music. All the channels . . . all the sport.'

We all looked at the TV. He was right. It was stupidly large. Ridiculously so. It was probably visible from space. But the picture seemed wrong. The colours seemed too bright and the picture had a soft sheen about it that was distracting.

'Which teams do you follow?' asked Steve.

'Arsenal,' said Tom. 'But I don't go to the matches.'

'Man City,' said Andy. 'Although I haven't been to a game in a few years.'

Steve looked at me expectantly. 'No one,' I replied feebly.

'I'm a Spurs man myself,' continued Steve quickly glossing over my lack of footballing allegiances. 'Although they haven't exactly had their best season have they?' He laughed. 'Anyway, there'll be plenty of European friendlies on during the week so you won't miss any of the action.' He paused and for a moment looked like an overgrown cherub. 'I hope you don't mind me asking, boys, but what made you choose Malia for your holiday?'

Tom pointed to Andy. 'It was his idea.'

'I only ask because . . . well, because we don't tend to get many people your age here.'

'What do you mean?' replied Andy shiftily. 'I'm twenty-eight.'

Steve-the-barman chuckled heartily. 'If you say so, mate.'

'Give it up, Andy,' said Tom. 'He knows we're over thirty because we stick out like a sore thumb – a thumb that's been battered senseless by a sledgehammer. Didn't you notice on the coach on the way over here that there wasn't a single person on it under twenty-five? They might call it an eighteen-thirty holiday but no one goes on these things past the age of twenty-five.'

'It's true,' said Steve-the-barman. 'Compared to ninety-nine per cent of the lads and lasses in Malia you are ancient.'

'Even if we are a bit mature,' replied Andy, 'it makes no odds. Charlie here managed to pull some cracking bird at the airport without even trying.'

'Only because it probably wouldn't have occurred to her that people as old as us would dream of going on to somewhere like Malia,' said Tom.

'Do you remember when we used to go out on the pull when we were at university and we'd see packs of greasy old men eyeing up the girls we were with?' I said to Andy with a sigh. Andy nodded. 'Well, I've got a horrible feeling that we're the greasy old men now.'

'Enough of me yakking on at you, eh?' said Steve-the-barman uncomfortably. 'I bet you want to get to your rooms and freshen up a bit.'

We all followed him back to the reception, through an open archway and up a flight of stairs. 'Here we go,' he said, unlocking the door to apartment six. 'This way.' We all stepped into what appeared to be the kitchen but then right in front of us was a small table so I concluded that it was a dining room too. Then just behind the table was a large uncomfortable-looking sofa-bed which was clearly for the third person in the party, making it also a bedroom. We exchanged worried glances. The main bedroom was much better. There were two single beds, a wardrobe and a dressing table and very little else but at least it was clean. The only worrying thing was the temperature in the room.

'How do people sleep in this?' I asked Steve-the-barman. 'It's like a furnace in here.'

'They don't,' he replied, 'not unless they pay the extra to have the air-conditioning turned on.'

'We'll pay,' I said, without consulting the others.

'A wise decision,' said Steve-the-barman, giving me a wink, 'I'll get you the key and the remote control for the unit in a minute.'

The rest of the apartment was equally uninspiring. There was a TV but it had only three channels; a very basic tiled bathroom with a shower which Steve warned didn't really give out any hot water until about three in the afternoon; and then finally he slid open the doors to the balcony.

'You've done well here, boys,' he said, 'you've got a sea view. Not that you can see it now of course.'

I looked at the skyline and at the very bottom where the dark blue appeared to meet the black I could just about make out the lights of a passing ship.

'He's right you know,' I replied. 'We have got a sea view.' I looked down below. 'And a view of the hotel pool too.'

'Well, I'll leave you to it,' said Steve. 'The bar will be open as late as you like tonight if you want a drink in a bit.'

Yassou

We finally made it downstairs to the bar an hour and much arguing later. The problem was that no one wanted the sofa-bed and we couldn't agree a fair way of solving the problem. Tom suggested a rota but Andy hated that idea. I suggested drawing straws, but Tom said that the way his luck was running at the moment he would be bound to draw the short straw. Andy suggested that we arm wrestle for it but as I hadn't been near a gym for years I shot down that idea. In the end Tom announced that he would volunteer to take the sofa-bed if it meant that we could all stop arguing. Andy just laughed and muttered something about Christian charity in action. Relieved that we wouldn't have to sleep in the kitchen, Andy and I promised to compensate Tom by making sure that he didn't have to buy a single round of drinks for the rest of the holiday.

'What are you having?' I asked my friends. The bar was virtually empty apart from a group of lads in one corner and the girls that had arrived on our coach in another. Maybe people were put off drinking there by Steve-the-barman's dress sense, or the Billy Joel greatest hits album that was playing over the sound system.

'I'll have a pint,' said Andy.

'We're in Europe,' I replied. 'It's litres and half litres here.'

Andy sighed and sat on one of the tall stools in front of the bar. 'I'll have a litre, then.'

'Me too,' replied Tom.

'I knew you'd guys would be down,' said Steve cheerfully. 'Oh, and sorry about bringing up the age thing. Just to give you boys a proper welcome – and to show you that the Apollo Bar welcomes anyone no matter how prehistoric – I've got something special for you.'

Intrigued, we watched as Steve walked over to a large chest freezer and pulled out a plastic bottle filled with clear liquid. He carried it back over to the bar and then set three shot glasses up in front of us and began pouring.

'It's Ouzo isn't it?' asked Andy.

'Close,' replied Steve. 'Raki.'

He pushed the glasses over to our side of the bar, poured himself a glass too. 'Yassou,' he said, holding up his glass, and then on his cue we all knocked back our shots.

The small explosion at the back of my throat was instant. And as the flames licked their way down to my lungs, up to my nostrils and tickled the back of my eyeballs, it was all I could do not to cough and splutter like a schoolboy trying his first cigarette.

'You get used to it,' said Steve. 'You sort of have to because they serve it everywhere around here.'

Still chuckling, he began pouring our beers while Tom and Andy asked him questions about the best places to go in Malia.

Feeling removed from the conversation I announced to my friends that I was going for a leak and made my way to the lounge area where I promptly sat down on one of the large sofas near the pay-per-go pool table. The truth was I didn't need the toilet at all; I just needed to be on my own for a while. As much as I was enjoying being with my friends, the prospect of spending all day every day with them over the coming week was already beginning to overwhelm me. Things had changed a lot since our college days when we'd lived in each other's pockets. I'd got older. More grumpy. Less likely to put up with other people's nonsense. Now I was thirty-five I'd completely lost the tolerance required for living with anyone other than the woman I loved. Unfortunately for me, somewhere during the decade we were together, the woman I loved had somehow lost the tolerance for living with me.

I reached into my pocket, pulled out my phone and reread Sarah's text message, imprinting every word in my brain. Then, taking a deep breath, I pressed 'delete', and she was gone.

DAY ONE: MONDAY

Reptilian sensation

I woke up shivering. I peered through the dim bedroom at the flashing light on the front of the air-conditioning unit that indicated that it was on (thanks to Andy) its maximum setting. Grimacing, I looked over at Andy and watched as he snored oblivious of the arctic chill in the air. With a sigh I pulled on my T-shirt from the floor and then looked at my watch. It was just after ten o'clock.

As I slipped out of bed and continued getting dressed, I wondered how long Andy had been asleep. It wouldn't have surprised me if it had only been a couple of hours. As it was, the three of us had remained in the hotel bar talking with Steve-the-barman until nearly four in the morning. Once again Tom had been the first to bed, followed half an hour later by me. But I could tell from the look of determination on Andy's face as he labelled me a lightweight and finished off my beer that he was prepared to see in the daylight, because he had a point to prove: that when it came to excess he was a giant amongst dwarves. It was a message wasted on me: I already knew this and was more than content with my vertically challenged status.

Still, it felt wrong being the first one of us awake – almost unmanly. On the original holiday to Malia there had been an unspoken daily struggle between Andy and me to win the coveted title of Last Man Up. Although I managed to beat him on a number of occasions, and once even clocked up a staggeringly tardy six-thirty in the evening, it was always Andy who was the more consistent winner. I was nothing more than his pace-maker. Now a decade on, here I was awake while Andy and *even* Tom were both still asleep. I felt like a genuine lightweight.

Other than the cold, the main reason I was awake was due in no small part to the vast array of things on my mind. Everything from my encounter with the girl-in-the-cowboy-hat to my alcohol consumption over the past few nights and right through to a genuine sense of excitement at being on holiday had managed to wake me up and get me thinking. But right at the top of the list, straight in at the number-one position, was Sarah and her text message.

What did she want? Should I reply? Did she know that I had gone on holiday? Did she know when I was getting back? Why hadn't she called me directly? And was it bad news? Or was it good news? Did she want me back? Did I want her back? Were things not going well with Oliver? Was it about money? Or bills? Or change of address cards? There were just too many questions and not enough answers. And although I knew all it would take to put my mind at rest would be to pick up the phone and dial her number I was also well aware that all it takes is a slight shift in perspective for the easiest things in the world to become the most difficult.

The one thing I wanted from this first day of my holiday was for it to be untainted by Sarah in any way, shape or form. Today was too special for that. Too hopeful.

Picking up my sunglasses from my bedside table I walked over to the patio doors, held back the curtains, opened the latch and stepped out on to the balcony. Instantly I was transported from the middle of the harshest winter on record to the kind of record-breaking temperatures that result in people dropping dead from heat exhaustion. The sun seemed a million times brighter and more intense than anything I'd ever experienced. I'm pretty sure it was my imagination but for a few moments I could have sworn that I smelt the hairs on my arms singeing in the sun.

The balcony furniture consisted of two white plastic chairs, a small round table, a clothes airer, and a bucket into which dripped water from a pipe connected to the air-conditioning unit. I sat down on one of the chairs and carefully manoeuvred myself so that I could peer over the edge of the balcony and get a better view of the swimming pool below. Though the pool itself was empty, the loungers around the edge – there must have been at least forty of the things lined up together – were occupied either by a vast array of bikini-clad girls of all shapes and sizes or large beach towels with colourful logos.

Feeling too fragile to cast anything more than a cursory glance across the girls below I adjusted my chair to its lowest reclining position, leaned back, closed my eyes and instead basked in the almost reptilian sensation of my sun-starved body being brought to life. Within minutes the sensation of being baked had shifted from pleasant but tingly, to searing and uncomfortable, as though I might be seconds away from bursting into flame. But I didn't care. This was it. I was warm. I was free. I was on holiday.

That's just it

I ended up spending the next few hours shifting between a range of activities that included getting a few chapters further into my book, staring aimlessly into the sky, and wondering what I could possibly wear that might make me appear cool for my 'date' with the girl-in-the-cowboy-hat. I would've continued like that for a few hours more, too, if a bleary-eyed Tom, wearing only a T-shirt and boxer shorts, hadn't put his head through the gap in the patio doors and informed me that he was hungry.

'What are we doing for breakfast, mate?' he asked. 'I'm starving.'

'I was waiting for you and Andy,' I replied.

Tom ducked his head back into the room. 'Andy's out like a light,' he said, reappearing. 'I'll die of hunger before he wakes up. What time did he make it to bed? Dawn?'

I shrugged. 'How about we give him another ten minutes and then go out and get something?'

'All right then,' said Tom joining me on the balcony. He sat down gingerly on the hot plastic chair next to me.

'How long have you been up?' he asked shielding his eyes from the sun.

'A few hours,' I replied. 'Couldn't sleep.'

'And you've been sitting out here all this time? It's like being grilled on a barbecue.'

'It gets all right, after a while,' I assured him. 'And even if it does burn you, to a sun-hungry Brit like me there's nothing better than being toasted like this.'

Tom laughed and leaned back in his chair. 'So when was the last time you went on holiday?'

'Last August. Sarah and me went to Malta. It was nice. The hotel was fantastic.'

'Isn't Malta meant to be big with the grey brigade?' asked Tom. 'I know my grandparents have been going there every summer for the last ten years. They meet up with a whole bunch of friends that they made out there and spend all their time visiting places they've already been a million times before.'

'It is a bit like that,' I replied. 'When we first booked the holiday, the girl at the travel agent's tried to talk us out of it. She was really polite, but you could see in her eyes she just wanted to say: "Look, you'll hate it. It'll be full of British pensioners sucking humbugs." But it wasn't like that at all. It was really chilled out actually. Sarah and I loved it. We ate great food. Slept late everyday. And in the afternoons we just lay on the beach and read. We didn't go to a single nightclub, get drunk or stay up past midnight once. It was fantastic.'

'Sounds great,' said Tom. 'Before Anne and I had the kids we spent a month touring around Tuscany. The trip was worth it just for the food, let alone the scenery and the weather.'

'We were supposed to go to Tuscany this summer,' I said despondently. 'Some friends of Sarah's parents had a villa out there and they were going to let us have it on the cheap. It would've been great too.' I paused and allowed myself the necessary indulgence of a small sigh. 'I can't tell you how different life is without her, Tom. It's like I've got all this time on my hands and no one to spend it on. When we lived together I always felt like I didn't have enough time to myself. If she ever went away for the weekend to see her parents I'd go mad trying to fit in all the things that I felt I was missing out on. I'd go to the cinema and watch stupid action films; I'd watch *South Park* box sets back to back; I'd eat takeaway food until it was coming out of my ears; I'd listen to music until the early hours. And then an hour before she was due back I'd steam around like a demon and tidy the whole place up. By the time she'd got back to the flat everything would be immaculate.'

'But that's good, surely?' said Tom. 'Now you can do all that stuff all the time.'

'That's just it,' I replied. 'Now I've got all the time in the world I don't want to do any of that stuff any more. Instead I just sit around hoping that Sarah's going to come back through the front door.'

Feeling suddenly self-conscious I opted to change the subject but before I could do so the patio door slid open and Andy appeared in the doorway, scowling at the sun and naked except for his boxer shorts.

'Now that is hot,' he said sliding a hand inside his boxers and scratching. 'How long have you two been up?'

'Half hour,' said Tom.

'A while,' I replied, in a bid to sound cool.

'Let's do breakfast,' said Andy firmly. 'I'm starving.'

'We were waiting on you,' said Tom. 'What time did you get to bed?'

'Half-five . . . maybe six . . . can't remember really.' He paused. 'I'm going to have a shower then.'

'Can't you do that after breakfast?' I asked.

'Nah,' he replied, 'after breakfast we should go straight to the beach.'

'So if you're going to the beach why would you bother having a shower?'

'You're joking aren't you? Now we're on holiday I can't take any chances. I mean, what if we bumped into the girl-in-the-cowboy-hat and her mates? No, from now on I'm on full-time duty, which means dressing to impress twenty-four-seven.'

I'll have what they're having

There is no greater sartorial challenge for the British male than deciding what clothing is appropriate for a day at the beach. Living in a country where the sun rarely makes an appearance has had the effect of shaking our confidence so much that when it comes to removing layers of clothing in the public arena we have no idea what to do. Show us a hail storm in deepest Aberdeen and we'll be appropriately attired in a matter of minutes. Put us in the sunshine in Crete and we'll be flailing through our suitcases for hours on end. Andy, for instance, interpreted the theme of 'dressing for the beach' as 'dressing for a game of five-a-side in the park' (white Reeboks, dark blue Adidas football shorts and a white England T-shirt). Tom took it to mean 'wear what you might put on if you were about to play a round of golf followed swiftly by some fell walking on the Yorkshire moors' (a pastel blue polo shirt, beige khaki shorts and a pair of chunky 'all-terrain'-style sandals). And I interpreted it as 'dress as if you're a thirty-five-year-old male trying to hang on to the last vestiges of his youth' (a T-shirt with a doctored image of Bruce Lee riding on a skateboard, a pair of cut-off camouflage print shorts, and a pair of knock-off Birkenstock sandals). Looking at the reflection of the three of us and our differing interpretations of the theme, the one thing

I was sure our individual looks didn't say was: 'We are going to the beach.'

Collecting together our essentials for the day (books, magazines, suncream) we made our way downstairs. In the hotel lobby there were a few lads milling about wearing only gold jewellery, shorts and trainers. Judging from the peeling skin on their backs they appeared to be veterans of this summer's assault on Malia rather than new recruits like us. Before we left the hotel I thought it wise to ask the Greek girl on the reception desk for directions to the beach. She just laughed and said: 'Out of the door, take a right, and follow the road to the sea. You can't miss it.'

Stepping outside into the intensity of the sunshine I immediately lowered the sunglasses on my head on to the bridge of my nose and looked around. Last night when we'd arrived I hadn't paid a great deal of attention to our surroundings. In the full glare of daylight I took it all in. The Apollo appeared to be lodged on one of the main roads in the resort as every other frontage was a hotel, car-hire shop or takeaway food emporium. Scattered along the pavements were various groups of young Brits chatting to each other, sipping water or simply posing. Occasionally a delivery truck laden with bottled water or the odd hire car went by but the main source of noise pollution (other than the constant club DJ mix albums being pumped out of speakers located inside every shop) was from the roar of chunky-wheeled quad bikes being driven by lads like the ones at our hotel.

'From scooters to quad bikes,' said Tom as two guys riding pillion passed by flicking the 'v's to their friends. 'Do you remember the scooters we hired last time we were here?'

'I still bear the scars from when I skidded off mine racing you and Charlie,' laughed Tom.

'Maybe we should hire one of these each for a bit of a laugh?' said Andy, enviously eyeing up a quad bike parked up in front of our hotel.

The last thing I wanted to do was let Andy talk me into hiring a quad bike so that we could relive our youth. My days of taking part in pointlessly reckless activities were long behind me. Now I no longer had a live-in girlfriend to look after me should the need arise I needed to be careful.

As we headed along the road towards the beach with the general aim of finding somewhere reasonably nice and cheap to have breakfast we played holiday resort bingo. Clothes shops selling T-shirts bearing comedic gems like 'I'm with stupid'? Tick. 'Authentic' Greek restaurants advertising 'English-style roast dinners with all the trimmings'? Tick. Grocery stores selling copies of the *Sun*, the *Star* and the *Daily Mirror*? Tick. Bars with ridiculously traditional English pub names like 'The Royal Oak?' Tick and bingo! Every cliché, everywhere, and they were all repeated on a constant loop along every single inch of the road. It was like a reproduction Blackpool but with better weather. It was a simulated Skegness without the North Sea. It was Little England in the sunshine.

We ate breakfast at Stars and Bars, an American-themed bar and diner with a British slant. The whole of the outdoor terrace had been empty when we'd sat down but the bar's owners had compensated for this by attempting to import a 'happening' ambience into the bar via three large TV screens positioned above our heads, showing various MTV channels. Their attempts were hampered by the fact that the sound had been turned down on all three screens.

Half distracted by the soundless MTV screen, we had barely glanced at the menus by the time our waiter arrived to take our order. Andy and I ordered lager (because it was cold and large) and then followed up with the 'Killer' English breakfast (bacon, eggs, sausages, tomatoes, mushrooms, hash browns, toast, tea and jam). Though Andy and I spoke to the waiter in English, for some reason Tom made the whole process more complicated by pulling out his *Rough Guide* book and earnestly murmuring a few sentences in Greek. At first we assumed that Tom's pronunciation was so awful that the waiter had failed to understand a single word he'd said but it turned out that Kevin wasn't Greek at all. He was actually from Bloxwich near Wolverhampton and was spending the summer in Crete helping out in his uncle's bar to earn some money before going to university. It was all Andy and I could do to stop ourselves from spluttering with laughter as Tom sighed and mumbled: 'I'll have what they're having.'

Susie

Following on from our late breakfast we ventured to a grocery store to buy bottled water and a couple of day-old English tabloid newspapers and continued on our journey towards the beach. At various junctures along the way, one of us would point out a landmark that we recalled from our last visit. Tom indicated Kato's, a small nightclub that Andy had once got thrown out of for falling asleep on the dance floor, which had now changed its name to Eden. Andy pointed out the once open ground where we had played mini-golf every afternoon, now a new block of holiday apartments. And finally I spotted Ming House, the all-you-can-eat Cantonese restaurant that was now Luigi's, a takeaway pizzeria.

'They've even renamed the beach,' said Andy as we finally reached our destination.

I glanced up at the official-looking sign above Andy's head. 'Laguna Beach – this way'. 'What was it called before?' I asked trying to recall its name.

Andy shrugged.

'I think it was just called "the beach",' said Tom. 'That's how sophisticated things were back then.'

Laguna Beach was exactly what I expected of the Malia I had encountered so far. It was less a beach in the traditional sense of the word and more an alfresco nightclub. Two huge speakers were carefully positioned at the top of the beach to ensure maximum exposure of the kind of club tunes that I spent my whole life trying to avoid.

Resignedly we began making our way across the beach in search of a patch of sand without a sun-lounger parked on it. Ten feet on to the sand, however, we were intercepted by a tall bare-chested bronzed guy wearing black wrap-around sunglasses, cut-off shorts and a bum bag.

'Five Euros each,' he said in heavily accented English.

'We've got to pay?' said Tom incredulously.

'For that you get a pass, a sun-bed and umbrella.'

'No thanks, mate,' I replied. The idea of paying to lie on a beach just seemed wrong on all kind of levels.

'Come, come,' he said confidently. 'I will show you someone who will explain.'

I looked at Andy and he shrugged and then Tom looked at me and he shrugged too and because we were English and didn't like to offend people if we could help it, we followed him across the sand to three empty sun-loungers. The man waved across the sand to a pretty blonde in a bikini top and cut-off denim shorts who came running across with all the urgency of a lifeguard in action. When she reached us the bronzed guy gave me a cheeky wink and then disappeared, leaving the girl to introduce herself.

'Hi,' she said. 'I'm Susie.'

'Nice to meet you, Susie,' said Andy shaking her hand. 'Is that a Newcastle accent I detect there?'

Susie nodded. 'I've just graduated so I thought I'd come out here for the summer. I'm here during the day and then in the evening I work at Eden.' She paused and smiled. 'So how long are you guys here for?'

'A week,' said Andy. He winked at Susie. 'But it could be longer if you play your cards right.'

Even I could see that Susie was merely chatting us up in order to soften the blow when she asked us for money for our so-called beach card but Andy was lost in a fantasy world where he imagined that this girl really fancied him. I was reasonably sure that his flirtatious manner was more out of habit than actual intention. But thankfully before he could get round to proving me wrong she got to the point.

For the princely sum of five Euros each we would receive a card that would entitle us to three sun-beds and umbrellas for a week, ten per cent off any meal at Spetzi's Chicken Grill and a free cocktail (choice determined by the barman) at the Cool Breeze beach bar. We all signed up without the slightest hint of struggle. It was pathetic really. The fact that this very attractive girl was even talking to us seemed to render our cognitive faculties redundant.

Susie thanked us for our money, assured us that she would see us later and then shimmied back across the beach to where the tall bronzed Greek guy was standing with some other tall bronzed Greek guys. Suitably emasculated we arranged ourselves on the sun-loungers (left to right: Andy, me, Tom) and took in the view.

There were literally hundred of girls on loungers. Girls of every shape, size, race, colour and, presumably, denomination. Some were tanned to perfection. Others lobster pink. It was as if a women-only container ship had run aground and carefully thrown up its precious cargo on the beach right in front of us.

'You can't even see the sea,' complained Tom as he pulled out his *Rough Guide* book from his rucksack and began reading.

He was right too. You couldn't see the actual sea at all

from where we were because there were too many bodies around us. But there was a sea in front of us – a sea of flesh, long legs, tantalising upper thighs, tattooed backs, toned midriffs, lower buttocks peeking out through g-string bikini bottoms, side breast and (yes) even the occasional full breast with nipple. And though technically it should have been a glorious sight to behold I couldn't help but feel intimidated. It was as if every single one of the young women who surrounded us was fully aware of the power and allure of the feminine form. And uncharacteristically I longed to see these women clothed, if only because it would have provided a moment's respite from the feeling that I was never going to stand a chance with any of them.

The three of us had been keeping ourselves to ourselves, quietly reading on the beach for over an hour when suddenly a group of yobs barely old enough to buy alcohol legally in England began play-fighting in front of us in a bid to impress a group of girls sitting across from us.

'This is like a school field trip from hell,' said Tom slamming down his *Rough Guide*.

'I know what you mean,' I replied peering at them over the top of my sunglasses as one of the yobs dropped his shorts and mooned his friends. 'I keep looking at them and thinking: "Where's your responsible adult? Who's actually in charge of you lot? Surely at some point someone's going to round them all up and take them back to whichever borstal or secure unit they've escaped from."'

'But it's not just these yobs that are winding me up,' replied Tom, warming to his theme, 'have you seen that lot over there?' Tom discreetly gestured to a group of guys, roughly in their twenties, who were all defined upper body muscles, tattoos and perfect tans. They were flirting with a group of girls who, with their perfect hair, bodies and flawless skin, appeared to be their female counterparts.

'That bloke there has got a washboard stomach,' I said squinting in the group's direction. 'I don't think I've ever seen an actual six-pack that wasn't on the cover of some sort of fitness mag.'

'But do you know what's worse?' added Tom. 'Look around us and what do you notice that makes us the odd ones out here?'

I did as Tom instructed but as far as I could tell there were so many things that made us the odd ones out that it was difficult to choose just one. 'Is it the fact that we're the only blokes on the beach who look like off-duty geography teachers?'

'Nearly,' replied Tom. 'It's actually that we're the only people here wearing T-shirts.'

I looked all around. Tom was right. Most of the girls were in bikinis and every guy was topless. 'Do you think we should de-robe so we blend in a bit?'

'You can if you like,' replied Tom. 'But I'm keeping my T-shirt firmly on. I thought I wasn't in bad shape until I saw this lot. But this bunch of body fascists will probably call the police on us.' Tom paused and adopted a high-pitched Monty Pythonesque voice: 'Hello, is that the police? I'd like to report three lumpy thirty-five-year-old men on the beach lying around making the place look untidy.'

Tom and I laughed and then fell into an uneasy silence.

'But it's easy to look like that when you're twenty-one,' I said after a while. 'You don't have to exercise, you can just eat what you want and burn it all off arsing about all day.' I paused as a different bunch of guys ran past, pursued by a group of giggling girls. 'Do you know what? I'm half tempted to whip off my top and yell: "Enjoy yourself while you can because this will be you in ten years time!"'

'So why don't you?' asked Andy, his first contribution to conversation.

'It wouldn't make any difference if I did. They're already enjoying themselves as much as they can. Anyway, one way or another they'll learn that the party's got to end sometime.'

Andy had just returned from a trip to the grocery shop near the top of the beach to get various essentials like water, crisps and sandwiches when he paused and said in reverent tones: 'Now *that* is a work of art.'

Tom and I sat up and followed his line of vision as a blonde minus the top half of her bikini strode past our loungers towards the outdoor shower.

'She might be a work of art,' I replied as the girl stood underneath the shower and turned it on, 'but she knows it.'

'Doesn't matter,' said Andy unashamedly standing up to get a better view. 'If I was a girl and I had a body like that I'd spend most of my life walking around completely naked. I mean it – *all the time*. I'd be there prancing around stopping traffic, watching guys crash their cars and blokes on motorcycles smash into lampposts. I'd cause mayhem.' Andy laughed and finally sat down. 'The world is so lucky that I wasn't born a woman.'

As Andy returned to his newspaper and Tom returned to his *Rough Guide*, I settled back in my lounger and momentarily found myself thinking about Sarah. On our last holiday I found myself staring at her while she was engrossed in some book that she'd bought at the airport. And I remember thinking to myself that she was mine. This beautiful woman lying next to me was mine and nobody else's. And unlike the girls around us playing frisbee in the sea or the girls sunning themselves on the loungers or even the girl my friends and I had just watched take a shower, Sarah didn't know how beautiful she was. I liked to believe she didn't think stuff like that mattered. And in my eyes at least that made her even more beautiful. As that thought began to fade, I deliberately tried to stop thinking about Sarah because I wasn't sure how much I could take. And so I closed my eyes and enjoyed the calming sensation of the heat of the sun on my eyelids. And though my head was still full of thoughts, my heart remained as broken and as empty as ever.

The rest of the day slipped away without a fight. We lay on our loungers, stared at the sea and watched the girls go by. And now that we had experienced our first full day in the sun I felt as if I could relax. I could easily imagine how our daily routine might go and because of that I was sure that for the 'daytime' section of our holiday there wouldn't be too many surprises to encounter ahead. The 'night time' section however would be a completely different beast altogether. And I was well aware that, like Dr Jekyll and Mr Hyde, daytime Andy and night-time Andy were two different creatures altogether.

Leaving the beach towards the close of the afternoon we headed back to the apartment and came up with a plan for the evening: 'free time' until nine o'clock, then a drink in the hotel bar, followed by a meal out at the nearest half-decent restaurant. Then the main event: the bars and clubs of Malia until the early hours. Tom called his wife and kids and then took himself off for a walk; Andy meanwhile went to bed and promptly fell asleep; and I returned to the balcony to continue with *Touching The Void*. A short while before we were due to leave I came in and had my first (vaguely warm) shower of the day and got ready to go out. By ten minutes past nine all three of us were standing in the kitchen (aka Tom's bedroom) in our best glad rags (me: T-shirt and jeans; Tom: button-down polo shirt and chinos; Andy: T-shirt and cut-off camouflage trousers).

It had felt good having some time to spend getting ready for our big night out. As if the effort I'd put into making myself look half-decent would somehow pay off in admiring glances. Ultimately, however, the focus of my efforts for the evening was the girl-in-the-cowboy-hat. In spite of some initial reservations I was beginning to believe that something might actually happen between us. So much so that I began to imagine her name on what I hoped would be a long list of women whom I'd always refer to as 'The ones that came *after* Sarah'.

Hiya, boys

It was now just after eleven and Andy, Tom and I were in a taverna near the beach called Taki's Place, having just consumed our first authentic Greek meal of the holiday: chicken souvlaki in pitta bread with chips and tatziki followed by a litre of Carlsberg. As we waited for the bill to arrive we watched as a continuous stream of shirtless revellers screeched by on their quad bikes yelling to each other at the top of their lungs whilst attempting to run over anything that attempted to get in their way. It was like watching a junior facsimile of a hell's angels rally.

Leaving Taki's we began our expedition towards what Steve-the-barman had referred to as 'the main strip' – the dozens of cafés, bars, clubs and takeaway restaurants that made up the heart of Malia nightlife. It was like on the streets around Wembley on Cup Final day: with each step we were joined by legions of merrymakers whose destination was the same as our own. Young guys and young girls, all ready to party like it was a Saturday night back home. We passed smaller bars and restaurants that tried to tantalise us with offers of cheap beer, football matches on TV and pirate films that hadn't even been released at the cinema yet but not a single one could match the allure of our objective. As we reached the crossroads at the heart of the resort we were finally able to see our promised land in all its neon glory and hear it in all its stereophonic disco splendour.

Crossing the road to the main strip was like journeying across a checkpoint between two different countries: in one there was law and order and in the other anarchy reigned supreme. Even before we'd reached the other side of the road we saw a girl throwing up on the pavement while her friends held her hair out of the way; two paramedics attending to a shirtless guy propped up against the window of a fried chicken takeaway; and a gang of guys with their trousers around their ankles mooning a group of giggling girls.

'I've got a horrible feeling that tonight is going to be pretty grim.' Tom shook his head in despair as we stepped over a patch of sick on the pavement.

'You are so wrong, my church-tastic friend,' countered Andy. 'I've got a feeling tonight is going to be a night to—' he stopped suddenly as an attractive dark-haired girl caught his eye with a killer smile and reeled him in right in front of us.

'Hiya, boys,' she said standing directly in our path. The accent was English and northern. 'I'm Tasha. Where are you guys from?'

'I'm Andy,' said Andy. 'And I'm from Hove.'

'I'm Tom,' said Tom uncomfortably. 'And I'm, er . . . from Coventry.'

'I'm Charlie,' I added nervously, wondering if all this personal information would be used against us. 'And I'm from Brighton.'

'I've been to Hove,' she said ignoring Tom and me and focusing her attention on Andy. 'I've got an auntie down there. I'm from Chorley in Lancashire. Do you know it?'

'Yeah,' replied Andy. 'I've got family there too.'

'That's brilliant.' Without any hesitation she reached out and held his hand. Unable to believe my eyes I looked to Tom to reassure me that this whole exchange was as weird to me as it was to him. He flashed me a puzzled look by way of return that said: 'Surely it can't actually be this easy to go on the pull in Malia?'

'How long are you here for?' asked the girl, still holding Andy's hand.

'A week or so,' said Andy coolly. 'Maybe longer if you're lucky.'

I couldn't believe it. Andy was recycling the lines that he had used on Susie from Newcastle right in front of us.

'So is this your first night out?' asked Tasha.

'We arrived late last night,' said Andy. 'I would've gone out last night but these guys weren't up to it.'

'Well at least you're here now,' said Tasha confidently. 'And as this is your first night out then you lads should kick things off tonight in style . . . at the Eclipse, where we've got a two-drinks-for-the-price-of-one promotion going on all night.' Without pausing for a reaction, Tasha started dragging Andy in the direction of a dark, empty neon-clad cavernous bar. I could see the dilemma writ large on Andy's face. On the one hand he was flirting with one of the most attractive girls we'd seen so far but on the other she was only talking to him in order to drag him and his hard-earned money into an empty bar. Though he was clearly offended that she was so openly exploiting her sexuality (and his own), at the same time it was quite clear that there was part of him that just didn't care.

Andy looked at Tom and me forlornly as though he couldn't bring himself to walk away without our assistance.

'I think we're going to have to give your bar a miss tonight, Tasha,' I said, wrestling Andy's hand away from her. 'We're going to Pandemonium. Maybe another time, eh?'

'He's right,' said Andy in a voice that registered genuine disappointment. 'Maybe another time, eh?'

It was as though Tasha had just flipped a switch. In the blink of an eye she went from sex kitten to ice queen. The flirting stopped. The smile turned to a grimace. And Andy's face free-fell into disappointment. If we hadn't forced him to start walking away I'm sure he would've rushed back to Tasha and begged her forgiveness. In fact, even when we were well out of her reach he couldn't help turning around to watch as Tasha waylaid a group of lads coming the other way using the exact same technique that she had so skilfully employed on him only moments earlier.

The situation was so tantalisingly ripe for Tom and me to use as ammunition against Andy that we didn't have the heart – it would've been too easy. Instead, taking into consideration the fragility of his ego, we made the decision to move briskly on without further comment. This was difficult, because in the space of the next three bars we were stopped by two bikini-top-wearing girls from south London offering us free introductory vodka shots on behalf of Bar Go-Go, virtually manhandled into Galaxy bar by three Scottish girls in pink sparkly hats who offered three drinks for the price of one, and nearly lured into Club H_2O by a gorgeous girl from Birmingham with huge false eyelashes and an offer of a free fruit cocktail.

'It's quite insulting really,' said Tom as we extricated ourselves from the grip of the girl-with-the-false-eyelashes. 'These girls think just because they have great bodies and are drop-dead gorgeous that they can get us to do anything they like.'

'Well they can,' said Andy. 'The only reason I'm not standing in that first bar drinking the second of my two-for-the-price-of-one beers is because of you guys. Alone, I'd have folded like a pack of—' Andy stopped and pointed across to the other side of the road. We were here. We'd finally reached our destination: Pandemonium. Yet another neon-lit bar that, while not exactly empty, wasn't all that full either. But that didn't matter. What mattered was that I was convinced that it would be here where my luck would finally begin to change. Here I would rid myself of the spectre of my ex-girlfriend. Here I would meet the girl-in-the-cowboy-hat.

'Are you ready, Charlie?' asked Andy.

I looked at my watch. It was five minutes to midnight. 'I'm as ready as I'll ever be,' I replied and then, taking a deep breath, I looked both ways and crossed the road to meet my date with destiny.

Budweiser, okay?

Even from my short experience of the strip so far I knew that most bars in Malia relied heavily on loud pounding club music to provide ambience. The difference with Pandemonium was that the music was turned up just that little bit louder, as though the extra volume might make it stand out from the crowd. It was only when we reached the bar and were pointed by a barman in the direction of some banquette seating that we discovered that Pandemonium had one further trick up its sleeve: waitresses in bunny-girl outfits.

'Now this is what I call a holiday,' bellowed Andy as a waitress resplendent in pink fluffy ears, hot pants, fishnet stockings and heels passed by our table carrying a tray of tequila shots. 'What do you think to that, church boy?' Tom didn't reply. 'The girls in the bunny outfits,' said Andy this time nudging Tom with his elbow. 'Fit or what?'

'Hmm,' said Tom in a noncommittal fashion. He turned his head slightly and gave the waitress a cursory once-over, shook his head and then looked away as if to ponder some higher vision. It was only when Andy and I followed his line of sight that we realised that the higher vision Tom was pondering was the highlights of the England test match playing on a miniature TV screen above the bar.

'I like sport as much as the next man, but how can you

be watching cricket when there are women like this . . .' said Andy indicating yet another waitress slinking by our table, 'less than three feet in front of you?'

'Leaving aside that I'm happily married with two kids,' said Tom, '. . . fact is we're doing really well.'

One of the bunny waitresses approached our table. 'All right, lads?' she asked in a pronounced Liverpool accent as she leaned in towards us in an effort to be heard over the music. 'What can I get you boys tonight?'

'Anything you like, darling,' leered Andy.

'Three beers will do,' I replied quickly, giving her an excuse to ignore Andy.

'Budweiser do you?' she asked smiling in my direction.

'Yeah,' I replied giving her the thumbs-up. 'That'll do nicely.'

She turned and headed in the direction of the bar to deliver her order.

'Why don't girls at home look like that?' wondered Andy as he turned his head to get a better view of the waitress's legs.

'Because all the girls at home who do look like that are here,' I replied. 'I'm guessing they come for a holiday and stay because they can't stand the thought of going back to another grey summer in England.'

'But do you think it's in the rules that you have to be a babe in order to be allowed to stay? Pretty much every girl who has spoken to us since we got here has been amazing.'

'Don't know,' I shrugged, 'but I don't suppose it can hurt can it?'

We both fell silent as we spotted our waitress wending her way through the now-crowded bar with an almost balletic grace.

'There you go, lads.' She set the bottles down on the table along with a bill. Andy snatched it up immediately and then, presumably possessed by the spirit of Hugh Hefner, handed her a large Euro note and told her to keep the change.

'What?' protested Andy once she was out of earshot.

'What do you mean, what?' I replied.

'So I gave that girl a tip, big deal!'

'No, Andy, you gave that girl a gigantic tip because she was wearing a bunny outfit. You've been like a dog on heat since we landed last night.'

Andy rolled his eyes in despair. 'For once in your life, Charlie, why don't you have a go at being a bloke? It's actually quite a bit of fun when you know how.'

'What's that supposed to mean?'

'It means stop being such a self-righteous eunuch and grow a pair, because you're beginning to drag me down,' replied Andy.

'I'm dragging you down?' I repeated. 'I thought this holiday was supposed to be for my benefit?'

'It is,' replied Andy, 'but as the saying goes "You can lead a horse to water . . ."' He paused and looked around the room. 'I'm just saying instead of moaning about being thirsty all the time why don't you get yourself a drink?'

'And *I* will do,' I replied, willing the girl-in-the-cowboy-hat to choose this moment to walk into the bar, 'but don't forget *you've* got a girlfriend.'

Andy nearly choked on his beer. 'Are you bringing Lisa into this?'

I wished I'd kept my mouth shut. I wished Lisa hadn't asked me to keep an eye on Andy. And I sort of wished this night was over because it was already becoming too much of a strain.

'Forget it,' I replied, realising I hadn't got either the energy or the inclination to argue. 'I shouldn't have said that. And I'm absolutely in the wrong.'

'Too right you are.' Andy looked genuinely infuriated. 'I'm here to have a good time so just leave Lisa out of—' Andy stopped as two things happened simultaneously: first, the guy behind the bar turned the music down so low that for a few moments we could actually hear the conversational hubbub in the bar, and second, a huge commotion erupted near the entrance.

'What's going on?' asked Tom as the bar was suddenly deluged by a huge influx of revellers dressed in swimming goggles, snorkels and cheap-looking white T-shirts.

'Finally,' said Andy, rubbing his hands with glee, 'the entertainment.'

'What's he talking about?' asked Tom.

'Check out the T-shirts,' I replied, pointing to a couple of guys standing by the bar.

'The Club Fun Big Night Out,' said Tom reading the slogan. 'You're telling me that after all this time the mother of all bar crawls is still going?'

'Makes you feel sort of proud doesn't it?' said Andy. 'And they say young people have no sense of tradition.'

The Club Fun Big Night Out organisers ended up commandeering the rear half of the bar near where we were sitting. A young guy wearing a blue version of the white T-shirt appeared to be leading the proceedings and after a short while he turned on the microphone. Tapping it several times to make sure it was working he then jumped on to a raised platform to the left of us and bellowed in a broad Yorkshire accent: 'Welcome to the Legendary Club Fun Big Night Out! Are! You! Ready! To paaaaaaaarrrrrrrrtttttttttyyyyyyyy!'

The crowd gave a half-hearted cheer, which wasn't good enough for the holiday rep. He put the microphone back up to his lips: 'That's rubbish!' he chided. 'You need to make more noise. Now on the count of three . . . one . . . two . . . three! Welcome to Club Fun! Are! You! Ready! To paaaaaaaarrrrrrrttttttttttyyyyyyyy!' The crowd cheered back but the rep still wasn't satisfied. 'One more time!' he boomed into the microphone. 'Come on! Give it all you've got. Club Fun Big Night Out! Are! You! Ready! To paaaaaaaarrrrrrrtttttttttyyyyyyyy!'

Clearly motivated by the need to have this idiot stop shouting at them, the crowd yelled, screamed and whooped at the top of their voices like game-show contestants.

'That's more like it! Now let's get things started with one of my favourite party games and I'm sure it's one of yours . . . you know what it is . . . the ice-cube game!'

My jaw dropped.

'How brilliant is that?' said Andy, laughing uncontrollably. 'Mate, we should get up and join them for old times' sake.'

'No way,' I replied. 'And neither should—' I stopped as I realised that the back pocket of my jeans was vibrating. I reached for my phone and looked at the screen. It was a phone number I didn't recognise.

'Who is it?' asked Andy.

I shrugged, wondering if Sarah had perhaps bought a new phone. 'It's too loud in here,' I said to Andy, 'I'm going to answer it outside.'

'See you in a bit,' he replied.

Tom was sipping his beer, still engrossed in the cricket and I whispered in his ear: 'Keep on eye on Andy for me and make sure he doesn't get into any trouble, okay?'

'Yeah,' replied Tom, his gaze fixed to the TV screen.

'Will do.' I moved away but then returned: 'Oh . . . and keep an eye out for the girl-in-the-cowboy-hat and her mates.'

'I'll keep an eye out for everybody,' said Tom, wincing as one of the England team was bowled out. 'Go and answer your call, and trust me, everything will be just the same by the time you come back.'

That's the problem

The strip was now so busy it resembled Trafalgar Square on New Year's Eve. There were gangs of lads singing football chants, groups of girls singing along to Kylie Minogue, young guys in cars blasting out music from their in-car CD players and, watching over the entire proceedings, a small collection of stone-faced police officers. In a bid to get away from the noise I ducked down a side street next to Pandemonium and answered the call.

'Hello?' I began.

'Charlie,' said a female voice. 'It's me, Lisa.'

It took a few moments for her voice to register. 'Lisa?' I replied eventually. 'What's going on? How are you? Is everything all right?'

'I'm fine, honestly,' said Lisa.

'You had me worried there for a second,' I replied, 'I thought something must have happened.'

'I'm sorry.' She sounded genuinely apologetic. 'I knew I shouldn't have called you like this. It was a bad idea. I'll let you get back to doing whatever it was you were doing.'

'No, no, no,' I replied. 'It's fine. I don't mind you calling at all.' I paused. 'I take it this is about Andy?'

'Am I that obvious?'

'Transparent.'

'This is so pathetic.'

'No it's not,' I replied. 'You're worried and you're looking for a bit of reassurance. It's better you call me up and find out what's going on than sit at home driving yourself mental.'

'So how has he been?' she asked. 'I hoped he might call me tonight but I've not had so much as a text message to let me know you guys got there okay.'

'Well, let me bring you up to speed,' I replied. 'The flight was all right, the accommodation is okay, the weather is glorious and most of today we spent hanging out on the beach.'

'And that's all?'

'Yeah,' I replied. 'That's—' A group of lads passing by at the end of the street let off an air horn, cutting me off mid-flow.

'So where are you now?' asked Lisa. 'You sound like you're at a football match.'

'I think a football match would be less crowded than this. I'm outside a bar called Pandemonium. When I left to take your call Andy was staring into space and Tom was watching the cricket.'

Lisa laughed. 'So you're telling me I've got nothing to worry about?'

'Yes,' I replied, 'I'm telling you you've got absolutely nothing to worry about.'

'And you'd tell me if there was something to tell, wouldn't you?'

'I promise you, Lisa, other than tales of excessive drinking, I doubt that there will be anything to report back to you. And you don't want to hear about that do you?'

'No,' replied Lisa. Her voice was lighter now and less anxious. 'I'm really sorry, Charlie. You've been a sweetheart. You really have.'

'Look,' I replied, 'it's no problem at all.'

'Thanks, Charlie. I'm going to let you go, but just promise me this one thing, will you? Promise me you won't tell Andy I called.'

'Of course,' I replied.

There was a long silence.

'Okay,' said Lisa finally. Her voice was shaky. She sounded small and lonely. 'Well, have a good night then.'

'We will,' I replied. 'And you can call me as much as you want to. You know that.'

We said our goodbyes and then I ended the call and made my way back to the main street. For a few moments I stood on the pavement, jostled by passersby in both directions, thinking about Lisa. I couldn't get over how much she loved Andy. She loved him so much that she couldn't even bear to think about losing him and despite his many faults her love remained. And I thought to myself that that is what love must be – resilience in the face of opposition; knowing when you should give in and refusing to do so. Andy didn't know what he had in Lisa. He didn't know that she had what it took to make love work. He'd taken her for granted and would always do so because, unlike me, he'd never had a Sarah in his life to show him just how tough life could be.

Still mulling the call over I returned to Pandemonium and worked my way across the crowded bar area to the seats where I'd left my friends. A few feet away from my destination I realised that half of them were missing.

'Where's Andy?'

Tom dragged his eyes from the cricket and looked at me. 'He said something about going to the—' he stopped abruptly and instinctively I followed his line of vision across the room to the other side of the bar. Andy was frantically kissing a tall, dark-haired girl who was wearing a Club Fun Big Night Out T-shirt while holding a glass full of ice cubes.

'This isn't going to be a relaxing holiday at all, is it?' sighed Tom.

'No,' I replied despondently. 'I'm guessing this is going to be as stressful as they come.'

DAY TWO: TUESDAY

Let's hope it doesn't last long, eh?

Déjà vu. That was the feeling I woke up with on the morning of my second day in Crete – the sense that I had pretty much already seen this day begin before. I looked at my watch. It was just after ten o'clock. I sat up in bed and the sheet covering me slipped off my shoulders exposing my skin to the arctic chill of the room. I glared at the air-conditioning unit gurgling happily on the wall as it continued on its mission to turn the bedroom into a glacial wasteland. Sighing, I pulled up my sheet and relaxed into my pillow, listening to the various sounds coming from outside: music from the bar down below, people laughing and shouting next to the pool, the occasional splash of someone jumping into the water. Everything was just like the day before . . . with one glaring exception: Andy wasn't here. His bed was empty and he was nowhere to be seen – a clear indicator, should I have needed one, that the events of the night before had been no passing nightmare. They were very real indeed.

Last night. What. A. Total. Disaster. Tom and I had watched slack-jawed as Andy had kissed, fondled and generally manhandled the tall girl with the dark hair for a good five minutes before we finally managed to tear our eyes away from the car crash that had occurred right in front of us.

I really couldn't believe that he had so unambiguously crossed the line. I knew that Andy liked to flirt with members of the opposite sex like most people liked to breathe, but I'd always assumed that when it came to The Line – between being technically faithful and technically unfaithful – he had enough sense to remain on the side that would bring least trouble. And yet there he'd been standing right in our line of vision, kissing a girl I'd never seen before only moments after I'd assured his teary live-in girlfriend that he would be faithful to her for the entire holiday.

Neither Tom nor I had any idea what we should do. It wasn't as if we could have dragged him forcibly from her clutches – although that was actually the first suggestion I'd come up with. So after taking time out to assess the situation over a stiff drink, we came to the conclusion that the only thing we could do was let him get on with it in the hope that he would come to his senses and return to the fold. After some time it became clear that Andy and the girl weren't going to come up for air any time soon. Just as we'd reassessed the situation and made the decision to issue Andy in his absence with a toothless NATO-style sanction ('If he doesn't stop snogging that girl in, say . . . the next hour or so I think we should register our protest by going back to the hotel') Andy and the girl stopped kissing.

'Finally,' I said, relieved, 'his conscience is kicking in.'

'He hasn't got one,' said Tom. 'I suspect he had it surgically removed years ago to make room for his ego.'

Tom was right. As the girl disappeared in the direction of the ladies' toilet Andy didn't look the slightest bit repentant. In fact he looked incredibly pleased with himself, as though he deserved a round of applause. Returning to our table, he picked up his beer and downed the remains of his Budweiser in one go.

'Now that hit the spot,' he said, setting down the bottle firmly on the table in front of me.

'Are we supposed to be impressed?'

Andy sighed wearily. 'I knew you'd make a big deal out of this. It's nothing, Charlie, okay? Just a bit of fun. There's no need to be concerned.'

'Come on, mate,' I replied. 'You don't have to do this. You've made your point. She was gorgeous and you're the king of pulling birds. Let's just leave now and call it a night before you get yourself in any more trouble.'

'Leave now?' said Andy. 'You must be joking. There's no way I'm going anywhere tonight without her. Have you seen her, Charlie? She's amazing.'

'You're right. She is amazing. And I can't believe that you're making me remind you but here goes: you've got a girlfriend.'

'Will you try and be a bloke just for one second?' snapped Andy. 'This is the kind of thing I'd expect from church boy Tom, not you. Come on, mate, we're blokes. This is what blokes do. Especially when they're on holiday.'

I looked over to see if Tom had any words of wisdom that might back me up.

'You want me to say something to stop Andy going off with this girl?' said Tom, reading my face. 'Maybe something about his girlfriend, and how he's risking losing her for a meaningless fling?' Tom shook his head. 'No, I'm afraid I won't be doing that.' He gave Andy a wink. 'Do whatever you want, mate. Just leave us out of it, okay?'

For a brief moment I was sure that I saw a faint flicker of doubt spread across Andy's face. And it might have taken hold had that not been the exact moment that Andy's kissing companion chose to stride across the bar and join our table.

'Are these your friends?' asked the girl, slipping her fingers between Andy's.

'Nina, this is Charlie and Tom,' said Andy neutrally. He then gestured to Nina. 'Charlie and Tom, this is Nina.'

Tom didn't take his eyes off the cricket during the whole exchange and as I felt bad on behalf of everyone involved I ended up issuing an overly enthusiastic hello.

'Hi,' I said, shaking her hand. 'It's really good to meet you.'

'It's nice to meet you too,' replied Nina.

Even in an ill-fitting Club Fun T-shirt there was no disguising how attractive Nina was. 'How long are you here for?' I asked.

'A week,' she replied. 'I'm here with my sister and some friends. You guys are only here for a week too aren't you?'

I nodded. 'Having a good time so far?'

'Great. It's just nice to take a break isn't it?'

'Yeah, it is,' I replied. 'Where are you from?'

'London. East Finchley to be exact. Are you from Brighton too?'

I nodded. 'Although I'm originally from Derby.' I paused and asked the six-million-dollar question. 'When do you go back home?'

'Wednesday,' she replied, even though I'd been willing her to go first thing in the morning so at least I could be sure of this nightmare not dragging on too long. 'And I'm back at work on the day after. It'll be murder.'

'Right then,' interrupted Andy, clearly bored with me and my small talk. 'I'll see you guys later.'

'It was nice to meet you,' said Nina, giving Tom and me a little wave which Tom dutifully ignored. 'Maybe I'll see you again.'

'Yeah,' I replied. 'That would be nice.'

Hand in hand Andy and Nina crossed the bar, pausing only to kiss at the exit before disappearing from view. Once they had gone I looked at my watch and realised that, thanks to Andy's antics, I'd been too distracted to realise that yet more bad news had managed to come my way without my even noticing it. The girl-in-the-cowboy-hat was nowhere to be seen. I'd been stood up.

'We can wait a bit longer if you want,' said Tom, reading my mind.

'No.' I finished off my drink in preparation to leave. 'Let's just go before this night gets any worse.'

We were about to move when I looked up to see a young woman approaching our table. She was wearing a tight black sleeveless top, dark blue jeans and heels. Three things immediately struck me: first, there was something oddly familiar about her; second, unlike everyone else in the club she didn't appear to be in her early twenties. Late twenties, yes. Early thirties possibly. Early twenties, definitely not. Third: she was very pretty.

'Excuse me,' she said, 'I know this is going to sound a bit weird but your friend who left a little while ago, is he an all-right-sort of guy?'

'Yeah,' I replied as I exchanged baffled glances with Tom. 'Why do you ask?'

'He's with my sister and, well, she sometimes doesn't have the best judgement in the world, if you know what I mean.'

'Believe me,' said Tom. 'We know what you mean.'

'So?' said the girl looking at Tom. 'Your friend?'

Tom licked his lips as though already relishing the sweet savour of his answer. 'Andy,' he began, 'is an—'

'Okay sort of bloke,' I interrupted.

The girl raised her eyebrows. 'Well, put it this way,' she said, 'is he the "okay sort of bloke" you wouldn't mind being with your sister?'

I had to laugh at the thought of my sister Jeanette (minus her husband and her two kids) together with Andy. 'I think I'd mind pretty much anyone being with my sister,' I replied. 'But yeah, Andy really is an okay sort of bloke.'

'Thanks,' said the girl. 'Well I'd better get off then. It was nice to meet you.'

'Yeah,' I said. 'Nice to meet you too.'

Thanks again for last night

As I lay in bed still shivering from the cold, having just reviewed the previous night's escapades, I found myself thinking about the girl from the club whose sister had gone off with Andy. There had been something about her that had immediately marked her out in my head as different, and it hadn't just been an age thing (although that did help), or that she had been attractive (although that helped, too). What had marked her out from the other girls in the club was that she looked as though she had a story to tell. Things had happened in her life. Things that had left their mark. I couldn't tell what that story might be. Whether it was happy or sad. But what I did know was this: I hoped that somehow I would get to hear it this holiday.

An electronic beep from my mobile signalled the arrival of a text message and broke my chain of thought. My pulse quickened. It had been a while since I'd spent any time contemplating Sarah's 'Call me' text message and I couldn't help but wonder if this were a reminder. I scrabbled around on the floor with my hands and eventually found my phone wedged in the back pocket of my jeans. I looked hopefully at the screen but was disappointed to discover that it was a text message from Lisa:

Message Lisa: Charlie, sorry about last night. Do you forgive me? Hope it didn't spoil your evening. Thanks for being such a treasure. Have a great rest of holiday. L x PS. Did you pull?

I sat up in bed and read it several times – just to make sure that I was fully aware of every single guilt-inducing nuance of the message – and then sent a reply in return.

Message Charlie: Hi, don't worry about a thing. Night out was pretty poor anyway. Your phone call was highlight. C x

I pressed send and then climbed out of bed and got my things together for a shower. On my return to the bedroom, naked and dripping water over the floor, I noticed that my phone was beeping again to let me know I had another message:

Message Lisa: Why pretty poor? L x

Feeling uncomfortable about her question I sat down on my bed and keyed in a response:

Message Charlie: Everyone here is decade younger than us. Feel like a mature student at university/school teacher. Delete as inapplicable. C x

I pressed send and then put on a clean pair of shorts and a T-shirt. Grabbing my book and sunglasses I decided to sit on the balcony and read until either Andy came back to the apartment or Tom woke up. As I slid back the patio doors I remembered that I'd left my phone lying on the bedside table and went back to get it. As I picked it up, it beeped in my hand once again.

Message Lisa: Don't you know that older men can be quite a novelty to youngsters?

And again:

Message Lisa: Don't put your back out though! L x

I was glad that she seemed to be in such a good mood. And I have to admit I was also glad to be the one helping her not to worry, even though I hadn't exactly kept Andy out of harm's way.

Message Charlie: Never mind mocking the afflicted, young lady. Why aren't you busy working for a living instead of hassling me? C x

I pressed send and waited expectantly for a reply. When one didn't come I decided that she had probably had enough and so I picked up *Touching The Void*. I'd scarcely got more than a few pages further into the book when I received another message:

Message Lisa: I don't leave for work until 8.30 a.m.! We're two hours behind you lot.

And another:

Message Lisa: But I promise am going to stop bothering you now. Okay??? So have a good day and stay out of the midday sun. L xxx

And another:

> **Message Lisa:** PS What are your plans for this evening?

I had no idea what my plans would be for the evening but I guessed that if Andy were still with Nina then there would be every chance that he would spend the evening with her. And as Nina had friends who (at least in Andy's eyes) would need entertaining, Andy would more than likely try to get Tom and me to come along. As I was in no mood to help Andy out like that, it was therefore looking highly likely that the evening ahead would consist of me and Tom moaning about Andy's behaviour over a quiet pint somewhere.

> **Message Charlie:** No plans as yet. Will probably go somewhere quiet that doesn't require the use of ear trumpet to hear conversation as I fear it puts girls off! C x

I didn't even get a chance to pick up my book again as a reply came back in less than a minute.

> **Message Lisa:** Have to go to work now. Thanks again for last night. And remember that you WILL meet someone nice soon. L x

For some reason the last line of her text message made me feel incredibly sad. Not for me, but for her. There she was, trying to cheer me up, oblivious of the mess Andy was making of their relationship. I think I ended up rereading it three or four times but just as I was about to put the phone away I received one last message from her:

Message Lisa: P.S. Can you remind Andy to reapply his sun cream too. He always forgets. L x

As I reached the end of the message I decided that enough was enough. I went through them all one last time and deleted them, because my overactive imagination had created a horrific scenario consisting of Andy picking up my phone by accident, seeing the messages and jumping to the wrong conclusion. That done, I switched off my phone, put my feet up on the railing in front of me, picked up my book and, for a short while at least, escaped into the pages of the true-life snow-covered-mountain adventure.

My 'cup-of-tea' face

Midday came and went with no sign of Andy. The thought of calling him on his mobile had briefly crossed my mind but I had rejected the idea on the basis that (a) I wasn't his mother and (b) the last thing I needed was him pointing this out to me. By this time Tom was up, showered and dressed but had yet to show any interest in Andy's whereabouts. Instead he lobbied constantly for us to go for breakfast despite the fact that one of our number was missing. By this point it was difficult for me to tell which one of my friends was annoying me the most: Andy, because he was being Andy, or Tom because he was annoyed at Andy for being Andy. I'd always felt that part of Andy's charm was his essential Andyness and to be anything more than moderately exasperated at him for being who he was seemed to be missing the point entirely.

'Come on, Charlie,' said Tom impatiently, 'he's probably still with that girl from last night having breakfast at her hotel while we're sitting here starving. If he really wants to find out where we are all he needs to do is call your mobile.'

'Okay,' I finally relented. 'You're right. Let's go.'

Without further protest I packed a small rucksack with a towel, my book and a bottle of water. Tom and I left the apartment and made our way to the downstairs lobby. We would have gone straight out but there were at least two dozen people crowded around as though a meeting was about to begin or had just ended. When Tom asked a girl standing near the pool table what was going on, she told him it was a welcome meeting organised by a Club Fun tour rep.

'Look at this,' said Tom, calling me over to take a closer look at a series of forms on the reception desk. 'They're doing day trips and organised events. All you have to do is sign your name and you can pay on the day. Leaving aside the stuff like boat parties, barbecues and bar crawls, some of this stuff looks okay.'

I wasn't convinced. 'Like what?'

'Well for starters there's a trip to Agios Nikolas.'

'Which is?'

'A town I read about in the *Rough Guide*. It's got a lake that locals claim is bottomless.'

Tom looked at me expectantly. I pulled a face that clearly said: 'Not really my cup of tea.'

'Okay, how about this one?' continued Tom, reading off the list. 'A visit to the palace of Knossos.'

'You want to go to a palace?'

'It's more ruins than anything,' explained Tom. 'It was supposed to have been home to the Minotaur.'

'That's the bull-thing isn't it?'

Tom nodded. 'Half-man and half-bull and liked to devour young virgins.'

'That'll be Andy then.'

'So what do you say? Fancy it?'

My 'cup-of-tea' face made an unwelcome return. 'Is there nothing . . . ?' I searched for the right word. 'You know . . . a bit groovier?'

'You want groovy? Okay, tomorrow they're organising a sixteen-kilometre trek through the Samaria Gorge, which is apparently one of the longest gorges in Europe. It'll be great.'

My 'cup-of-tea' face made an immediate reappearance.

'It'll be good exercise,' countered Tom.

'It might be,' I replied. 'But isn't sixteen kilometres quite far? I didn't really pack with hiking in mind.'

'Neither did I,' said Tom. 'I've done hiking in my trainers before now, you'll be fine. It says here that a coach would pick us up outside about eight and we'd be back sometime around five.'

Tom looked at me expectantly but my 'cup-of-tea' face was still firmly fixed in place.

'You don't want to go do you?' asked Tom.

'Not really,' I replied.

There was a long pause.

'Fine,' said Tom eventually, 'I'll go on my own.'

Suddenly I felt bad. Tom didn't ask much from me (in fact a lot less than Andy) and it seemed like a million different types of wrong to turn him down, but the truth was, hiking along a gorge in the heat of the Cretan sun seemed like madness to me.

'Look, I'll come,' I replied, making the decision to try to be a better friend to Tom. 'You can put my name down at the top.'

Tom picked a pen up off the desk and hovered over the form, but then he put it down with a resigned sigh. 'It's nice of you to offer,' he began, 'but to be truthful if you're not into it, it'll just bring me down. I'll be fine. I'll go on my own.'

'Are you sure?'

'Yeah,' he replied. 'I'm sure.'

As Tom scribbled down his name at the top of the list I looked through the lobby towards the pool where a group of girls was screaming and laughing as they took it in turns to be thrown into the pool by a couple of lads. Every last one of them looked as though they would no sooner spend the day walking along a gorge in thirty-six-degree sunshine than they would spend the day reading *War and Peace*.

'What about Andy?'

'What about him?'

'Maybe he'll want to go with you.'

Tom laughed. 'Do you know what, I'll put his name down on the off-chance that between now and then he completely loses his mind.'

King of the road

Leaving the Apollo, Tom and I made our way along the same route to the same diner that we'd eaten at the previous day, where we were served by the same waiter. We then ordered the same breakfast and beer combo and ended up watching MTV again with the sound off. And at the end of the meal we even left the same amount of money as a tip as we had done the day before. As we stood up to leave, I found myself thinking that we'd been in Malia only one full day and yet we were already in danger of finding ourselves stuck in a rut.

'What are you thinking?' asked Tom as we lingered at the entrance to Stars and Bars, roasting in the afternoon sun. 'Back to the beach?'

'We could do,' I replied, conscious of the fact that we had done just that yesterday. 'What do you reckon?'

'I'm easy either way,' said Tom, 'although if I'm honest I quite fancy doing something a bit different.'

'Different,' I echoed determinedly. 'You're right. We do need to do something different. Any ideas?'

Tom thought for a moment. 'I've got it,' he said eventually, 'let's rent a couple of those quad bike things and visit somewhere else for the day.'

'That, my friend . . .' I began as a gang of youths passed by yelling and shouting to each other, '. . . sounds like a great idea.'

Renting the quad bikes was the best thing we could've done to get us out of our post-Andy funk. Riding along with our throttles wide open and the wind in our faces we were young again and we were free. We cruised along the coastal road out of Malia and headed for Stalis, the next resort along. Every now and again, as we sped along, we would pass girls on lower-powered quad bikes than our own and as we'd overtake them I'd feel, if only for a moment, as though I really was king of the road.

As Tom and I sat down on the beach that we didn't have to pay for and got out our books, it occurred to me that if Malia was a metaphor for youthful excess then Stalis was its older, wiser sibling who had long since given up late nights and all-day drinking for the delights of good food and family life. The contrast couldn't have been greater. Slightly less Anglo-orientated than Malia (on our walk through the town centre we passed a Dutch-owned bar, saw German translations on several menus and passed a couple arguing in French), Stalis itself was populated solely by couples and families. The only people we saw under twenty-five were kids on holiday with their parents or other quad-biking migrants from Malia.

Although neither of us said it aloud, I could see that Tom was thinking the same as me: 'This is where we should've come on holiday.' Not that the attraction of Malia to the eighteen-to-thirty crowd was lost on me but the fact was neither Tom, Andy nor I *was* between the ages of eighteen and thirty any more and as we hadn't been for a long time, there was no point in pretending anything else. Stalis was a resort built for grown-ups. People who had left their twenties well behind and moved on. But as I sat there on the beach devoid of loudspeakers and club music and surveyed the couples and families that surrounded us, it hit me that I actually didn't belong here either. Tom, with his family, yes. Possibly even Andy with Lisa. But me without Sarah? There was no place in this holiday world for a thirty-five-year-old single man. There was no resort designed for those recently dumped but disinclined to party until dawn. There was no middle ground at all because people like me simply weren't a big enough demographic to cater for. Market forces had dictated that we were invisible – we didn't exist. We weren't young and we weren't settled. And because we weren't at the beginning of our stories or in the happily-ever-after end zone, we'd been simply edited out all-together.

'So what's your take on last night?' I asked Tom in a bid to derail this particularly depressing train of thought.

'I think Andy's an idiot,' replied Tom putting down his book. 'I haven't got much more to add than that.'

'I suppose,' I replied. I thought for a moment. 'How old do you reckon that girl Nina was?'

'Twenty-three or twenty-four,' suggested Tom. 'I can't really tell how old anyone is these days.'

There was a long silence. Taking this to be the end of the conversation Tom returned his attention to the *Rough Guide* but I was far from finished with the topic of Andy and his infidelity.

'Lisa asked me to keep an eye on him you know,' I said looking out to sea. 'When she dropped him off at mine on Saturday night. She said she'd sort of guessed what he wanted to get out of the holiday and asked me to try and stop him. And ironically, the reason I didn't manage to do what she wanted was because at the crucial moment I was on the phone with her.'

'Lisa called you?'

I nodded. 'She wanted to know how things were going. And what's worse is that I told her everything was going to be okay. She even sent me a couple of text messages this morning too.'

'You didn't tell her anything about last night did you?'

'Of course not but I feel bad about making out like everything's okay when it obviously isn't. I know Andy is my friend but . . .'

'But what?'

'But part of me feels like she deserves to know.'

Tom nodded. 'I know what you mean, but if you want my advice I'd say don't get involved.'

'I know but—'

'She won't thank you, Charlie. And I doubt that Andy would either. Just stay clear. These things usually have a way of coming out without anyone's help.'

'I know you're right,' I replied. 'But it just feels wrong. No one likes being the last one to find out do they? No one ever likes to be the last one in on the joke.'

Tom and I ended up staying in Stalis for the rest of the afternoon. He carried on reading his *Rough Guide* while I dozed in the sun, flicked my way through a day-old copy of the *Daily Mail* and went for a number of contemplative footwear-free walks along the shoreline. At around five o'clock the beach began to empty so we took that as our signal to return to the madness of Malia. As we handed the quad bikes back in at the hire shop I couldn't help but feel slightly disappointed that we hadn't managed to cultivate a single envy-inducing anecdote during the day that might provoke Andy to jealousy. All we'd done was hire quad bikes, travel the short distance to Stalis and then sit on a beach that had a lower ratio of beautiful girls to middle-aged German men than the one we had left behind. Andy meanwhile had probably spent all morning and all afternoon feasting on a rotating diet of drinking, sex and post-coital napping. Of course he'd be gutted.

It was just an observation

As I opened the front door to the apartment, I half expected to see Andy and his new lady friend entangled in convoluted sexual congress on the kitchen table because that would've been Andy all over – an exhibitionist in need of a shockable audience – but there was nothing on the kitchen table save a half-empty bottle of water and two plastic carrier bags from the local minimarket.

'You'd think he'd call us just to let us know he's not dead,' I snapped as we walked through the kitchen into the bedroom.

'Not Andy,' replied Tom, choosing to stretch out on our absent companion's bed. 'He's far too self-involved to worry about what we think.'

I sat down on my own bed and looked over at Tom. 'Do you think we should call him?'

'And let him think we've got nothing better to do than sit around and wait for him to turn up?' asked Tom. 'You can do what you like but leave my name off the petition.'

Tom was right. Calling Andy would be a bad move which would only serve to further inflate his ego. At the same time, I had to admit that I was beginning to miss having Andy about. This was the conundrum faced by everyone who invited Andy into their lives: he was twice as entertaining as he was annoying but it was impossible to separate one part of the equation from the other.

'Okay,' I replied, 'you're right, I shouldn't phone him. It's a bad idea. But the thing is I feel like I ought to at least try and do something, because I've got this horrible feeling the longer this thing carries on, the worse the consequences are going to be.'

'I'm not so sure myself,' said Tom. 'My guess is Andy will carry on seeing Nina until she goes home and then he'll hang out with us for the rest of the holiday. Come Sunday night he'll fly home and carry on as though nothing happened. And what's more, he'll get away with it. Because Andy always gets away with everything.'

'Maybe you're right,' I sighed. 'I don't even know why I'm that bothered what he gets up to. I mean, why do I care?'

I'd meant the question rhetorically. I didn't really want to know why I cared at all. But then I looked at Tom as I said it and there was something about his face that changed just for an instant, that made me curious.

'What?' I asked.

'Nothing.'

'*What?*'

'Look,' said Tom, 'you didn't mean it as a proper question so it doesn't matter.'

'No,' I replied. 'Come on. Let's hear what you've got to say.'

'Fine. I think you care because you sort of wish it was you that had pulled last night and you're sick and tired of always being envious of Andy.'

'That's rubbish,' I replied. 'I'm not envious of Andy.'

'Fine,' said Tom. 'It was just an observation.'

'But I'm not.'

'I said, fine.'

'But you don't believe me.'

'It doesn't matter what I believe, does it? All that matters is what's true.'

'And you think it's true that I'm envious of Andy?'

'Why else would you still be hanging out with him after all these years when most of the time all he does is rub you up the wrong way? He does the things you wish you could do.'

'You've never liked Andy though have you?' I countered. 'It's been the same ever since college.'

Tom shook his head. 'You're wrong actually. It's not him I don't like. He's an idiot and nothing much is ever going to change that.'

'So who is it you don't like then?'

'You . . .' said Tom fixing me with a disappointed stare '. . . when you've been round him too long. That's always been your main problem. You lose sight of who you are too easily and let Andy lead you around like a lost sheep.' He sighed and then climbed off the bed as I looked on speechless. This wasn't like Tom at all. Yes, he was sometimes confrontational with Andy but he'd never been like that with me before.

'What's wrong?' I asked. 'Why are you being like this? This obviously isn't about me or Andy, so what's it about?'

'Nothing,' sighed Tom. 'I was well out of order.' He paused and laughed. 'You'd think someone had died and made me minister of home truths the way I've just carried on. It's not like I couldn't be told a few myself.' He shrugged and looked at me. 'Are we all right?'

'Yeah of course,' I replied. 'But don't you want to talk about whatever it is that's bothering you?'

'No,' said Tom. 'I'm fine. I'm probably just tired or something.'

There was a long silence.

'So what now?' I asked eventually.

'I thought I'd have a shower, call Anne and the kids and then have a sleep,' said Tom. 'Assuming his lordship is otherwise engaged tonight what do you want to do later?'

I shrugged. 'I don't care, really. Just not the strip if we can help it.'

'Well, this might not be your thing,' began Tom. 'But I was reading in the *Rough Guide* this afternoon about a little village not too far away from here called Mohos.' Tom reached down to the floor, pulled the book out of his bag and flicked through it until he got to a page where he had turned down the corner. 'We could get a taxi there, have a bit of a wander round, a drink and something to eat. What do you think?'

'Sounds okay,' I replied. 'Be ready to leave about eight?'

'Sounds good to me,' said Tom. 'So what are you going to do until then?'

I looked around the room for inspiration and spotted some through the patio doors. 'Finish the day the way I started it,' I replied pointing to the balcony, 'making the most of the sun.'

Look after my man

As Tom began getting ready for his shower I finally got off my bed and plucked *Touching The Void* from my bag. I was getting tired of all the tension between the two friends on their snow-covered precipice. I wanted something a bit lighter . . . a bit less full-on and so I opened my suitcase, pulled out *The Da Vinci Code* (the second of my three holiday reads), went out on to the patio and closed the door behind me.

Sitting down in my favourite patio chair with my feet up against the railing, I began reading the first paragraph of my book. A few sentences in, Tom turned on the shower and so distracted me that I stopped reading. I tried again a few moments later but then a group of girls talking loudly passed by underneath the balcony and I stopped again. When I eventually picked the book up some five minutes later, my heart was no longer in it. I was bored but I didn't want to read. I wanted to be entertained without actually leaving the comfort of my balcony seat. And then the answer came to me. I pulled out my mobile phone from my pocket, typed out a text message and pressed send.

Message Charlie: Hi, just thought you'd like to know I'm lying on a beach, drinking fluorescent cocktails served by topless hula ladies. How about you? C x

A minute later I got the following reply:

Message Lisa: I'm at work. My back aches, I have a headache and it's raining. Keep holiday chirpiness to yourself! L x

To which I replied:

Message Charlie: I'm actually sitting on the balcony of our apartment watching (in strictly non-pervy way) a bunch of nineteen-year-old girls have a water fight. C x

To which she replied:

Message Lisa: What have you guys been up to today? Did you remind Andy about the suncream? L x

To which I replied:

Message Charlie: Hung out on beach all day. And yes, I did remind Andy about suncream. C x

To which she replied:

Message Lisa: What are you up to tonight? L x

To which I replied:

Message Charlie: Haven't decided. What about you? C x

To which she replied:

Message Lisa: Staying in wishing I was sunning myself in Crete too. L x

To which I replied:

Message Charlie: You should guilt-trip Andy into taking you away. C x

To which she replied:

Message Lisa: Can't. He has no conscience. L x

To which I replied:

Message Charlie: I'll get him one for Christmas! C xxx

To which she replied:

Message Lisa: I'd better go. Have a great rest of holiday. PS. Look after my man. L x

The time that elapsed between the first text message and the last was just under an hour and during all that time I didn't return to *The Da Vinci Code* even once.

It's not *Match of the Day*

The sound of keys rattling in the front door signalled Andy's return to the apartment. I looked across at Tom. Though neither of us spoke, I knew that we both wanted to achieve the same thing: to look as sufficiently uninterested in Andy, Nina (should he have brought her along), and his whereabouts for the last twenty-four hours as was humanly possible. Tom opted to frown at his book as though mulling over a particularly well-structured paragraph, while I chose to un-mute the TV and stare at it, looking vaguely bemused.

'You can call off the search party,' said Andy striding into the bedroom. 'I'm back.'

Tom (who I have to say excelled in his attempts at projecting general uninterest) finished the sentence he was reading before looking up at Andy. I preferred to stare blankly as though I only vaguely recognised him.

'Okay, I get it,' said Andy bullishly, 'you're both wound up at me for being away so long.'

'Yeah, that's it in a nutshell,' replied Tom. 'We've been lost without you.'

Ignoring Tom, Andy deliberately focused his attempts at ingratiation on me. 'Come on, Charlie,' he nearly but not quite pleaded. 'You can understand can't you, mate? I mean you've seen her right? She's amazing.'

Without replying I got up, walked over to the chest of

drawers, put my sunglasses back inside their case and began sorting out my suitcase.

Realising I was ignoring him, Andy sighed in my direction as though he was really disappointed in me. 'How long are you two going to be like this?' he asked.

'Like what?' I replied.

'Like you're my dad,' he said. 'Do you know what? Nina didn't want me to leave her and come here.'

'So why did you?' I asked.

'Because I hadn't seen you guys all day.'

Tom laughed. 'And are we supposed to feel flattered?'

'You're not supposed to feel anything,' replied Andy. 'Look, I—' He stopped suddenly, rolled his eyes in frustration and tried a different approach to the problem. 'Hey, Charlie,' he began. 'Did that girl you were supposed to meet last night ever turn up?' he asked. 'You know, the one in the cowboy hat?'

'No,' I replied.

'Bad luck, mate.'

'It was no big loss.'

'Still, you shouldn't give up yet. How about this? Why don't you come out with me tonight and meet Nina's mates? We're going to Flares. Do you remember it from last time? It's that seventies bar we used to go to sometimes where they played that *Match of the Day* theme tune and then everyone would do that dance – do you remember?'

'It's not *Match of the Day*,' corrected Tom. 'It's *Ski Sunday*.'

'Same difference.'

'No,' replied Tom. 'I think you'll find that one is dedicated to the sport of football and the other skiing.'

I wanted to laugh but I could see that Andy was running

out of patience. 'Come on, guys,' he said adding a hint of joviality to his plea, 'both of you come out tonight. I guarantee you we'll have a laugh. Nina's mates are good fun.'

'What about her sister?' I asked, hoping that Andy wouldn't make a big deal about it. 'Tom and I met her last night after you left Pandemonium: shortish, dark-hair, nice-looking, dry sense of humour. More our sort of age than most girls in Malia.'

'That sounds like Donna all right.' Andy grinned. 'You don't fancy her do you?'

'Of course not,' I lied, making a mental note of her name. 'She just seemed nice, that's all.'

'I haven't had much to do with her,' said Andy. 'But since I'm currently in with her sister I'm sure a word from me could put you in good stead.'

'No thanks,' I replied. 'I'm good.'

'You're nowhere near good,' said Andy, 'Look, mate, unlike some people . . .' he paused and looked pointedly at Tom, '. . . I haven't forgotten what this holiday is all about – it's about you moving on. And the best way of doing that would be for you to come out with me tonight. Forget Sarah. Forget the girl-in-the-cowboy-hat. And forget Nina's sister too. Because I've spent all day telling Nina's mates about how wonderful "my mate, Charlie" is. Mate, I guarantee they're practically gagging for you. I've built you up so much they already think you're the greatest thing since sliced bread. All of which means at least one of them has got to be a dead cert.'

'A "dead cert"?' I repeated disdainfully at the thought of Andy's selling me to Nina's friends as though I was a sack of potatoes past their sell-by date.

'Yeah,' replied Andy stubbornly refusing to pick up on my sarcasm. 'A "dead cert".'

'Well, much as I'd like to be the beneficiary of your charitable efforts to get me sex,' I replied, 'I'm going to have to say no this time.'

'Why?' asked Andy.

'Because Tom and I have already got plans.'

Andy looked confused. 'What plans?'

At this point it would have been perfect if the plans Tom and I had in mind had been the type that involved excessive drinking, lap-dancing clubs and the possibility of rubbing shoulders with a female celebrity or two.

'We're going to a village up in the hills that Tom's *Rough Guide* recommends,' I explained feebly. 'It's got a church . . . and some shops . . . and a taverna. You can come if you want.'

'Let me get this right,' said Andy his eyes straining with incredulity. 'You're turning down a night out with hot girls for a trip to a village with a Christian?'

'Well, if you'd given us a bit more notice . . . like this morning . . . or even this afternoon we might have been able to come,' I replied. 'But the fact is we've made plans, mate. It's just the way it is.'

'Fine,' snapped Andy, 'you stick to your village people plans and I'll stick to mine.'

There was a long uncomfortable silence while we all sort of stared at each other.

'Anyway,' I began softly in a bid to appease Andy. 'I'd be rubbish company for girls tonight anyway. I'd just end up cramping your style.' I paused and, a diversionary tactic I'd cultivated over the many years I'd known Andy, I decided to flatter his ego. 'Nina's a bit spectacular,' I said raising my eyebrows suggestively. 'Tell us about her.'

'Like what?' said Andy, making a token effort to resist my flattery.

'Like what does she do?'

'She works in TV.'

'Doing what?'

'She's a production secretary.'

'How old is she?'

'Twenty-five.'

'When's her birthday?'

'November the—' Andy stopped suddenly and began laughing. 'All right, Mansell, you've had your fun. Let's move on with the questions.'

'Hang on,' said Tom, 'I've got one I'd like to ask.'

'Go on then,' said Andy.

'I know I said I wasn't going to get involved but I'm curious to find out how long you're going to carry this on?'

Andy turned to face Tom but neither man spoke for several moments.

'I'm not in the mood for this, Tom,' said Andy coolly. 'So for your benefit and the benefit of Charlie I'll say it once: this is just a holiday thing. It's not going to last forever so there's no need to tell anyone anything. I know you two think that you're somehow morally superior to me but this is something I've got to do, okay? And none of it is any of your business—' Andy stopped abruptly and pulled out his mobile from his back pocket. 'It's Lisa,' he said looking at the screen. 'I'll be back in a minute.'

Tom and I exchanged wary glances as Andy left the room to take the call on the balcony.

'I think we're being too hard on him,' I whispered to

Tom as Andy slid back the patio doors. 'After all, none of this is our business.'

'Look,' said Tom, 'if you want to go to the club with Andy then you should go. But whether you come or not my plans for this evening involve going to Mohos.'

'I'm still coming to the village,' I replied. 'Nothing has changed there. All I'm saying is I think this night out Andy has planned is his way of saying sorry for being away all day. I think he really wants us to come out tonight.'

'Maybe he does,' said Tom. 'But do you know what, Charlie? I don't think I could put up with his nonsense tonight even if I wanted to.' Tom smiled mischievously. 'But you should go, mate, if you really want to.'

'What are you smiling about?' I asked.

'You, and your big speech about Andy wanting us to go with him. You just want to see Nina's sister again, don't you?'

'Yeah right,' I replied. 'I only met her for about five seconds.'

'There's no need to be defensive, mate. She seemed really nice. I can see why you'd be into her.'

'And why would that be?'

'She's just your type.'

'And my type would be?'

'Oh come on,' protested Tom. 'You've always had a type. Even back in college. They were always pretty but not too pretty. Usually dark haired. Good dress sense. Look like they might be able to hold their own in a conversation about the meaning of life until the early hours . . . you know the sort of thing.'

'Okay, okay,' I grinned. 'You're right. I have got a type and Nina's sister did pretty much fit the bill. But I'm not going out with Andy tonight and that's final. Tonight it's just you, me and a village—' I stopped as Andy opened the patio doors and returned to the room, yawning.

'Everything okay with Lisa?' I asked.

'Yeah, fine,' replied Andy. 'She was just ringing for a chat. I kept it short though. Told her we were going out in a minute.'

'So what did you tell her?'

'I said we'd spent the day hanging out by the hotel pool and then—'

'You said what?' I spluttered.

Andy looked confused at my concern. 'I told her we'd spent all afternoon by the hotel pool,' he repeated. 'Which it so happens is actually what me and Nina did when we weren't—'

'But why did you tell her we'd been by the pool?' I asked nervously.

'Why shouldn't I have?' replied Andy. 'It's not like she's going to know any different is—' Andy stopped abruptly and looked at me. 'What aren't you telling me?'

It was a good question. There were a million things that I wasn't telling him. But at this moment everything would be a lot easier if I kept it down to just the things he needed to know.

'Lisa sent me a text message this afternoon.'

Andy looked confused. 'Why's she sending you text messages?'

'It was something to do with Sarah,' I lied. 'But you're sort of missing the point. In my reply to her message I told her that we'd spent the day at the beach.'

'So?'

'Well you've just told her we spent the whole day by the pool.'

'So I mixed up swimming pool and beaches, so what?' said Andy. 'I do that kind of thing all the time. Honestly, Charlie, you nearly gave me a heart attack acting like that.'

'But aren't you even a little bit worried that she knows what's going on?'

'Not at all,' said Andy sighing with relief. 'I guarantee you, my friend, that she does not suspect a thing.'

Useful phrases

Andy had long since gone back to Nina's when Tom and I finally left the apartment just after nine. As we waited for a taxi by the roadside I noted that as usual the streets of Malia were buzzing with young Brits on their way up to the strip. As they passed by I found myself scanning them in what I considered a detached academic manner, as though I were a TV documentary maker scouting locations for a reality TV series called 'Malia Uncovered'. This pseudo-anthropological stance was, of course, simply a cover for me to stare at attractive girls in short skirts in the hope that one of them might be the girl-in-the-cowboy-hat.

I'd been wondering on and off all day why she hadn't turned up when it had been she who had made the initial contact. My more cynical side presumed that it was all part of some elaborate joke but my more optimistic side was willing her to have been run over. I guessed that the truth would be somewhere in the middle.

A white Mercedes with a taxi sign on the roof came by after a ten-minute wait and we jumped in the rear seats and asked the driver – a grim-faced local in his late fifties – to take us to Mohos. He did a sort of comedy double-take. As he pulled away from the pavement he checked several times that Mohos was definitely our destination and even tried to put us off making the journey. 'No nightlife in Mohos,' he said brusquely. Once we'd reassured him that we weren't expecting dancing girls and wild parties from a village in the hills he just shrugged and turned on his car radio.

Because there were so many revellers on the streets we had to drive through the strip at a snail's pace on our way to the motorway. I wondered briefly whether the taxi driver had taken this route deliberately as if tempting us to stay where we belonged. If so, the implied message of our detour was: 'This is what you'll be missing out on tonight: tall girls, short girls, fat girls, thin girls, girls with dark hair, girls with light hair, girls with short skirts, girls with long skirts . . . in fact every kind of girl you can think of.' And I'll admit for a moment there I was tempted to yell out, 'Stop the car. You've made your point and it's a good one.' I didn't, of course, even though I was well aware a night out in the hills would inevitably mean one fewer opportunity for me to meet someone. Sighing inwardly, I kept my mouth shut until we'd left the deafening music and neon haze of Malia long behind and replaced it with the comforting xenon glare of motorway streetlights and the gentle purr of Goodyear radial on bone-dry tarmac.

Slowly negotiating a long narrow residential street, the taxi finally emerged into a small village square. Though I tended not to have much of an opinion on matters aesthetic when it came to village squares, even I appreciated that this one was indeed pretty. Everything about it from the trees glinting with decorative fairy lights to the quaint old church was picture postcard perfect. In fact, had the girl-in-the-cowboy-hat and I ever made it to a second date, this would've been the perfect place to take her.

As Tom dug around in his pockets for money to pay our taxi driver, he attempted to engage him in some Greek banter culled from the 'useful phrases' section of his *Rough Guide*. To say that the taxi driver wasn't interested would be something of an understatement. In fact he seemed to be bordering on the outskirts of outrage, as though the very act of Tom attempting to speak Greek was somehow permanently soiling his mother tongue.

Still somewhat stunned by his naked contempt for us, we headed first to a small gift shop across the road from the taverna, because it seemed as though it might have the fewest people in it who hated us. We had become aware that we were the only non-locals in the square and the row of elderly men sitting on a bench outside a butcher's shop blatantly watching our every move as though we were the evening's entertainment did little to make us feel less self-conscious.

The gift shop was filled with standard tourist items: Greek lace, a million different kinds of olive oil, little dolls in 'traditional' Greek clothing, the lot. As we walked around, Tom voiced his concern that the tendrils of commercialism had extended so deeply into the countryside that there was a real danger of losing any sense of authentic Crete. I didn't want to argue with Tom because it was hard enough arguing with Andy all the time, but I was sure that his idea of simple peasant people, living simple peasant lives, untainted by the modern world hadn't existed anywhere other than in the heads of tourists searching out the 'real' Crete for some time.

Still closely observed by the old men on the bench we left the shop and headed over to the church. There appeared to be some sort of service going on so we didn't go in, but as we turned to leave an old lady standing in the vestibule at the back spotted us and nudged her friends: as one they all turned and stared at us for an uncomfortably long time.

Bemused by the interest we seemed to be creating we finally made our way to the taverna and sat down at one of the many outdoor tables. Much to our great relief, within seconds of sitting down a friendly middle-aged man came over and took our order. Still keen to try out his phrase-book Greek, Tom relayed our choices from the menu as best he could. And although he struggled greatly with a whole gamut of unfamiliar words and phrases, our waiter seemed to be genuinely pleased that Tom was making the effort.

The food and drinks arrived quickly and were a definite improvement on anything we had eaten so far. There were spinach and feta pies, meatballs, stuffed vine leaves and a few dishes that we couldn't match to the menu but tasted great anyway. Just as we ordered a second round of beers to wash down the remains of the meal, a couple of guys carrying acoustic guitars emerged from inside the taverna and began playing a batch of songs that some of the locals spread across the other tables seemed to know well. Within a few moments virtually all the customers were clapping and singing in unison.

'Charlie?' whispered Tom in my ear as we finally overcame our natural reserve and joined in with the clapping to a particularly upbeat song. 'If I tell you something, I need you to promise that you won't make a big deal out of it, okay?'

'Of course,' I replied, still clapping. 'It'll be a small deal all the way. What's on your mind?'

Tom stopped clapping and I did likewise. 'You know earlier today you asked me if I was okay?' I nodded. 'Well the truth is I'm not.'

'What do you mean?' I replied.

'I mean I've had something on my mind for a while that I haven't told a single soul about and it's sort of driving me mad.'

'What is it?' I asked.

'It's like this,' he began. 'The day we fly back home I've got to make a phone call.'

'What kind of phone call?'

'It's nothing really it's just . . .' his voice faltered. '. . . It's just I'm supposed to call my doctors' surgery to get some test results.'

'Test results?' I said a little too quickly. 'For what?'

'I really don't know how to say it,' said Tom fixing his eyes on the guitar players in front of us. 'I really don't. I haven't even dared to say the word aloud even when I'm on my own.'

'This is me you're talking to,' I replied. 'You know you can tell me anything.'

'Cancer,' said Tom quietly as the song came to a close. 'I've got to phone my doctor to see if I've got cancer.'

DAY THREE: WEDNESDAY

She is a holiday

Through the dimness of the darkened bedroom I could just about make out the shape of a figure at the bathroom door. I squinted at my watch. It was just after seven in the morning. The good news from my perspective was that for once during this holiday I wasn't the first person awake. The bad news was that had I not been woken up, I'm sure I would have slept on for hours. Realising that I was unlikely to get back to sleep any time soon I climbed out of bed and, without saying a word, slipped on my shorts, opened my suitcase and pulled out my 'Death To The Pixies' T-shirt.

'Morning, mate,' said Andy, emerging from the bathroom wearing shorts and a T-shirt. His hair was wet and he was frantically rubbing it dry with a towel.

'You woke me up,' I replied cheerlessly.

Andy fixed me with a hard stare. 'I've just had a shower. Since when was that a crime?'

'Since you started stealing my towel to do it,' I said snatching the damp towel from Andy's hands. 'What are you doing up so early anyway? I didn't expect to see you until tonight. That's how it goes doesn't it? Every twenty-four hours you check in with us just to make sure we're still alive.'

'I'm back because Nina and I agreed that we're both

knackered,' said Andy, side-stepping my early morning fractiousness. 'And my plan – if it's actually any of your business – was to have a shower and then sleep until late in the afternoon but if you want me to go back to Nina's I can do that just as easily.'

'Well if you really want to go,' I replied. 'Be my guest.'

There was a long silence. Andy stared at me as though trying to work something out. All of a sudden his face suggested he'd found the answer and he whispered knowingly, 'I get it.' He looked pointedly over at the kitchen door. 'This isn't about me at all is it? It's about you having to spend all this quality time with Hans Christian Andersen, visiting villages, hiking up hills and talking about Jesus.' He paused and laughed. 'This is great. You're finally as sick of it as—'

'Just leave it, Andy,' I threatened cautiously. 'Today is most certainly not the day for you to be saying all this.'

'Really? And why would that be? Tom's never been my biggest fan and I'm certainly not his so what's the point in pretending anything else? If you ask me he's a—'

'Look,' I interrupted, 'I've asked you once and now I mean it, drop it.' I stepped towards Andy and pushed him in the chest as if to punctuate the point.

'Tell me you didn't just do that,' said Andy as his face flushed with anger.

'I did it,' I replied, even though I could feel that the situation was beginning to get out of control, 'and do you know what? I'll do it again if you carry on talking about Tom like that.'

'Is that right?' said Andy squaring right up to me as though he might actually throw a punch in my direction.

'Yeah,' I replied firmly, 'that's right.'

I'd never stood up to Andy like this before. I don't suppose I'd ever needed to. And I could see in his eyes that even though he was used to getting his own way, he actually wanted to back down as much as I did. Unfortunately I wasn't sure Andy actually knew how to back down so the only way it was going to happen was if I did it first.

'Look,' I began. 'I shouldn't have pushed you like that, Okay? I'm just a little weirded out that's all.'

'Weirded out by what?'

'By Tom,' I replied. 'Last night he told me that he thinks he might have cancer.'

Andy's face fell in shock. The tension between us immediately evaporated. The confrontation was finally over.

'Cancer?' said Andy barely able to get the words out. 'How can Tom have cancer?'

Walking over to the patio doors I opened them up and gestured for Andy to follow me on to the balcony. There I sucked in a deep breath of air and held it in my lungs and looked around me. It was odd being outdoors this early in the day. The morning air seemed fresher. The sun, though bright, had yet to reach its usual intensity. All the loungers beside the pool were empty. Everything familiar seemed as though it had been turned on its head.

'Listen,' I began, as I closed the patio doors behind Andy, 'I'm not sure that I'm supposed to tell you about what Tom said. He didn't say one way or the other. I suppose given how you've been on at him all holiday he didn't think the occasion for a heart-to-heart would come up somehow.'

'I know, I know,' said Andy shamefacedly, 'I have been a bit of an arsehole. But that's not the point is it? The point is how can Tom have cancer? He looks fine to me.'

Andy sat down on one of the plastic chairs while I took the other and I told him the whole story, the same way Tom had told me.

One morning about a month earlier Tom had been to the toilet before breakfast and noticed afterwards that the water in the bowl had a slightly pinkish tinge to it. He ignored it for a few days, hoping it would sort itself out, but it didn't; it got worse and gradually became pinker by the day until one day he saw spirals of red. He made an appointment to see his doctor that same morning, without telling his wife and she immediately referred him to a specialist at his local hospital. The doctor checked him over and informed him that they'd have to run a whole batch of tests to rule out the worst-case scenario – cancer of the bladder.

'So they don't know for sure what he's got?' asked Andy.

'No,' I replied. 'But I don't know whether you know this, but cancer of the bladder is what Tom's dad died of . . . and he was only fifty-two.'

Neither of us spoke for a few moments.

'When do his results come back?'

'The morning we land back at Gatwick.'

Andy thought for a moment. 'That's why he agreed to come on the holiday with us, isn't it?'

I nodded. 'He told me he thought he'd be better off being distracted by the two of us than moping around at home waiting for the results.'

Andy stood up and went back inside the bedroom, reappearing with his cigarettes and a lighter. He lit a cigarette and handed it to me, then lit one for himself. As the balcony briefly filled with a pale blue haze of smoke we sat looking out at the misty horizon in front of us.

'My nan died of cancer,' said Andy quietly. 'It was in her liver. Saddest fucking day of my life.'

'You lived with her, didn't you?'

'From about seven, when my dad left and my mum lost the plot, to when I left to go to college. Honestly, Charlie, my whole life she was such a strong woman – a real tower of strength – nothing ever fazed her. Not raising my brother and me. Not working two jobs. Not my granddad dying. She took everything in her stride. She used to bang on about God all the time and about how he would look after her because he always had done in the past. But he didn't. As she gradually got sicker she was like a different person. She wasn't my gran any more. She was a frail old lady. I'd never thought of my nan like that – as being an old lady. But the first time I saw her in hospital after her first round of treatment that's what she was.

'She'd always been this woman who wasn't scared of anything or anyone. I remember this one time her house got burgled – they nicked a video recorder and some cash that had been sitting on the fireplace – and she had a pretty good idea which one of the kids in our close had done it, because my nan had lived there all her life and knew everyone's business. She must have been pushing seventy at the time but that didn't stop her from walking round to this kid's house and banging on his front door until his parents opened up. Right there on the door step she threatened to batter the mum, the dad *and* the kid black and blue unless the video and the money were returned to her by the end of the day, along with a bit extra to cover the cost of a pane of glass that had been smashed. And do you know what? She got it too. That was my nan, a force of nature.' Andy paused to flick the long stem of ash from his cigarette and then took a long drag. 'But you wouldn't have recognised her in hospital. You really wouldn't. And every time she had a treatment she looked worse not better. And then one day a few months in, I'd been to visit her and it just dawned on me that despite all the talk she was never actually going to get better. And after that I never went back. My brother did. He was with her at the very end. But me?' Andy shook his head. 'I just couldn't stand to watch her go like that.'

I didn't know what to say. I'd known bits about Andy's background. The stuff about being raised by his gran (although he'd never mentioned anything at all about his parents before) and just how much his gran had meant to him, although that was mainly through the way he reacted after her death. It knocked him sideways. It really did. He stopped eating. He drank to excess. And was so obnoxious to pretty much everyone in his life that along with losing his job, he lost nearly every friend that he had made in the last decade with the exception of me and Lisa. It was nearly a year before he was able to get himself together, and only because Lisa threatened to leave him. And while it had long since occurred to me that there had to be a reason why Andy was so anti-religion, and anti-Tom especially, now that I knew, or at least could guess his reasoning, I couldn't say that I felt any wiser. He had his reasons and I'm sure they felt justified to him but that didn't make him right.

'Do you think he'll be all right?' said Andy, stubbing out his cigarette on the balcony railing.

'Yeah, of course,' I replied. 'He'll be fine.'

'How old are his kids again?'

'I think one's four and the other is three.'

'And he still believes in God?' said Andy shaking his head in disgust. His response was posed as a question but also as a statement of fact. But whatever it was I chose not to respond.

'You think I'm being an idiot cheating on Lisa, don't you?' he asked.

I left a gap of a few moments before replying in the hope of convincing Andy that I was wavering between two options. 'Yeah,' I replied eventually. 'I think you are.'

'You think she deserves better.'

'I think if you don't want to be with her, fine, end the relationship and move on. But if you have any respect for her at all then you'll stop this thing with Nina now.'

'Or . . . ?'

I looked at him, puzzled.

'You make it sound like you're going to do something about it if I don't,' he said.

'What could I possibly do?' I replied. 'It's not like I'm in any position to force anyone to do anything.'

'Lisa is what I want,' said Andy calmly. 'And I know that we'll have kids and all the rest of it.'

'But?'

Andy smiled ruefully. 'There's always a but isn't there? And for me it's the routine. I can't stand it. Mondays: work and the gym. Tuesdays: work and then TV in the evenings. Wednesdays: work and one of her mates will come over for dinner. Thursdays: work and she goes out with her mates and I'll go for a drink with you. Fridays: work and then a takeaway in front of the TV; Saturdays: gym, shopping, and if we can be bothered we might go out in the evening; Sundays . . . who knows what happens to Sundays? Every day just melts away into nothingness because before you know what's happened it's Monday again and you're right back where you started. Who wouldn't want a holiday after that?'

'Is that what Nina is? A holiday?'

'It's as good a word as any,' replied Andy. 'She is a holiday . . . from real life . . . from routine and yeah, even from Lisa. Everybody needs a holiday, mate. Even you.' He paused, picked up his cigarettes and stood up. 'I'll see you, later, maybe?'

'Are you going to bed?'

'No,' he sighed. 'I'm going back to Nina's.'

I ❤ Malaysia

It was ten o'clock and I was back on the balcony, lying in the sun, with my nose stuck between the pages of the *The Da Vinci Code*. Tom had long since set out on his trip to the Samaria Gorge leaving me alone for the day.

Things had been awkward between the two of us to say the least. I didn't know how to behave around someone who'd just told me they might have cancer. I was so confused by the situation that I ended up alternating between being overly concerned about his well-being and acting like his personal court jester in order to lift his spirits. By the time he left the apartment (having turned down a constant barrage of offers from me to come to keep him company) he must have been over the moon to see the back of me.

With a full day alone ahead of me and no one to distract me from indulging in thoughts of Sarah, I knew that it would only be a matter of time before she took up her usual residency in my thoughts. So, resting my book on the table at my side, I decided that if thinking about Sarah was inevitable then the best thing I could do would be to get it out of the way. Without any further ado I settled back in my chair and commenced thinking.

I never told this to anyone but on the day Sarah left me I actually went out to book a holiday. It had been a day full of arguing and shouting and crying (on both our parts) and then she had delivered the final blow with the words: 'I don't think I love you any more.' I knew straight away she wasn't bluffing. It was just like when I was a kid and I'd been up to no good, deliberately doing something that I knew would get me in trouble. My dad would catch me in the act and he'd say something like, 'Right, that's it,' and from the tone of his voice I'd know straight away that this wasn't an empty threat. Within seconds I'd feel the effect of my dad's open palm connecting with the bare flesh of my upper legs long before I'd hear the sonic boom of the slap. And that's exactly what it was like hearing Sarah tell me she no longer loved me. It was a blow to the heart followed by a sonic boom. A slap so hard that I thought it would never stop stinging. My head was reeling, my heart was racing and my life was lying shattered in tiny shards at my feet.

As Sarah slammed the door at her exit I remember feeling strangely calm. People who have nearly died on operating tables in hospitals sometimes say, as they're lying there with doctors and nurses screaming all around them trying to bring them back to life, that they can feel themselves leaving their bodies and floating up above the scene of what they think are their last moments. Well that was me. I was floating out of my own body watching myself slumped lifeless on a chair at the dining-room table only there was no one trying to bring me back to life. There was just me, an empty flat, and too many memories. And in that state I heard myself saying the words, 'You've got to do something,' over and over again and I couldn't work out whether I meant I'd got to do something to get Sarah back or that I should just stop sitting there and take some action. And while I sat there trying to work out exactly what I meant, out of the corner of my eye I spotted a holiday brochure in a magazine rack by the TV. It was called something like *Luxury Holidays Plus*, and was filled with expensive five-star breaks to places like Barbados, the Seychelles and the Maldives – holidays that we could never have considered under normal circumstances. That was when I realised that Sarah hadn't picked up the brochure with the two of us in mind at all. Within seconds of this bombshell dropping, I'd put on my shoes, grabbed my coat and was heading into town.

The travel agent's I went to were called Holidays Now. Above the door to the shop was a sign that said: 'The home of holidays', and stuck to the windows with Blu-Tack were dozens of marker-pen-inscribed cards featuring late-booking offers. My eyes lit up as I reviewed the offers in the window: fourteen nights in Costa Rica, ten nights in Ibiza, seven nights in Gran Canaria, a fortnight in Portugal and eight days in Malta but there was a problem with every single one of them. All the discount prices were offered on the basis of two people sharing. And yet here I was, just one person, looking for a way to escape.

The moment I entered the travel agent's I felt as if all eyes were on me. It was as if I'd tripped some sort of infrared alarm. The three of the female sales agents had looked up and flashed me their whitest, toothiest, shiniest smiles. For a few moments I genuinely felt loved, and then I realised that they were not so much smiling as responding to some sort of Pavlovian trigger they had been taught on one of those long-distant training schemes at the beginning of their careers. They reminded me of the androids in *Blade Runner*. Human, but not quite human enough.

A deftly manicured finger pointed me in the direction of their waiting area – a space in the centre of the store somewhat bizarrely made up to look like a beach-style café bar. There were three aluminium café-style tables with chairs and sunshades and in the middle of them was a pile of sand, a bucket and spade, a beach towel and a Jackie Collins novel.

Unsure whether this was an art installation or a genuine waiting area, I looked enquiringly back at the saleswoman and she gave me a hearty smile and a wink. Taking a deep breath I crossed the floor and sat down at one of the tables, feeling peculiarly self-conscious. Here I was, a now single, thirty-five-year-old man, sitting alone at a fake outdoor café, next to a fake beach, in a travel agency in the middle of a busy Brighton shopping centre on a wet July afternoon.

As I poured myself a cup of water from a dispenser I tried to work out which one of the sales girls would serve me first. My guess was the one nearest the entrance, as there was something ridiculously efficient about her manner that told me she was probably the store's top sales person. But as I looked around the room I noticed that the assistant sitting at the desk at the rear of the shop was actually quite pretty. She had dark brown hair, caramel-coloured skin and a killer smile. Even in her work uniform of purple polyester skirt and red checked blouse she looked amazing.

The pretty sales assistant must have sensed she was being watched because for no reason at all she looked up and caught my eye. Our eyes met for a few moments and then instinctively I looked away, which only served to make me look guilty. To balance things out I looked at her again but then incorporated this look into a whole batch of long stares around the room to make me look less suspect. I stared at the large banner above her head, featuring soft focus families walking across an idyllic palm-tree-strewn beach; I stared at three men in the queue at the Bureau de Change (one of whom was carrying a large carrier bag emblazoned with the slogan: I ❤ Malaysia); and I stared at the Jackie Collins novel in the display.

Having sufficiently distanced myself from any deviant-seeming behaviour, I hedged a glance back at the pretty saleswoman. She was still deep in conversation with a young couple she was serving and didn't look in my direction once in the three seconds I spent imagining what it might be like to kiss her. And so with the heat off I took a long sip of my water and studied the rows of brochures on the rack behind me. Just as I was about to pluck out one about skiing holidays (even though I didn't ski and hated the idea of skiing) I stopped. A young couple, laden with fashionable shopping bags and dressed as if they were going out on a Saturday night, sat down at the table next to mine. Our eyes met, and I was temporarily frozen in embarrassment until a female voice entered my consciousness.

'Hello there.'

The pretty sales assistant was talking to me. She was barely into her twenties and was even prettier up close.

'I'm Denise,' she said cheerfully. 'How can I help you today?'

There was a long pause as the cogs in my brain began to rotate, reminding me of several key factors I'd neglected to consider that would considerably hinder any attempt to book a holiday: first, it was three weeks until pay day, second, I hadn't checked with work when I could get the time off, and third, I didn't want to go on holiday alone.

I smiled. 'I'm afraid I've wasted your time. I've just realised that I'm in completely the wrong place to book a holiday.'

Then I stood up and left.

Camera phone

Around midday I came to the conclusion that if I was going to enjoy this holiday at all then I was going to have to stop thinking about Sarah. I briefly contemplated going down to the beach with *The Da Vinci Code* but I was getting tired of reading about religious conspiracies and wanted to do something that required physical exertion of some description. Looking around the room for inspiration, I spotted Tom's beloved *Rough Guide* that he'd inadvertently left on the table on the balcony and began flicking through it. There was a whole host of 'must see' cultural suggestions from museums and ruins right through to hills and famous birthplaces. Though Tom had circled a number of his favourites in blue Biro, most held no interest for me whatsoever.

The only place I was even vaguely interested in visiting was Heraklion, the capital of the island. And that was because I thought it might have proper shops and things to buy that weren't just the usual old tourist tat. In essence what I wanted from Heraklion was a small glimpse of England – a homogenised city centre that despite its architecture, culture and customs would have the same chain stores, brands and regular 'old tat' shops of any high street back home. Why? Because what I wanted more than anything was a little retail therapy. And with several hundred pounds' worth of holiday Euros doing very little other than securing me access to alcohol, ice cream and local cuisine, I was now desperate to exercise my real buying power.

I took a taxi into Heraklion and my hunch that it might be a modern city, with modern shopping facilities, paid off. It was just as I had hoped. The downside was that once I was there, I couldn't actually find a single thing I wanted to buy. I visited electrical shops and computer shops, clothes shops and book shops, and I visited a bunch of One-Euro shops and a market and left all of them without buying a single thing.

Coming to the conclusion that my excursion had been a mistake, I made my way down a back street in a bid to find the taxi rank where I had been dropped off. After a quarter of any hour, it became clear to me that I was well and truly lost. Nothing in my surroundings seemed even vaguely familiar and with the midday sun beating down on my head I was beginning to feel quite disorientated. In a last-ditch attempt to find out where I was, I took a left down a narrow passageway that opened up into a large civic square dominated by a grand-looking cathedral.

As I edged my way further into the square, the cathedral's bells chimed twice as if beckoning me towards it. Reasoning that I had nothing better to do I made my way across the shady square and up the steep steps to the entrance to the church.

In contrast to the intense warmth and brightness of the day outside, the inside of the cathedral was dimly lit and cool and seemed like the perfect sanctuary. Sitting down on an old wooden bench at the back of the church I looked around me. The cathedral was just as I expected. It had grand painted ceilings, colourful stained-glass windows, ageing frescoes and hundreds of ornate woodcarvings.

Closing my eyes, I took a deep breath and as the peace and quiet of the building began to filter into my head I wondered whether I might ever find myself approaching a religious conversion similar to Tom's. Though it was probably my imagination, for a few brief moments I began to feel as if the weight of my worries was being lifted off my shoulders. Just as I was beginning to explore this new sensation an electronic-sounding camera click broke my reverie. I opened my eyes to see a middle-aged woman armed with a camera phone frantically taking pictures of everything around her as if she was shooting a front cover for *What Cathedral Weekly*.

Even though I was pretty sure I didn't believe in God, on Tom's behalf and behalf of people like him, I was grabbed by the impulse to smash this woman's phone into a million pieces. Fortunately for me, a priest approached her and after a brief exchange she left the building. I felt as though I could finally relax and for a short while that's just what I did. I stared at the characters depicted in the frescoes, I watched a stream of people lighting candles for their loved ones and I thought long and hard about Tom and his situation. And although I felt none the wiser by the time I came to leave, I did at least feel in some small way more at peace with the world. And while I wasn't sure whether it was the right thing to do or not, I lit a candle for Tom.

As I turned round to leave, I noticed a young dark-haired woman standing by the bench in front of me. And recognised her immediately.

'You're Andy's friend aren't you?' said the woman. 'Charlie, isn't it?'

'Yeah,' I replied shaking her hand. 'And you're Nina's sister Donna.'

Why would anyone want to kill a pixie?

'Are you Catholic?' asked Donna.

'No,' I replied. 'I was just . . . it's a long story.' I paused and looked at her. 'You're not Catholic are you?'

Donna shrugged. 'I think the rules say you're one for life even if, like me, you haven't stepped foot in a church since you were a teenager.' She paused. 'I don't even know what made me decide to come in. It's one of those things you do when you're in a foreign country, isn't it? I'd never think for a minute to look around my local church just because I was passing by.' She smiled awkwardly. 'Are you here alone?'

'Yeah,' I replied. 'My mate Tom has gone hiking and I'm guessing Andy's with your sister. You're not here with them are you?

'Those two?' laughed Donna. 'I doubt they're even up yet. No, I came in on my own. We fly home tomorrow so I thought I'd buy a few presents and see something other than the beach. How about you? What brings you to Heraklion?'

'Same as you really,' I replied. 'Malia can feel a bit small after a while.'

'You're not wrong there.'

'Where are you off to next?' I asked.

'I don't know. How about you?'

'I've got nothing planned as such. In fact I was thinking about heading back.' I paused. 'Look, I don't suppose you fancy getting a coffee or something do you? I haven't eaten yet and could do with grabbing a quick something.'

'That would be great,' said Donna. 'On my way here I saw a café across the square that looked quite nice. It's in the shade, too, which is a blessing in this heat.'

With Donna leading the way, we made our way outside.

'You forget how bright it can get,' she said slipping on a pair of black Jackie O-style sunglasses. They suited her perfectly. With the blue-striped T-shirt and grey skirt she was wearing, she looked like a glamorous sixties film star.

'They suit you,' I said to Donna as I put on my own sunglasses.

'Thanks,' she replied. 'I bought them on holiday last year. They're my favourite thing I own. I love them.' She peered at me closely so that all I could see was my own reflection in her sunglasses. 'Yours suit you too. You look like you ought to be in a band.'

We walked a few steps in silence and then Donna spoke. 'So do you live in Hove like your friend Andy?'

'Brighton, actually,' I joked. 'How about you?'

'North London,' she replied. 'Archway to be exact.'

'I know Archway,' I replied. 'I used to have a mate who lived there for a while. His place was just on the edge of a really rough council estate.'

'Henmarsh?'

'Yeah,' I replied. 'I think so.'

Donna laughed. 'That's where I live.'

'That's so typical of me,' I said, wincing. 'It's a wonder I haven't started randomly insulting members of your family.'

'It's fine,' replied Donna. 'It *is* a bit of a rough estate. But Sadie and I won't be there forever.'

'Sadie?' I asked.

'My daughter.'

As we reached the tables outside the café, some kids behind us rode their bikes towards a large congregation of pigeons, sending them flying into the air. Donna ducked in towards me and instinctively I put my arm around her to protect her.

'Sorry about that,' said Donna as she realised that she was clinging on to my T-shirt. 'I hate pigeons. Can't stand them. My worst nightmare is one of the vile things getting their feet caught in my hair.'

'I don't mind them really,' I replied, 'although I admit I get a bit freaked out when I see the ones with missing limbs hopping about. Does that make me evil?'

'No,' smiled Donna. 'At least not in my eyes.'

We sat down and I plucked a plastic menu, sandwiched between a container of sugar packets and a paper-napkin dispenser, and handed it to Donna.

'Are you just snacking or having a proper meal?' she asked.

'It's too hot to eat a proper meal,' I replied. 'I just want something to fill the gap.'

'I'm going to have the waffles and ice cream then,' said Donna handing me the menu. 'They sound really nice.'

I scanned the menu. 'I'll have that too. And I think I'll have a Coke to wash it down.'

'Good idea,' said Donna, taking off her sunglasses and resting them on the edge of the table. 'Full fat or diet?'

'Full fat,' I replied. 'You?'

Donna smiled. 'Full fat all the way.'

A waitress appeared almost as soon as I returned the menu to its resting place and took our order. As soon as she left Donna turned to me and pointed at my T-shirt. 'So you like the Pixies then? I saw them once at the Brixton Academy when I was eighteen.'

'Were they good?'

'They were brilliant. Have you seen them?'

'I saw them back in Brighton when I was at college. They were okay but I wouldn't call myself a massive fan. I liked the T-shirt more than anything. It just seems like such a mad thing to proclaim don't you think? "Death to the Pixies". Why would anyone want to kill a pixie?'

'Maybe it's like my thing with pigeons,' smiled Donna. 'Maybe somewhere in the world there's a woman wearing big sunglasses who has an acute fear of getting pixies stuck in her hair.'

There was a brief lull in the conversation as we watched the kids on bikes continuing to harass the pigeons who had regrouped to peck the ground around the cathedral steps.

'What do you do for a living?' I eventually asked.

'I'm a paediatric nurse at Whittington hospital,' said Donna. 'I've been there nearly ten years now and I still love it. I just wish it paid more, that's all, so I could move out of Henmarsh. How about you?'

'Try not to yawn, but I set up schemes to help businesses and housing trusts start up in run-down areas around Brighton and Hove. It's an all-right job as they go and the people I work with are good to be around so I don't worry about it too much.'

The waitress returned with our drinks and set them down in front of us. I hadn't realised just how thirsty I was and had to stop myself gulping down the entire glass straight away. Donna meanwhile sipped her Coke through a straw in a slow considered manner as though she were savouring every drop.

'Can I ask you a question?' said Donna setting aside her drink.

'Depends what it is.'

'It's about your friend Andy,' she began. 'He's got a girlfriend hasn't he?'

I studied her face, trying to work out if she knew this for a fact or was trying to trick me into confirming her suspicions but then I realised that I didn't actually care one way or the other.

'Yeah,' I nodded, 'he has.'

'I thought so.'

'Does your sister know?'

'Any time I ask her about it she gets cagey – which is a sure sign of guilt in my family. She keeps telling me it's just a holiday thing. As if that makes it all right.' She frowned and bit her lip. 'It doesn't does it?'

'It's hard to say.' I shrugged. 'There's that phrase Americans always say when they go to Las Vegas in a big group isn't there? Something like, "What happens in Las Vegas stays in Las Vegas". Malia's a bit like that for us Brits. It's a place where people go a little bit mental just because they can. I think it must be something that's hardwired into the human brain – the need to escape the normal rules sometimes.'

'So is it a case of what happens in Malia, stays in Malia with you and your friends?' asked Donna. 'Or will you be telling Andy's partner what he's been up to?'

I thought for a moment. 'It'll be staying in Malia,' I replied.

Donna nodded. 'And I'm guessing the trade-off is that he won't be telling your partner what you've been up to either?'

'There's no partner for him to tell.'

The information registered on her face. A raise of the eyebrows, some curiosity in the eyes, a small movement in the lips and then . . . gone.

'You don't look single,' said Donna matter of factly.

I had to laugh. 'So what do I look like?'

'You look like the partners of my friends back home – well turned out and looked after.'

I sighed heavily. 'Well, it's not been that long since that was actually the case.'

Donna winced. 'Looks like it's my turn to put my foot in my mouth. I'm really sorry. I went a bit far there didn't I?'

'No, it's fine,' I replied. 'It's not like it happened yesterday.'

'So is that what this holiday is about?'

'Is it that obvious?'

Donna smiled. 'Come on, three guys in their mid-thirties in a place like Malia? What could be at all obvious about that?'

'Well, for starters I can assure you that it wasn't my plan.'

'Let me guess,' said Donna. 'It was Andy's.'

'When he gets an idea in his head it's difficult to say—' I stopped mid-sentence as the waitress returned with our waffles and ice cream and by the time she had left it no longer seemed like a sentence worth finishing.

With the conversational flow between us interrupted we both retreated to our separate corners and tucked into our waffles in a polite silence. I wanted to carry on talking to her. I didn't want this to end. I decided that the best thing I could do was jump in with both feet.

'Okay,' I said, after Donna forked the first mouthful of her dessert into her mouth. 'You know about how I ended up here but you've still to explain about *you*. After all you're . . . what . . . ?' The face. The hair. The clothes. I had her pegged somewhere roughly in her early thirties but decided to err on the side of caution. '. . . late twenties?'

Donna grinned. 'Early thirties – as if you couldn't tell.'

'Early thirties?' I laughed. 'Then you belong in Malia about as much as I do. Shouldn't you be out renting villas in Tuscany or going on diving holidays in the Maldives or at the very least living it up in Ibiza?'

'I would've loved to have done any of those things you mentioned this summer, but beggars can't be choosers. Nina and I are half-sisters and even though there's nine years between us we're really close. Anyway, about a month ago she told me she was planning to come here with her friends and wanted me to come along. With work and Sadie I don't get to see her as often as I'd like so I thought why not?'

'So who's looking after your daughter now?'

'Her dad. He's a teacher. We're not together any more.' She paused and then added: 'These things happen, don't they?'

'Yeah,' I replied. 'I suppose they do.'

We both picked up our spoons and returned to our waffles and ice cream.

'So how old's Sadie?' I asked after a while as Donna pushed her empty plate to one side.

'She was six in April.' Donna reached into her bag, pulled out her purse and took out a passport-sized photo of her daughter. She too had dark hair, big brown eyes and a huge smile.

'She looks just like you,' I said staring at the photo.

'A lot of people say that,' replied Donna. 'But I don't see it myself. Have you got any kids yourself?'

Her question took me by surprise. Then I realised that at my age it was a valid question, given that most of my contemporaries were now fathers or at the very least thinking about becoming fathers.

'No,' I replied.

'Were they ever on the list?'

'I think so,' I replied. 'Once upon a time they were, anyway.'

Donna and I talked in general about the holiday and a bit more about our lives back home but then our waitress returned to clear our table and I could feel that our time together was over. We split the bill and then, tucking the money we owed underneath the sugar dispenser, stood up and made ready to leave.

'Thanks for that,' said Donna quietly. 'That was a really nice way to spend an afternoon.'

'It was, wasn't it?' I replied. 'Maybe I'll see you around later in Malia? Andy was saying that you were all going out tonight as it's your last night.'

'Nina did mention something like that. You and your other friend should definitely come along if you're free.'

'Cool,' I replied. 'Well, I'll see you later then, hopefully.'

Donna waved goodbye and as she crossed the square back to the city, the cathedral bells began to chime, sending the pigeons that had been resting in the bell tower soaring one last time into the sky.

Happy face

It was just after six-thirty when Tom returned to the apartment. He came out on the balcony where I'd been sitting and I offered him one of the two remaining cans of Heineken I'd brought out with me. Though worn out from his day walking he looked happy, almost carefree and we exchanged highlights of our day apart with none of the awkwardness of earlier. He was back to being Tom and I was back to being me. And everything between us was just fine.

'So is it too crass to ask the big question?' asked Tom.

'Which big question would that be?'

'The one about you and Donna,' he said, smirking. 'Do you think anything will happen tonight?'

'I've no idea,' I replied. 'It's not like I got any sort of positive vibes from her . . . not unless you count agreeing to eat Belgian waffles with me.'

Tom shrugged. 'Well I wouldn't discount it altogether. Back when I was single I knew plenty of girls that wouldn't even talk to me, let alone eat waffles in the same vicinity.'

'You see,' I sighed, 'this is the bit I always found difficult, back in my single days: the "how to tell if they're interested part".'

'What does the evidence say?' asked Tom.

'Well, other than the waffles she did say that I should come out with her sister and her friends tonight.'

'That's all the evidence you need right there,' said Tom.

'Do you think so? She told me to bring you along too.'

'Even better,' said Tom. 'That's a clear case of using me as a smokescreen to hide her true motive.' He paused. 'So what's Andy got organised for tonight anyway?'

'Nothing too excessive . . . you know . . . a few beers and a bit of a laugh. Tell me you're coming.'

'I can't,' said Tom, wincing. 'This walk really took it out of me. I was at the front of the entire walking party there and back. Tonight all I want to do is have a shower, phone Anne and the kids, and then sleep. Just give Andy a ring and tell him you're definitely coming tonight. If he gets a little too Andy even for you then at least you'll have Donna to chat to.'

'I think I'll do it,' I said reaching for my phone. I dialled Andy's number and he answered after three rings. 'It's me. I'm just calling to see what you're doing tonight. Tom's knackered from his hiking thing so he's going to—'

'Brilliant!' yelled Andy down the line. His voice became muffled but I could still just about hear him informing Nina that 'my mate Charlie is coming out tonight'.

'We're starting off at Club Tropicana,' said Andy coming back on the line. 'It's an eighties-themed bar and restaurant on the main strip, just past Pandemonium. We'll be there around nine-thirtyish. How does that sound?'

'Cool,' I replied. 'Nine-thirtyish. Club Tropicana.'

'That's the one.' He added cheerfully, 'Charlie?'

'Yeah?'

'Make sure you bring your happy face with you, okay, mate?'

'Happy face?'

'You know . . . give misery the night off for a change. It's the girls' last night in Malia. They want it to be a good one and I just want to make sure that everything is in position.'

'In position for what?'

'For you to have the best night of your entire life.'

What plan B?

As I sauntered into Club Tropicana at close to twenty to ten I was quite sure that it wasn't going to be the best night of my life. For a start, my clothes didn't feel right. I'd wanted to wear the same clothes I'd worn on our night out at Pandemonium (a tried and tested ensemble that was virtually my going-out-on-the-town uniform back in Brighton) but after all that time in the bar the shirt stank of cigarette smoke. My back-up ensemble, a pair of beige trousers and a white patterned shirt, had never been matched together before and though technically they should have had no trouble getting on together, for some reason the whole thing didn't quite work. Secondly, on my way to the strip that night I'd been waylaid by two Geordie girls who looked about seventeen. The first girl cheered me up immensely with the greeting: 'You're gorgeous, you are,' but then a second girl leered drunkenly into my face and tittered: 'Stay off the Bacardi Breezers, Tina, he's at least forty.' Thirdly, though not completely up to speed on the rules and regulations for having the best night of your life I was pretty confident that it wouldn't be sound-tracked by a Jive Bunny mega mix.

I found Andy and Nina sitting at a table on the club's outdoor terrace surrounded by Nina's friends, but there was no sign of Donna.

'Charlie!' said Andy, greeting me like I was his long-lost brother. 'How are you, mate? Come and sit down and meet the girls.'

One by one I was introduced to Nina's friends: Stacey, Melissa, Hattie and Beth. They all seemed nice enough and several of them were actually incredibly attractive but none of them sparked off anything in me the way Donna had that first night in Pandemonium – none of them looked as though they had stories to tell.

'I thought there were six of you?' I asked as I settled down in a chair between Andy and Melissa. 'Who's missing?'

'That'll be my sister Donna,' said Nina. 'She wanted to have some time by herself so we said we'd meet her around midnight in Bar Go-Go.'

'Couldn't you have told her we were going somewhere else?' said Andy.

'Why would you do that?' I asked.

'Andy thinks Donna doesn't like him,' said Nina. 'But he's wrong.'

'How can I be wrong since I was there when she took me aside yesterday and said to my face: "I don't like you."'

'It's not that she doesn't like you,' said Nina breezily. 'She's just looking out for her kid sister that's all. Trying to make sure that I'm not being corrupted by an older man.'

Andy stood up and began taking orders for the next round of drinks. But because I was determined to make a good impression I told him that I would get the next round in. We then proceeded to bicker in a pantomime fashion before agreeing to a compromise: I would pay while Andy would come to the bar with me and give me a hand getting the drinks back to the table. It was a perfect rendition of our 'how-to-look-good-in-front-of-the-opposite-sex' routine lifted straight from our college days and could only have been improved if Donna had been there to witness it.

'So what do you think of the girls then?' said Andy as we made our way to the bar.

'They seem nice enough.'

'Well, my friend, you're in for some luck tonight,' said Andy. 'With them going home tomorrow there's a bit more of a party atmosphere in the air than usual. And if you want my advice I think Hattie – the tall girl in the black dress – is your best bet. She hasn't pulled all holiday so might be up for some last-minute action. If Hattie's not your thing, try Stacey – blond hair, red top, white skirt. Nina says Stacey's pulled a different bloke every night so if you don't mind being number seven you could be well in there. I think you might be out of luck with Melissa – dark hair, black top, white skirt – because she's got a boyfriend back home but I reckon if you turn on that old Mansell charm to its maximum setting she might be persuaded to forget about him. Finally there's Beth – red hair, blue dress – she's actually single but to be truthful, mate, she is so out of your league it hurts. I only say this because she's pretty much out of my league too. I suppose if you're feeling ambitious she might be worth a go but I reckon you'd be wasting time that could be better spent charming Hattie out of her knickers.'

'What are you talking about?' I asked, even though I knew *exactly* what he was talking about.

'You came out tonight to pull didn't you?' said Andy.

'No,' I replied, reasoning that there was no point in weakening my argument with the truth, 'I came out tonight because I spent today, the third day of a holiday we're supposedly on for my benefit, on my own while Tom went hiking and you hung out with Nina.'

'Well, I'm here now aren't I?' said Andy. 'And the girls are here too. All you've got to do is give it a bit of the old chat and you'll be away.'

'Fine,' I said glancing over to our table in the hope that Donna might have arrived. 'I'll get the drinks and you—' I stopped as I felt my mobile phone vibrate in my back pocket. I pulled it out and looked at the screen.

'It's Lisa,' I said locking eyes with Andy guiltily.

'Why is she calling you again?' he asked staring at the screen on my phone.

'How am I supposed to know?' I replied. 'Do you want me to answer it or let it go to voicemail?'

'Answer it,' said Andy quickly. 'Speak to her. Find out what she wants.'

'Look,' I replied as the phone continued to ring. 'I've been thinking about this and I'm really not comfortable at getting into the middle of all the stuff with you and Lisa.'

'I know, I know,' he said urgently. 'Look, I've got a Plan B sorted that will solve everything, okay? Just answer the call and it'll be the last thing you have to do with her I promise you.'

'What do you mean you've got a "Plan B?"'

Andy winked at me. 'I'd tell you but I think I'd prefer to see the look on your face when I pull off my masterstroke. Now just answer the phone and talk to her for as long as you need to, okay?'

'Fine,' I replied. 'But you'll have to get the drinks in.'

It's not Malia

'Lisa,' I said breezily into the phone as I watched the hordes of late-night revellers milling in the street outside Club Tropicana. 'How are you?'

'Where are you?' she asked quickly. 'It sounds noisy.'

'Outside a bar,' I replied. 'It's quite crowded around here so—'

'Is Andy with you?' she interrupted.

'He's at the bar getting the drinks in.' I paused. 'Look, Lisa, what's with all the questions? Are you okay? Is something wrong?'

'I'm really sorry, Charlie.'

'Sorry about what?'

'I've got it into my head that you're hiding something from me. You're not are you?'

'What makes you think that anything is wrong?' I asked, side-stepping the issue.

'Nothing really. It was just a small thing that you said earlier that didn't quite add up. You remember the text message you sent me? You said you and Tom and Andy spent the day on the beach, didn't you?'

'Yeah, I did.'

'Well, are you sure about that?'

'Of course I am.' Then I paused and, employing my best acting skills, corrected myself. 'Well . . . actually . . . come to think of it . . . we actually spent most of the day by the pool because we were too wrecked to go anywhere else, but then we did make it to the beach a bit later in the afternoon once our strength was up. But you know how it gets when you're on holiday, everything sort of merges into one doesn't it?'

'You're right.' The acute relief in Lisa's voice was clearly audible. I felt like the lowest of the low. 'You're absolutely right.' She paused. 'I really am so sorry, Charlie. I should let you go. I feel like I'm single-handedly ruining your holiday.'

'You don't have to go,' I said quickly. Her guilt was making my own spiral out of control. 'It's not like I'm missing out on much. I think they're playing Tears For Fears at the moment.'

'Okay,' laughed Lisa. 'Leaving aside Tears For Fears for the moment . . . how has your day been?'

'How has my day been? All right . . . I suppose. Nothing special. It started pretty crappily but then—'

'Why did it start crappily? Andy's not being a real pain is he?'

'No,' I replied. 'It's not Andy . . . it's just that . . . well last night I heard some bad news and it was pretty much the first thing on my mind when I woke up this morning—'

'It was Sarah wasn't it?' said Lisa with genuine pity in her voice. 'She's finally told you.'

'Told me what?'

There was a long pause. I could feel Lisa panicking at the other end of the line.

'It's . . . it's nothing . . .' she stammered. 'I thought that . . . look, it doesn't matter.'

'What do you know about Sarah that you're not telling me?' I demanded. 'She sent me a text message on Sunday but I didn't reply. You know what she wants to talk to me about, don't you?'

'Please, Charlie, don't make me say any more,' pleaded Lisa. 'I'm begging you. I've said too much as it is. It's the sort of news that you need to hear straight from Sarah not me. Call her and I'm sure she'll tell you everything.'

'Just tell me, Lisa,' I snapped. 'Whatever it is I'm not going to blame you, okay? This is Sarah's fault. Not yours. So tell me what she wants and we can move on.'

'I can't,' she said.

'Just tell me.'

'I can't,' she repeated.

'Look, I'm not going to hang up until you do.'

'She's pregnant,' she said finally. 'Sarah's pregnant.'

There was a long silence.

'I'm so sorry, Charlie.'

Silence.

'Charlie, you have to forgive me. You should never have heard this from me.'

Silence.

'I'm sorry.'

'I know you are,' I said softly and then without saying goodbye I switched off the phone.

DAY FOUR: THURSDAY

Voicemail

It was just after midnight. I was sitting on my own in a booth overlooking the strip in the McDonalds at the crossroads. In front of me were a cold cup of coffee (mine) and the remains of a Big Mac Meal (someone else's).

I pulled my phone out of my back pocket and switched it on. Within seconds it beeped frantically to let me know that I had several voicemail messages. I dialled the mailbox and listened to the messages:

> **Message one:** 'Charlie, this is Lisa. Where are you? I'm so sorry for what happened. Please call back and let me know you're okay.'
>
> **Message two:** 'Charlie, it's Andy here. It's nearly half ten. Where are you, mate? I know I said talk to Lisa as long as you want but this is ridiculous. Come back quick. Nina's mate Hattie is definitely interested in you.'
>
> **Message three:** 'Charlie, Andy here again. It's half eleven. You've chickened out on me and gone back to the apartment haven't you? Is it because of Hattie? Well you've missed out there. She's pulled some Scottish guy with an armful of tattoos. Just come back okay? The night's still young and even Beth – the one I said you didn't stand a chance with – is looking a bit desperate. We're off to Bar Go-Go in a bit so look sharpish.'

> **Message four:** 'Charlie, whatever time you get this message please call me to let me know you're all right. I've tried calling Andy to find out where you are but his phone is switched off. I'm starting to get worried that something bad has happened. Please call.'

I put my phone down on the table and took a moment to look through the window in front of me. A large gang of lads in Newcastle United shirts were passing by the restaurant singing at the top of their voices. Sighing heavily, I picked up my phone again and typed out a text message for Lisa:

> **Message Charlie:** 'Hi, don't worry. I'm fine.'

As I switched off my phone and looked out of the window again a huge tidal wave of emotion crashed over me, threatening to engulf me completely. My heart began racing and I felt as though every last one of my internal organs was being slowly crushed inside.

The intensity of my reaction took me by surprise. I couldn't work out what it meant or why it was happening. Even after Sarah first left me I'd been more angry than upset. I'd been more interested in exacting revenge than in responding in any kind of emotional way to her actions. I almost took comfort from the fact that she simply didn't push the button. Yes, she had the power to make me depressed but *she* wasn't the trigger that opened up the flood gates. And for that small mercy, at the time at least, I was grateful because it made me feel as if I was superhuman. She had gone and wrecked my life in the process and yet I didn't feel a thing. I was bulletproof. I was invincible. I was Superman. But as I wiped the tears from my eyes in the crowded restaurant I realised that even Superman had his Kryptonite, and thanks to Lisa I'd now discovered mine.

I dumped my cold coffee in the bin by the exit and strode into the street outside with such purpose that I almost bumped into someone coming the other way.

It was only when I looked to apologise that I realised that the person standing in front of me was Donna. She was dressed in a white top and skirt with matching sandals. Her hair was tied back in a pony tail.

'Charlie,' she said surprised. 'Aren't you going the wrong way for Bar Go-Go or have I missed something?'

'I'm not going,' I replied.

'Are you all right?' asked Donna as though she had a sixth sense for troubled minds. 'Has something happened?'

'I'm just not in the right mood to be here tonight.'

'You're not the only one,' said Donna. 'I'm missing Sadie like crazy and on top of that I'm really getting sick of this place.' Donna paused and looked at me again as if trying to see inside my head. 'I was only going to show my face at Bar Go-Go so that Nina wouldn't keep on about me being miserable,' she began. 'Why don't you come too? We wouldn't have to stay long and if you came I'd at least have someone nice to talk to.'

'Thanks,' I sighed. 'But—'

'Are you sure?'

'Yeah, I'm sure.'

Donna nodded carefully. If she was offended by my sullen mood she did a good job of hiding it. 'Okay, well I think I'll still pop in anyhow.' This was it. This was goodbye. 'Well, it was nice to meet you anyway.'

'Yeah,' I replied, willing myself to say something that would make her stay. 'It was nice to meet you too. Hope everything goes well for you and Sadie back in north London.'

'Look after yourself, Charlie.' She reached up and kissed me on the cheek. 'And make sure you have a great life.' With that she turned and walked away in the direction of Bar Go-Go and for a few moments I stood rooted to the spot, unsure of what I should do next. That was the moment I realised that I couldn't let her walk away without at the very least explaining my behaviour. I ran after her, calling out her name until she stopped and turned around.

'Listen, Donna,' I said unable to take my eyes off her. 'I'm sorry for what just happened. I know it's no excuse but the thing is I've just had a bit of bad news that's sort of turned my whole world upside down.'

'Was it about your ex?'

'Is it that obvious?'

Donna smiled and shook her head. 'Do you want to talk about it?'

'I don't know,' I replied. 'Do you want to listen?'

'How about we take it in turns to do both?' said Donna smiling.

'Now that,' I began as she took my hand in her own, 'sounds like a good idea.'

Heads or tails?

At Donna's suggestion, we made our way back up to the strip in the direction of all the main bars and clubs, but as we passed the Camelot club we turned right up a street with a slight incline that I'd failed to notice on my previous visits. The early part of the street consisted mainly of fast-food outlets and amusement arcades but those died out the further we walked along and were gradually replaced by small grocery shops and bakeries. Near the end of the street, opposite a taxi rank, was a small bar called Mythos. As we walked in it was obvious that Mythos didn't cater for the tourist crowd: the décor was that of a traditional taverna, the music on in the background was Greek and with the exception of a couple of middle-aged locals the entire bar was empty.

Donna and I sat down at a table near the door and when a waiter came over to us we ordered two beers which he brought to us straight away.

'So how did you find this place?' I asked.

'On my travels,' replied Donna. 'One afternoon when the girls were all down at the beach I took myself off for a walk. I spotted the bakery next door first and bought a few pastries and then saw this place. It just seemed really nice and quiet so whenever I could get away during the day for a little while I'd nip up here and have a drink and write a postcard to Sadie.'

'You wrote more than one?'

'Two a day for every day that we've been here,' she laughed. 'I told you I was missing her.'

There was a long silence.

'Heads or tails?' said Donna after a few moments.

'What do you mean?'

Donna laughed. 'I thought it might make it easier to work out which one of us would be talking first.'

'Heads you go first,' I replied.

'Okay,' said Donna handing me a one-Euro coin. 'But you'll have to be the one to flip it because I'm rubbish at that kind of thing.'

I flipped the coin and caught it moments later in mid-air, wrapping my fingers around it tightly. Donna and I stared expectantly at my clenched fist. I opened my hand and Donna laughed, clearly delighted with the result.

'Over to you then.'

'Fine,' I replied, 'but I'll keep the coin.'

With that I took a long sip of my beer and told Donna everything about my break-up with Sarah, beginning with the day she left and finishing with Lisa's phone call less than a couple of hours ago.

'No wonder you looked so shell-shocked when I bumped into you,' said Donna. 'I'm surprised you're still standing at all after what you've been through.'

'Maybe,' I replied. 'I think the real killer is that I didn't even see it coming.'

'There's no reason you should have done, Charlie. I think it's just one of those things. The important thing is what you do next.'

'There is no next,' I replied. 'That's it. It's all over.'

'But what about the baby?'

'It's not mine. It's his. Oliver's.' I caught Donna's eye and could see that she was curious how I could be so sure. 'We hadn't touched each other in months,' I explained. 'I assumed it was just a phase, but we never seemed to come out the other side.'

A million years

'For a long time after Sadie's dad left I thought about taking an overdose,' said Donna.

'You're joking?'

Donna shook her head. 'I wish I was.'

'But you didn't do anything did you?'

She shook her head, scanning my face for a reaction. 'I think it was just me not thinking straight, that's all. My GP had prescribed me antidepressants and I wasn't coping very well.' She paused and looked at me. 'You don't think I'm weird do you?'

'No, of course not.'

'I don't think I was serious about it,' she continued. 'I know I'd never willingly leave Sadie in a million years. But there were times after he'd gone when I didn't know how I'd make it through the next minute, let alone the next day. I missed Ed so much I didn't know how to cope. In the end my mum and dad had to come and stay with me to help out with Sadie. Ed walked out because he said he couldn't cope with being tied down. He said that I wanted more from him than he had to give and that he needed his own space.' She paused and laughed. 'He said a lot of things actually. But none of them ever made sense.' She took a sip of her lager. 'It's been two years since it happened and I get on with him now for Sadie's sake rather than my own. If I didn't think that she would hold it against me, I'd never have anything to do with him again. He's okay now that he's managed to get over his mini-life crisis, find himself a new girlfriend, and finally get his head around the idea of being a parent. But I just can't find it in my heart to forgive him for what he did. He broke my heart, Charlie. Smashed it in two and I never thought that I'd recover.'

My way of coping

'What's the single thing you miss most about Sarah?' asked Donna.

'Just one thing? Her not being around,' I answered. 'Until she left I don't think I was ever quite aware just how much space she filled in my life.'

Donna nodded. 'No one ever tells you what a lonely place the world can be when you go from being two to one, do they? I think the only reason I managed to cope with the situation was because I had Sadie to look after.'

'I suppose Andy and Tom are my way of coping,' I said, avoiding Donna's gaze. 'It's not so much that they've said or done anything special since I split up with Sarah – I didn't even tell Tom that Sarah had gone until he arrived at my flat the day before we flew here.'

'So what is it they give you?' asked Donna. 'How did they help you to cope when Sarah left?'

I paused and thought for a moment. 'They gave me somewhere to belong,' I replied eventually. 'And I think that's pretty much all I needed.'

The middle of it

'Where do you think you'll be this time next year?' asked Donna.

'What kind of a question is that?'

'The kind of question I ask all the time,' smiled Donna. 'I think about the future all the time. Probably even more than the present. I never used to be like this. I think it must be something to do with having a kid because you always have to plan ahead – meal times, clothes to wear, everything. Now I love thinking about the future because it's a place where, until you arrive there, anything can happen.'

'I used to think about the future quite a bit when I was at college,' I replied. 'But you do when you're that sort of age don't you? You constantly feel like your whole life is ahead of you.'

'And now?'

'Now I'm in the middle of it. This, right now, this is life and most of the time I've got enough problems dealing with the now to think about anything else.' I paused and laughed. 'I sound like the king of doom.'

'That's because you're too bogged down in the daily struggle.'

'Okay,' I replied. 'So with all your thinking about the future, where do you think you'll be this time next year?'

'Somewhere out of London,' said Donna. 'I don't know where exactly. Maybe somewhere in the country, or near the sea. A few years ago my parents moved to Aberdovey in Wales. Where they live is only five minutes from the sea and it is absolutely amazing there. Sadie and I try to see them at least every other month and any time we go it's just like being on holiday. That's where I'd like to be if we could afford it.'

'And what about next year's holiday?' I asked mischievously. 'Any chance of you coming back here with Sadie?'

'You may laugh but she'd love it here,' said Donna. 'She'd be telling all of her friends how sophisticated she is.'

'So where then?'

'Do you know what? I haven't actually thought that much ahead. But if you pushed me for an answer I think I'd be happy going on holiday anywhere. Anywhere at all.'

Let's go

'It's late,' said Donna, looking at her watch. 'Let's go but not home.'

'Another bar?'

Donna shook her head. 'I'm done with bars.'

'How about the beach?'

Donna's face lit up immediately. 'Definitely. I think it's the one thing I'll miss about this place when I've gone.' She stood up, finished off the remains of her drink and then took me by the hand.

'Let's go.'

The two of us

It was just after two in the morning as Donna and I headed along the crowded strip in the direction of the beach while everyone else was heading in the opposite direction. It felt good swimming against the tide like this. As if it was the two of us against the world. Every step we took towards our destination seemed to bond us closer together just as every step the crowd took seemed to push them further away.

'Do these guys really think girls who look like that actually fancy them?' asked Donna as we watched with some amusement as a girl in a tight white vest and red sparkly hot-pants waylaid a group of lads who looked as if they had only just this second turned eighteen.

'They're not completely stupid,' I explained. 'They're just willing participants in the fantasy.'

'You sound like you're talking from experience.'

'Lurking inside most men is a spotty prepubescent teenager who thinks he'll never get a girlfriend.'

'Even you?'

'Especially me.'

A gang of girls carrying glow-in-the-dark batons passed by, closely followed by a similar-sized gang of lads chanting (rather than singing) 'Happy Birthday'.

'So was that ever you?' I asked as one of the girls carrying the glow-in-the-dark batons suddenly turned around and lifted up her skirt to flash the boys behind her.

'I wouldn't like to say.'

'So you've been on holidays like this before?'

'Full-on, all-girls-on-the-razz type resort holidays?'

I nodded.

'A few,' replied Donna coyly. 'The last one was about seven years ago. Some girls from nursing college and I went to Fuerteventura. We partied so much we inevitably all came back suffering with the symptoms of Fuerteventura 'flu: extreme exhaustion brought on by burning the candle at both ends for fourteen nights on the trot. It took me a good six months before I felt anything near back to normal and a year before I could look a Mai-Tai in the eye without feeling like I was going to throw up. My friends all went back the following year. I would've gone with them too but by then I'd got together with Ed, and the two of us went to Sardinia instead.'

'Was that a good holiday?'

Donna shrugged. 'It was okay, I suppose. We were young and in love and this was the first time that either of us had ever been away on a couple's holiday. When my friends came back from Fuerteventura and I heard about everything they'd got up to I remember feeling for a while like I'd missed out on something special. But when they all went back the year after I didn't have any regrets at all. It was definitely a case of been there, done that.'

'I met Sarah ten years ago here in Malia on an all-boys holiday with Andy and Tom,' I confessed.

'A holiday romance? I'd never have guessed that in a million years. I suppose because I've never done the holiday-romance thing myself.'

I was surprised. 'Not even when you went to Fuerteventura?'

'Not even when I went to Newquay with my parents when I was fifteen,' she replied. 'I don't know . . . I think I always thought they were a bit of a waste of time. My friends all had them and they never worked out. They'd fall massively in lust with some guy and a few weeks later when they were back at home and he hadn't phoned or called they'd be heartbroken.' Donna paused and smiled. 'Still, it worked for you. You must have been one of the good ones that kept the dream alive.'

Donna paused as we returned to the crossroads near McDonalds. There were quite a few cars on the road and no sign of a break in the traffic. As we waited, Donna squeezed my hand and smiled. A closeness was growing between us. And it didn't seem forced or even flirtatious. It seemed natural. As if the only logical place in the world for her hand to be was in my own.

Typical Libran

As we passed by a late-night grocery shop a few hundred yards from the top of the beach Donna suggested that we stop and get a bottle of wine. Without waiting to hear my reaction she led me into the brightly lit store where a middle-aged woman with a sad face sat at the till, staring into space.

I followed Donna to the wine section where she asked my opinion about what kind of wine to get.

'Let's go for a mid-priced red and a cheap one for afters,' I suggested reaching for a merlot and a cheaper bottle of Rioja. I offered both bottles up for her approval.

'They'll do fine,' said Donna. 'I hate choosing which wine. If you'd left it up to me we would've been here for ages and then I would've spent all night thinking that you secretly hated my choices.'

'Ah,' I joked, 'so instead I'm the one who's got to spend all night worrying?'

'No,' said Donna squeezing my hand. 'Right now, my friend, I don't think you could do a single thing wrong if you tried.'

Along with the wine we bought some chocolate and Pringles in case we became hungry and then left the grocery store with the bottles clanging together in a blue plastic carrier bag. Within minutes we had left the road behind and were on the path down to the beach.

It was odd being at the beach so late at night. The moon was quite bright and in its light I could see the shadowy outlines of the sun-loungers and umbrellas packed away behind a fenced-off area. The rest of the beach was completely empty.

'Do you think I should call Nina and tell her where I am?' asked Donna.

'Definitely.'

Donna took off her sandals and walked barefoot across the sand until she was out of earshot but just about visible.

I don't know why but I suddenly felt like talking to someone too. I pulled out my phone and dialled Andy's number.

'Charlie?' he said, answering the phone after six or seven rings. 'What happened to you? One minute you've gone outside to talk to Lisa and the next you've vanished into thin air.'

'It's a long story,' I replied.

'To do with Lisa?'

'No, to do with Sarah.'

'Oh, right,' said Andy solemnly. 'Bad news?'

'You could say that.'

There was a long pause.

'So where are you now?'

'I'm with Donna down at the beach.'

'Donna who?'

'Nina's sister, Donna.'

Andy burst out laughing. 'You're a sly one. How did that happen?'

'I bumped into her. We got talking.' I paused basking in the glow of being momentarily enigmatic. 'That's pretty much it.'

'Never mind all that,' said Andy. 'Have you and her—?'

'No.'

'But you are going to—?'

'No.'

'What do you mean no? This is it, Charlie. This is your moment. Don't screw it up by being Mr Nice Guy okay?'

I sighed. Andy was draining my batteries down to nothing. 'Look,' I replied, 'I only called to say sorry for running out on you like that.' I looked across the sand in Donna's direction and she waved at me. 'I'll see you later, okay?'

'Yeah,' replied Andy chuckling. 'I will see you later. And you'd better be prepared to tell me everything.'

I pressed the end call button and slipped my phone into the back of my jeans just as Donna beckoned me towards her.

'I think I've just completely freaked my sister out,' said Donna gaily, as she grasped my hand. 'She can't believe that I've gone off with you like this. It's so funny. Normally I'm the one trying to stop her doing crazy stuff.'

'I was on the phone to Andy and I think I freaked him out too. Which is probably a good thing.'

'Well I've got some good news for you,' said Donna. 'You'll be pleased to know that my sister's friend Beth apparently fancies you something rotten.'

'I'll make a note of that for later,' I said laughing.

Hand in hand we walked across the beach until we were about twenty yards from the edge of the sea.

'How about here?' suggested Donna. 'We'll be able to see the water but won't be under threat from getting soaked by the waves.'

We sat down cross-legged on the sand and I proceeded to open the more expensive bottle of wine by pushing the cork back into the bottle using the keys to the apartment.

'I think you should try it first,' I said, handing her the bottle. 'You can let me know if it's to your liking.'

Donna took a long swig and swallowed. 'It tastes fine to me; see what you think.' She handed the bottle back and I put it to my lips.

'Tastes pretty good to me too,' I replied.

For a few moments we sat lulled into a hypnotic silence by the waves breaking on the shore. I would have been content to stay like that much longer but Donna must have felt self-conscious because for no reason at all she asked me when my birthday was.

'Pardon?'

'Your birthday,' repeated Donna. 'When is it?'

'You're not going to ask me my star sign are you?' I asked warily.

'That's such a sexist thing to say. Not all women are obsessed with astrology. I'm just curious that's all.'

'Okay,' I replied. 'It's the first of June.'

'I knew it. A Gemini. That explains everything.' She paused and then admitted, 'I don't know anything about astrology. I only know you're a Gemini because an old boyfriend of mine used to be into it. He was forever trying to explain away my actions as being down to my star sign. In fact it got to the stage where I promised myself that if he ever said the phrase "Typical Libran", to my face again I was going to dump him. A minute after I made the decision he said it and I told him it was over that very second.'

'That's a bit harsh, isn't it?' I said leaning in closer to her face so that my lips were only inches away from her own.

'I don't think so at all.' She was smiling.

Waves

I don't know how long we kissed. A minute. Maybe two. In my head it seemed all too short although I suspect for Donna it was just long enough for the conscious side of her brain to gain control of the subconscious side.

'Is something wrong?' I asked as she pulled away.

Donna shook her head and leaned against my shoulder. 'There's nothing wrong. It's just me.' She reached across and held my hand, carefully interlacing our fingers. 'Do you mind if we just sit like this for a while and talk?'

'No,' I replied. 'That's fine.' And so pulling closer together, we sat in silence, watching the waves crash in front of us, wrapped in our own thoughts in our own worlds.

Foot prints

'What time is it?' asked Donna sleepily.

'Just after six,' I said reluctantly removing my gaze from the hazy rising morning sun to my watch. 'How rock and roll are we staying up all night?'

'Not very.' Donna stretched her arms above her head and yawned. 'Right now I think I could easily sleep the whole day away.' She looked at me and smiled. 'Are you hungry?'

'Starving.'

'Shall we go and find somewhere to eat?'

'I know just the place,' I replied. 'You'll love it.'

We stood up, stretched our limbs, brushed the sand off our clothes and made our way hand in hand across the beach.

'Look,' said Donna. 'Are those our foot prints from last night?'

'Yeah,' I replied.

'It seems like such a long time ago since we made these,' said Donna. 'It's almost as if they were made by two different people.'

'But they weren't two different people,' I replied. I pointed to the ground. 'Look, there's your foot print and there's mine. Side by side going in the same direction.'

'And now we're going back,' sighed Donna. 'It almost makes me wish we could turn around and just keep going forwards until we fall off the edge.'

Like infinity

The road near the beach was the quietest I'd ever seen it. No Brits, no club music and no quad bikes. The only signs of life were from delivery trucks dropping off supplies and tired-looking shop keepers opening up their stores. Stars and Bars, however, was a different story. Clusters of shattered-looking clubbers were scattered around the various tables as if it had somehow become the final port of call for Malia's more hardcore hedonists before they finally said goodbye to the night before.

Donna and I managed to find a table at the rear of the bar and ordered two of the 'Killer' English breakfasts along with two beers. Falling into an easy silence we were content to eavesdrop on the gang of student-looking types in front of us retelling the story of their night with all its attendant highs and lows. For the first time during the holiday I realised that I was no longer looking on with envy at their lives. I no longer wanted to be them at all. Finally I was happy being me.

'Why can't real life be like this all the time?' I asked as our waiter arrived at our table with our breakfasts.

'Do you really want a life where you're always out eating breakfast at six in the morning?' asked Donna laughing.

'No,' I replied, 'I mean why can't holidays last for ever?'

'Because then they'd stop being holidays and would start

being real life,' replied Donna. 'Holidays are holidays because they're a break from the norm.'

'When I was a kid I used to wonder if people who lived in Spain went on holiday,' I said squeezing a dollop of tomato ketchup on to my plate. 'If people like my next-door neighbours went on holiday to Majorca, then what did people who lived in Majorca do when it came to holiday time?'

'What answer did you come up with?'

'None,' I replied. 'I probably got distracted and accepted that it was just one of those weird conundrums that you're faced with in life – like infinity, or when time began. I must have come to the conclusion that it's probably easier to not think about things like that at all.'

'The head-in-the-sand philosophy?'

'Yeah,' I replied. 'But don't knock it if you haven't tried it.'

So what now?

'I can barely keep my eyes open,' said Donna as the waiter came to take our empty plates away.

'We should probably think about going.' I looked up at our waiter and asked for the bill. A few moments later, he placed it in the middle of the table but before I could reach for it Donna snatched it up and passed it back to him along with a handful of notes.

'You didn't have to do that,' I said as we stood up.

'But I wanted to,' replied Donna.

'Okay, but next time breakfast is on me.'

It was just a throwaway comment. A joke and nothing more. But I could see from the look of worry that flashed across Donna's face that it carried more weight than I'd intended. How would there ever be a next time when Donna was leaving Malia for good?

'So what now?' We were standing outside the bar basking in the gentle warmth of the early-morning sun.

'This is really difficult for me, Charlie.' Donna took my hand.

'I know.' I changed the subject. 'What time do you leave?'

'I think the coach to the airport is supposed to arrive about nine. I'm going to get some sleep but why don't you come to my hotel about six and at least then we can maybe get something to eat.'

'I'll see you at six then.' Donna stepped towards me and I automatically put my arms around her and we kissed. It was different from our earlier kiss, though. More awkward and self-conscious.

'I'll see you later,' she said waving goodbye.

'Yeah,' I replied. 'I'll see you later.'

Tell uncle Andy everything

'Go on, Tom. Poke him awake.'

'You poke him awake.'

'But you're closer.'

'And you're obviously more interested than I am.'

'I'm not that interested.'

'So wait until he wakes up then.'

'You're joking. He's been asleep ages as it is. I can't be hanging around here all day. I've got stuff to do.'

'Well, if you want him awake, by all means be my guest.'

'Okay, I'll do it myself but I think it's worth pointing out that there's no need for you to be such a—'

Andy stopped mid-sentence as I blinked open my eyes to see his unshaven face leering inches away from my own.

'Ah, so it lives,' he said smirking at me. 'Nice to see you're awake finally.'

'How could I not be with you two yelling over me like that?' I sat up and yawned. 'What time is it?'

'Ten past three.'

I immediately leapt out of bed and began throwing on clothes.

'What's the big rush?' asked Andy.

'I only meant to sleep a couple of hours,' I said as I struggled to pull on my shorts. 'I'm supposed to be meeting up with Donna again at six and I've got a few things I need to sort out before that.'

'What kind of things?'

I shrugged. 'It doesn't matter what. Just stuff.'

Andy rolled his eyes in despair. 'This is so typical of you when it comes to girls. You were just the same at college: always pointlessly secretive about everything.'

'Look,' I said, grabbing a clean T-shirt from my suitcase, 'I'm not being secretive about anything. In fact I'm actually sort of keen to tell you both what happened last night because I could do with some advice.'

'At last.' Andy rubbed his hands together with mock glee. 'Tell your uncle Andy everything.'

Leaving out the contents of Lisa's call, I told Andy and Tom everything that had happened from the moment I'd met up with Donna right through to our breakfast at Stars and Bars.

'So that's it?' Andy looked at me with an odd mixture of amusement and disbelief. 'All you did was talk?'

'With the exception of the odd kiss, yes.'

'Well there's your problem right there.'

'I knew you wouldn't get it.'

'What's to get?' replied Andy. 'She's obviously not interested.'

'That's rubbish,' said Tom. 'She sounds to me like she is interested but just wants to take things slowly that's all.'

'So slowly that she's not even mentioned seeing him again?' said Andy shaking his head. 'No, mate, you're being blown out, but if you want my advice you're best off out of it anyway. With the kid and her ex and all the rest of the stuff she sounds like she's too high maintenance for you.'

'You couldn't be more wrong,' I replied.

'So if she's that great why didn't you bring the subject up yourself?'

I shrugged. 'Because the timing's so off. We missed the boat on being a "holiday thing" that turns into something more . . . and we're too early for anything else. The choice is either say nothing and risk losing her or say something and risk coming across like some kind of stalker.'

'She's just a girl,' said Andy. 'There'll be others.'

'You just don't get it do you?' I replied.

'Look,' said Andy, 'I'm only telling you this for your own good. You should've stayed with me last night and worked your magic with Hattie like I said. She was so desperate by the end of the night that she ended up pulling some kid in a Newcastle United top. That could've been you there with her. Instead, you were off having moonlit chats on the beach with some girl who may or may not be interested in you. You're thirty-five, Charlie, not fifteen. You should've grown out of this teen-angst melodrama years ago.' He tutted and then, more to himself than to me, added, 'And you wonder why Sarah left you.'

If I'd wanted to hear a pin drop on our tile flooring now would've been the time to do it. Though Tom looked shocked, I could tell Andy was the more horrified. In the past I had allowed him a certain amount of leeway with regard to the offensive and childish stuff he said to my face simply because we were friends, but this time he knew he had overstepped the mark.

'Look, mate—'

'Just go,' I said. 'Go before I say something we'll both regret.'

I could see him weighing up the situation. On the one

hand he didn't want to lose face in front of Tom, but on the other he knew that he had gone too far.

'I'll talk to you when you've calmed down a bit, yeah?' He picked up his rucksack from the floor, slung it over his shoulder and left the apartment.

'Tell me again why you're friends with him?' said Tom as Andy slammed the front door.

'Do you know what? You should give him a break sometimes. The reason Andy's an arsehole to the people who love him is the same reason we're all arseholes to people who love us . . . because it's only the ones who stick around when we haven't given them a reason to that are worth keeping.'

Tom grinned. 'So how are you today, you useless bag of crap?'

'Me? You fat tosser. I'm fine.' I paused and looked at Tom. I wanted to ask him about the cancer thing without actually talking about the cancer thing.

'Are you sure you're really okay?' I asked.

'I wouldn't say I'm great,' shrugged Tom, 'but I'm not down either. I'm sorting of hanging on in there with grim determination.' He flashed me the same look of examination that I'd given him. 'And how about you?'

'About the same.'

'Made a decision?'

I shook my head. 'And if that's not bad enough she's off in six hours.'

'So what are you going to do? Play it by ear?'

'No,' I replied. 'Right now I'm going to try to see if I can buy myself some more time.'

I'll be fine by myself

The look of surprise on Donna's face when she spotted me pulling up in front of her hotel in a white Fiat Punto, spot on six o'clock, said it all.

'What's this?' she asked, peering over her Jackie O sunglasses as I wound down the window.

'It's a car,' I replied, 'new invention, great for getting from "a" to "b" with.'

'Okay,' said Donna, laughing. 'What I meant to say is . . . why are you driving it?'

'Tom hired it yesterday and put me down as a named driver,' I lied. 'I thought as you're leaving in a few hours it was pointless to let some surly coach driver have the pleasure of your company when I could have it all to myself.'

The disappointment in Donna's face couldn't have been more apparent. 'I don't know what to say,' she said.

'All I'm offering you is a lift to the airport,' I replied.

She didn't look convinced. 'I'm not sure,' she said, as though the mere thought of getting in a car with me was causing her much unneeded stress. 'I'll have to talk it over with my sister, okay?'

'Fine,' I replied tersely, 'you talk to your sister and I'll wait here.'

As Donna walked back across the road to her hotel I

wished that I hadn't bothered hiring the car. Despite my efforts to downplay my big romantic gesture, Donna had spotted the significance of it straight away and run a mile in the opposite direction. Rather than sweeping her off her feet, all I'd succeeded in doing was confirming her worst fears – that perhaps I wanted more than she was willing to give. I couldn't help but think that perhaps Andy had been right. Maybe I was acting like a lovesick teenager. Maybe I had blown my feelings completely out of proportion. Maybe I should've stayed with him last night and tried to pull one of Nina's friends after all.

I looked across the road. Donna was coming out of the main entrance, but much to my disappointment she didn't look any happier than when she'd disappeared inside five minutes earlier.

'So are you coming or not?' I asked brusquely.

Donna gave me a reluctant nod. 'But we can't be late for the check-in, Charlie . . . I really mean it.'

'Fine,' I replied, 'you tell me what time you want to be there and I'll get you there.'

'Ten at the latest.'

'Then ten it is.'

'I'd better go and get my luggage then.'

'I'll give you a hand.'

'There's no need,' said Donna coolly. 'I'll be fine by myself.'

It's all in the past

'Are you going to tell me what's wrong?' I asked as we finally pulled up on an open piece of rough land near the harbour walls in Heraklion. 'You've barely said anything the whole journey.'

Donna had seemed wrapped up in her own thoughts and as I hadn't wanted to give her any more of an excuse never to see me again, much of our hour-long journey had been spent in silence. Occasionally she'd make a polite comment or two but then as soon as we'd batted the topic around for a while she would immediately fall back into silence. Even when we reached the outskirts of Heraklion and the roar of jet engines became so frequent that barely a minute passed by without hearing one screeching overhead she said little. Instead she stared out of the car window while the roar of every engine made me increasingly aware of just how little time I had left with Donna.

'I know I've been quiet,' said Donna. 'I'm sorry.'

'Is it me?' I asked dreading the answer. 'Have I done something wrong?'

'No.' She touched my hand. 'It's all me. I've got a lot of things on my mind.'

'Can we talk about it?'

Donna shook her head. 'I think it's probably too late for

that, but it's no excuse for me being such a misery though. I feel I'm spoiling everything.' She ran her hands over her face as though trying to wake herself up from a dream. 'Thanks for doing this, Charlie,' she said, turning towards me. 'I know it's only been a short time but you really have made this holiday special.'

We climbed out of the car, bought a parking ticket and made our way towards the restaurant I'd discovered in Tom's *Rough Guide*. Donna seemed brighter. She was more talkative, and making jokes and seemed much more like the person I'd got to know the night before.

The restaurant was right next to the harbour wall. There were scores of tables set up underneath a canopy and we were shown to one that the waiter assured us had the best view of the harbour. Instead of sitting opposite each other we sat side by side so that we could watch the same sun set that we had seen rise.

We left the restaurant after an hour, having shared everything from home-made tatziki to fried Mako shark and made our way back to the car hand in hand. The silence had a different quality now. Less gloomy and more hopeful – as if we'd stopped speaking because there were too many things to say rather than too few.

'Last night and this afternoon have been really special,' Donna said, as we reached the car. 'I don't know the last time I spent this much time in someone else's company . . . not since . . . well you know. Anyway, I just want to say thanks.' She reached up towards me, wrapped her arms around my neck and then placed her lips on top of my own. We kissed the sort of long slow kiss that had the ability to transport me right back to the night before.

'I think it might be time to go,' said Donna, once the kiss had ended.

'Yeah, you're probably right.'

I've forgotten my sunglasses

Our time was over. The day had come to an end. And Donna was heading home. But the big question, in my mind at least, was had I succeeded in making Donna want to commit to seeing me again? As we pulled into the car park at Heraklion airport and I looked across at her I couldn't help but feel like the answer to the question was a resounding yes. Surely, I told myself, she had to be feeling what I was feeling?

Still, as we climbed out of the car into the still-baking heat and unloaded Donna's luggage on to the tarmac, I made up my mind that if all really was fair in love and war, then now would be the right time to pitch one last all-out assault. Timing, I reasoned, was everything and fortunately for me I had been dealt the perfect hand: a 'departure gate goodbye'. I prepared the speech in my head: stuff about her being 'special', our need to 'overcome obstacles' and 'how we could make it work if we really wanted to'. It was all made for this moment. Victory was assured.

'I've forgotten my sunglasses,' said Donna, when we were only a few metres away from the entrance to the departure lounge. 'I must have left them in the car.'

'Carry on and check in,' I replied, 'I'll go back and get them.'

'I couldn't ask you to do that,' said Donna. 'You've done enough already. I'll go myself.'

'No problem,' I replied, handing her the keys to the car. 'I'll just wait here for you.'

Sitting on the kerb outside the entrance to the airport with her suitcase and bags by my side, I watched her until she disappeared behind a row of cars. She was gone longer than I expected but soon returned wearing her beloved Jackie O sunglasses.

As we entered the airport we went in search of Nina and her friends amongst the hundreds of British holidaymakers who were heading back home. Each one of them, standing in line at the various check-in desks, was dressed as though they thought that the warm weather of Crete would stay with them forever. My mind flicked back to the tanned and T-shirted hordes I'd seen arriving at Gatwick in the rain – people stuck so solidly in their holiday state of mind that they had forgotten that any climate existed other than the one they had left behind.

'Won't you be a bit cold when you reach England?' I asked, as we studied the departure board to find her check-in desk.

'I put a warmish jumper in Nina's bag before I left,' said Donna who herself was wearing a long skirt, a sleeveless top and flip-flops. 'She'll have it with her now.'

'Right now I wish I was wearing a jacket so I could do the gentlemanly thing and give it to you.'

Donna opened her mouth to reply when a voice yelled her name from across the hall. We both turned round to see Nina waving at us frantically from the front of the furthest check-in desk from where we were standing. Dragging her suitcase behind her Donna rushed over to join them. Nina and her friends all huddled around her immediately, while some threw a bemused glance in my direction.

Once the girls were all checked in they collected themselves together at the side of the queue while Donna made her way back to me.

'Everything okay?' I asked.

'Yeah, fine,' said Donna. 'Nina and the girls are going to meet me on the other side of passport control in a minute or two but I'm just going to the loo first.'

There was something about her face when she spoke to me that didn't seem right. I let it go, reasoning that perhaps this was a good sign: that she was finding it as difficult to leave me as I was finding it to accept that she was going. At this rate, I told myself, our departure gate good-bye could be nothing short of a resounding success.

After about five minutes or so with no sign of Donna's return I became uneasy, so I headed towards the ladies' toilets in search of her. When she failed to emerge after a further five minutes I began to be convinced that something was wrong. Aware that I was once again possibly going too far I approached a couple of English girls on a flight bound for Manchester and asked if they could check the toilets for any sign of Donna. When they emerged a minute later without her, a real panic set in and I searched the whole of the airport frantically, even briefly considering contacting the airport's security. In the end I decided that the best thing to do would be to return to the spot where we had parted and wait. And there I remained for over an hour before I finally accepted that she had gone.

With Donna still occupying my every thought, I made my way back to my hire car. As I opened the car door a folded sheet of paper on the driver's seat fluttered down into the footwell. I reached down and opened it up:

I know you'll think this was the coward's way out and you're probably right. And I know you probably hate me right now. But the truth is I just can't think of any other way of saying goodbye that won't make things more complicated than they are (and believe me they are complicated enough already). I'm sorry for everything, Charlie. I really am.

Donna xxx

With my heart still racing, I started up the car and wound down the window. A warm gust of night air caused Donna's letter to flutter on the dashboard. I read it one last time, as though saying a final goodbye to both her and the notion that there was any fairness in the world. Nice guys did finish last. Sarah had taught me that and now Donna had rammed the point home.

I told myself that I was tired of being a doormat to the world at large. From now on I was going to switch off my brain and act on instinct. I wasn't going to agonise over every decision or wallow in the past. In short I was going to take a leaf out of Andy's book and start putting myself first.

And so as I tore up Donna's letter into a fistful of confetti, dropped the pieces out of the window and watched them flutter to the ground, there was no doubt in my mind that it was the right thing to do.

DAY FIVE: FRIDAY

Why break the habit of the holiday?

I cracked open my eyes. The bedroom was still shrouded in darkness although chinks of light coming through the curtains indicated that morning had broken. I sat up in bed and two things happened: first, the covers slipped down my body resulting in legions of tiny goosebumps springing to life as my skin came in contact with the arctic air. Secondly I was temporarily overwhelmed by a sudden feeling of biliousness that had me racing to the bathroom. I wasn't sick but I wished I had been because then at least the nausea currently gripping me might have gone away. Instead it stayed with me, clinging tightly to the pit of my stomach with a fist of iron.

As I left the bathroom I looked over at Andy's bed. Although it was empty it had clearly been slept in. I carefully opened the kitchen door. Tom's bed was empty too. I opened the fridge, pulled out a bottle of water and attempted to rehydrate myself. It was just after midday.

I threw on some clean clothes and then looked around the room for inspiration as to what to do next. I spotted *The Da Vinci Code* on my bedside table and decided to read for a while. Picking up the book along with my sunglasses I drew back the curtains over the patio doors to reveal Tom lounging in one of the white plastic chairs with his feet up on the balcony. In one hand was his beloved *Rough Guide* and in the other a cigarette. What was strange about this scene was that Tom didn't smoke and never had done.

'All right?' I said as I opened the patio doors and stepped out into the midday sun. I stared pointedly at Tom's cigarette. 'Anything you'd like to tell me?'

'I'm experimenting.' He paused and inhaled heavily, then slowly expelled the smoke from between his lips. 'I found them on the table,' he said, holding up a pack of Andy's Benson and Hedges. 'I was sitting here looking at them and I thought to myself: if I have actually got cancer then at least the cells that are screwing me up will be too busy attacking my bladder to worry about my lungs.'

'And what if it's something else?' I asked.

'Well, if it is and I've gone through all this for nothing,' Tom plucked the cigarette from his lips, 'then I think the very least I deserve is a cigarette.'

I sat down next to Tom, slipped on my sunglasses and squinted at the sky. 'So – fledgling cigarette habits notwithstanding – how are you this bright and sunny afternoon?'

'I feel like crap,' said Tom. 'Which is I'm guessing how you must feel too.'

'I feel like I'm dead from the neck downwards,' I groaned. 'Any chance you could take me through the details of last night because some of them are more than a bit foggy?'

'I think it started when you came back to the apartment after your evening with Donna and didn't speak for ages,' began Tom. 'I asked you what was wrong and you said that you didn't want to talk about it. So then I suggested that we go for a drink because I was sick of thinking about this cancer thing and you said, "Good idea let's do it." Nine bars, roughly six hours and many, many, many drinks later we crashed out here.'

'Was Andy with us? I don't seem to remember much about him last night at all.'

'Bizarrely, he chose to stay in,' said Tom. 'Something about wanting to catch up on his sleep.'

'So where is he now?'

Tom shrugged and lit another one of Andy's cigarettes. 'When I was in bed this morning I heard the door open. I assumed it was Andy either coming in or going out but I don't know any more than that.' Tom stubbed out his cigarette. 'That's me done with smoking for now,' he said cheerfully. 'Maybe I'll see what other vices I can succumb to before the holiday's out.' He stood up and picked up his book. 'Hungry?'

'Starving.'

'Stars and Bars?'

'Of course,' I replied. 'Why break the habit of the holiday?'

The substance of things hoped for

'So,' said Tom, as the waiter brought our 'killer' breakfast and lager combo, 'I think we've now skirted round enough diverse topics for me to ask the billion dollar question.'

'Me and Donna?' I replied. 'It was a disaster. A near-perfect disaster.'

'You told her how you felt and she turned you down?'

'Worse than that,' I replied. 'Much worse. I hired a car, took her out for dinner and then to the airport, only to have her do a runner when my back was turned.'

'You're kidding me,' said Tom looking gratifyingly outraged.

'I wish I was,' I replied. 'Now come on, what she did was a bit harsh wasn't it? Women always talk about how men hate confrontation and will do anything to avoid it . . . but if what Donna did wasn't avoiding confrontation I don't know what is.'

'Obviously I'm not taking her side or anything,' said Tom cautiously, 'but I can't imagine that she did it for a laugh. It must have been hard for her. It's not like it's that long since her kid's dad left her is it? Maybe she's a bit gun shy.'

'Gun shy?' I replied. 'I'll tell you who should be gun shy – me. I found out the night before last that Sarah's pregnant.'

Tom was stunned. 'I don't know what to say.'

'There's nothing *to* say,' I replied, 'other than that I know for a fact that it's not mine.' Suddenly I didn't feel quite so hungry any more and so I pushed my breakfast plate away to one side. 'I really loved her you know.'

'I know you did,' replied Tom quietly.

'So how could she do this to me after being together so long? A whole decade, Tom. Surely that has to count for something?'

Tom looked on blankly.

'Right now,' I continued, 'I feel like the only thing that has any real substance is the moment you're in right now. That's what Andy thinks, doesn't he? He lives in the moment and that's all he believes in.'

'And look where that's got him,' said Tom. 'He's no happier because of it. He just spends his life chasing something that he's never going to get. I know it's difficult for you right now but you can't always think the worst will happen. Sometimes you've got to have a bit of faith that everything will work out in the end.'

'Faith?'

'The substance of things hoped for.'

'How can I have faith when everyone always lets me down?' I replied. 'How can I have faith in anyone when I haven't got any in myself?'

'Maybe believing in yourself is the best place to start,' said Tom.

'Maybe,' I replied, glancing over at my plate in the hope that my appetite might return sometime soon. 'Then again, maybe not.' My appetite was nowhere to be seen, so instead I took a long sip of my lager and changed the topic of conversation. 'What do you think Andy's up to then?' I asked. 'I've got a bad feeling that he's up to something.'

'Maybe he went out last night after all and hooked up

with some new girl,' suggested Tom. 'You never really know with Andy do you?' Tom paused and looked at me. 'Anyway, why all the curiosity about Andy?'

'I don't know,' I shrugged, 'I guess I'm tired of being annoyed at him.'

Tom smiled. 'Do you remember that time the two of you fell out after you had a go at him for bouncing a cheque on you for his share of the rent for the third time in a row? He didn't talk to you for days.'

'How could I forget it? I was the one out of pocket and yet he was the one who went around slamming doors like it had just gone out of fashion.' I contemplated my drink absent-mindedly. 'You don't really think Andy's with another girl do you?'

'Like I said, with Andy anything's possible, isn't it?'

'Don't ask me why but I kind of get the feeling that he's not going to do it again. I mean, why would he? This thing with him and Nina was about proving to himself that he'd still got it. There wouldn't be anything to be gained by doing it again.'

'I'd agree with you,' replied Tom, 'if Andy was a subscriber to regular logic. But he isn't, is he? He just makes this stuff up as he goes along. Who knows how his mind works? Maybe he wants to get caught out? Maybe he thinks it'll be easier if Lisa dumps him than the other way round. All I know is that there's always been something in Andy that just seems . . . I don't know . . . unhappy. You must have noticed it too.'

'It'd be hard to miss,' I replied.

'Do you think he'll ever get over whatever it is he's got to get over?'

'I hope so for his sake,' I replied. 'I really do.'

Tom finished his breakfast and I ordered another beer. Leaving Stars and Bars just after one-thirty, we headed back to the Apollo stopping off at a mini-market to stock up on bottled water, beer and assorted crisps and confectionery. As we reached the lobby we noticed that there were about half a dozen guys scattered around the sofas by the pool table watching the highlights of a football match on the widescreen TV and we joined them for five minutes or so and bonded briefly over a discussion of England's performance in a friendly match earlier in the week. Eventually we left our new friends to their football highlights and made our way up the stairs to our apartment where we were surprised to discover that the door was open – either our room was being cleaned or Andy was back. My gut instinct told me to go with the Andy option.

I still hadn't quite managed to work out how I was going to behave with Andy following our argument the day before. Part of me wanted to continue being annoyed at him because he deserved it, but the rest of me knew that maintaining any kind of frostiness would end up being too much like hard work in the face of his constant effervescence. In the end I decided that I would go with the first emotion that sprang to mind.

Tom and I unloaded our bags on to the kitchen table and then made our way through to the bedroom. When I saw Andy, the first emotion that registered on my internal radar was complete and utter shock and surprise. My mind shot back to Tom's comment that 'with Andy anything's possible' and I suddenly realised just how was right he was, because standing next to Andy in a vest, a denim skirt and flip-flops – looking for all the world as though she was on her way out to the beach for the day – was Lisa.

Could you just rub some on my back, babe?

Andy couldn't have looked more pleased with himself if he'd won the national lottery. 'All right, boys?' he announced cheerfully as we looked on slack-jawed. 'Don't just stand there staring like a pair of idiots. What sort of welcome is that to give a lady?'

'Oh, Andy,' said Lisa, as the penny dropped. 'How could you not tell them I was coming?'

'What fun would there be in that?'

'But you promised me you'd clear it with them first. No wonder they're looking at me like I'm some kind of freak. I'm really sorry about this, guys. I'd understand completely if you wanted me to stay somewhere else.'

'We're absolutely fine with you staying here,' I said finally getting my mouth into gear. 'It's just that . . . well . . . we're a bit surprised to see you that's all. Don't take this the wrong way but . . . what *are* you doing here?'

'Yesterday morning Andy called me up out of the blue and told me he was missing me so much that he'd bought me a cheap flight to Crete over the internet,' explained Lisa, still glowering at Andy. 'One call into work faking food poisoning and an early morning trip into Gatwick and here I am.'

I had to give Andy the credit that was due him. Inviting Lisa over to Crete was a masterstroke of strategic thinking on his part. The perfect win/win scenario. He'd had his fun during the first part of the week and now at a stroke he'd allayed her fears and banked himself a tonne of perfect-boyfriend points in the bargain. It was genius really. Utter genius. And I probably would've given him a standing ovation had his actions not made me feel like the lowest of the low. How did he think he could pull off such barefaced deceit without being crippled by guilt? He obviously didn't know the meaning of the word. But I did, and thanks to him I felt forced to take on the burden of his guilt for cheating on her as well as my own for hiding the fact from her.

'It doesn't matter how you got here,' I said, squeezing Lisa in my arms. 'It's great anyway.'

'That's really nice of you,' said Lisa. 'Even if you don't actually mean it. I know this was meant to be a bit of a boys' holiday and now here I am messing things up. I promise you I'll do my best not to cramp your style.'

'Look, Lisa,' said Tom grinning, as he too greeted her with a hug, 'we've been about as rock and roll as a bunch of old age pensioners. Your presence can only improve matters, believe me.'

'Right then,' said Andy as if he hadn't got a care in the world. 'Who's coming down the beach?'

'That sounds great.' Tom exchanged glances with me warily. 'I could do with a day in the sun.'

'Me too,' I replied acknowledging Tom's look. 'It'll give me a chance to catch up with my reading.'

As we made our way down to the beach there was a certain amount of tension between us. Lisa was obviously conscious of having gate-crashed our holiday. Tom seemed on edge because despite not wanting to get involved he had now been covertly sucked into keeping Andy's secret from Lisa. And I was anxious because not only had it been me who had promised to keep Andy on the straight and narrow and failed to do so, but in addition I had my own private source of tension with Lisa due to our last conversation on the phone. The only one of us who seemed to be anywhere near relaxed was Andy.

Because of all this apprehension, we all made an effort to talk as a group rather than splitting off into our natural pairings. But the route to the beach was so busy that it was impossible to walk along four abreast. At one point near Stars and Bars, the pavement got so crowded that Tom and Andy broke off and I found myself walking a few paces alone next to Lisa. As I didn't want to talk to her about my mission with Andy, or indeed about Sarah's pregnancy, as she opened her mouth to speak I started fake frantic coughing while carefully speeding up my pace to join the others. When it happened again a few yards later, I was forced to pretend that I had a stone in my sandal. And a few yards after that my solution was to get in first with conversational topics that couldn't be construed as personal. And while these were possibly the least subtle methods I could have chosen to keep Lisa at arm's length – bar my obtaining a loudhailer and yelling the words 'Don't come any further!' – they did at least do the job.

As usual the beach was heavily congested with young sun-worshippers. But whereas before the three of us had felt like intruders into a world of youth and beauty, with Lisa in our midst I felt as though we now had as much right to be there as anyone else. Although at thirty-one Lisa was probably one of the oldest – if not the oldest – women on the beach, she easily looked five years younger and had the body to prove it. So suddenly we were no longer just a bunch of sad thirtysomething blokes spending the whole day with their noses pressed up against the sweet-shop window, instead we were three thirtysomething blokes who had a three-in-one chance of being mistaken for Lisa's boyfriend. I couldn't have asked for more. And as the three of us trooped across the sand towards the sun-loungers, I could see gangs of younger guys straining to get a better look at Lisa's magnificent figure. It really was all I could do not to turn round to them with their sinewy bodies, their perfect tans and stupidly youthful haircuts and kick sand in their faces.

Gathering together four spare sun-loungers, we set up camp for the afternoon. Andy lay down on his lounger first and then Lisa lay down next to him. At this point Tom looked at Lisa and then at me as if to say, 'You know her better than me,' and so I stepped forward to take the lounger next to her and Tom tucked himself on at the end.

'This is fantastic,' said Lisa, as she undressed down to her bikini. 'I wish Andy had invited me to come earlier.'

'I know what you mean,' I replied eyeing my best friend's girlfriend's perfect bikini-clad figure from behind the privacy of my sunglasses and then immediately wishing I hadn't. I closed my eyes and tried to delete the image from my retinas.

'Charlie's only saying that because you're here now,' said Andy mischievously. 'Secretly he's really enjoyed being one of the lads this week. Isn't that right, Tom?'

'Hmm,' said Tom who was already engaged as usual with his *Rough Guide*. 'Definitely, mate.'

'Has he managed to pull any "birds" while you've been here?' asked Lisa pouring a small amount of sun lotion into the palm of her hands.

'Was that your attempt at being one of the boys?' laughed Andy.

'Don't you call girls "birds" any more?' asked Lisa as she began to rub the lotion into her arms. 'I know it's a long time ago but I quite liked being a "bird" when I was young free and single.'

'You're still a "bird" to me,' said Andy. 'Isn't that right, Charlie? Lisa's still got "bird" status, hasn't she?'

'Yeah, of course,' I said wincing as I covertly watched Lisa rubbing suntan lotion into her thighs. 'She's a "bird", all the way.'

'Thanks, guys,' said Lisa. 'That's just what I needed to hear.' She turned to Andy and handed him the suntan lotion. 'Could you just rub some on my back, babe?'

'No problem,' replied Andy as Lisa lay down on her front and deftly untied her bikini top to reveal the full allure of her naked back.

'So, Charlie,' said Lisa as Andy straddled her back and began to massage the lotion into her shoulder blades. 'What's the talent been like?'

'What are you asking him for?'

'Because he's the only one of you that's legally licensed to check out the women here,' grinned Lisa. 'Come on, Charlie, remember I'm "one of the boys", now. You can tell me anything.'

'It's been . . . all right,' I replied.

'The man's on fire, actually,' interrupted Andy who was now massaging the middle of Lisa's back. 'He managed to pull at the airport before we'd even collected our bags.'

'He's exaggerating,' I replied. 'All that happened was that a girl came up to me while we were waiting for our bags . . . she said she wanted to meet up in some bar. It must have been a practical joke or something because she didn't turn up . . . it's all a bit embarrassing, really.'

'Rubbish,' said Andy. 'She definitely fancied him. She had a look in her eyes like she really wanted a morsel of Mansell. I think something must have happened to stop her coming that night.'

'Was she nice?' asked Lisa.

'Gorgeous,' said Andy, working the sun lotion into Lisa's lower back. 'Like a young Naomi Campbell.'

'Wow,' said Lisa. 'A babe like that could be just the thing you need, Charlie. Maybe we'll bump into her tonight. Talking of which, what exactly have we got planned for tonight?'

I shrugged and passed the question over to Tom in a bid to distract myself from Lisa's glistening back.

'What do you reckon, Tom?'

'My vote is somewhere quiet,' he replied. 'I don't mind having a big night out tomorrow but after last night I could do with taking it easy.'

'This is what I've been up against all holiday,' said Andy climbing off Lisa's back. 'Some people wouldn't know a good time if it bit them on the backside.'

'Actually I think Tom's right,' said Lisa struggling to retie her bikini top. 'Maybe we should save ourselves for the last night and have a big blow-out then? Tonight we could go out for a nice meal and then maybe have a bit of a drink and a chat on the balcony when we get back. It's nice out there.'

'Sounds okay to me,' said Tom.

'I suppose that's all right,' added Andy, 'as long as we're definitely going out tomorrow.'

Lisa turned and looked at me expectantly. 'What do you think, Charlie?'

'Sounds like a great idea,' I replied even though I was already beginning to get the feeling that this quiet night out might turn out to be more eventful than we'd bargained for – Lisa was an unknown quantity in what was already a pretty volatile mix. 'Count me in for sure.'

Mine has a little extra kick!

It was now just after ten in the evening and we were all sitting at a table on the vine-covered terrace of Taverna Stefanos. The taverna was tucked away in the older part of Malia, far enough from the hectic pace of the main strip to imagine that we might be somewhere rural. Much of the tension from earlier in the day now seemed to have evaporated. Tom was talking to Andy. Andy was talking to me. And I was even talking to Lisa. Everybody seemed to be getting on and the meal, the wine and the entertainment (halfway through our second course a couple of bouzouki players dressed in traditional Greek costumes emerged from the rear of the restaurant) seemed to bind us all closer.

'Now that was a fantastic meal,' said Tom to Georgiou, the owner, as he brought our bill. 'We'd be back in a shot if tomorrow wasn't our last night.'

'Well if you were to bring this lovely lady back with you tomorrow night,' grinned Georgiou, 'you might get yourself a free bottle of wine.' He paused and gave Lisa a cheeky wink. 'What do you say?

'It's tempting,' said Lisa, allowing Georgiou, who had complimented her on both her beauty and her dress sense at regular points throughout the meal, to steal a kiss on the cheek. 'We'll have to see.'

I couldn't blame Georgiou – a middle-aged father of three – for trying it on with Lisa as she was absolutely stunning in her black backless dress. Sitting with the three of us at the table she was the perfect definition of a rose amongst thorns.

'I feel I have died and gone to heaven,' said Georgiou swooning theatrically from Lisa's kiss. 'To which one of you lucky men does this stunning lady belong?'

'This is my boyfriend,' said Lisa, pointing to Andy. 'And these two handsome gents are just friends.'

'Well, my friend,' said Georgiou in a mock whisper as he leaned in towards a clearly embarrassed Andy, 'I hope you know that you are a very lucky man.'

We piled up a small mountain of Euros in the middle of the table to cover the bill and as Georgiou was about to sweep the cash away, Andy asked if there were any chance that we could buy a bottle of raki from him to take away. Georgiou immediately called for one of his waitresses to get a bottle.

'I make it myself,' said Georgiou as she returned with a plastic litre bottle of the clear liquid. 'I make the best raki on the island.' He thumped the table dramatically. 'Mine has a little extra kick!'

'That's good to hear,' said Andy. 'A little extra kick is just what we all need.'

We thanked Georgiou for the meal and then slowly made our way out of the taverna to the quiet street outside.

'What have you bought that rot-gut for?' asked Tom as we made our way through the winding back streets. 'We've still got some beer back at the apartment.'

'I'm not touching a drop of that stuff,' I said, adding my weight to Tom's objections. 'That stuff is lethal.'

'Will you two stop acting like old ladies?' said Andy. 'This stuff is brilliant.'

'What is it?' asked Lisa taking the bottle from Andy's hands to examine it closely.

'Have you ever had ouzo?' asked Tom.

'Not since I was seventeen and my parents went away for the weekend,' replied Lisa. 'A couple of friends came over to keep me company and things got a bit out of hand. We ended up dumping a whole bottle of ouzo that my parents had brought back from a holiday in Athens into the remains of a two-litre bottle of Coke and split it four ways.' Lisa shook her head in shame. 'Before long some boys got invited round, my friend Katie ended up getting a huge love bite from a boy called Kevin and we all ended up in my parents' bathroom taking it in turns to be sick.'

'Well,' said Tom laughing, 'it's just like that . . . only stronger.'

Lisa looked at Andy. 'Do we really have to do this?'

'Of course we do,' he replied. 'It's a rite of passage. You know as well as I do that every holiday needs a good hangover story.'

'Like you haven't got enough already,' sighed Lisa. 'Fine. Count me in. Only because I don't want you moaning that I spoilt things by not getting into the mood. But when you wake up in the morning with a screaming headache don't come running to me.' Shaking her head in disapproval, Lisa joined Tom who was walking slightly ahead of the group. She looped her arm through his and started asking him lots of questions about his kids, which forced Andy and me into walking together. Neither of us spoke for quite a long time but as we paused waiting to cross a road Andy eventually broke the silence.

'Listen, mate,' he began, 'I'm sorry about yesterday. What I said was absolutely out of order.'

'It's okay,' I replied. 'It's no big deal.'

'So we're all right, then?'

'Yeah . . . we're all right.'

There was another silence.

'So, did you always know you were going to bring Lisa out here?'

'Yeah,' replied Andy. 'Pretty much so.'

'So this holiday was never about me?'

'Of course it was about you. But it was about me too.'

'And you don't feel guilty?'

'About Lisa?'

'Of course about Lisa.'

Andy shrugged. 'I don't think about it.'

'I guess that's the big difference between you and me.'

Andy checked that Lisa and Tom were out of earshot.

'Nina called me today,' he began quietly. 'Said she wants to carry on seeing me when I get home.'

'You've said no though, haven't you?'

Andy shook his head. 'It's difficult.'

'What's difficult?'

'I think I might want to see her again.'

'What about all that stuff you said to me yesterday?'

'I think that was more for my benefit than yours.'

There was another long silence.

'Being with Nina . . . it makes me feel like I'm alive again.'

'So what about Lisa?'

'I need her too,' said Andy. 'Like I said, it's difficult.'

'Look,' I said pointing to Lisa and Tom up ahead. 'Just look. That beautiful woman there is your girlfriend. And more than that she loves you. Why would you want to risk losing all that?'

'I wouldn't be risking anything,' said Andy evenly. 'She'd never find out. All Nina's suggesting is that we meet up once in while.'

'You'll get caught.'

Andy shook his head. 'No we won't,' he said confidently. 'I've thought it through.'

'People who cheat always get caught,' I replied. 'It's a fundamental law of the universe. You take one risk, and then you take another and another until you've convinced yourself that you're invincible. Then one day you'll take a risk too far . . . or you'll get careless . . . or you'll end up hating Lisa so much for not catching you out that you won't care if she finds out . . . but whichever way it happens, the truth will come out because it always does. Just like it did with me and Sarah.'

Andy stopped and looked at me. 'I thought you said you only found out when Sarah left you.'

'That wasn't true,' I replied. 'I lied to you because I didn't want to look stupid. But the truth was I knew Sarah was cheating on me long before she left.'

'How?'

'I went through her things one morning after she left for work. I went through everything – her bags, clothes, underwear, diary – even her computer. I was trying to find evidence that might explain why she had changed so much in the past few months. I felt terrible. I really did. It felt like a real intrusion. Until I found something. It was a letter from him folded inside an empty compact in her make-up bag. It had all the stuff you'd expect. And it was quite obviously not the first letter of its type either. So I had to ask myself what was so special about this one? I read it and reread it a million times and I couldn't work out why she'd kept it when she'd obviously disposed of the earlier ones. And then it hit me . . . she'd kept it because the thought of destroying the letter upset her more than the idea that I might find it. That's when I knew that it wouldn't be long until she left me.'

'So, why didn't you say something?' said Andy. 'You shouldn't have let her walk all over you like that.'

I could've predicted Andy's reaction down to the letter. He didn't understand because he couldn't understand. And he couldn't understand because he'd never been in love.

'I didn't say anything because I knew that would mean she would leave me sooner rather than later. So I put all of her stuff back exactly where I'd found it and carried on as if nothing had happened. A month later she left me anyway. And do you know what? I don't regret not confronting her about it for a second because the thing you won't understand – I don't think you *can* understand – is this: when you love someone and you find yourself living on borrowed time, you're just too grateful for every last moment you get to worry about anything else.'

Good friends

When we finally reached the apartment, the first thing Andy did was raid the kitchen cupboard in search of receptacles for the raki. Failing to find any shot glasses he chose to improvise and brought four white 'I ❤ Crete' mugs out to the balcony. Carefully pouring a double shot's worth of raki into each mug, Andy distributed them out amongst us and then on his cue we raised our mugs in the air and simultaneously knocked back our shots in one. Our reactions were instant: Andy's eyes began to water, Lisa and I coughed so violently I thought we might choke and Tom gritted his teeth like a tough TV detective and immediately poured himself another glass.

That first drink marked something of a watershed for the four of us. It was as if we had unanimously decided to give our minds a night off from our various individual troubles and just have fun. And with each shot of raki we consumed, having fun seemed to become a lot easier. Encouraged by Lisa, Andy, Tom and I wheeled out all our old favourite stories from the past. Everything from how we'd met during our first week at college, through our post-college years right up to and including the 'edited' highlights of our first night out in Malia only a few days earlier. Anyone watching this scene would have immediately assumed we were not just friends, but good friends. People who cared about each other. People who loved each other.

The night is still young

It was just before midnight and we'd been drinking, smoking and talking for well over an hour. Andy was sitting on one of the patio chairs with Lisa lodged on his lap, Tom was sitting on the other chair with his bare feet propped on Lisa's lap, and I was sitting cross-legged on the table looking round at my friends and grinning like an idiot. This was one of those moments that I wished would last for ever. It was the kind of moment that makes a holiday feel like a holiday.

'Never let it be said that I won't admit when I'm wrong,' I said drunkenly to Andy. 'You were absolutely right about the raki, mate. This stuff is spot on.'

'You're telling me,' said Andy. 'For the past half an hour I've been shocked by just how entertaining Tom can be when he's drunk too much.'

Tom raised his mug. 'And with every double shot of raki, Andy, you somehow become a lot less obnoxious.' Tom then walked over to me and gave me a drunken squeeze. 'I'm off to bed,' he announced. And after proceeding to embrace both Lisa and Andy, he slid back the patio doors and disappeared inside.

'And then there were three,' said Andy sharing out the last of the raki.

'How can we have drunk a whole bottle already?' said

Lisa staring disappointedly into the bottom of her mug.

'Maybe it's a sign that we should call it a night,' I said conscious of the fact that this was the second night in a row that I had drunk too much. 'Maybe we should quit while we're ahead.'

'There'll be no talk of quitting,' said Andy. 'The night is still young. Don't worry, for the greater good I'll nip out and get some raki and fags, too, as we seem to be running low on B&H. I won't be long . . . half an hour.'

'No, mate, don't,' I pleaded as I realised that with more raki in the apartment there would be little chance of any of us getting to bed before dawn.

'Too late,' said Andy, standing up, 'I'll be back before you know it.'

Through my raki-addled brain I did a quick calculation: one Tom (already in bed) minus Andy (to get raki and fags) plus me and Lisa would equal an opportunity for an uncomfortable conversation (or two). I did not want this to happen, especially as the alcohol had already done a pretty good job of loosening my tongue. 'I'll come with you,' I said, struggling to my feet. 'Keep you company.'

'Charlie Mansell!' screamed Lisa in mock outrage. 'Anyone would think you're scared to be left alone with me.'

'I'm not scared of anything,' I lied. 'I just fancied a walk that's all. You could come with us if you want.'

'No way,' exclaimed Lisa. 'It's hard enough walking in my heels when I'm sober, let alone in this state. Nope, I'm staying here and you're staying too.'

'You stay,' said Andy. 'I'll be back in a bit.' He patted his pockets as if looking for something. 'Have you seen my keys?'

Lisa shook her head. 'You must have had them earlier because you let us all in.'

'They must be around somewhere, but I can't be bothered to look for them right now. I'll just call you on my mobile when I'm back and you can let me in, okay?' He leaned across to Lisa and kissed her on the lips. 'Oh, and make sure he doesn't sneak off to bed, okay?'

Lisa nodded. 'I'll try my best.'

'Right then,' said Andy sliding back the patio door. 'You two try to be good and I'll be back ASAP.'

Show me how it's done

'Tell me something I don't know.' Lisa turned to me with a grin as I sat down in the chair next to her.

'I don't understand what you mean,' I replied. 'Tell you something I don't know about what?'

'About you,' she replied, 'tell me something I don't know about you.'

I was confused. 'But why do you want me to do that?'

'Because if you don't then we're both going to have to sit here and endure the mother of all awkward silences. Come on, Charlie, you've been trying to avoid me since I arrived.'

'What are you talking about? I've done no such thing.'

'So that wasn't you practically clutching on to Andy's leg, yelling, "Don't leave me alone with this woman?" I know why you haven't wanted to be around me. The last time we spoke was horrible. I feel terrible about it, I really do. And I know what you guys are like . . . you all hate talking about awkward stuff. You'd sooner chop off your head than talk about how you're feeling. But one way or another, Charlie, we're going to have to talk about these things because I need to . . . if only to apologise for my part in them. So for now I thought I'd warm you up – so to speak – with a much lighter conversation.'

'One where I tell you something about myself that you don't know?'

'Anything at all,' said Lisa. 'The first thing that pops into your head.'

'I'm terrible at these sorts of things,' I explained. 'Nothing's "popping" into my head at all. I'm a complete blank.'

'That's the second rubbish bloke thing you've said in as many minutes,' said Lisa. 'I thought you were better than that.'

'If it's so easy then,' I replied, 'why don't you show me how it's done?'

Lisa laughed. 'You've got me there. There are millions of things you don't know about me: how can I choose just one without you reading too much into it?'

'My point entirely.'

Lisa took a sip of raki. 'Okay, here's one. When I was twelve my parents bought me a Girl's World for my birthday – do you know what that is?'

'My best mate's sister had one,' I replied. 'They look a bit like the head of a shop-window dummy and you're supposed to use them to practise hair and make-up skills.'

'That's the one,' said Lisa. 'So at least you know what one is . . . because my revelation is a bit tragic really . . . I now confess right in front of you that I used to practise French kissing on mine.'

'But it hasn't even got a tongue.'

'I know, I know, I know,' said Lisa momentarily burying her face in my shoulder in shame.

'And did all that practice turn you into an amazing kisser?'

Lisa laughed cheekily. 'I've had no complaints if that's what you mean.'

Right,' I said knocking back the last of my raki. 'So I

need a revelation that's as good as snogging a plastic replica head . . . ?'

Lisa nodded.

'Haven't got one I'm afraid.'

'Nothing?'

'Nope, nothing. You've won revelation of the day, hands down with your Girl's World story. But you can consider me warmed up if you like.'

There was a long silence.

'I just really want you to know how sorry I am about what happened,' said Lisa quietly. 'I can't tell you how much I wish I'd kept my stupid mouth shut. You should never have had to hear news like that the way you heard it. I could barely sleep that night for thinking about you and what I'd done. I was really worried about you.'

'There was no need,' I replied. 'I was fine.'

'And now?'

'I'm still fine. In fact it was probably the best thing that could've happened because it forced me to do the one thing I hadn't managed to do: move on.'

Lisa reached across and touched my hand. 'Are you saying you were still in love with Sarah?'

'I don't know what I'm saying,' I replied, aware of the warmth of her touch. 'When you've been with someone for as long as I was with Sarah it becomes quite difficult to tell when love stops being love and starts being habit. Either way, it doesn't really matter now does it? She's definitely moved on. And so have I.'

'I can't tell you how shocked I was when she told me,' said Lisa, still touching my hand. 'She and Oliver had only been together five minutes.' She paused and added: 'I'm not sure I should tell you this, but at one point she actually asked me if she was doing the right thing having this baby.'

'And what did you say?'

'What could I say?' replied Lisa. 'I told her she had to do whatever she thought was right.'

Momentarily lost for a response, I chose to stare into the bottom of my empty mug in the vain hope that it might have replenished itself. The only thing I found lurking at the bottom of the mug was a change of subject.

'It must be weird for you,' I said looking out towards the sea. 'Yesterday you were in Brighton in the cold – today you're in Crete in the sun.'

'It's been great to get away,' said Lisa. 'I'm loving every second of it. I know I seem to be doing a lot of apologising but I really am sorry if I've spoilt your holiday. It's not enough that I've been calling you and sending you text messages about Andy, now I'm here in person spoiling things up close.'

'You're not spoiling anything. In fact it's been nice having you around today.'

Lisa squeezed my hand. 'That's really sweet of you.'

'Well, it's true.' I was silently willing Lisa not to release my hand. 'How are things with you and Andy now you're here?'

'Okay, I suppose,' replied Lisa. 'It's funny, but my first reaction when he told me he'd bought me a ticket to come over was that he was trying to make up for something. Isn't that a horrible way to think?'

We both stopped talking for a moment, content to look out towards the sea where a far-off ship was passing by. Meanwhile underneath us we could hear a group of girls – all clicking heels and laughter – passing by the pool.

'So, what about this girl that you met at the airport?'

asked Lisa with a mischievous tone in her voice. 'The girl-with-the-cowboy-hat? Andy said she was a bit of a babe.'

'She was, and right now she's probably getting chatted up by some tall, dark, handsome twenty-year-old bricklayer with abs of steel.'

'I think you're doing her a massive injustice,' said Lisa. 'Girls don't always go for the physical . . . not that there's anything wrong with you like that, but you know what I mean.'

'Come on, Lisa, which would you rather have – me or the bricklayer?'

Lisa grinned. 'Abs of steel you say?'

'Yeah.'

'Personality?'

'Of a house brick.'

'But he's got abs of steel?'

'Steel covered in burnished bronze.'

'And then there's you?' said Lisa pulling a face.

'Less abs of steel and more abs of custard.'

'But a great personality.'

'I can definitely tell a joke or two if that's what you mean. Two fish walk into a bar—'

'That wasn't a question,' replied Lisa, cutting me off with a grin. 'It was a statement. And on top of that you can talk on the phone without resorting to a series of grunts, you're a good listener, especially when the person at the other end of the phone is in tears . . . and to cap it all you're nigh on perfect at making insecure girlfriends feel that bit less insecure when their useless boyfriends decide to go on an all-boys' holiday. You won't know this but I've always said to Andy that you really would make some girl the perfect boyfriend.'

'I doubt that strongly.'

'Because of Sarah?'

'No,' I replied, 'because . . . oh . . . it doesn't matter.'

'Is this to do with this other girl you met out here? Donna?'

'And they say that women are the worst gossips! What did he say exactly?'

'Well, this is all through an Andy filter so I'll take some, if not all, of it with a huge pinch of salt, but he said that you had some sort of an intense twenty-four-hour thing with her where nothing actually happened.'

'That's pretty much it.'

'I bet it wasn't.'

'She was still getting over her ex.'

'A pretty big obstacle, I'll grant you but not an impossible one.'

'She told me that holiday romances never work out . . . maybe she was right. After all, technically speaking that's what Sarah and I were.'

'Maybe they do work out and maybe they don't,' replied Lisa, 'but they can be a lot of fun while they last.'

As Lisa's words echoed around my head I realised that there was a certain inevitability about what was about to happen. It was as though everything in the past week had been conspiring to bring about this moment. Everything from our embrace in my kitchen, to the easy intimacy of our text messages, to the news about Sarah's pregnancy had had the effect of bringing us closer together. But it had been Andy himself who had ultimately united us through his friendship and through his lies.

I touched Lisa's face with both hands and she didn't shy away. For a moment I wavered, telling myself that what I was about to do was wrong. But before I could retreat I recalled Andy's response when I told him not to contact Nina: 'I wouldn't be risking anything,' he'd said. At the time he had seemed so sure of the odds and so confident of the outcome that I wanted to know what it would be like to take the risk. Just as Andy had done. Just as Sarah had too. And that was the moment that thought turned into action.

DAY SIX: SATURDAY

BBC Breakfast News

Most mornings when I wake up, the first thing that hits me is a strong sense of déjà vu, which is only natural, I suppose, because most mornings are exactly the same. Radio clock alarm goes off, I get out of bed and have a shower. Dripping water over the bathroom floor I shave badly in front of a steamed-up mirror and then return to the bedroom where I finally get dry and pull on some underwear. Clad only in boxer shorts I take out the ironing board and proceed to iron one of the five white work shirts I've washed over the weekend. I slip on the shirt, still warm from being pressed, quickly followed by my grey work suit, before heading to the kitchen where I pour myself a bowl of cereal (usually cornflakes but occasionally muesli – I got a taste for it after Sarah moved out). I eat the cereal in front of *BBC Breakfast News* then return to the kitchen, slip two slices of bread into the toaster and take out the margarine from the fridge in anticipation of my toast's arrival. Lurking in the living room, I continue watching TV until I hear the toast pop up, then head back to the kitchen, slap the margarine on the toast and return to the TV. Approximately sixteen bites later breakfast is over and so I put on my shoes, grab my coat and I'm out the door. Sometimes I think I hate this routine. It makes me feel that I'm boring. So occasionally I'll vary it (iron my shirt the night before or buy a different cereal or watch GMTV) and I'll feel great. Vibrant even. But no matter what happens, the very next day I'll be back to my normal routine with no deviations or variations. It's almost as if the day before had never happened. And that's exactly how I felt when I woke up following my raki-fuelled late night.

Staring at the darkened ceiling I strained my ears listening to noises coming from outside: water splashing in the hotel pool, laughter from fellow holidaymakers and the electronic warning beep of reversing delivery trucks. Lying there with all these familiar noises swirling round the room I thought to myself, 'This is just an ordinary day. A day like yesterday and the day before that,' and for a few seconds I felt a real sense of relief. That nagging feeling of discomfort was wrong. The sick feeling in the pit of my stomach was mistaken. I even smiled at the air-conditioning unit when I realised that once again it had been left on its maximum setting all night.

And because nothing was wrong and everything was okay I reasoned that today was going to be a day just like any other on the holiday so far. We'd get up. We'd have breakfast. We'd go to the beach. In the evening we'd go out, drink too much and go to bed in the early hours. Everything was predictable. Everything was safe.

Just as I finally allowed myself the luxury of relaxing, something – possibly my burgeoning sense of guilt – made me turn my head in the direction of Andy's bed where he and Lisa lay fast asleep and that was the moment that I knew for sure that this wasn't going to be a day like any other. This was the day after the night before. And I'd never seen this script before in my life.

Unwilling (or unable) to start thinking too deeply yet, I climbed out of bed and quietly got dressed in my usual holiday attire of shorts and T-shirt. Grabbing my sunglasses and the keys for the hire car, I made my way from the bedroom into the kitchen. Tom stirred briefly on the sofa-bed but soon fell back asleep, so opening the front door as quietly as I could I stepped into the bright morning light and made my way downstairs.

The big question on my mind was where to go. The beach seemed like the most obvious place. It became less appealing, however, once I imagined it filled with its usual clientele flirting with each other against a backdrop of loud club music. Of course, now I had transport I could go anywhere I pleased. And so without thinking about my eventual destination, I made my way to the car, started it up and pulled into a break in the traffic in the direction of the Malia crossroad.

With only a handful of road signs for guidance, I knew I had to make a decision. Amongst the signs for nearby villages and the motorway, there was one with the symbol for a tourist attraction next to it that said 'The Palace of Malia: 3km'. I had no idea what The Palace of Malia might be given that I was having a hard time imagining that Malia, even in ancient times, had been anything other than the alfresco night club that it is today. Whatever it was, I reasoned that it was as good a destination as anywhere else and so followed the road signs in that direction.

It took no time at all to get there. As I climbed out of the car the first thing I noticed was the intensity of the sun. Despite it being relatively early, the temperature was already so hot that the car park tarmac had begun to melt and felt sticky underfoot.

I locked the car and made my way along a path to the entrance where a sign said: 'Welcome to the Palace of Malia – a Minoan treasure.' Looking over the fence I could make out various huge lumps of sandstone. Next to the sign was an elderly woman wearing a straw hat who was sitting in a chair reading a book. I asked how much it was to come in and she said something in Greek and pointed towards a doorway a few yards away.

Inside the room along with some literature about the Palace, there was a small ticket booth. As no one was there, I pressed a buzzer mounted on the top of the counter. A small woman with a cheery smile arrived almost immediately and sold me a ticket, which I then handed to the woman in the chair outside. As I gave her my ticket, she muttered something in Greek and then pointed me in the direction of a building behind her.

The building was part of a permanent exhibition that told the story of the palace's excavation. Large black and white photos from the 1900s were mounted on the wall, and reading from the panels underneath them I learned that the first palace of Malia had been built by the Minoans in 1900 BC only to be destroyed some two hundred years later. It was later rebuilt and destroyed again and then in 1450 BC they rebuilt one last time.

This final version must have been the most impressive, because when I followed the exhibition trail through an archway into an interconnected room, I found a scale model of the palace on a table, under a large glass case. It looked like those models of planned shopping centres and housing developments that I used to see at work before everything became computer generated. I stood for quite a long time, imagining miniature Minoans going about their daily lives. It was sad thinking that all the people who had lived in the palace were no longer alive. And it was a stern reminder of how much things can change in a relatively short space of time.

More knowledgeable about the Minoans than when I'd entered the exhibition, I made my way to the exit, stepped outside and began to pour with sweat. In the short time that I'd been out of the sun the outside temperature had sky-rocketed to unbearable proportions. With the realisation that I might die of dehydration, I wiped the sheen of sweat from my forehead and began looking around the ruins of the palace in earnest. I looked around the remains of court-yards and cellars. I ventured around workshops and dwelling rooms. And somewhere around the court of the tower I decided that it might be time to take a look at the ruination of my own life.

Coming to a huge lump of sandstone that was probably of great archaeological significance, I took the opportunity to take the weight off my feet and sat down. As the sun beat down on my scalp, I took a deep breath and, with much relief, finally let the guilt bottled up inside me run its course.

Here's to hot summer nights

The kiss on the balcony. That was where it had begun. But it had ended somewhere entirely different. Though we had stopped speaking by this point, there had been no doubt in my mind about how far we intended to go. Guilt didn't even get a look in as we negotiated the short distance from the balcony to my bed and I knew that unless Andy returned any time soon, nothing short of a miracle would stop my betrayal.

Everything that happened once we reached our destination was lost in the blur of sensory overload. (Although later that night as Lisa and Andy slept peacefully in their bed next to my own, I could recall perfectly the sense of urgency that had gripped me at that moment; the actions it inspired however had faded too swiftly to make a lasting impression. It was a moment within a moment. It was everything and then it was nothing.)

Afterwards, as we disentangled our bodies and readjusted our clothing, I found myself waiting expectantly for the arrival of some sort of sense of regret. After all I had just slept with my best friend's girlfriend. But there was nothing. And the longer I thought about it the more I began to wonder whether this was down to the simple fact that I wasn't sorry. Whatever the reason, the deed was done. Events had been set in motion. And no matter what we did to cover up our actions, something fundamental had changed about the world we both inhabited and could never be changed back, no matter how much we adjusted the sheets of my bed, straightened our clothes and wiped away smeared make-up.

The tension was unbearable. Every knock, creak, scrape or groan of the infrastructure of the apartment building set my heart racing even once we were ready for Andy's return. And as the minutes passed, and the distance between our shared moment and our current state of readiness grew, we became more tense rather than less. I was almost more desperate for him to return and sense that something had gone on than I was to wait for his arrival and escape the consequences of my actions. What I didn't want – what I couldn't stand – was the waiting. It was the not knowing if my betrayal would be exposed that was the real torture.

When Andy finally called to let us know he was back I was convinced that if his senses hadn't been dulled by the raki then he would have guessed straight away that something was wrong. Through my now sober eyes it was as though everything that had been witness to my actions and Lisa's was emitting a steady fog of guilt that only the sober could see. The whole apartment seemed eerily sinister, like the scene of a murder long after the body had been removed.

'Victorious,' said Andy, holding up not one but two bottles of raki. 'Sorry I took so long, kids. On the way back from the mini-market I bumped into Steve-the-barman downstairs and we got talking and so I bought him a beer.' Andy set down the bottles, arranged our mugs in a huddle, poured out a double shot into each one and handed them out. 'Here's to hot summer nights,' he said raising his mug in the air. 'May there be many more of them.'

The three of us stayed out on the balcony for another hour or so, during which time I amazed myself by remaining calm in such a chaotic situation. I made jokes at Andy's expense, I chatted with Lisa about the everyday stuff of life and I breathed calmly at every opportunity. In short I acted as though nothing had happened. But as the night progressed I realised that my ability to fool Andy had less to do with innate acting skills than my fear of being discovered. I just couldn't let that happen. I had betrayed my best friend in the cruellest way possible. So if it meant I had to crack jokes, if it meant I had to make small talk with Lisa, if it meant that I had to callously act as though I hadn't just committed the crime of the century, then that was exactly what I would do.

For the most part, however, as we whiled our way through to the early hours, my mind was focused on two questions: why had Lisa done what she had done? And more importantly, where would we go from here?

Not a single thing

No one batted an eyelid on my return to the apartment following my sojourn to The Palace of Malia. Tom and Lisa were out on the balcony, while Andy was in the bathroom taking a shower. They all assumed I'd gone down to the beach for a morning constitutional and as it seemed as good an excuse as any I didn't correct them.

Fear of being discovered aside, my biggest worry about the day ahead was centred on how Lisa might act around me in the cold harsh light of day. In my more egotistical moments I'd been imagining that she might be in need of some form of reassurance that last night had meant as much to me as it had done to her. I imagined a whole day of longing looks and secret smiles. Perhaps even a few unexplained tears and temper tantrums. Lisa, however, was as far from giving the game away as possible. From the moment of my return all she did was laugh, joke and be her usual effervescent self. And that was even when Andy wasn't there. As we made our way down to Stars and Bars, Andy told an anecdote about an anti-student loans demonstration we'd gone on in a bid to chat up a couple of girls we both fancied; I tried desperately to catch Lisa's eye as if to say, 'Last night was real wasn't it?' but when I did, though she held my gaze unflinchingly, there wasn't even the faintest flicker of guilt or recognition. It was as though she had wiped the memory from her mind. And without her corroboration to back up my version of events it began to feel as if last night hadn't happened at all.

'That was excellent,' said Andy lighting up a post-breakfast cigarette following our usual Stars and Bars breakfast. 'I'd suggest that we get the waiter to give our compliments to the chef but I'm guessing he'd think we were being clever.' He yawned and stretched his arms in the air. 'So what are we going to do tonight, boys and girls? It's our last night of freedom. After tonight there's just a plane ride between us and another twelve months of day-to-day grind.'

'Very poetic,' teased Lisa. 'Is that what life is like with me?'

'Of course not,' grinned Andy. 'It's much worse.'

'Well . . . though I'll hate myself for saying it, given last night's excesses,' began Tom, 'I think we sort of owe it to ourselves to head out in Malia tonight.'

'Did Tom just suggest that we have a bit of fun?' asked Andy doing a comedy double take. 'I tell you what, Charlie, he's more fun than you these days.' He paused and took a drag on his cigarette. 'So Malia it is then,' he continued. 'There are still loads of bars that we haven't been in that look like a right laugh . . . in fact there's a club I read about that's throwing a "foam party" tonight.' Andy looked at us all expectantly but we all looked equally nonplussed. He reached into the back pocket of his shorts and pulled out a page torn from a magazine. It was an advert for the Camelot Club featuring a series of photos of young (mainly female) clubbers waist deep in white foam as if an industrial washing machine had exploded only moments before the pictures had been taken.

'Now that,' said Andy waving the advert, 'is a foam party. Tell me that doesn't look like fun.'

'When you say "fun",' said Lisa drily, 'I take it you mean, "Largely populated by twenty-one-year-old girls in bikini tops and cut-off denim shorts?"'

'Not at all, but if there are girls like that around, then that can't exactly be a bad thing for our friend here.' Andy gave my shoulders a squeeze – his physical shorthand for sincerity. 'Come on, babe,' he continued, 'have a heart will you? Let's not forget that Charlie here – the only single person amongst us – has yet to get any action this holiday. We have to go to this party . . . for his sake.'

'Thanks and all that,' I said to Andy in a more determined voice than usual, 'but it really doesn't sound like my thing. Let's just go out, have a few beers and a laugh, okay?'

'You say that now,' replied Andy, 'but when the foam's flying—'

'I'm not interested, honestly.'

'You will be. Trust me.'

'Trust *me*,' I replied as my exasperation edged its way into my voice, 'I won't.'

'Come on, Andy,' intervened Lisa on my behalf. 'If Charlie said he's not interested then you shouldn't force him.'

Andy rubbed the top of my head patronisingly. 'See this guy here? This is my mate Charlie Mansell and there's not a single thing in this world that I wouldn't do for him. Not a single thing. So that's why we're going to the Camelot Club tonight. And that's why we'll have a good time. And that's why I'll make sure that whatever happens he won't leave that party alone.'

To talk

It was mid-to-late-afternoon, the sun was marginally less intense than it had been all day (which meant that you could still probably just about fry an egg on the sand) and the four of us were lying on our sun-loungers. Lisa had yet to drop a single hint about the events of the previous night, despite my giving her various opportunities to do so. After leaving Stars and Bars I'd deliberately lingered behind Tom and Andy so that Lisa and I could walk down to the beach together without arousing any suspicion. But before she had noticed me she had playfully called out to Tom and asked for a piggyback as far as the mini-market. At the mini-market I announced that I was going to buy a couple of bottles of water and might need a hand. Although Lisa could've easily volunteered, Tom was forced to come to my aid because Andy had simply ignored my request and Lisa took the opportunity to reapply some suncream on her shoulders. Once we were settled on the loungers, I'd asked if anyone was interested in going for a walk – knowing full well that Tom was too engrossed in his *Rough Guide* and Andy too lazy to stand up – but again she declined preferring to have Andy undo the strings to her bikini, douse her back in suncream and vigorously massage it into her skin. By the time I returned from my walk Lisa was dozing in the sun with one hand resting gently on Andy's arm and the two of them looked like the perfect picture of togetherness.

'Do you know what?' said Tom resting his *Rough Guide* on his chest. 'It's just occurred to me that none of us have actually been in the sea all holiday.'

'What's the point?' said Andy. 'All that happens is you go in, you get wet, you come out, sand sticks to you and then you have to have a shower – sounds like a proper pain in the arse if you ask me.'

'I'd love to go in,' said Lisa, 'but my suncream isn't waterproof and I'd have to reapply the lot.'

'What about you, Charlie?' asked Tom. 'Fancy a swim?'

'Nah,' I replied eyeing Lisa from behind my sunglasses. 'I've always felt there's something undignified about men walking round topless. It's the snob in me.'

Andy sat up, yawned loudly and stretched. 'I'm going to get some more water. Anyone else want anything?' Lisa asked for an ice cream while Tom requested a can of Coke. I declined. All I really wanted was an acknowledgement from Lisa that what had happened last night wasn't a figment of my imagination, so that I could stop feeling as if I was losing the plot.

'Do you need someone to give you a hand?' Tom said. 'I could do with a walk.'

'Actually I've got it sorted,' said Andy quickly. He turned and looked at me and even though he was wearing his sunglasses I could tell that something was going on. 'Charlie will give me a hand, won't you, mate?'

My heart froze mid-beat. 'Yeah, of course.'

'Oh, I see,' joked Lisa. 'You want to have a quiet word with Charlie, is that it?'

'Course not,' said Andy coolly. 'Feel free to come if you want.'

Lisa looked over at me and I saw a flash of anxiety in her blue-green eyes. 'No thanks,' she replied. 'You two go and do your boy thing.'

We trudged barefoot across the hot sand until we were out of earshot.

'So what's going on?' I asked.

'Nothing really,' said Andy, looking over his shoulder at Lisa and Tom. 'I just couldn't think of any other way of getting you on your own.'

'On my own for what?'

'To talk.'

'About what?'

'Nina.'

'So what have you decided? Are you going to carry on seeing her or call it quits?'

'Well, that's sort of what I wanted to talk about.'

Without waiting for my response Andy walked out of the entrance to the beach, crossed the road and sat down on the wall outside the mini-market. There were a couple of girls chatting to each other just to the left of him. Neither of them noticed me as I sat down only a few feet away from them. I was invisible.

'I know I don't act like it,' began Andy, 'but the truth is Lisa really does mean the world to me. You won't understand but this holiday and the things I've done . . . they aren't anything to do with her at all. It's all been about me.' Andy paused and stared at me as if trying to judge whether I was buying into his argument. What he saw I don't know, but when I looked into his sunglasses in a return bid to see his soul, all I could see was my own reflection.

'Well if all that's true,' I replied, 'why are we talking now?'

'Because somehow things have got messed up,' said Andy. 'Last night I came up with the excuse of getting those extra bottles of raki so that I could call Nina and tell her that I wouldn't be seeing her again. But as soon as I told her she started telling me how good we were together and how we ought to at least give things a try. And even though I kept telling her "no", at the back of my mind I knew that I wanted to say "yes".'

'So you're going to carry on seeing Nina behind Lisa's back?'

'No,' replied Andy. 'I've decided that when we get back from holiday I'm going to leave her.'

It is what it is

Andy waited for my reaction.

'So what do you think?' he asked eventually. 'Am I losing it? Am I doing the wrong thing? Tell me what I should do?'

I wanted to tell him to leave her. I wanted to tell him that he didn't deserve her. I even wanted to tell him about what had happened last night. But I didn't say anything. Instead I remembered that despite everything Andy was still one of my closest friends in the world and deserved the best advice I could give irrespective of its consequences to me.

'If you leave her it will be a mistake,' I said firmly.

'Maybe, but right now I feel it's the only thing I can do.'

'You're not thinking straight. You can't be. You're talking about leaving someone you've been with for nearly seven years for a girl you've known only a few days. Does that sound like the action of someone who is thinking straight?'

'It is what it is,' said Andy.

'What does that mean?' I replied. 'It doesn't mean anything. It's one of those meaningless phrases people say when they can't justify whatever ridiculous act of self destruction they're about to do next.'

There was a long silence and the two girls sitting next to Andy stood up and walked away. I couldn't think of what else to say. I couldn't think of how I wanted things to turn out. It was all a mess.

'I thought you of all people would understand,' said Andy, looking down at the pavement.

'What's that supposed to mean?' I replied.

'Nina told me about you and Donna. Nina said that reading between the lines Donna seemed to think that you might have fallen in love with her.'

I tried to hold back all of the feelings brought to the surface just by hearing Donna's name. 'Recently dumped guy falls in love with girl on holiday,' I replied sarcastically. 'Has all the hallmarks of a relationship that – even if she hadn't dumped me at the airport – would've lasted . . . what? Five . . . maybe . . . six seconds after we'd got back home and she'd realised that I'm not the bloke she thought I was, just a dull bloke with a dull job . . . and a dull flat . . . still licking his wounds following a savaging by his ex-girlfriend.' I paused and looked at Andy. 'So what was your point?'

'My point was . . .' his voice trailed off. 'Look you know what I'm like. I'm hardly perfect boyfriend material, am I? Lisa deserves someone better than me.'

'And Nina doesn't?'

'It'll be different.'

'How?' I replied. 'What makes you so sure you won't do the same with her too?'

'Because that's the whole point of starting again,' said Andy, 'to give yourself a clean slate in the hope that maybe this time around you'll get it right.'

I could see from his face that his mind was made up, so we made our way into the mini-market in silence, bought all the things we were after and then left the shop. On our way back to the beach neither of us mentioned Nina or Lisa again. Instead we talked about recent films we had seen, TV we had watched and famous women we found attractive. And that small host of conversations managed to occupy the void between us right up until we got back to the beach. I retreated to my corner and Andy retreated to his and even though neither of us spoke again we both knew that the conversation was far from over.

. . . and that was all it took

Lisa was holding Andy's arm aloft so that she could look at his watch. 'Time to go, boys,' she said disappointedly.

'What time is it?' asked Tom.

'Just coming up to five.'

'So that's the end of beach life for us for a while,' said Andy. 'I was actually kind of getting into it.'

'We could still come down tomorrow,' said Lisa. 'What time are we supposed to be out of our rooms?'

'Eleven,' said Andy.

'Midday,' I corrected.

Andy shrugged. 'Either way we'll have nowhere to wash once we've been kicked out so I doubt if I'll be bothering with the beach tomorrow.'

'That's a shame,' said Lisa. 'So what time's the actual flight home?'

'Eleven o'clock at night,' said Andy.

'Actually it's just after midnight,' I corrected again. 'And the coach picking us up for the airport is coming some time around nine.'

As Andy and Lisa began collecting their things together, it became clear that the tension between me and Andy hadn't gone unnoticed because Tom lifted up his sunglasses and raised his eyebrows in querying fashion. Andy and Lisa were still too close for comfort for me to respond so as they began making their way towards the top of the beach I lingered by the loungers with Tom.

'So what's happened now? You've barely said a civil word to each other since your trip to the shops.'

'I don't even know where to begin,' I replied. 'It's all wrapped up so tightly together it's almost impossible to unravel. I'm not even sure where the beginning of the story is . . . but I'm pretty certain what the end will be if Andy finds out.'

'This doesn't sound good at all. What has he done now?'

'It's actually all my fault this time,' I replied. 'I slept with Lisa.'

'You *what*?'

'I know,' I replied. 'I shouldn't have done it but I did.'

'When did this happen?'

'Last night, after you went to bed. Andy went out to get some more raki and I don't know . . . we started talking and it all snowballed from there.' Tom couldn't have looked more disappointed in me if he'd tried. 'I promise you, if I'd thought for a second that Andy even remotely cared for her I would never have let it happen.'

'That's easy to say,' said Tom. He looked up ahead to where Andy and Lisa stood waiting at the top of the beach. 'I take it he doesn't know?'

'No,' I replied.

'So why all the tension this afternoon?'

'Well that sort of brings me to the twist in the story . . .'

'Nothing you say could surprise me now.'

'Not even if I told you that not only is Andy going to carry on seeing Nina when we get back home, but he's decided that he's going to leave Lisa?'

'This whole holiday is a mess from beginning to end.

We would've all been better off staying at home.' Tom bent down and picked up his bag. 'So where does all this leave you and Lisa?'

'I don't know,' I replied. 'We haven't had a chance to talk yet.'

'And if you had, what would you say?'

'I don't know,' I replied. 'I really don't know.'

It's not going to blow over

It was evening now and the four of us were making ready to leave The Bengal Castle (one of the few Indian restaurants in Malia and yet another one of Tom's discoveries). Our next stop was the strip, where we planned to visit a few bars before heading off to Andy's beloved foam party at the Camelot Club.

So far the evening had been uneventful. Andy and I had barely spoken to each other until we all sat down to dinner, when we both mellowed significantly for the sake of the evening that lay ahead of us. As for Lisa, I was still none the wiser about her feelings about last night. She hadn't said a single thing to me and there hadn't been the opportunity for me to say a single thing to her. Instead, while the others hung around the bedroom watching TV, I sat on the balcony alone under the guise of reading *The Da Vinci Code* when in reality all I was doing was staring out to sea and thinking about Lisa.

'So come on then, Charlie,' said Tom as he pushed his chair underneath the table and leaned on the backrest, 'what do you think will be the first thing you'll do once you get home?'

'I don't know.' I hadn't been particularly talkative all evening. I glanced at Lisa. 'Maybe you should ask someone else.'

Tom turned to Lisa and smiled. 'You'll give me an answer won't you, mate?'

'Okay,' replied Lisa. 'The first thing I'll do is open the post. I love it when you go away and there's a ton of stuff waiting for you. It's almost like it's your birthday . . . only there aren't any cards . . . only junk mail and utility bills and letters from your auntie telling you how well all your cousins are doing.' Lisa batted the question back to Tom. 'What about you? What will be the first thing you do when you get home?'

'It's a bit boring,' replied Tom. 'I'll kiss Anne and the kids. That's the first thing I always do when I walk through the door.'

'That's not boring,' said Lisa. 'It's sweet. I'd love to come home to a family like that one day.'

'Ask him what the second thing is,' said Andy. 'I bet it won't be quite so cuddly.'

'He's right,' laughed Tom. 'The second thing will be to check all my work e-mails in case there's anything important in there. Last time Anne and I went away I came back to an in-box groaning under the cyber-weight of two hundred-and-sixty-seven unopened e-mails and attachments. Ninety per cent of them were the usual: "It's Brian's leaving do on Friday – please make the effort to come along."'

'That sounds like my place too,' replied Lisa.

'What about you, Andy?' asked Tom. 'What will be your first move when you get home?'

'I can answer that one for you,' said Lisa. 'It's easy. The first thing Andy always does is go around the house checking every single room to see if anything's changed. It's a weird sort of superstition he's had going for as long as we've been living together.'

'She's making this up,' said Andy, clearly embarrassed, 'I don't do that at all.'

'He does,' teased Lisa. 'He even does it in the same order every time. It's living room, kitchen, front bedroom, back bedroom and then bathroom. It's like he's checking for burglars or something.'

'Look,' interrupted Andy, 'can we stop talking about going home and start having some fun here? Tonight's our last night together. And I'm pretty sure that none of us is ever going to come back here again. So let's just enjoy ourselves okay?' He patted me on the back. 'And that means you too, mate. Tonight is going to be a night you're never going to forget.'

Things were busy now. The pavements were packed with so many young Brits that it was hard to imagine there could be anyone between the ages of eighteen and thirty left at home. They were all here, fuelled with booze and ready to party.

The bar girls of the strip were in force. It was easy to pick them out amongst the streets crowded with holidaymakers because they stood out a mile: long legs, incredible bodies, cheeky personalities, provocative dress sense. It was all there and it was all working for them. We watched in admiration as a stunning girl in a pink top, short skirt and cowboy boots managed to single-handedly herd about ten guys into Bar Logica in a matter of seconds. Meanwhile across the way three girls wearing tight jeans and matching polka-dot bikini tops were picking off groups of guys at random and leading them into Hotshot's cocktail lounge at such a rate that there was a huge backlog of blokes crowded in the bar like sheep waiting to be shorn. But despite the strong bar-girl presence, unlike on our previous visits, not a single one of them even looked in our direction. The message was clear. Even though there were three of us – and only one of Lisa – in their eyes at least, we all belonged to her. We were no longer strays as I'd imagined at the airport. We had an owner. A leader. Someone in charge. And the girls in their short skirts and tight tops knew and respected that. And although I didn't miss the attention – my mind was too focused elsewhere – I did resent the assumption that Lisa owned all three of us, even if in truth they were actually only one third out.

Lisa's presence affected my perception of the strip too. Bathing in the neon glow of the bars and the clubs we found ourselves jostling with rowdy gangs of youths shouting and swearing at the top of their voices; we were breathing in the hot fat smells of a thousand and one takeaway meals, and we were forced to endure the constant thump of countless anonymous club tracks. Thanks to Lisa, I suddenly saw Malia with new eyes and felt embarrassed that we had brought her here at all. Everything around us was evidence of both my and Andy's lack of maturity – the exact opposite of the dictionary definition of 'sophistication'. We were Beavis and Butthead at thirty-five. Grown men in schoolboy trousers. Overgrown teenagers trying desperately to hang on to the last vestiges of our youth. And I realised (albeit too late) that some activities in life, like holidaying in Malia, skateboarding or drinking until you throw up over your shoes, are too youthful for a man this deep into his thirties to participate in without looking like a fool.

'Let's try this place.' Lisa came to a halt as if she had overheard my thoughts and was now desperate to compound my shame. 'It looks like fun.'

'Are you sure?' replied Andy, staring at Pandemonium's

eye-catching neon sign. 'I mean, it looks a bit tacky, don't you think?'

'Cheesy, yes,' corrected Lisa. 'Tacky? No. What does everyone else think?'

'I don't mind,' said Tom.

Lisa looked at me expectantly, but I had long since given up trying to hide how I was feeling.

'Right then,' said Lisa, 'Pandemonium it is then.'

Pandemonium hadn't changed since we were last there. The music was still loud, the bar was still packed and the waitresses still wearing very little. We set up camp in the same seats that we had occupied on our first night, Tom and I facing the bar and Andy and Lisa sitting opposite. A bunny-girl waitress came and took our drinks orders and once they arrived we tried several times to start a group conversation but soon tired of yelling over the music. Out of necessity, then, Lisa and Andy fell into their own private conversation while Tom and I fell into our own.

'It's like history repeating itself,' said Tom as he looked up at the TV screen above his head showing highlights of the day's test match. 'At least tonight should be less eventful than last time.'

'Maybe,' I replied.

'What do you mean, "maybe"?' asked Tom looking at me suspiciously. 'You're not going to start something tonight are you?'

I took a sip of my beer. 'I really like her, Tom. I really like her.'

'Lisa?'

I nodded.

'Do you mean you like her in the same way you "really liked" Donna?' said Tom, playing devil's advocate.

'That's hardly fair is it?' I responded. 'I *did* like Donna . . . but she didn't want me. What should I be doing instead? Sitting around crying into my beer?'

'No,' replied, Tom, 'but I just don't think Lisa's the answer. Think about it, Charlie, you haven't even spoken to her about last night yet and you're already thinking about rocking the boat with her and Andy.'

I glanced across the table. It seemed too bizarre for words that I could be discussing my feelings for her so openly with her sitting less than three feet away and yet so oblivious.

'You're absolutely right.'

'Absolutely right about what?' asked Tom.

I didn't reply. Instead I stood up, walked around to Andy and Lisa's side of the table and tapped them both on the shoulder.

'All right, mate?' said Andy. 'What's up?'

'You're right about me putting some effort into having a laugh tonight. In fact I'm so in the right frame of mind that I actually fancy a dance . . . which is why I was just wondering if I could borrow your girlfriend for a bit.'

Andy laughed. 'How much have you had to drink? I've never seen you on the dance floor unless you're practically slaughtered.'

'I know,' I replied. 'But there's a first time for everything.'

'In that case you have my full blessing, mate.'

Lisa looked on helplessly as I took her by the hand and led her in the direction of the Pandemonium's packed dance floor. At the last minute, however, I changed direction and instead guided her through some large glass doors to the bar's outdoor patio area where dozens of couples sat at tables talking by candlelight.

'I'm sorry for dragging you away like that,' I said as we came to a halt next to a row of potted olive trees. 'I didn't know what else to do.'

'This is insane, Charlie,' protested Lisa. 'What if Andy came out here right now?'

'I know, I know,' I replied, fighting hard the urge to kiss her. 'But what could I do? I've got to know what last night was about.'

'It was a mistake,' she said quietly.

'A mistake?'

Lisa nodded. 'I wish with my whole heart that it had never happened.'

I walked over to an empty table, sat down and closed my eyes in a bid to block out what was happening. As I squeezed my eyes shut a million and one emotions washed over me.

'It can't have been a mistake,' I said desperately. 'I felt something for you last night and I know you did too. I can't have got it that wrong, surely? It wasn't just all in my head.'

'You're right,' she replied. 'I think when Andy told me he was flying me over here I was more excited about seeing you than I was him. You were there for me when I needed you. I wanted to be there for you, too. But I took things too far. You're Andy's best friend. I should never have put you in that position.'

'But you did,' I replied. 'And even though I'm Andy's friend I don't regret anything about last night.'

'You and Andy have been friends too long for me to believe you mean that.'

'You don't need to tell me what's at stake,' I replied. 'I already know. And maybe Andy will never get over it or maybe he will. But all I know is that it's worth the risk. Last night wasn't just about sex. It was about something more than that. It must have been.'

'I don't know what to say.'

'Say you'll leave him.'

I could see from Lisa's face that she hadn't seen that coming. 'You don't know what you're saying, Charlie.'

'Maybe not,' I replied. 'But I know you don't love him.'

There was a long silence.

'You're right,' she said eventually, 'I don't, at least not like most people would mean it. We're probably more like a car crash. We're too mangled together to tear apart without doing ourselves some permanent damage.' Lisa paused as a group of girls carrying luminous cocktails came out through the glass doors and filled the patio with cackling laughter.

'We'd better go back inside, Charlie,' said Lisa, standing up. 'Andy could start looking for us any second. Are you coming?'

'You carry on,' I replied. 'I'll see you in a minute.'

Lisa headed back inside the bar while I looked up into the night sky and contemplated what had just happened. She was right, of course. What had happened was just a messy situation in which some degree of misery was inevitable for everyone involved. But what she didn't know was that she was living on borrowed time, just like I had been with Sarah. Andy was going to leave her and yet she had chosen him over me. This didn't seem right or fair. Once again he was going to walk away with everything he wanted while everyone else cleared up the chaos behind him.

I crossed the patio towards the door back into the bar but stopped when I saw Tom coming the other way.

'Are you all right?' he asked. 'When Lisa came back to the table alone I thought something might be up.'

'She's not going to leave him,' I said succinctly.

Tom sighed. 'I know it must be tough for you but it's probably for the best.'

'How can that be true when he's going to leave her anyway?'

'You don't know that for sure, do you? Andy says a lot of things he doesn't mean. And even if he does, there's no need for you to get involved is there? If he does leave her then maybe there'll be a chance you and Lisa can get together when all this has blown over.'

'It's not going to blow over,' I replied. 'Can't you see that? This whole thing is a mess. I didn't mean for it to happen but I don't regret it because it wasn't me who cheated on Lisa in the first place. And it's not me who's planning to leave her when we get back home. And while this might not be the best way for me and Lisa to get together, now it's happened there's no going back. The only thing I regret is all the lies. It's time for me to be honest, Tom. It's time that someone told Andy the truth.'

'You're not thinking straight,' said Tom grabbing my arm. 'This is going to cause nothing but trouble. What about Lisa?' Tom increased his grip. 'You haven't even talked it through with her.'

'I know all I need to know,' I replied.

When I look back at that moment when I broke free of Tom, stepped back inside the bar and began making my way over to Andy and Lisa, the two things I remember most clearly are the sound of blood rushing to my head and the feeling of urgency fuelling my actions. This was something I needed to do, regardless of the consequences.

'All right, mate?' Andy grinned as I reached our table. 'So how was the dance floor?'

'I wasn't on the dance floor,' I replied much to Andy's confusion. 'We need to talk.'

'No, he doesn't,' said Tom, catching up with me. 'Just ignore him, Andy.' He grabbed me by the arm again and tried to pull me away but I was too determined to carry out my mission to budge an inch.

Lisa flashed Tom a look of concern. 'Is he all right?' she asked, as though I was unable to speak for myself.

'I'm fine,' I replied. 'I just need to talk to Andy alone, that's all.'

'This isn't the time or the place, mate,' said Tom. 'Why don't you leave it until later?'

'Leave what for later?' said Andy standing up. 'I feel like I'm missing out on something. What's this all about?'

'It's about you,' I said calmly.

Andy's eyes flitted from me to Tom and back again as he tried to weigh up whether this was to do with him and Nina, or something else altogether.

'Let's take this outside, mate,' said Andy, hedging his bets.

'You'd like that, wouldn't you?' I replied. 'Is it because you don't want Lisa to hear what I've got to say?'

'You'd better watch yourself, Charlie,' warned Andy. 'You're going too far.'

'You're wrong,' I replied. 'I've already gone further than I thought I ever would and now I'm here I'm not going to back down. I've always backed down with you, haven't I? I used to back down with Sarah too. I feel like I've spent my whole life backing down from everything and everyone. But not this time. This time I'm going to stand my ground.'

'Look, mate,' intervened Tom. 'I'm begging you, please don't do it. You'll regret it. You know you will. Just leave it and walk away.'

'I can't, Tom,' I replied. 'I have to do this.'

'You have to do what?' said Andy defiantly.

'Tell you that last night I slept with Lisa,' I replied, facing Andy head on.

Andy didn't say anything for a few moments. He didn't need to as it was all written across his face: the relief of realising that this had nothing to do with Nina, followed quickly by the hurt of a double betrayal, and then finally the anger and indignation of being wronged.

Before he could ask Lisa the question on his lips, she grabbed her bag, and brushed past me and ran towards the entrance to the bar. Pausing only to throw me a look of pure distilled hatred Andy followed after her, while Tom and I stood by in silence.

DAY SEVEN: SUNDAY/MONDAY

It's good for the soul

It was early morning and I'd been sitting on a towel in the middle of an empty Laguna beach watching the tide come in for well over an hour. Sensing that I was no longer alone, I turned to see an elderly Greek guy standing less than five feet away from me. He was wearing a white sun-hat, sunglasses and pale blue swimming trunks and was carrying a towel and a bundle of clothes underneath his arm.

'You like early swim too?' he asked in heavily accented English.

'Yeah,' I replied, even though I was startled at the sight of a genuine old person. I didn't know that Malia had any genuine old people and this guy with his leathery sun-beaten skin and silvery body hair looked to be at least in his seventies. 'I do like swimming early in the morning,' I continued, 'it's good for the soul.'

'I swim every morning,' said the old man, carefully laying out his towel on the sand by his feet and placing his clothes on top of it. 'It makes me feel good about the day ahead.' He took off his hat and sunglasses and laid them on his towel. 'Enjoy the water when you get there,' he said, giving me a gentle wave of his hand, 'the Mediterranean is the best sea in the world.' With a sudden burst of energy – particularly for a man verging on his seventies – he gently jogged towards the sea. Within a few moments he was chest deep in the blue-green waves and soon all I could make out was the shape of his head bobbing in the water.

Seeing the old guy enjoying the water like that was like a challenge to me. If he could get into the water then so could I. As I'd arrived at the beach already wearing my trunks, all I needed to do was kick off my sandals and slip my T-shirt over my head. Feeling the warmth of the early morning sun against my skin made my whole body feel alive again and now I was back from the dead I was more than ready to begin my journey to the water. Walking across the warm sand I came to a halt once the sea was lapping at my feet and watched, momentarily hypnotised by the rise and fall of the water. A few yards in front of me a large wave crashed on the shore sending a huge surge of water over my ankles. As the sand underneath my feet began to give way, and I felt myself sinking, without further encouragement I took my first steps into the water.

The sea felt cool but not cold and with the sun overhead getting warmer with each passing minute, the water gradually became more inviting. The deeper into the water I walked the more quickly I became acclimatised to its temperature and within moments I too was nothing but a head bobbing above the water. So there I was, treading water, facing out towards the open sea, while being gently buffeted from side to side by the swirling currents around me, grateful for the opportunity, if only for a few moments, to feel weightless.

It had been a long night. Tom and I had waited at Pandemonium in the hope that Andy and Lisa might come back. We must have made a ridiculous sight for the bar's usual 'up for it' clientele: two miserable-looking guys in their mid-thirties not talking or drinking while everyone else in the bar partied at their very hardest.

When it became clear after an hour and a half that Andy and Lisa weren't going to return Tom and I headed back to the apartment, hoping to find them there. They weren't of course. The empty apartment was shrouded in darkness. Tom suggested that we go out and look for them, in case anything had happened. In retrospect I can see that this idea was more about making me feel like I was actually doing something than it was about finding our friends. Malia was a big resort and Andy and Lisa could have been anywhere in it. A search party of two stood no chance at all. In the end we both agreed that the best thing we could do would be to get some sleep but once Tom had retired to his sofa-bed I dropped all pretence of getting ready for bed and instead opened up the doors to the balcony, positioned myself in front of the horizon and tried my best to work out how once again I had managed to get things so completely and utterly and spectacularly wrong.

By organising the holiday, Andy had given me the one thing I needed most in my life: hope. His holiday plans had set me in a completely new context, one where I could forget about the past and could allow myself to be more optimistic about the future. Because of this newfound positivity, I'd seen opportunity at every turn and regardless of the consequences had pursued it to the end. The girl-in-the-cowboy-hat had got things going but it had been Lisa's phone calls and text messages where I'd really begun to hit my stride towards lunacy. So by the time Donna had arrived in my life I'd been so ready for action that not even the setback of Sarah's pregnancy could stop me from my mission. But when all my efforts with Donna came to a halt, all I did was refocus on Lisa. That's the only way I could find to explain what had happened. Sleeping with friends' girlfriends wasn't the kind of thing I did normally. It wasn't me at all. I had succumbed to the ever-present holiday temptation to take leave of my senses.

I sat out on the balcony for most of the night and as each hour passed without heralding Lisa and Andy's return I felt increasingly worse about my role in the night's events until somewhere around seven in the morning I could take no more. From my vantage point on the balcony, I looked around for something to do and found a huge blue-green expanse of inspiration right in front of me. 'That's it,' I thought, as the sun continued its rise over the horizon, 'for the first time this holiday I'm going to go in the water.'

In total I spent just under an hour in the sea – far longer than I'd expected – but every time I contemplated leaving the comforting buoyancy of my surroundings I kept imagining how every step towards the shore would bring me closer to the burden of carrying my own weight. When I eventually came out of the water I felt ungainly. Beached almost. And it took a few moments to get used to the sensation of supporting my own weight on dry land. Returning to my towel and clothes I found myself wondering about whichever one of my evolutionary ancestors it had been who had first come up with the idea of leaving the safety of the ocean. I was convinced that if I had been in their shoes (or flippers) at the time, as soon as I'd experienced the unbearable strain of life on land I would've turned my salamander-like tail right around and headed straight back into the ocean.

The beach was already beginning to fill up. The guys who ran the sun-lounger business were setting out their wares and a few early-bird sunbathers had already laid claim to the best spots on the beach. Not wanting to get changed in front of even the smallest audience I used my beach towel to soak up as much of the water as possible, pulled on my T-shirt, shoved my feet back in my sandals and left.

There were few people on the streets although Stars and Bars, as usual, was home to a number of young clubbers determined to deliver a two-finger salute to the supposedly moribund concept of sleep. A few of them waved at me as I passed by and I waved back, even though it may have been a joke at my expense. It was a good sign, however. I was feeling positive again. The night before had represented rock bottom but now I was definitely on my way up.

This is between me and Charlie

I was beginning to flag by the time I reached the front door to the apartment. As I put my key in the lock I was yawning and barely able to keep my eyes open, so as I opened the door and slipped past Tom on his sofa-bed my intention was to throw myself into my bed even though I was in desperate need of a shower. Once in the bedroom I realised that I wasn't going to be getting any sleep any time soon. Standing in front of me, packing their suitcases, were Andy and Lisa.

'You're back,' I said inanely.

'Not for long,' replied Andy. 'We'll be out of your way in a bit.'

'Look, Andy,' I began, 'I just want you to know that I'm completely aware how much I've messed up. What I did was . . . well . . . it was unforgivable. I've let you down in the worst possible way. And I completely understand if you want nothing more to do with me. I just want you to know that it was nothing to do with Lisa. It was all me. I'm the one to blame.'

Andy stopped packing. 'Have you finished?'

'Yeah,' I replied. 'That's all I wanted to say.'

'Good,' said Andy, 'I can carry on with my packing.'

'Look,' I said. 'Can't we at least go somewhere else and talk this through?'

'I'm not interested in hearing anything you've got to say,' said Andy. 'So I suggest that you leave me alone before I show you just how unimpressed with you I really am.'

'Please, Charlie,' said Lisa stepping in between us. 'Just do what he says.'

'Come on, Andy,' I pleaded, 'this is me and you we're talking about here. Surely there has to be a way that we can work this all out?'

'Are you joking? Tell me, Charlie, how do you think we're going to work this all out? You slept with my girlfriend. How are we going to resolve something like that?' He then struggled past Lisa and pushed me in the chest with such force that I staggered backwards into the side of his bed.

'Calm down, Andy,' I yelled, struggling to my feet.

'I'll calm down when you answer the question,' said Andy through gritted teeth.

Tom entered the room. 'What's going on?' he shouted as Andy made another lunge for me and connected with my chest, sending me flying on to the bed again.

'Just stay out of it, Tom,' spat Andy as he drew back a fist ready to thump anyone who got in his way.

'If you think I'm going to let the two of you batter each other senseless, you've got another think coming,' barked Tom.

'Stop it all of you!' yelled Lisa grabbing on to Andy. 'Just stop it.'

Lisa's intervention seemed to have the effect of bringing us to our senses.

'I understand that you're angry, Andy,' began Tom in his role as peacemaker, 'and from where I'm standing you have every right to be. What Charlie did was . . . well, you know what it was. But fighting each other won't change a single thing, you know that.'

'So why don't you help us out here?' suggested Andy. 'Come on, Tom, you're the Christian. Tell me what would you do if you were standing in my shoes? What would you do if our friend here had slept with your wife? Would you turn the other cheek? That's what you're supposed to do isn't it? Come on. I really want to know the answer. Would you forgive him?'

'No,' replied Tom, his eyes filling with disappointment. 'I don't think I could forgive him—'

'See that, Charlie?' replied Andy. 'Even Tom thinks you're scum.'

'That's not true,' said Tom. 'You didn't let me finish. What I wanted to say was that if I was in your shoes I didn't think I could forgive Charlie . . . *on my own*. But that doesn't mean that it's impossible. It just means that I'd need help to do it. We all need help sometimes – even you.'

No one spoke for a while. We all stood staring at each other, wondering how this was going to end.

'You're probably right when you say there's no way back from this.' I finally found my voice. 'I should know that better than most. When I found out Sarah was cheating on me, it really did feel like my life was over and to have done the same to you was the lowest thing I could've done to anyone. So you don't need to tell me how hard it is to forgive, because I already know. But do you know what though? That doesn't mean I can't ask.'

'You can ask all you want but the answer will always be no,' said Andy.

'Will it?' Lisa turned to Andy. 'Is that really the way it

is? You know it's not that straightforward, Andy. We're all as bad as each other. And to make out Charlie is somehow worse than anyone else makes me think that you didn't mean a single thing we talked about last night. They weren't just words, were they?'

There was a long silence.

'No,' said Andy eventually, as he avoided Lisa's gaze. 'Of course they weren't.'

Lisa reached out and held his hand. 'Well then, if you really did mean it when you told me you wanted for us to start over, if you meant it when you said that you wanted to give us another go, then for our sake I think that you have to find some way to forgive Charlie, because otherwise you'll always be holding on to the past.

'I know you, Andy. You won't be able to move on if you don't deal with this now. You'll just end up hating Charlie, and hating me and hating yourself at the same time and I don't want that for you or me.' Lisa paused and looked from Andy to me and back again and then, leaving Andy's side, she walked over to Tom. 'It's up to you,' she said. 'If you want us to work this will be the only way it will happen.'

Not the way we were

The balcony was a tip. Our solitary week of occupation had taken its toll. There were beach towels draped over the chairs, ashtray overflowing with cigarette butts, abandoned crisp packets and beer bottles littering various surfaces and right in the centre of the table, gently warming in the mid-morning sun, lay the dregs of Andy's second bottle of raki from two nights earlier.

'Looks like someone had a bit of a party out here,' said Andy moving a towel from one of the chairs and hanging it over the railings.

'A party?' I replied. 'More like a wake.'

We sat down and slipped on our sunglasses but neither of us spoke. It had been my idea to come out here while Tom and Lisa went for a walk. I felt I'd done some of my best thinking during this holiday while looking out across our perfect sea view and hoped that the power of the balcony would assist Andy and me in the seemingly impossible task ahead.

Lowering my sunglasses on to the bridge of my nose I stared down at the swimming pool. A new batch of twenty-something girls had taken up residency on the prime spot of sun-loungers opposite our balcony and were gently grilling themselves in the sun.

'New Arrivals,' I said, in a bid to start us talking.

'Looks that way,' replied Andy. He reached into his pocket, pulled out a pack of cigarettes and offered me one which I declined.

'Given up?'

'Never really started.' I paused and then added, 'It was just a holiday thing more than anything.'

There was a long silence as we both realised that once again one of us was using the holiday to excuse some form of anti-social behaviour. We both knew it was ridiculous. The holiday wasn't to blame for anything. We were.

Looking out to sea, Andy lit his cigarette, took a long, deep drag and held his breath before sending a swirl of smoke into the morning sky.

'Let's get this straight,' said Andy lowering his cigarette. 'I'm out here because of Lisa not you.'

'I know.'

'If it was up to me I'd never say a word to you again.'

He meant it too. He meant every word.

'So what do you want to do?' I asked. 'Sit here until Lisa comes back and then make out like we've sorted things out?'

'Have you got a better plan?'

'No.'

'Well then that's what we'll do.'

There was a long silence. We both looked down at the pool as a couple of guys who could have been Andy and me in our younger days simultaneously dive-bombed into the water, making such a huge splash that all the girls lounging at the side of the pool looked at them.

'So where do we go from here?' I asked as, mission accomplished, the two young lads swam across to the steps on the other side, exiting the pool to the cheers of their friends.

'I don't know,' said Andy. 'I think the best we can do is try making it up as we go along. But one thing I know is we will never be friends again. It just won't happen.'

Still hungry

Content to be amused by the antics of the young guys showing off below, Andy and I sat quietly on the balcony for some time. Eventually we both stood up and made our way back indoors; Andy continued packing while I finally had a shower. By roughly midday the four of us were all standing in the bedroom with suitcases packed ready to leave the apartment.

Although we had only been living in our apartment for just over a week, somehow during those seven days it had managed to transform itself into a home. As we checked all the rooms one last time in case we had forgotten anything, I knew that I would soon end up feeling nostalgic about the lukewarm/cold shower and the uncomfortable single bed, the overzealous air-conditioning unit and the TV with its three crappy stations. But the one thing I would miss most of all was the balcony – the few square metres of private outdoor space that had provided the backdrop for so much of the holiday. Grabbing my camera, I slid back the patio doors and stepped out on the balcony. Breathing in the outside air I tried to capture the view in my head: the perfect blue of the sky meeting the perfect blue-green of the sea and illuminating it all the perfect summer sun. I took the picture in my mind's eye. Then I took the picture with my camera and although I was sure that there would be a discrepancy between the two, I was content to make do until the day when I could see it once again with my own eyes.

The photo taken, I returned to the others, who had been silently observing my eccentric behaviour from the kitchen doorway. No one made any comment and we made our way outside where Tom handed me the keys, allowing me the honour of locking the door one last time.

Downstairs there were already quite a few people waiting by the reception desk to check out. I recognised some of the people in the queue ahead of us: the young lads and the two girls who had arrived at the Apollo at the same time as us as well as a group of student-looking types who'd been lingering by the pool most days. Eventually the queue whittled down and we handed in our keys, settled our quite extensive bar tab, paid the extra we owed for the use of the air-conditioning unit and put our luggage in the hotel's storage room.

'So what are we going to do for the rest of the day?' asked Tom as we all gravitated towards the steps at the front of the Apollo. 'I could murder some breakfast.'

'Me too.' I tried to read Andy's face but he wasn't giving anything away, nor was Lisa. 'What do you guys reckon?'

'Actually,' said Andy coolly, 'Lisa and I have got a few things to do. How about we meet you guys back here later this afternoon, around three? The coach to the airport isn't coming until about nine so we'll still have time to do some stuff later.'

'Okay,' I replied. 'We'll see you in a few hours then.'

Andy and Lisa turned left out of the hotel and headed in the direction of the strip.

'What do you think that was all about?' asked Tom.

'I don't know,' I replied. 'Maybe they just need some more time on their own to sort stuff out.'

'So what are we going to do until three?'

I looked at Tom and smiled. 'Still hungry?'

'Ravenous.'

'How does a "Killer" English breakfast followed by a litre of lager chaser sound?'

'Perfect. Stars and Bars?'

'Of course.' We descended the steps to the street. 'And after that . . . well who knows? We're still on holiday so we might as well make the most of it.'

A great plan

At three-thirty in the afternoon, Tom and I were sitting in the hotel lounge drinking beer and watching the sports channel on the big screen TV. Since our final breakfast at Stars and Bars all we had done was wander around Malia hunting for souvenirs that might be appropriate for Tom's kids. It was a harder task than we'd assumed as most shops seemed to specialise in little more than glow-in-the-dark-condoms, T-shirts with slogans even students would be embarrassed to wear and statuettes of Priapus, the ridiculously over-endowed Greek god and symbol of fertility. In the end we managed to find a One-Euro shop and bought two packs of felt-tip pens and two T-shirts emblazoned with a map of Crete.

'Do you want another beer?' said Tom looking at his watch. 'Or should we hang on until they arrive?'

'We might as well have another,' I replied. 'Who knows how long they'll—'I stopped mid-sentence as I spotted Andy and Lisa entering the lobby.

'I'm really sorry, guys,' said Lisa. 'We sort of lost track of time.'

'No worries.' I could tell straight away that there was something different about Andy even without him speaking. His black mood from this morning seemed to have completely disappeared. He almost looked as though he was happy. As though he had made some sort of life-changing decision.

'What have you guys been up to?' asked Tom.

'It's a long story,' said Andy, 'which we'll explain later.' He paused and looked at me. 'Look, Charlie, I think we should both put everything that's happened in the past now. Agreed?' He held out his hand for me to shake.

'Agreed,' I replied shaking his hand even though I knew this charade was for Lisa's sake, not mine.

'And the same goes for you, Tom,' continued Andy, offering his hand to Tom. 'I know I've been a bit of an arsehole in the past and I'm sorry.'

Tom looked at me perplexed. 'Yeah, okay,' said Tom shaking Andy's hand warily. 'Who are you again?'

'He's still the Andy we know and love,' said Lisa rolling her eyes, 'believe me.'

'And now that you've finished dissecting my personality,' said Andy, 'do any of you mind if we actually get on with the rest of the day?'

'What have you got in mind?' asked Tom cautiously.

'Nothing that you need worry about,' replied Andy. 'It's just that Lisa has come up with a great way to kill the afternoon: we all choose one thing we really want to do and then we do it.'

'Sounds like a great idea,' said Tom. 'Where's the catch?'

'There is no catch,' replied Andy. 'And just to show that there isn't, I think you should go first.'

'You mean I get to choose somewhere to go and we'll all go without any arguments or moaning?'

Andy nodded. 'Anywhere at all.'

Tom thought for a moment. 'Well, there is somewhere I actually do want to go but I guarantee you'll hate it.'

'We'll enjoy it, okay, Tom?' grinned Andy. 'But whatever it is just spit it out because time's running out.'

'Okay,' said Tom, 'I want to go and see a tree.'

'A tree?' said Andy, incredulously.

'Yeah, a tree,' replied Tom. 'It's two thousand years old. Apparently its circumference is so wide that it would take sixteen adults linking hands to span it. I'd really like to see it. Charlie's still got his hire car until tonight. And it shouldn't take longer than a hour to get there.'

'Well, if Tom wants to see a two-thousand-year-old tree,' said Andy, shaking his head in mock despair, 'let's take him to see a two-thousand-year-old tree.'

It's not an olive tree

It took just under an hour for us to reach the village of Krassi. We pulled up in a dusty car park on the outskirts that was all but empty apart from us and one other car.

'Are you sure you've got the right place?' asked Andy leaning out of the rear passenger window. 'Or could it be that there's not exactly a huge demand amongst tourists to see some knackered old olive tree?'

'It's not an olive tree,' said Tom.

'So what kind of tree is it?'

'How am I supposed to know?'

'It could be an arse tree for all I care,' replied Andy. 'How interesting can any kind of tree be?'

'Give it a rest, Andy,' said Lisa calmly. 'Think about it, how often do you get to see something that's as old as this tree's supposed to be and still be alive?'

'Nice try,' said Andy. 'But I guarantee you that this tree is just going to be a tree, no matter how old it is.'

We climbed out of the car into the searing sun and began making our way up the steep hill to the village. On the way up we were all on constant tree alert but other than the occasional gnarled-looking oak we didn't see anything at all that fitted our expectations. As we reached the top of the hill with no sign of it, however, we began to wonder if we had somehow missed it.

'Do you think it was the pine tree by that house on the hill?' asked Tom. 'That was pretty tall, after all?'

'It can't have been,' I replied. 'Surely a two-thousand-year-old tree is going to be more substantial than that?'

'Well, how about that chestnut tree by that gate?' suggested Tom.

'That can't have been it either,' said Andy. 'Two of us linking arms could've spanned that easily.'

'I give up then,' said Tom. 'I have no idea where this thing is.'

'Maybe we should ask someone,' suggested Lisa.

Andy, Tom and I looked at her blankly. It was clear that none of us wanted to do anything as potentially embarrassing as asking people for directions to a two-thousand-year-old tree.

'Okay,' said Lisa pointing across the road at a shady terrace the size of a small football pitch. It was surrounded by a line of trees (none of which looked to be over thirty years old let alone two thousand) and had tables and chairs set out as if it were some sort of outdoor café. 'Why don't we go over there, get a drink and cool down a bit and work out what to do next?'

Following Lisa's lead we all crossed the road and made our way to a table at the edge of the terrace. A waitress came over to us and handed out menus and we were in the process of deciding what to order when Andy froze and pointed across the way. And there it was, right in front of us: a two-thousand-year-old tree looking exactly like you'd expect a two-thousand-year-old tree to look – tall, stately, ancient and wise.

'If you'd told me this morning that I'd be impressed by

a tree I'd have called you a nutter,' said Andy quietly. 'But I have to admit, Tom, you were right, mate, because that . . . really is one amazing fucking tree.'

The small thumb

'So come on then,' said Andy on our return to the hire car. 'It's your choice next, Charlie, what's it going to be?'

'How come it's me next?'

'Well, we could do mine if you like,' conceded Andy. 'But I think it'd be more fitting if we did it last.'

'It isn't dangerous is it?' asked Tom.

'I wouldn't say it was dangerous,' said Andy, revelling in the mystery. 'At least not if it's done properly. But there'll be no backing out of it okay? I've seen your tree, we'll do Charlie's thing next and finish up with mine.' Andy turned to me. 'So come on then, hurry up.'

'What I really want to do,' I said having now rejected over a dozen different ideas in my head, 'is sit on a beach where there aren't massive speakers blasting out music, people trying to flog you loyalty cards to use sun-loungers, hot girls in bikinis or cool boys with six-packs. That's what I want. Just us and a beach and as much peace and quiet as we can manage.'

Unsurprisingly the criteria for my beach excursion proved difficult to fulfil given that all the decent beaches were next to densely populated resorts and therefore packed with people. Any stretch of water that had sand next to it seemed to be either too grim for words (broken bottles in the sand, plastic bottles washing up on the surf, chockful of sinister-looking seaweed) or right next to some smoke-belching industrial plant. Just as we were about to give up and return to Malia, Tom spotted a sign for a stretch of beach that wasn't visible from the road and suggested that we give it a try.

In front of us was a small lagoon that was empty apart from a mum and dad watching their young son skimming stones across the surface of the still water. There was no sand, only large, perfectly smooth pebbles.

'Is this good enough for you, Charlie?' asked Lisa as she slipped off her sandals.

'I think this is what I've been looking for all holiday,' I replied. 'A bit of peace and quiet and a nice view.'

Andy laughed. 'Are you sure you're actually a bloke, Charlie? Because you do a brilliant impression of a girl sometimes.'

'Don't listen to him,' said Lisa, 'this place is fantastic.'

I turned to Tom. 'What do you think, mate?'

'I think we need to get our shoes off and get in that water,' said Tom.

Barefooted, all four of us walked down to the water's edge and then in unison waded into the cool shallows right up to our knees.

'You don't get pebbles like these on Brighton beach,' said Lisa dipping her hand into the water and picking up a large smooth grey stone with a long white swirl in it. 'This one looks like a bar of soap,' she said, offering to me. As I took it, my fingers grazed her warm skin, sending a shiver down my spine. 'You keep it,' said Lisa. 'It'll be something to remember the holiday by.'

'Have you got your camera on you?' called Andy as he skimmed a handful of stones across the water. 'We should take a picture.'

I pulled out the camera from my bag and handed it to Andy who walked over to the small boy and asked him to take a picture of us all.

Knee deep in the water we lined up in a row with our arms around each other – Tom, me, Lisa, Andy – and then in his best English the boy yelled: 'Cheese' and took the picture. He handed the camera back to Andy before running off to rejoin his parents and we all grouped around to get a better look at the camera's display. Though it might not have been the most brilliantly composed picture of all time – a small thumb was clearly visible in the corner of the picture – it still managed to capture the essence of what we were about: four people who were connected with one another more closely than any of us might like to admit.

Dragons aren't really me

It was just after six o'clock by the time we made our way back to Malia. And even as we parked the car a few doors down from Stars and Bars, Andy still wasn't giving much away about our final task.

'So where is it we're going next?' asked Lisa, yawning.

'I'm afraid there's no "we" in this next bit,' replied Andy. 'This one's strictly for the boys.'

'It's not a strip club is it?' asked Tom.

'Of course it isn't,' said Andy rolling his eyes. 'It's better than that.'

'So what then?'

'It's over there,' said Andy, pointing to the Angel tattoo parlour across the road. 'And it's the perfect way to commemorate this holiday.'

I'd never given much thought to the idea of paying to have my skin permanently scarred in order to make some sort of indelible fashion statement, but if I had I would've definitely have been one of those people who rejected it on the grounds that: 'It might look great now but what about when you're eighty-five, and about to take residency in a nursing home?'

This was the argument that I attempted to present to Andy and Tom as we crossed the road to check out various pictures of the proprietor's (a Mr Rodney Cross, originally from Dulwich, East London) handiwork. There were full colour 6"x4" pictures of arms, legs, calves, backs, faces and full bodies covered with everything from animals and Celtic symbols right through to sportswear logos and film stars.

'Look, Charlie,' said Andy, 'if you do end up in a nursing home with a tattoo on your arm it'll be a fantastic reminder as you freefall into dementia that once upon a time you actually had a life worth living.'

Tom laughed. 'I'm with Andy on this one. If you make it to eighty-five and all you've got to worry about is a tattoo you had done over fifty years ago then as far as I'm concerned, you're doing pretty well.'

'So that's two against one,' said Andy. 'Are you in or out?'

'I'm in,' I replied. 'One hundred per cent.'

'For the record,' said Lisa, 'can I just say that I think this is one of the stupidest overly bloke ideas the three of you have ever had?'

'Your objection is duly noted, babe,' replied Andy. 'But what you don't understand is that sometimes a man's gotta do what a man's gotta do. And right now what these men have to do is choose a cool tattoo design.'

Agreeing that Mr Cross's work was of a sufficiently high standard to let him loose on our skin, we made our way into the shop and told the woman standing by the till our requirements: three reasonably straightforward tattoos, no colour, done as soon as possible. In return she took our money, booked our time slots and handed us several large portfolios of designs to look at.

'I've found my design,' said Andy after five minutes of flicking backwards and forwards.

'Me too,' said Tom.

They both looked at me.

'I haven't seen anything so far that says, "Please be on my skin forever," I replied. 'I could be here a while.'

'Not that I'm endorsing what you're all doing in any way at all,' said Lisa, taking the portfolio in Andy's hand away from him and flicking back a couple of pages, 'but I have to admit I quite liked that one.' She pointed to a design in black ink of a Celtic-looking sun. 'It's quite subtle and wouldn't look too hideous.'

I wasn't convinced.

'How about this one then?' said Andy turning the page to a small circular Chinese-looking design of a dragon chasing its own tail. 'I was seriously considering having it for myself before I found the one I really wanted.'

'Cheers,' I replied, 'but I don't think dragons are really me either.'

I looked at Tom. 'Come on, mate, you must have some sort of suggestion too?'

Tom shook his head. 'I think you already know what you want but you're just too scared about making the decision.'

I couldn't help but laugh. Tom was spot on. 'Okay, you're right,' I replied. 'I was just playing for time but my mind's made up now. So let's go and get ourselves a tattoo.'

When I emerged from the back of the tattoo parlour three quarters of an hour after Andy and Tom had had theirs done, all Andy would say was that his tattoo was in the middle of his shoulder blades while Tom told me that his was on his right shoulder. Given that we were all being so secretive, I suggested that we have a grand unveiling in a few weeks' time as a sort of post-holiday reunion. Tom thought that was a great idea but Andy just laughed and said that he would have to see.

As good a place as any

'What time is it?' asked Andy as we emerged from the tattoo parlour. The early evening sun had long since disappeared and we were now standing right in the middle of the constant bustle of night-time Malia.

'Dinner time,' said Tom looking at his watch. 'I'm starving and we've only got half an hour before the coach arrives to pick us up.'

'What kind of food do you want?' asked Andy.

'The fastest food possible.'

As we headed back to the Apollo feasting on takeaway McDonalds we were laughing and joking so much that the events of the morning seemed as though they had happened a million years ago, to someone else entirely. Were Andy and I back to being friends? It was hard to tell. The damage we'd inflicted on each other was hardly going to heal overnight. The important thing to me, though, wasn't that we were back to normal. Rather that it seemed that we were both willing to make the effort to fake our friendship until such counterfeit feelings were no longer necessary.

Liberating our suitcases from the Apollo's secure room we sat on the steps outside to wait for the coach. Within five minutes the Club Fun tour coach finally reared into view and it pulled up directly in front of us.

'We should have said goodbye to Steve-the-barman,' I said as the coach driver opened up the vehicle's storage bay and began loading up a small mountain of luggage.

'No worries,' replied Andy, 'I'll do it for you later.'

'How are you going to do that? You'll be—' I stopped and looked at Andy's face and suddenly realised what he meant. 'You're not coming back home are you?'

'No,' said Andy, 'we're not.'

Lisa's face confirmed that Andy wasn't joking. Andy reached across and gently traced a small line along Lisa's right hand. It was a small gesture. A gesture of love, I suppose. But even though I tried to fight it the gesture broke my heart.

'What are you saying?' asked Tom. 'That you're extending your holiday?'

'We're thinking something more permanent,' said Andy.

I don't know why I was surprised. If I'd learned anything from this holiday it was this: given the right degree of provocation, anyone could lose the plot. All it took was a partner leaving, a doctor diagnosing cancer, or the betrayal of a close friend and it appeared the rule book for normal behaviour could be abandoned completely.

'I know it's a lot to take in,' began Lisa. 'We can hardly believe it ourselves but we've talked about nothing else and it's what we want.'

'To stay here?' I asked.

'It's as good a place as any,' replied Andy.

There was a long silence. I could feel the time slipping away.

'I know it's none of my business but are you really sure?'

'There are just too many distractions at home,' explained

Lisa. 'Too many ways to get lost. That's what went wrong with me and Andy: we both ended up being too focused on things that didn't matter. We need to take this time out together if we're ever going to make things work between us again.'

'We're thinking a year to begin with,' added Andy. 'And if we're still happy . . . maybe we'll even make it permanent.'

'What about your jobs?' I asked.

'We'll sort something out,' said Lisa.

'And your house?'

'We were sort of hoping you'd keep an eye on it for us,' said Lisa. 'We've rented somewhere here for a few months – that's what we were up to this afternoon – it's not much but I can't see us needing to do much in there apart from sleep. And as for work . . . look where we are . . . there must be hundreds of bars and restaurant jobs going. And if there aren't, well, we'll just have to sort something else out.'

The more I tried to reason the whole situation out in my head, the more I came to realise that every hole I tried to find in their plan seemed to point out my own inadequacies rather than theirs. The truth was I was jealous of their spontaneity. I was envious of the fact that they had succeeded where I'd failed. For both Andy and Lisa, whether they stayed together forever or split up after a week, this would always be the holiday that changed their lives. The Andy standing in front of me right now was different from the one who had left England over a week ago. And that's what bothered me. He had changed and I was still the same. I'd be going back to the same flat, job and life that I had left behind seven days ago.

'Are these going to the airport?' asked the coach driver pointing to our luggage.

'Yeah,' I replied. 'Just these two please.'

'Are you sure?' he asked eyeing Andy and Lisa's luggage. I looked at Andy and then Lisa waiting for their confirmation.

'Yeah,' replied Lisa. 'We're sure.'

The driver shrugged, loaded up the last remaining suitcases on to the coach and closed the hatch. There was no going back now.

'So this is it,' said Andy thoughtfully.

'I'll say my goodbyes first,' said Lisa. She put her arms around Tom and squeezed him tightly, burying her face into his chest. 'I hope everything goes well tomorrow. I'll be thinking of you.'

Initially confused, Tom looked at me and the guilt must have been written on my face. 'I told Andy earlier in the week,' I apologised.

'That's okay,' said Tom. 'I'm glad in a way. It'll be nice knowing I've got friends rooting for me.'

'Well, count me among them,' said Andy shaking Tom's hand firmly.

'Look after yourself, Charlie,' said Lisa embracing me.

'You too,' I replied. 'I really do hope everything goes well for you guys.'

'It will,' she replied. 'I'm sure of it.'

'Look after yourself, mate,' said Andy stepping towards me.

'I will do,' I replied. 'And if you need anything at all while you're out here, just let me know and I'll sort it out for you.'

'Cheers.' Andy paused as if he wanted to say something

else but then at the last minute his face changed and he shook my hand. 'Don't go thinking things will change,' he said. 'Because they won't. From now on you're dead to me. Absolutely dead!'

I'm sure you really are a nice guy

At the sound of the electronic ding the seat-belt light over my head switched off, thereby setting off a commotion of seat-belt unclicking. Even though it had been half an hour since the plane had taken off, my mind was still very much on the ground, wondering from minute to minute what Andy and Lisa were up to and when might be the next time I would see them. Releasing my seat-belt I stretched my arms in the air, yawned and turned behind to see if I could see what Tom was up to. Due to a computer error, we'd been allocated seats in different parts of the plane and Tom was now sandwiched between a dour-looking youth wearing multiple gold chains and a smiling middle-aged woman with painted-on eyebrows and a deep orange tan. Looking at Tom's companions, I realised I'd fared much better: a pretty but hassled-looking mother, with a sleeping baby on her lap and a napping toddler on the seat next to her.

As people began passing by on the way to the toilet I reached under the seat in front of me and pulled out *The Da Vinci Code*. With all that had been happening over the past few days I'd somehow managed to neglect the book so much that I suspected I'd have little chance of getting back into it. So I pulled out the third and final choice for my holiday reading: *White Teeth* by Zadie Smith – a book

I'd selected less because I was desperate to read 'an epic comic tale telling the story of immigrants in England' and more because the bespectacled authoress on the cover looked quite foxy. I only managed to get as far as the end of the first paragraph before I had to stop as I'd become aware that somebody was lurking by my side. I looked up to see a man roughly my own age, with a few days' worth of stubble and a slightly drawn complexion, staring down at me.

'Sorry to trouble you,' he began, 'but I was wondering if you wouldn't mind swapping seats with me? It's just that my wife and kids are here.' We both looked across at his wife and she gave me the same wearily apologetic smile that her husband had just given me. I smiled back, somewhat surprised to find myself feeling envious of the guy who had just spoken. He was where I was supposed to be at thirty-five. But where was my hassled wife? Where were my sleepy children? Where was my family holiday? 'We were all supposed to be sitting together, you see,' the husband continued, 'but they made a cock-up at the check-in desk and said that we should wait until take-off to see about swapping seats.'

Envious or not, I wished them happiness. 'Of course you can have my seat,' I replied as I bundled my things together. 'Just show me where you were sitting.'

Cringing from the huge amount of appreciation that the couple lavished on me, I followed the husband back to his original seat – a middle seat – some five rows in front of my own. As we approached, an austere-looking woman, who had obviously spent too much time in the Cretan sun, stood up making little effort to hide her annoyance at being disturbed for a second time. Apologising again the man quickly grabbed his things, thanked me and made his exit, leaving me to squeeze into my middle seat and re-organise my things.

'Sorry about this,' I apologised as I knocked the girl in the window seat next to me several times with my elbow. 'They don't actually give you very much room to do anything in these seats beyond breathing.'

'That's a good thing you've done,' said the girl. 'He'd been fretting about moving seats ever since—' She stopped abruptly and a horrified look spread across her face. And though it took a few seconds, I suddenly realised the reason.

'You're not wearing your cowboy hat,' I said, unable to believe my luck. It was the girl-with-the-cowboy-hat or rather the girl-formerly-known-as-the-girl-with-the-cowboy-hat.

'Oh, it's you,' she began. 'I really am sorry for what happened.'

'There's no need to apologise,' I replied. 'It's fine.'

'It wasn't really me,' she continued. 'You see I was being egged on by my friends.'

'Honestly,' I replied. 'It's all fine.'

'Look, I'm really sorry if I embarrassed you.'

'I wasn't embarrassed,' I replied grinning. 'I was flattered.'

'But you didn't turn up at the bar, did you?' I shrugged and she buried her face in her hands. 'Oh, you did, didn't you? You must think I'm a terrible person. I'm so sorry. I did sort of think about going but I lost my nerve. I feel awful now.'

'And so you should. I waited all night for you to turn up.'

'You didn't, did you?'

'No,' I replied. 'As it happens that whole night went a bit weird so I probably wouldn't have been much fun anyway . . . *even if you had turned up*.'

There was a long silence. Fully aware that in terms of conversation etiquette a choice was being presented to us – to continue chatting or not – the girl-with-the-cowboy-hat chose to stare pointedly out of the window into the darkness. Accepting that our conversation was now officially over, I pulled out my book again and began reading. She did the same with her book. Just as it seemed that we would both spend the entire flight not talking I became convinced that I was looking a proverbial gift horse in the mouth. Here I was, sitting next to an attractive girl who had selected me to ask out on a date following a dare. Conversational openers didn't really get much better than that.

'Just in case you've forgotten,' I said, closing my book, 'I'm Charlie.'

She turned and looked at me, embarrassed. 'Look, Charlie,' she began hesitantly, 'I don't want this to come out the wrong way . . . and I'm sure you really are a nice guy but I think I ought to tell you I met someone . . . in Malia . . . and we're sort of together.'

'Oh,' I replied. 'Well, that's good to hear.'

There was another long silence. The girl-in-the-cowboy-hat smiled at me uncomfortably. It was difficult to know which of us was more desperate to get away from the other.

'I'll be getting back to my book then,' I said, after a few moments.

The girl-in-the-cowboy-hat half nodded, dug into her bag and plugged a set of headphones into her ears.

I folded back the cover of my book and read page one all over again.

We landed at Gatwick ten minutes early because of something to do with wind speeds and early time slots. As we taxied along the runway, I tucked my book into my bag. I would never finish *White Teeth*. Not because it was a bad book, but rather because judging from the little I'd read I'd come to realise that, along with being quite foxy, the author was also incredibly talented and most definitely out of my league. This news depressed me: once again, by virtue of just being me, I was ruling out yet another one of the several billion women alive on planet Earth.

As the cabin crew switched off the seat-belt sign there was once again a frenzy of activity among the passengers. The austere-looking woman next to me was out of her seat and rummaging in the overhead locker in an instant but the girl-in-the-cowboy-hat, I suspect keen to give me a head start off the plane, remained in her seat looking out of the window.

Along with everyone else, I shuffled into the narrow central aisle of the plane towards the exit. Welcome home. There was a chill in the air and floodlights were glistening in a dozen puddles dotted across the wet tarmac.

Waiting for me at the bottom of the steps was a tired and drawn-looking Tom. I looked at my watch. 2.38 a.m. There was now roughly six hours until he would be making the call that could change his life forever.

'How was it for you?' I asked as we boarded the bus that would take us to arrivals.

'I slept for most of it. How about you?'

'It was . . . interesting.' My eyes flitted across the tarmac to the girl-in-the-cowboy-hat who was waiting for her friends.

'Is that who I think it is?' asked Tom.

'Yeah,' I replied. 'But don't get your hopes up.'

'Why not?'

'Because I did and I ended up severely disappointed.'

Tom laughed. 'If it wasn't to be then she probably wasn't right for you.'

'Maybe not,' I replied, 'but if she isn't, who is?'

I could tell from the look on his face that Tom wasn't interested in discussing his feelings about making the call. So instead we walked in easy silence until we were through passport control and out the other side.

We both turned on our mobile phones. 'Any messages?'

'Looks like it,' replied Tom as he dialled his voicemail. Positioning himself out of the way of fellow passengers, Tom's face lit up as he listened to voicemail messages that were obviously from his family.

Tom grinned. 'One from Anne, two from the kids . . . and one from Andy.'

'What did he say?'

'Even though he doesn't believe in God, on the off-chance there is one, he said he'll say a little prayer on my behalf.'

'That doesn't sound like him.'

'No,' replied Tom. 'That doesn't sound like Andy at all.'

We made our way through to the luggage carousels and waited patiently for our bags to arrive. Once again I spotted the girl-in-the-cowboy-hat pushing a trolley with her equally attractive friends but on seeing me she steered them to the opposite end of the carousel.

It took over half an hour for our luggage finally to emerge, by which time most of the passengers (including the girl-in-the-cowboy-hat) had claimed their bags and disappeared through customs. I could feel all the good work that my seven days of relaxation had achieved slowly beginning to unravel. And as we finally pushed our luggage through the brightly lit 'Nothing to Declare' channel at customs, I was gloomily convinced that by the time we reached the long-stay car park, I would be back to my usual hassled and severely stressed state of mind.

Stepping through the large doors from customs into the arrivals lounge, Tom and I were forced to walk the gauntlet of waiting husbands, wives, boyfriends, girlfriends, parents and minicab drivers all scanning constantly for a glimpse of the people who mattered to them most. We had no one waiting for us. Or so I thought. But right at the end of the crowd queuing behind the security barrier was Donna.

It was odd seeing her in the flesh, here. As I walked towards her, I was forced to readjust the picture of her in my head that had grown somewhat blurred these past few days. She was prettier than I remembered, and her hair was different. And while I was still wearing shorts and a T-shirt appropriate to summer in Crete she was wearing jeans and a coat more appropriate to autumn in England. The oddest thing of all was that she was wearing glasses.

'You hate them, don't you?' said Donna, as I came to a halt in front of her.

'What?' I replied.

'My glasses,' said Donna. 'All day I've been agonising over whether to wear them or my contacts. Nina said contacts because she's pretty vain, so that immediately made me want to go for my glasses.'

I didn't know how to respond to her glasses, the knowledge that she had been preparing all day to meet me from the plane or the fact that she was here at all.

'What are you're doing here?' I said, eventually.

Donna opened her mouth to reply but paused and looked expectantly over my shoulder where a clearly embarrassed Tom was lingering with our luggage trolley.

'I just wanted to say that I'm going to get a coffee,' said Tom.

'Cheers, mate,' I replied. 'I'll see you in a bit.'

As Tom headed off in search of a café, Donna and I stood watching the people around us: an elderly man pushing a trolley piled high with suitcases; a young couple kissing next to a newsagent's; and a group of young lads taking photos of each other with their mobile phones.

'I'm sorry about leaving like that,' said Donna quietly. 'There was no excuse for it. I should have been more honest with you.'

'So why did you do it?'

'Do you want the truth? Because you seemed more sure of me than I was.'

'So it was my fault?'

Donna shook her head. 'I got scared, Charlie. Really scared. I was beginning to feel things for you that I haven't felt for anyone in a long while. I just wasn't sure that I was ready for anything this big this soon. Sadie's dad and I were together a long time. And we had a child together. And even though everyone thinks I should be moving on and looking for something new I couldn't do it. I felt like I was stuck in the past and I just couldn't find a way of moving forward.'

'So what changed your mind?'

'You did,' said Donna, looking into my eyes. 'You changed my mind. I don't know how you did it but you did. You've been in my head every second since I left you. I've replayed the time we spent together a million times and that's when I realised that the feelings I have for you weren't going to go away just because you weren't there. So last night I called my sister to get Andy's number and called him to find out what time you guys were landing at Gatwick. And now here I am. That is, if I'm not too late?'

It was a good question. Was she too late? Did what had happened between Lisa and me make a difference? Had my feelings for Donna just been a holiday thing? All I had was questions and not enough answers that I could be sure of.

'You met someone else, didn't you?' whispered Donna, observing my indecision.

'It's complicated,' I replied. 'But yes, I was with someone else after you left. It was a real mess and it's over now.'

'So why do I feel like there's something you're not saying?'

'Because there is . . . being here with you . . . having you here right now . . . hearing you say these things. It's like having my dreams come true in an instant. But the thing is, Donna, we're not on holiday any more. We're back in reality. And when I left seven days ago the one thing I wanted most of all was to come back different . . . to come back changed. And I've done it. I'm not the person who went on holiday any more.'

'I don't understand,' said Donna. 'So what's the problem?'

'The problem's this.' I let go of her hands and pulled

off the top I was wearing. I rolled up the right sleeve of my T-shirt to reveal the cottonwool dressing fixed over my tattoo. I pulled it away gently and showed Donna what was underneath.

'It's a question mark,' said Donna. 'I still don't understand.'

'I'm not sure I do either.' I shrugged. 'I've never tried to reduce myself down to a symbol before . . .' I paused and peered down at the black ink of my bold 18pt Helvetica question mark '. . . and looking at this I don't think I'll ever do it again.' I taped the dressing back in place, rolled down the sleeve of my T-shirt, then looked at Donna. 'The thing I need you to understand is that once upon a time I used to think I was an okay boyfriend . . . but then Sarah left and I realised I was wrong about that. I used to think I was a pretty good friend, too, but things have happened this holiday that have made me rethink that too. The truth is: I actually have no idea who I really am any more. Not in a real sense. I can't guarantee that the guy you met on holiday really is me and not just some faker. I can't guarantee that you won't wake up one day and hate my guts. And what hurts most is that I can't even guarantee that I won't do something that might hurt you one day. I can't offer you any guarantee of any kind at all, Donna. So why would you want to get involved with someone like that?'

'Because I don't need your guarantees,' she replied. 'I've got my own.' She paused. 'I know I don't know you that well. And maybe you're right about what you're saying. But what I do know is this: you're the first person I've met in a long time who has made me feel like wanting to trust again.'

There was a long silence.

'So where does this leave us?' I asked.

'It's up to you,' she said.

So there it was, right in front of me. A big decision that, as Donna had pointed out, was indeed 'up to me'. And I wanted to do the right thing . . . whatever that might be.

'This is all wrong,' said Donna, interpreting my reticence as the awkward silence before the delivery of bad news. 'I feel like I'm crowding you into making a decision, which isn't what I want to do at all.' She sighed. 'I should go.'

'Maybe you should,' I replied with a smile.

Donna looked confused.

'You drive, don't you?' I asked.

She nodded.

'And you know Brighton pretty well too?'

She nodded again.

'Good.' I rummaged in my pockets and pulled out the keys to my car and my flat. 'Well, I don't know what your plans are for tonight but I'd really like it if you'd take my car back to Brighton and stay at mine.'

'While you do what exactly?'

'I've got something I need to sort out. I'll tell you everything when I get back in the morning. But for now you'll just have to trust me.'

Donna smiled softly and looked at the keys in her hand. 'Just like you're trusting me?'

'Exactly,' I replied. 'Sometimes you've just got to have a little bit of faith.'

I gave Donna the details of where the car was parked and how to get to my flat and told her to ring me if she needed anything at all. With that done we made our way outside and joined the queue for the shuttle-bus to the car park.

It was raining and cold and I realised why Donna was dressed so warmly. Though it was technically August, the weather was more late September. I began to shiver as the cold quickly made its way through my thin summer clothing. Donna put her arms around me. As she pressed her body against mine she looked up and we kissed. While part of me was sure this was a bad idea, given we still had so much to sort out, most of me was simply happy to be caught up in the moment.

As we parted from the kiss Donna bit her lip guiltily and without saying another word, jumped on to the shuttle-bus. As she settled into a seat at the rear of the bus, I was conscious of being scrutinised by her fellow passengers as though I was part of some new form of reality television. I didn't care though. Standing my ground, I shivered patiently until the bus finally pulled away and then, taking in a long, deep breath of cool night air, I made my way back inside the terminal to find Tom.

Five hours and forty minutes and counting

'How did that go?' asked Tom when I found him sitting at an empty table in the only café still open.

'Okay, I think. I hope you don't mind, but I've sent her off to mine in the car. I thought we could wait here to make the call if that's okay?'

'Here's as good a place as any.'

'We could always get a hotel or something,' I added. 'There must be loads around here.'

'Here's fine,' said Tom. 'I doubt I'll sleep much anyhow.'

'So we'll just sit here until morning?'

'Probably not here, exactly,' replied Tom. 'The guy at the counter said he's shutting up shop pretty soon.' I looked at my watch. It was twenty minutes past three. 'Five hours, forty minutes and counting,' said Tom meeting my gaze. 'Doesn't seem all that long since I woke up this morning,' he paused and laughed. 'I guess time really does fly fast when you're having fun.'

I told Tom everything that had happened with Donna. When the café finally shut we ended up moving from the arrivals concourse to departures and eventually set up camp on a bench overlooking rows of closed check-in desks. Other than the occasional cleaner pushing large industrial floor sweepers back and forth no one took much notice of us and so we were free to sit and talk uninterrupted for the rest of the night. We talked about our university days, reminding each other of several embarrassing occasions best forgotten, we talked about what we both wanted from life and how we might get it, and then finally as night turned into early morning, we talked about Tom's beliefs and my own. It was an interesting and at times heated discussion and Tom made a number of points to which I genuinely could find no retort. I can't say that he changed the way I thought about religion, because he didn't; what he did was change the way I thought about him. Regardless of my opinions, Tom's faith worked for him in a way that I truly envied. And that's not to say that he didn't seem scared about how the call to the doctor's might go, it was more that I could see in his eyes that – even if the news was bad – the things he believed in would somehow give him comfort.

The café reopened at 6.00 a.m. and we were its first customers of the day. But as the hours passed things gradually became busier until sometime around 8.00 a.m. the café reached critical mass – every table occupied, huge queues at the tills, and the café staff beginning to look hassled.

With only twenty minutes left before Tom made his call, he decided to phone Anne and the kids.

I wondered whether I too should use this opportunity to make a call. The events of the early hours seemed so far away that I almost feared they were an elaborate dream. Though I was happy imagining Donna asleep in my bed, part of me (possibly all of me) wanted to call her and wake her up just to say good morning. Now that a new day had begun I wanted to make a new form of connection with her. But even though I took out my phone several times I just couldn't bring myself to make the call, for fear that things wouldn't be the way I hoped.

When Tom returned to our table he looked even more tired and drawn, as if he had suddenly driven headlong into a brick wall of mental exhaustion.

'Everything okay?'

Tom shook his head and for the first time I thought he was going to break down. 'I just can't believe that any of this is really happening,' he said. 'I feel fine. I feel healthy. Surely if I had something bad I'd feel sick, wouldn't I? I keep telling myself to expect the worst because at least then I'll be prepared for it. But I can't do it. The worst is just too terrifying to think about.'

We sat and stared at our collection of empty coffee cups.

'How are the kids?' I asked, eventually.

'They're fine,' replied Tom. 'They've been playing their gran up big time this morning, which can only be a good thing. Anne and her mum took them to a butterfly farm yesterday. Apparently Katie now wants to be a butterfly farmer when she grows up and Callum wants to be a caterpillar . . . because they get to spend all day eating.'

'Does he like his food, then, Callum?'

'He can eat for England.'

'I'd love to see them again. I bet they've grown loads since I last saw them.'

'They'd love to see you, too. They're really curious about you. When I told them I was going to Crete with my friend Charlie you took on this strange mystique in their heads. Now they think you live in Crete and for some reason they've got hold of the idea you're very tall.' Tom stopped abruptly. 'Will you do something for me?'

'Yeah, of course,' I replied. 'Whatever you want.'

'If this does turn out to be bad news, will you promise me you'll always keep in touch with my kids?'

'Of course.'

'It's just that they're young. They'll forget.'

'Of course they won't. You're their dad. And anyway Anne will remind them about you all the time.'

'I know. And she will do a great job. But I want them to know *all* about me. I want them to know what their dad was really like. I want them to know that I struggled with life just like they'll have to. I don't want them to grow up thinking I was perfect.' Tom looked at his watch again. 'It's time,' he said quietly.

'Where do you want to do this?'

'Here's fine.'

'Are you sure?'

He nodded, almost glaring at his phone in anger. I found myself holding my breath as he began dialling his doctor's number. Even though the air was ringing with the constant chatter of dozens of different conversations, I could still make out the high-pitched tones of each number pressed on his keypad. I couldn't begin to imagine what he might be going through. At least not on any meaningful level. How would I know how it might feel to have everything that I loved balancing precariously on a knife-edge? I didn't have a wife. I didn't have kids. There was only me.

Entering the final digit into his phone Tom breathed deeply and put the phone up to his ear. His face contorted in rage and he threw the phone down on the floor. 'They're fucking engaged,' he said kicking the empty chair next to him with such force that it toppled over. Everyone in the café turned and stared at him.

'It's all right, mate,' I said grabbing him by the arm in a bid to calm him down. 'Look, I'll make the call and as soon as someone answers, I'll pass them over to you when they answer.'

Tom nodded and calmed down. 'Thanks,' he replied as he rescued his phone from the floor. 'I'm sorry about that.'

'Don't worry about it,' I replied. 'You wait here and I'll keep trying until I get through.'

Making my way out of the café, I headed in the direction of the nearest newsagent's in search of a morning newspaper as a distraction. On the way I tried the number twice and each time got the engaged tone. In a bid to try to calm myself down, I told myself that I wouldn't try again until I'd read the headlines on every single newspaper in the shop. And that's just what I did. It was the usual mix of politics and celebrity scandal, although one newspaper headline was dedicated to the poor weather the nation had been suffering in recent days. Even after seven days away, none of it was a surprise. Just more of the same.

I pulled out the phone again and pressed redial. And my heart began to race when, instead of the engaged tone, I finally got a connection. As I ran back to Tom at full pelt a voice at the other end of the line answered my call.

'Brookdene Road Surgery,' said a female voice brightly.

'Hi,' I replied, as I finally reached the café. 'Could you just hang on a second?'

I barely dared to breathe as Tom took the phone from my hand and told the woman his name, the reason for his call and his date of birth. And I continued to hold my breath as Tom closed his eyes as he waited for the news.

In a split second everything changed. He'd been given the test results. And the news was good. To this day I've never seen an expression more life affirming than the one on Tom's face. What the customers in the café must have thought as I threw my arms around Tom I don't know. And I don't care either. All that mattered was that he was okay.

A brand new start

I felt exhilarated as Tom and I grabbed our suitcases and made our way towards the train station. I was so euphoric that I wanted to stop complete strangers and tell them his good news.

At the station I bought a single ticket back to Brighton, while Tom bought a ticket into London so that he could get his train back to Coventry.

'Thanks for everything, Charlie,' said Tom, as we arrived at his platform just as the service into central London came to a halt and the doors opened. 'I wouldn't have been able to get through any of this without you.'

'You did it all yourself, Tom,' I replied. 'I didn't do a single thing. I'm just glad you're okay.'

'You'll come up and see us though won't you?' He picked up his bags. 'Anne was saying this morning that she would love to see you again.'

'I'll definitely come up. And you should bring them all down to Brighton one weekend too. Brighton beach might not be quite up to the standard of the ones in Crete but it'll do for a half-term break.'

We shook hands and Tom looked at me thoughtfully. 'I hope everything goes well with Donna,' he said. 'You deserve to be happy.'

As Tom boarded the train I remained on the platform,

lost in my own thoughts, long after it had departed. I was thinking about the holiday again, and about Donna, Lisa and Sarah too but most of all I was thinking about Andy. I still couldn't believe what I'd done to him. I still couldn't believe that I'd betrayed him like that. And even though I knew it was likely that I would never see him again I couldn't stand the thought that I'd let him down so badly. As I made my way out of the station to get a taxi I pulled out my phone. *'It'll be mid-morning now in Crete,'* I thought as I looked at my watch and I couldn't help but raise a small smile as I wondered whether Andy would be up yet. I dialled his number and determined to find out. The phone seem to ring forever but eventually someone answered.

'Hello?' said a groggy female voice.

'Lisa, it's me, Charlie.'

'Oh, Charlie . . . I'm sorry, I was fast asleep. Are you back home? How's Tom? Has he had his results yet? Is he okay?'

'He's fine. The results were negative.'

'That's fantastic!' There was a long pause while I heard her relay the news to Andy. I found myself smiling as I heard Andy let out a huge roar as though he'd just scored a goal in a world cup final. 'I'm so pleased, Charlie. I really am. If you speak to Tom tell him we'll ring him soon.'

'I will do.'

There was a short pause.

'I wasn't just calling about Tom's news,' I continued. 'I was sort of hoping to speak to Andy too if that's okay.'

'Of course,' said Lisa. 'I'll put him on.'

As I listened to the static at the other end of the line I began to wonder if this call really would give me the absolution that I felt I so desperately needed. The facts of the matter at hand hadn't changed now that I was back home; the feelings they had generated, though less intense on my side, were bound to be still boiling over inside Andy. And though my self loathing was riding at an all-time high, I still wasn't at all sure I had what it would take to face yet another rejection of my efforts to make things right. *Maybe I'm just making things worse*, I thought. *Maybe we'd all be better off if we just let this go*. I was about to put the phone down when Andy finally came on the line.

'Charlie,' he said evenly. 'It's good to hear the news about Tom.'

'Yeah it is,' I replied.

There was a long pause.

'Is Lisa still there?' I continued.

'No, she's gone for a shower. Why?'

'Because I want . . . I need to talk to you.'

'I know,' said Andy. 'I do too. I was going to call you later in the week. This feels wrong doesn't it? I want to hate you and I feel like I've got good reason to but I just can't quite do it . . . and last night I think I worked out why. The fact is after everything that happened I could've lost Lisa . . . someone who has been with me through all the bad times in my life . . . and if I had I couldn't have blamed anyone but myself. Not you. Me. No one but me. I've treated her badly so many times and always left you to clear up the mess so it's hardly surprising that she turned to you in the end.'

'But it was my choice wasn't it? I didn't have to do anything, did I? I could've stayed away from her.'

'I think you saw how I was treating Lisa and convinced yourself you'd be the one to step in and fix things. She told me everything you said to her. How you wanted her to leave me and be with you.'

'She wouldn't though. She chose you.'

'You could've made your job a lot easier if you'd told her about Nina. But you didn't. So why didn't you?'

'I'd been lying to her about what you were up to. What else could I do?'

'Nice try,' said Andy. 'But I don't believe you for a second. You could've easily talked your way out of looking guilty. You were only covering for me because you had no choice. You didn't tell her about Nina because you hoped I'd come to my senses. She would have understood that because seeing other people's point of view is what Lisa does best. And you're not stupid, Charlie. You knew that.'

'I don't understand. What are you trying to say?'

'I'm trying to say what I know to be true: that even after everything that happened you still couldn't bring yourself to betray me. That night in the bar you didn't tell Lisa what I'd done. You told *me* what *you'd* done. Even though you could have betrayed me you didn't, you betrayed yourself. And that's why I can't hate you, Charlie. I know better than most about letting people down.'

'I know what you're saying,' I replied. 'You're saying I let you down.'

'No,' replied Andy. 'You've got it all wrong. You've always had standards and yet you let yourself get dragged down to mine. That's my problem here. It's not me you've let down, it's yourself. And I know in my heart that it's a lesson learned. You'll never do it again because now you know how it feels. So don't beat yourself up about it. What's done is done. Pick yourself up and do like me: make a brand new start and promise yourself that you'll never go back there again.'

Just us

As the taxi I'd caught from the station pulled up outside my flat and I saw Donna standing on the doorstep, all the doubts that had pushed their way to the front of my mind melted away. As I struggled to pull my suitcase out of the cab, she descended the steps from my door down to the street so quickly that by the time I was free of the taxi her arms were around my neck and we kissed.

'I thought you were never going to come,' she murmured.

'And I thought there was a chance that you might not be here,' I replied.

'I'll always be here if you want me to be,' smiled Donna.

'Well in that case,' I replied, taking her hand, 'I think you should know that the way I'm feeling right now I will always want you to be here.'

'I don't need any guarantees from you, Charlie,' said Donna scrutinising my face.

'Then what do you need?' I asked.

'For us to be able to start again. You and me, right here, right now. No baggage. No worries. Just us.'

I thought about Andy. He was right. New beginnings. A brand new start. And now here was mine.

'Hi, I'm Charlie Mansell,' I said holding out my hand for Donna to shake. 'Pleased to meet you.'

'Hi, Charlie Mansell,' replied Donna shaking my hand,

'I'm Donna Finch and I'm pleased to meet you too.'

'How was that for a new start?' I asked.

'Good,' replied Donna.

'Really?' I replied. 'I think there's room for improvement.' Grinning I leaned across and kissed her firmly on the lips. 'And how was that?' I whispered as our lips parted.

'Better,' replied Donna. 'Much better.'

EPILOGUE

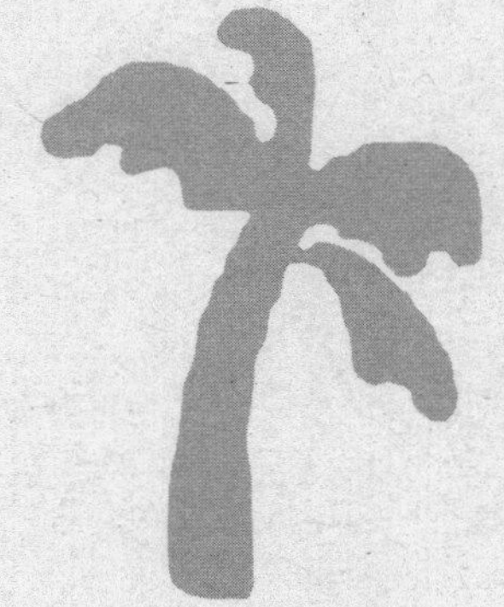

As long as we're together

So that's it really. The story of how, a year ago, a cheap package holiday changed my life. Changed it for the better. And it is better. By a long way. Donna and Sadie (a great kid, by the way, whom I couldn't love any more if she were my own) ended up moving from East London to Brighton after we'd been together six months. I offered to move to London, but Donna reminded me that Sadie had always fancied living by the sea and after a lifetime of land-locked living was ready to try something different. We talked briefly about moving in together, but with Sadie and Donna's ex to consider, we decided that it was a bit too early for all that and she ended up renting a flat three doors down from me. She got a new job too, working in a bookshop in the centre of Brighton because she wanted a break from nursing. She took a cut in pay and has to work every other Saturday but she enjoys it much more than her old job and the people that she works with are fun to be around.

As for me, I carried on working at the council, even though after the holiday I daydreamed about packing the whole thing up and moving permanently to a country where at the very least you were guaranteed decent weather in August. Helped by Donna, I ended up doing quite a bit of work to the flat: all the things I'd been meaning to do but had never got round to. So now every single room has been painted from top to bottom; I've had new kitchen and bathroom suites installed and finally got round to replacing the furniture that Sarah took with her when she moved out. Guests no longer have to sit on dining chairs or the carpet when they come round. I have a proper sofa, and a dining table and loads of other stuff that civilised people have in their homes.

Donna and I bought the sofa one Saturday morning in the early part of the new year. Sadie was spending the weekend with her dad and Donna had come down to Brighton for the weekend. Feeling good that we had finally managed to tick 'Buy Charlie a sofa' off the long list of things 'To Do' we'd decided to go for lunch at a really nice café in the Lanes. Just as we were about to go in, the door opened and a couple pushing one of those trendy prams that looks like a lunar landing vehicle emerged. It was only when Donna and I stepped aside and the couple pushing the pram looked up to thank us for doing so, that I realised that the woman was Sarah.

Though I'd been expecting to have an inevitable 'ex-encounter', as time passed and she faded from memory, I assumed (or should that be hoped?) that Sarah had left Brighton altogether. So when I saw her that day I have to admit it took me by surprise. Donna said that I acquitted myself pretty well but I'm not so sure. Surely the sharp pang of pain I felt must have shown on my face? I don't know what caused it. Whether it was the shock of seeing Sarah, or Oliver, or even their baby, a little girl they'd called Daisy, I don't know. But I know it did hurt. Probably more than it should have done.

Sarah and I talked for a while and did all the introductions required. She appeared happy and healthy and I have to say that they seemed more suited as a couple than we'd ever been. After five minutes or so of polite catch-up chit-chat we parted company. But it was very much a case of, 'Good to see you, have a nice life.'

Donna and I carried on into the café and I was grateful that she didn't make a big thing about it, even though she would have had every right to. In fact, Donna didn't mention it at all until I brought it up one evening about a month later. We were standing in my kitchen talking about nothing in particular when I came out with it. I told her I was sorry for the way I'd reacted and how seeing Sarah had taken me by surprise. Donna seemed to understand what I was trying to say and it sparked a discussion that went on until the early hours. Things from our pasts that we'd never spoken about before emerged and although at times it was upsetting, the end result of this tidal wave of confession was a declaration from Donna that she loved me and one in return from me that my feelings were the same.

As winter turned to spring and even Brighton got a bit warmer, we talked about going on holiday together – the three of us – Donna, Sadie and me. Initial thoughts ranged from a week at a posh hotel in St Lucia right through to a fortnight camping in south Wales. We just couldn't make up our minds. Then, around Easter, Tom and his wife and kids came to stay for a few days and they made us an offer neither Donna nor I could refuse.

'How about we all go on holiday together?' suggested Tom, as we all sat eating chips on the beach overlooking the old Brighton pier. 'Andy and I have been e-mailing each other about it for a while and he says there's a villa in Stalis owned by a friend of his. He thinks he might be able to get it for us all for a week on the cheap. It's got four bedrooms, a swimming pool and is only five minutes from the beach. What do you reckon?'

Things had remained pretty awkward between Andy and me. We hadn't spoken much at all. Neither of us was particularly suited to long telephone calls and I had more to say to him than I could ever limit to an e-mail. And although I'd seen them both at Christmas when they had returned to the UK to see their families and tie up a few loose ends to do with putting their house on the market, the time had flown by so quickly that I felt I'd barely seen them at all.

'You want to go, don't you?' asked Donna.

'Yes, of course,' I replied. 'But I'd understand if you didn't. After all, it's our first holiday together.'

'You're mad,' said Donna smiling. 'Of course I want to go. It doesn't matter where we go as long as we're together.'

So that was that. The plans were made for us all to stay at Andy's friend's villa in August. The night before the flight, Tom and his family stayed at mine and the next day we drove together to Gatwick and boarded a midday flight to Crete. From the moment I spotted Andy and Lisa waiting for us at arrivals it was clear that their new life in Crete agreed with them. With their matching deep bronze tans, and their T-shirts advertising 'Andy's Bar – the number one night-spot in Stalis', they looked every inch the perfect couple.

The whole week was faultless from start to finish. The weather was great every single day; the villa really *was* only five minutes from the beach and we all got on together better than we'd ever done. Andy was no longer quite as cocksure as he used to be; in fact for the whole of the holiday he was almost (but not quite) consistently likeable. Of course we had the odd bit of conflict (Tom and Andy argued over the best way to barbecue fish and Andy and I argued over who would win the premiership next season) but other than that things were fine. The three of us even managed a quick trip to Malia one evening for old times' sake, but we didn't even get out of the car. Instead we sat with the windows wound down, content to watch the teeming hordes of young Brits having the time of their lives.

Building sandcastles on the beach with the kids on the morning of the final day of the holiday, we were all shocked when Andy suddenly shouted out: 'What about the tattoos?'

Since we'd had them done, none of us had remembered to look at each other's tattoos. Eager to get the ball rolling, Andy promptly took off his T-shirt to reveal a Chinese symbol between his shoulder blades. 'It's the Chinese symbol for love,' said Andy. 'But my Chinese is terrible so it could say pretty much anything.'

Tom then rolled up the sleeve of his T-shirt to reveal three names on his bicep, one under the other: Anne. Callum. Katie. Anne laughed. 'You couldn't have just had an anchor or a dragon, like everyone else in the world, could you?'

'Don't you like it?' asked Andy. 'I think it looks great.'

'It's not that,' replied Anne, blushing. 'It's just that in seven months' time he's going to have to add another name to his list.'

'That's great news,' I said, patting Tom on the shoulder as everyone else joined in with the congratulations. When the commotion died down Tom demanded that I reveal my tattoo.

'I'm going to have a bit of a problem with that,' I replied, as I rolled up the sleeve of my T-shirt.

'Where is it?'

'I had it removed.'

'How come?' asked Andy. 'It had better be for a good reason.'

'It was actually,' I replied, looking over at Donna and Sadie and smiling. 'It was for the best reason possible: I just didn't need it any more.'

At this Tom laughed and Andy rolled his eyes in despair and as I walked over to Donna and kissed her on the lips I made a mental note to book us all on another holiday as soon as this one was over.

Acknowledgements

A round of applause to the following: Sue, Phil P, Swati and all at Hodder for their hard work on the book; Simon and all at PFD for making stuff happen; The Fitz for being such a great travelling companion; Euan, Jane, Jackie, Danny, Cath, Chris, Nadine, Vic, Elt, Ruth, Richard, Andy, Phil, Shelia, Alexa, Rod, John and Charlotte (for general mate/advice/family stuff); Arthur, Steve, Kaytee, Gary, Marcus, Ian D, Ian H, Jo, Amanda for being the Sunday Night Pub people; everyone at the Board for being there 24/7; and finally, for actions above and beyond the call of duty: Team Gayle.

The Life and Soul Of the Party

MIKE GAYLE

If you have enjoyed WISH YOU WERE HERE,
here is a taster of Mike Gayle's next novel,
THE LIFE AND SOUL OF THE PARTY,
available in trade paperback in August 2008
from Hodder & Stoughton.

Ed and Sharon's New Year's Eve Party December 2005

Melissa:

It was just after six on New Year's Eve and I was in my bedroom in the flat that I shared with 'creepy' Susie, my flatmate/landlady. I call Susie 'creepy' not out of any particular malice towards her but because that's exactly what she is. Despite being ten years my senior, Susie has a creepily large collection of teddy bears and a creepy boyfriend called Steve, who somehow always manages to be lingering outside the bathroom whenever I emerge from the shower. On top of all that I'm convinced she snoops around my room when I'm out which I'm pretty sure is the definition of creepy.

The only reason I put up with Susie's creepiness is because, as a thirty-four-year-old mature student with no boyfriend and money, I've no choice in the matter whatsoever. And anyway, having lived in enough nightmare houseshares in the fifteen years I've been in Manchester I know that as bad as Susie is, there are a lot of people out there who could be a good deal creepier.

My plan for the night ahead was simple: along with my friends Vicky, Chris, Cooper and Laura, I was heading to Ed and Sharon's house for their annual New Year's Eve party. And even though as a rule I hate New Year's Eve and can't think of many things I'd rather do less than celebrate the arrival of yet another twelve months heralding the arrival of yet more debt, more university assignments and a greater sense of being left behind by my peers, the only thing I hate more than New Year's Eve itself is the thought of spending it alone.

Looking down at the bed in front of me I tried to make my mind up about the various potential outfits I had laid out there for the party. There was a black floaty top and trousers; a green dress I'd bought last summer in the sales teamed with opaque black tights and boots; and a dark blue dress that I was 99 per cent sure I could no longer fit into and green shoes with a bit of a heel. Unable to decide, I tried to imagine myself in the clothes without having to go through the ordeal of actually putting them on. The longer I pored over them, however, the more I realised that actually nothing I had chosen was quite right. All the clothes seemed just a little bit too showy for a house party . . . which might have been okay for Vicky and Laura – who could pull off 'showy' – but would make me seem for all the world as though I was trying too hard.

Returning the rejected clothes to the wardrobe, I spotted a black long-sleeved top that had fallen off its hanger and was lying crumpled across a pair of black pumps that I hadn't worn in years. I was slipped off my dressing gown and tried it on. It just felt right, so I searched around some more and found a green knitted cardigan from Oxfam I'd bought a couple of months earlier; it went perfectly with the top, and, inspired, I made a final trip to the wardrobe and rejected all manner of trousers and skirts and even trouser/skirt combos, before closing the door in defeat. That was when I spotted the jeans that I'd been wearing all day. They were lying on the floor by the door. I straightened them out, slipped them on and checked myself in the mirror. I couldn't believe it. They looked great. The whole outfit was coming together very nicely indeed. Now all I needed was the right footwear. After some moments of deep deliberation I opted for my Converse baseball boots, which I eventually found by the radiator underneath the window swamped by a large mountain of ironing.

My baseball boots were almost as frayed and worn-out looking as my jeans. They were a faded brick red colour and so heavily scuffed and battered that I couldn't wear them in the rain because the seam on the right one had a tear in it. Still, grateful that it wasn't actually raining I slipped them on, tied the laces and surveyed my new outift in the mirror one last time. I looked like a student—which wasn't exactly the look I was going for—but I took some solace in the fact that at least I didn't look like I was trying too hard.

I tied my hair back in a ponytail and then began searching for my make-up bag which I eventually found underneath a stack of magazines by the side of my bed. Rooting around for an eyeliner that hadn't spoiled I finally tipped the whole lot out on to the bed in frustration, just as my mobile phone rang.

'Hey babe, it's me.'

It was Vicky.

'Hey you,' I replied. 'How are things?'

Vicky sighed. 'I've just put William to bed and told him mum's babysitting tonight and he went off on one as though I was leaving him in the care of the big bad wolf. I wouldn't mind but his Gran will spoil him to death like she always does.'

Of all my friends here in Manchester, I'd known Vicky

the longest. We met during the first year that I'd spent studying Business and Economics at UMIST before I was kicked off my course for being completely and utterly hopeless. Vicky and I had both lived in the same halls of residence and I'd been drawn to her because, unlike most of the other eighteen year olds I met during freshers' week, Vicky didn't act like she was trying to cram several years' worth of repressed teenage rebellion into seven days of debauchery. In fact she didn't act like she was eighteen at all. She seemed older and wiser somehow and even though she'd only been in the city for the same amount of time as me, she seemed to know the clubs and bars around Manchester like the back of her hand. So, rather than following the student hordes to grotty pubs and clubs playing the same music you heard everywhere, thanks to Vicky we ended up in clubs in the depths of rough housing estates, warehouse parties in the middle of industrial estates and the kinds of bars you had no chance of finding without being in the know. In short, back then, she had been an education in how to be cool. Fifteen years on, she was a wife, mother to William, my four-year-old godson, and hadn't set foot in a nightclub since the late nineties, but to me, she would always be the girl who knew everything.

'Anyway,' continued Vicky. 'I'm just calling about the plans for tonight. Chris talked it over with Cooper earlier and they've decided we're all meeting at eight in the Old Oak.'

'I thought eight was when the party started?'

'It is, but you know what the boys are like. Apparently it's far too emasculating to arrive at a party at the time actually written on the invitation.'

'That's fine by me.' I paused to consider what tone of

voice to use in order to ask the question on my lips. I decided to go with casual indifference. 'And what about Paul and Hannah? Are they coming?'

'I don't know. Chris left a message on Paul's mobile but he hasn't got back to him yet. I'm sure he'll turn up though. I don't think there's ever been a New Year's Eve that we haven't all spent together. And somehow I can't imagine Hannah is going to change all that.' Vicky paused. 'You are okay about him coming aren't you?'

'Of course I am,' I replied. 'I'll see you later, then, yeah?'

'Yeah, see you later.'

Vicky:

After I put the phone down I couldn't get the picture of Melissa out of my head. She'd be sitting alone in her tiny bedroom, thinking about Paul and Hannah, worrying about where her life was going and why he was now so happy and not her. And much as I loved Paul as a friend, I couldn't help feeling angry with him on Melissa's behalf. It was awful the way things had ended between them. Absolutely awful. And even though five years had passed since they split up, for all the moving forward Melissa had done it might as well have been yesterday.

I was with Melissa when she and Paul first met. We were both twenty-three, living in that post-student nether world where you're no longer in full-time education but you don't exactly feel like a fully paid-up member of the workforce either. Mel and I were living in a houseshare in Longsight and spent most of our time buying clothes and records and above all chasing boys. One night a bunch of us met up for a drink in the Horse and Jockey in Chorlton with the plan of moving on to a club night in Hulme afterwards. However, just after last orders, we heard about a party going on round the corner from the pub and we decided we'd give it a try; if it was any good we'd at least save ourselves money on the cab fare getting over to Hulme.

I'd never seen so many people crammed into such a small space. It was only a two-bedroom terrace, but it felt as though the entire population of the pub had transferred to the party too. I wanted to leave straight away and probably would have done had I not managed to lose Melissa within moments of arriving. I eventually found her half an hour later out in the garden, even though it was freezing cold. She was talking to a couple of guys I'd never seen before and called me over.

'Vicks, this is Paul and Chris,' she said with a grin. 'They lured me out here with the promise of a hidden stash of booze.'

'She's lying,' protested Paul. 'It was her banging on about "hidden booze" that lured us out here!'

Paul and Chris seemed cool and funny without being pompous and annoying and they were good-looking enough to make me want to join in with the conversation. I could tell straight away that Melissa was doing her best to try and impress Paul which was fine by me; Chris—tall and handsome, thoughtful without being morose—was more my type anyway.

Later, around three in the morning, with the party showing no signs of flagging, the four of us decided to leave and headed towards Chorlton Park for a change of scenery. We climbed over the gate and sat on the kids' swings, knocking back lukewarm Red Stripe that we'd liberated from a sink full of melted ice in the kitchen at the party, and for the next hour or so we put the world to rights with the kind of heated political debates that you can only have when you're drunk and in your early twenties. Eventually we calmed down and started talking about the future.

'So, where do you see yourself in ten years' time?' asked Paul, directing his question at Melissa.

Melissa shrugged. 'Why do you ask?'

'Curiosity.'

Melissa thought the question over. 'Ten years from now I'll be . . .' she paused '. . . what? Thirty-three? That sounds like a lifetime away.'

'So what will you be doing "a lifetime" from now?' prompted Paul.

Melissa took a swig from the can in her hand. 'Okay, okay. Ten years from now I'd like to be . . . right here.'

'What, in Chorlton Park?'

'No, in Chorlton. By then I'll have gone back to university and finished a degree in something more interesting than Business and Economics like—I don't know—Art History. I always loved the academic part of my Art 'A' level more than the sitting around drawing stuff bits. I like knowing the stories behind paintings, the reasons why artists create the things they do.'

'So what would you be doing for a job?'

'I don't know. Something worthwhile I hope. Maybe something for a charity. And I'd be living in one of those sweet little terraces on Beech Road.'

'On your own?'

Melissa laughed. 'No, with my bloke.'

'And what's he like, this bloke?'

'He's nice and caring and funny. Likes animals and is

good to his mother.' She paused, then added: 'And he never ever, ever forgets my birthday.'

'Sounds like a made-up bloke to me,' said Paul, grinning at Chris.

'Nope,' replied Melissa. 'He's out there somewhere. And do you know what? One day I'll find him.'

The interesting thing was that although two relationships started at that party, they both went in completely different directions. Chris and I were rock solid from day one, moving in together after nine months and then getting married a few years later, but Melissa and Paul's relationship was always volatile. In the early days it seemed like every other week they would have one kind of argument or another, only to make up by the end of the night. Thankfully, after a year or two they appeared to calm down and for a long while things were good between them. I remember them laughing. I remember them being happy. I can even remember thinking to myself when they moved in together (partly out of love but mostly out of convenience) that this was it. They would settle down into the kind of comfortable groove that Chris and I were already in. Finally there would be no more fights, no more arguments, and no more conflict. I even thought that one day the two of them might actually get married and have kids. And like I said, for a long while it really did look as though things were working out for them.

Quite when they began to fall apart I was never really sure, but Melissa always claimed that it was somewhere around the time that Paul turned thirty. It started with small rows about nothing, which eventually progressed into bigger rows about everything. Paul would get annoyed at Melissa and then Melissa would get annoyed right back, thereby guaranteeing that every petty quibble ended in full-scale war. As bad as it was though I never guessed that Paul would want to get out of the relationship: by this time—to me at least—they came as a pair. You never got one without the other. And I found that comforting because that was exactly how things would always be with Chris and me.

I assumed the arguments were just a 'phase' or a 'bad patch' or 'one of those things' that all couples go through, only to come out of the other side stronger. I'd lost count of the times when friends of ours would appear to be on the verge of splitting up, only to announce a few weeks later that they were getting married or having kids or leaving their jobs to go travelling for a year. I didn't realise that Paul was so genuinely unhappy with the way things were between him and Melissa. And certainly not that he was capable of speeding up the demise of their relationship with a catalyst so lazily constructed that to this day I still find it hard to forgive him.

Out one night with Chris and Chris's brother Cooper and some other mates, Paul got talking to a girl in a club and went home with her. He didn't know that one of the girl's housemates, Sara, was a friend of our friend Laura, and although Paul hadn't recognised her when he'd chatted to her next morning as she left to go to work, she had recognised him and told Laura everything. Laura then checked the story with Cooper (who lied) forcing her to ask me to check the story with Chris (who told a different lie) which in turn validated the story enough for Laura and me to present our evidence directly to Melissa.

Melissa was devastated; it really cut her to the bone. She challenged Paul the moment he got in from work and the second he confirmed it, she packed her bags and came to stay with me and Chris.

For most people that would have been the end of the story, but not Melissa. Because she was still in love with Paul, she just couldn't seem to let go. Paul must have felt the same, because about six weeks after the split Melissa told me that she had had a long talk with Paul and, despite all that had happened, they were going to try to be friends. I assumed that this was just her way of saying that they would carry on sleeping together but it wasn't that at all. She really did want them to be friends and nothing more. And even though in the months that were to follow she stayed over at his house on numerous occasions, sometimes even sharing the same bed, nothing ever happened between them. According to Melissa all they ever did was talk with an honesty and openness that they had never been able to achieve when they had been together. With the single-mindedness of a scientist on the verge of making a medical breakthrough, Melissa made it her mission to discover why things hadn't worked between them. Taking Paul's confessions and half-mumbled revelations, she did her best to make sense of them all and then, not far off the first anniversary of when things had fallen apart, she made a pronouncement that seemed to take even her by surprise. She said to Paul: 'You think you don't want what other people want. You think that all you want is to be alone. But it's not true. The day will come when you'll be so sick of being alone that you won't know what to do. And when that happens, come and find me and we'll pick up right where we left off.'

When Melissa told me what she had said, I got so angry that I lost it completely and told her to her face how pathetic she was being letting Paul walk all over her. The last thing she should do was promise to hang around waiting for him to get his act together. I told her straight. Paul didn't deserve her. He wasn't going to miraculously turn into some kind of Prince Charming overnight. And if she was under the misguided notion that she was the woman who was going to fix whatever was broken inside Paul and make him want to settle down, then she was wrong. The best thing she could do was move on to someone else as soon as possible. Melissa got up, walked out and didn't speak to me for the best part of a month.

Billy:

It was just after seven, I was on the phone and my New Year's Eve was not off to a good start.

'So what are you up to tonight?'

'Gina and Danni have got me tickets for some club in town,' said Freya. 'Apparently it's going to be really good.'

'What sort of thing?'

'Don't know.'

'Dancey or indie?'

'Indie.'

'Which club?'

'I don't know.'

There was a long pause.

'What about you then?' she asked. 'Are you hitting the town with the gruesome twosome?'

She meant my housemates Seb and Brian.

'Yeah,' I lied.

'Anywhere good?'

'Some club in town.'

'Indie or dancey?'

'Dancey, I think.'

There was another long pause.

'Well, have a good New Year, yeah?' she said. 'I'll be thinking of you come midnight.'

This was far from true. Freya would not be thinking about me at all. She would be thinking about whichever tight-trouser wearing, big-haired, 'Look at me I'm in a band' loser she'd have selected as her next victim. 'And I'll be thinking of you too,' I replied, realising just how much I didn't want this call to end. 'Are you going to make any resolutions?'

'No,' said Freya firmly. 'I'm not into all that. You?'

'I'm making a few.'

'Like what?'

'You know, the usual.'

Freya briefly considering digging a little deeper before she finally said: 'Well good luck with all that then. And we'll catch up soon yeah? Go for a drink or something, yeah?'

'Definitely. Let's catch up soon.'

I put my phone down on the empty computer printer box that doubled as my bedside table, picked up the remote for my CD player, and pressed play. As 'A River Ain't Too Much To Love' filled my ears, I lay down on my bed, closed my eyes and wondered whether Bill Calhoun had ever had problems with 'the ladies' when he was twenty-four.

I'd never been entirely convinced that what I'd felt for Freya had been love (after all, how could it be real love if she didn't love me back?) but what I felt now was torture.

I first got to know her when she took a job at the Duke and Drake in Chorlton. At that time Brian, Seb and I virtually lived there, and we'd got to know most of the staff, so when I turned up one Saturday night and saw Freya standing behind the bar it sort of took me by surprise. She was absolutely amazing. She had shoulder-length black hair that, along with the way she dressed, made her look as if she had just stepped out of a time machine from 1963. She had that whole Bridget Bardot, sexy indie-chick thing going on and the most beautiful face I had ever seen.

I guessed that she was into music so over the course of a couple of conversations as I got my round in, I'd drop in the names of a few bands that I thought she might like and when those worked I dropped in a few more and then a few more. One night, after about a month of name-dropping bands like crazy, she mentioned that a band we'd both been raving about recently were playing at Night and Day and asked me if I fancied coming along. I couldn't believe it. A date. With Freya. This kind of luck was absolutely unheard of. I was completely over the moon.

Though we'd arranged to meet at Dry on Oldham Street at eight, Freya didn't turn up until minutes to nine.

'I'm really sorry I'm so late.'

'It's fine,' I replied.

'No, it's not, you see the thing is . . .' she started to get a bit tearful, '. . . I've just had a massive row with Justin.'

'Who's Justin?'

'My boyfriend.'

The news that she wasn't single knocked me sideways, even though it made perfect sense that a girl like Freya would have guys throwing themselves at her left, right, and centre.

On the way to Night and Day, Freya gave me a potted history of her and her boyfriend, right up to and including the fight that they had just had. I listened attentively and gave her advice, even though this guy sounded a lot like some of the idiots who had been on my course at university—all rock star poses and daft haircuts without a shred of personality between them.

At about ten o'clock, when the headline band came on stage, Freya suggested that we move towards the front, grabbed me by the hand and led me right to the front of the stage. And from the band's opening song to their closing encore she didn't let go of my hand once.

At the end of the night we filed out of the venue and headed to a fast-food place for curry and chips, which we ate sitting on a bench next to the bus stop before getting the 192 back to Withington. As we got out to go our separate ways, she told me she'd had a great time and that she would call me in the morning. The call never came.

The next time I saw her was about a week after the gig, when I turned up at the Drake with Seb and Brian to see her behind the bar.

'I'm sorry,' she said. 'I didn't call you did I? It's just that . . . well . . . Justin and I sort of got back together.'

'Great,' I replied, with as much enthusiasm as I could muster. 'I'm really, really pleased for you.'

'Well, good because it was all down to you.'

'To me?'

'I followed your advice to the letter and before I knew it we were having this massive heart-to-heart and we realised that we were both really wary of getting hurt, that's all. Ever since that night things have been just perfect.'

It didn't last. Like most devastatingly pretty girls, Freya had spectacularly bad taste in men and soon Justin was superceded by a whole litany of posers who could smell her lack of self-esteem and father-issues from a mile away. And although the names changed (Oscar, Tom, Jamie and Lucien) the pattern always remained the same. They'd fancy her, she'd fancy them; they'd get off together at some crappy indie club in town, then a few weeks later she'd find them snogging some other girl; or she'd find out they already had a girlfriend; or they would simply stop calling. Upset and distraught, she would turn to me for comfort and support. And while I'd be hugging her and telling her how it'd all be all right in the end, she'd be telling me how special I was and how different I was from the other guys. And all the time I'd be thinking 'If I can just hang on a little longer, maybe she'll finally see just how mad about her I really am.'

So anyway, to cut a long story short, a few nights before Christmas Eve, following the demise of yet another short-lived hook-up with a skinny, scruffy, waste of skin and bone called Luke, Freya dropped round at mine to claim both consolation and a free bottle of wine. We joked about how love was a game for losers and made plans for a perfect New Year's Eve.

'How about I come to yours?' she said. 'We can order a takeaway.'

'And drink as much as our livers can take!' I added.

'And then when we're well and truly wrecked,' said Freya really getting into the rhythm of things, 'we can watch *Eternal Sunshine of the Spotless Mind* for the millionth time.'

At that particular moment we were the closest we had been, so I decided that six months of unrequited love was more than enough for anyone and attempted to convert a good-night embrace into something more. Honestly, I couldn't have misjudged the situation worse if I'd tried. The second my lips touched hers, Freya pulled away and was all 'I'm really flattered Billy, but I don't really see you like that', and I couldn't say a thing in reply because I was too busy willing the earth to open up and swallow me whole.

With five hours to go before midnight, I still had no idea what I was going to do with my New Year's Eve. I called Seb and Brian to see if there were any tickets left for the club night they were going to but apparently the whole thing had sold out months ago and tickets were now changing hands for ten times their face value. I didn't really fancy the idea of bankrupting myself just so that I didn't have to see the New Year in watching *Jools Holland* so I told them to have a good time and decided to put on more suitably melancholy music, turn off the lights, climb back into bed and allow myself the minor indulgence of feeling totally and utterly depressed. After a few minutes realising that I wasn't exactly being a man about all this, I got out of bed and called my older sister Nadine to find out what she was up to.

I chatted about life in general for a bit, to give her the illusion that I wasn't after anything (covering topics as diverse as our parents, the love life of my middle sister Amy, and Nadine's own impending thirty-fifth birthday) before jumping in with both feet and asking her the big question.

'So, sis, what are you up to tonight?'

'I'm off to a party.'

'You're nearly thirty-five!' I exclaimed. 'Do people your age still have parties?'

Nadine laughed. 'You're such a cheeky little sod sometimes.'

'But you love me for it don't you? So this party,' I continued. 'Is it local?'

'It's in Chorlton—my friends Ed and Sharon. Why do you ask?'

'It's just that . . . well . . . I'm sort of at a loose end and I was wondering if I could come with you.'

'You'll hate it,' said Nadine.

'I won't.'

'You will. I'm not saying it'll be a bunch of people standing around talking house prices and swapping notes from the Habitat catalogue but it's not far off, Billy. There won't be any drugs, raids by the police or young girls throwing up in the bathroom.'

Looking around my sad bedroom, my eyes came to rest on the portable TV sitting on top of the chest of drawers in the corner. *Jools Holland* could wait. A boring party full of boring people my sister's age it might be, but at least it was somewhere to go.

'It sounds perfect,' I replied. 'Give me ten minutes to sort myself out and I'll be ready.'

Melissa:

I arrived at the Old Grey just after eight. The pub—a favourite with the older crowd in Chorlton—was packed out like it would be just before last orders on a Saturday night. Vicky and Laura were sitting at a table near the jukebox, hemmed in on all sides by large groups of what Helena liked to call 'People like us' but which could have more accurately been labelled 'Slightly worn at the edges, *Big Issue*-buying, left-leaning, thirtysomething graduates who still feel like they're still students even if they aren't.' I eventually managed to find an empty stool, and made my way over to join Vicky and Laura.

'So where are the boys?' I asked.

'At the bar,' replied Laura. 'Although they seem to be taking forever about it.'

'And still no word of Paul and Hannah?'

Vicky shook her head. 'Not yet but I'm sure he'll be here sometime soon.'

It must have been obvious that I couldn't work out whether I was relieved or not, because Laura reached across the table and touched my hand. 'What do you want to drink, babe?'

'I'm fine for the minute,' I replied. 'Maybe I'll get one a bit later.'

'Don't be silly. Getting drinks is what boys do best.' She pulled out her mobile and dialled. 'Coop it's me. Melissa's here now, can you get her a drink?'

Cooper and Chris, patiently waiting to be served, smiled and waved at us.

'What are you drinking?'

'I'll have a Becks, if that's all right?'

Laura rolled her eyes as though my politeness was trying her patience. 'Melissa wants a bottle of Becks and a packet of prawn cocktail crisps and be quick about it!'

I poked Laura in the elbow. 'You tell him right now that I don't want any crisps, least of all prawn cocktail.'

'You might not, but I certainly do. I'm starving.'

Vicky looked perplexed. 'I thought you were on that Courtney Cox diet? Are prawn cocktail crisps part of the bargain?'

'Tomorrow,' grinned Laura. 'The diet starts tomorrow.'

Laura and I had been friends for as long as she had been going out with Cooper, which was roughly six years. Cooper had met her when he first moved to Manchester after splitting up with his girlfriend. I hadn't been too sure about Laura at first, she seemed much more of a 'boy's girl' than a 'girl's girl,' thriving on any male attention that was available. And although she'd probably be the first to admit that this was true, she was also a lot of other things besides and over time these made me warm to her. For starters she could be really funny, which I considered to be a good sign as beautiful people like Laura rarely bother cultivating a sense of humour. She was also burdened with more than her fair share of insecurities (she hated her nose, was a borderline bulimic through her teenage years and constantly put herself down for not being smart enough). Once I discovered what I considered to be her human side, I found it much easier to like her and with the minimum of adjustment, space was made in the tight bond that existed between Vicky and me to include Laura in our gang.

While we waited for our drinks we began exchanging stories about our various days.

'Well the highlight of my day,' Vicky began, 'was watching Chris trying to teach William how to fly the kite we got for him for Christmas. It would've been hilarious if it hadn't been so cold. Chris was running around the park like a demon trying to get the thing in the air and William kept asking if it was time to go home because he was freezing to death.'

'Well, given the fact that I only got out of bed about four hours ago,' began Laura, 'I'm guessing this is probably the highlight of my day.'

Vicky was incredulous. 'You only got out of bed four hours ago?'

Laura nodded sheepishly. 'I went out with a few of my old work friends from the teaching staff at Albright High last night and it turned into a bit of a late one and I didn't get in until three.'

'How about you, Mel?' asked Vicky. 'What have you been up to today?'

'Nothing much,' I sighed. 'I read about ten pages of that Monica Ali book that you lent me, watched a double episode of *Deal or No Deal* and finished off the entire top layer of the selection of chocolate biscuits that my evil stick-thin sister gave me for Christmas. Not exactly the most fruitful of days but I'm not complaining.'

Vicky grinned. 'I'd kill to spend the afternoon watching Noel Edmonds and eating biscuits.'

'You're welcome to my life anytime you want it,' I replied. 'Really, just say the word and it's yours. You have my life and I'll move into yours and raise William as my own.'

'If you're going to be me then you do realise you'll have to sleep with Chris?'

I pulled a face. 'Ours would be a chaste marriage.'

'So anyway,' said Laura, 'moving on from that distasteful picture, how are we all feeling in general about the year ahead? Optimistic?'

'As you know,' I began, 'I hate New Year's Eve and thinking about the future so it would be fair to say that I'm pretty pessimistic.'

Vicky smiled. 'I love the idea of being handed a clean slate every year and setting myself a whole new set of goals.'

'There speaks Wonder Woman. So what's your goal for this New Year then, Vick? Something involving those cook-books of yours? Maybe it's time you finally applied to *Ready Steady Cook*. You'd be ace on that.'

'Cheeky cow! No *Ready Steady Cook* for me.'

'Well then you should have another baby,' suggested Laura. 'You and Chris make great babies. It's a proven fact. William is quite possibly my favourite human being on the entire planet.'

'Well I'm afraid you're not his.' Vicky gave me a wink. Before we came out tonight it was Auntie Mel this and Auntie Mel that. I think he's got a massive crush on you, Mel.'

'Fine by me,' I replied. 'What is he, four? I'm more than willing to hang on another twenty-six years for the right one.'

'That is so wrong on about a million different levels,' protested Vicky.

'So, are you going to have another baby then?' Laura probed.

Vicky shook her head. 'I've only ever wanted one.'

I looked at Laura. 'Looks like you and Cooper will have to take up the slack, then.'

'Cooper would have kids at the drop of a hat,' said Laura despairingly. 'Your William's so much like a walking advert for procreation that I've lost count of the times Coop's dropped subtle-as-a-brick-hints like, "How great would it be to have one of those around the house?" and I'm like, "Are you insane? I can barely look after myself let alone another human being."'

'So you don't want kids then?' asked Vicky.

'There's too much I haven't done for me to even think about any of that. In fact if there's one thing I want to do this year it's go travelling. I want to see a bit more of the world, spend a bit of time in a place where it isn't always raining, live a little. Do you know what I mean?'

I nodded. 'You and Cooper should definitely do it.

Grown-up gap years are all the rage for the discerning thirty-something.'

'Tell that to my boyfriend. If it wasn't for the fact that he's making us save up a stupid deposit for a stupid house I'd do it in a heartbeat.'

Vicky sighed. 'You know you really shouldn't give him such a hard time. Cooper's just doing what Cooper does. He wants the best for you both.'

Laura shrugged and fingered the label of the beer bottle in front of her. 'I don't know, maybe he does. But why does he have to be so boring about it?'

'Look,' Vicky tried to lift the mood around the table, 'let's not get all depressed. It's New Year's Eve and we're all together so let's just enjoy ourselves.'

Chris:

It was just after nine by the time we left the Old Grey and made our way to Sharon and Ed's. On the way I tried Paul's mobile a couple of times but kept getting his voicemail. This was 100 per cent typical of Paul. He never returned people's calls if he could help it and when he turned up and you had a go at him, he'd just look at you like you were acting like some kind of girl making a big deal out of nothing and say: 'I'd let you know if I wasn't coming wouldn't I?'

Whilst hitting redial I thought about how long I had known Paul. We first met through mates of mates one summer night outside the Black Horse in the days before they knocked down Shambles Square and moved it over the road. I was in my second year of my law degree and I'd just finished my exams, so a whole bunch of us had been drinking on the benches outside the pub since late afternoon. Heading up to the bar to get a round in I'd ended up standing next to Paul. We had both drunk quite a bit by this point in the evening and out of nowhere Paul turned around and told me a joke about a nun and a polar bear that was so ridiculously puerile that even thinking about it now can put a smile on my face.

We got talking and he told me a bit about himself. He was in the second year of a Social Studies degree at MMU and though he was born in Telford he had moved around the country quite a bit with his parents before ending up back where he started at around the age of fifteen. That was pretty much it for biography, because after that all we talked about was football and motor-racing before the conversation as a whole disintegrated into the usual mix of music and films, clothes and trainers, in fact all the stuff employed by certain types of men to separate the wheat from the so-called chaff.

Despite us both proving our credentials to each other with talk of obscure Italian horror films, the back catalogue of the Stones and several shared sitcom favourites, we didn't have a great deal to do with each other after that night out, apart from the odd nod of the head or short conversation whenever we bumped into each other (usually either coming in or out of Piccadilly Records). It wasn't anything personal. I doubt either of us had given it any consideration, but I'm guessing if we had it would have been along the lines of if we were meant to be friends then it would happen whether or not we did anything about it.

A few months later, on an unseasonably mild afternoon at the beginning of our final term, we once again found ourselves sitting outside the Black Horse. But this time we somehow ended up making plans to go for a drink, and go and see bands and we somehow both followed through with these haphazard arrangements and gradually became mates.

I tried his number one last time. Sure enough it switched to his voicemail. Ending the call without leaving a message I returned my phone to my pocket and caught up with the others.

Melissa:
There were already quite a few people lingering outside Ed and Sharon's tiny two-bedroom terrace by the time we arrived. Some were congregating by the door saying hello to each other, while others were enjoying the first of many 'last' cigarettes before they resolved, once again, to give up forever at midnight. I recognised two of the smokers as Fraser and Helen, who I'd shared a house with in our early twenties. The boys claimed it was too cold to stand outside talking so they headed straight inside, taking Vicky and Laura with them. As I hadn't seen Fraser and Helen since they'd gone travelling over a year and half ago, I stood chatting for a while. It was good to see them and I was dying to hear their travelling stories; although they were a bit self-conscious at first, wary of coming across like the kinds of people who constantly evangelise about the wonders of travelling, they seemed so much happier with their lives in general and with each other specifically that it made me sort of hopeful about my own future too.

I left Fraser and Helen finishing their cigarettes outside and entered the house. The hallway was crammed wall to wall with party-goers. Even though I didn't know most of them, they all appeared to be the same vintage as me, which was comforting. At least if I got drunk and ended up dancing I would feel my peers' sympathy rather than their embarrassment.

In my search for Vicky and the others, I ended up bumping into an inordinate number of people I hadn't seen in ages. I once read a newspaper survey that each person in the UK knows at least 120 people. I remember thinking at the time that that seemed like a lot but standing here at this party maybe it wasn't such an outrageous figure after all.

I eventually found Vicky and Laura talking to Sharon and a group of her friends I'd never met before. They all seemed nice enough and encouraged me to join in the conversation, but conscious of the fact that I hadn't got a drink in my hands and that my plan for the evening was to drink myself stupid, I made an excuse and made my way to the kitchen.

Ed and Sharon's kitchen was, like the rest of the house, packed with people but eventually I spotted all the booze lined up on the kitchen counter next to the sink. I'd asked Vicky to give Sharon and Ed my contribution to the party—a bottle of Sancerre that had cost me nearly a tenner—when we first arrived and I was dying to try it. Scanning the various bottles and cans, I eventually found it, empty and minus its cork, poking out of a green recycling box on the floor at my feet. Resigning myself to the situation I selected a sophisticated looking oak-aged Chardonnay with a posh label as compensation, even though there was an open bottle of Sainsbury's own label right in front of me.

Just as I was cringing at how much I was letting myself down by three-quarter filling a plastic pint glass (I couldn't find any others) with wine that I had no proper claim on, a male voice said: 'All right, fella, what are you looking so guilty about?'

I spun around, almost spilling the wine all over me, only to find Chris and Cooper grinning like idiots. 'Okay, okay,' I replied. 'You caught me in the act. Someone drank the whole of that bottle of wine I brought with me. It wasn't like I was going to keep it to myself but I didn't even get a sip.'

'So now you're wreaking your revenge by searching out the most expensive bottle you can find?' 'What are you? Some kind of student waster?'

'You're such a git to me sometimes.'

Chris put his arm around me. 'You know I only do it because I love you.'

Chris and Cooper were more like older brothers than friends. The pair of them often teased me mercilessly (their jokes focusing mainly on the notion that I was a bit flaky, lack ambition and hopeless with men), but the flipside of this abuse is that as their honorary little sister it is their duty to protect me. I'd lost count of the times that one or other of them had walked me home in the rain, picked me up from the airport, put up shelves in my bedroom, even sorted out dodgy guys giving me hassle.

Obviously I'd known Chris longer than Cooper. In fact it was hard to remember there was ever a time that Chris was apart from the unit I'd come to know and love as 'Chris and Vicky.' He was the complete opposite of Paul. Whereas life with Paul was like being on a rollercoaster with highs that thrilled every nerve ending in your body and lows that took you to the very depth of despair, Chris was a lot more even and steady. You always knew exactly where you stood with him and how he would react in any given situation. He seemed to give off this aura of authority—so much so that whenever any of us had a real world problem, like when I was being hassled by a debt collection agency over an unpaid mobile phone bill, I didn't take my problem to Paul, or Cooper, I took it straight to Chris, and he sorted the whole thing out in a few phone calls.

Chris picked up a bottle of champagne from behind my back and held it aloft. 'Still,' he said, giving me a wink, 'if you're going to do this revenge thing at all, at least do it properly.'

'You can't do that!' Chris pulled off the foil and began removing the twisty metal surrounding from the cork. 'What if Ed and Sharon are saving it for midnight?'

'It's okay, Mel,' Cooper chipped in. 'No need to get your knickers all bunched up, mate. Laura and I brought it with us. We've had it sitting in our fridge since last summer, but you can consider it your belated Christmas present if you like.'

Before I could protest Chris popped the cork. Everyone in the kitchen looked at us with disdain, as though we were acting like a bunch of yobs, which I suppose in a way we were.

Chris took a swig then handed the bottle to me. 'Happy new year, Mel.'

'I really shouldn't be doing this, you two are always leading me into bad ways.'

Chris laughed. 'Us? Never.'

I took another swig. 'So, are either of you going to make any New Year's resolutions?'

Chris shook his head. 'Don't believe in them. I mean, what's the point?'

'They're only supposed to be a bit of fun.'

Chris didn't look convinced. 'Okay, so what's yours?'

'I've got a list as long as my arm: I'm taking up jogging, I'm going to start cycling into uni, I'm going to cut down on takeaways and read more books, watch less TV and . . . do you want me to carry on?'

Chris did a mock cringe. 'Please don't.'

I turned to Cooper. 'What about you? Unlike your useless brother here I know you must have a few.'

'No resolutions as such, just some plans.'

'Like what?'

'To buy a house. I'm sick of renting. It's money down the drain. Laura and I should have enough saved by the middle of the year for a deposit as long as house prices don't carry on going through the roof.'

I thought about Laura's comments back at the Old Oak. Knowing both of them as well as I did, I sensed trouble on the horizon but said nothing.

'Still,' I replied, 'getting a house of your own isn't the be all and end all, is it?'

'I think you're making Mel feel bad about the fact that she's wasting valuable time playing at being a student again rather than getting on the property ladder,' Chris teased.

I punched him on the shoulder as hard as I could. 'It's unbelievable how much of a tosser you can be sometimes.'

'Just ignore him, he's not worth the effort.' Cooper looked at me sheepishly. 'I suppose you're right: getting a house isn't the be all and end all but it's a step forward isn't it? And that's all I want really, a couple of steps forward.'

There was something about the look on his face, like a child desperately trying to hide a secret, that made me curious.

'What other "steps forward" are you thinking about?'

Cooper smiled enigmatically.

'You're not . . .?'

'What?'

'Going to ask Laura to marry you, are you?'

'Yeah, right. Do I look like a mug?'

'What do you mean? You and Laura make a brilliant couple. Plus, it's been ages since I've been to a good wedding where I actually cared about the couple getting hitched. You should do it.'

Cooper rolled his eyes. 'Well, much as I'd like to help you out by throwing a good party, Mel, I'm afraid that won't be happening any time soon. But I'll be sure to let you know if I do change my mind, okay?'

I looked at Chris in the hope that he might back me up but he just shrugged and offered me the champagne bottle again. I took a swig then set it down on the counter, glancing up at the clock on the wall. It was twenty minutes past eleven and there was still no sign of Paul and Hannah.

'So where's his Lordship then?' I asked, directing the question at both Chris and Cooper.

'Haven't heard from him.'

'But he is still coming isn't he?'

Chris shrugged. 'That's what he told me but you know what he's like, your guess is as good as mine.'

'Maybe Hannah didn't fancy the idea of spending the biggest night of the year with a bunch of her boyfriend's friends who don't really like her,' suggested Cooper. 'I don't think I'd be here if I was her. After all, she's not you, is she?'

'Cheers for the solidarity Coop, but she's Paul's girlfriend so we should be nice to her. He's always been nice to the guys I've seen in the past.'

'Maybe to your face,' said Chris solemnly.

'What do you mean?'

Chris shook his head. 'Look, I'm saying nothing. But take it from me he's never been anywhere near as happy as he makes out when you're seeing someone.'

This didn't exactly make me feel any better.

'Doesn't matter anyway,' I replied. 'The truth is I like her, and I can definitely see what Paul sees in her.'

'Well that's hardly rocket science, she's very easy on the eye.'

'I mean above all that superficial stuff,' I replied. 'I was talking to her round at Chris and Vicky's and she was telling me about some of the stuff she's doing on her MA and I didn't have a clue what she was talking about. It was like she was speaking a different language. She's so clever it's frightening.'

Chris put an arm around my shoulder as though he was drawing me close to impart an important piece of wisdom. (One of the downsides of being Chris and Cooper's little sister was that every once in a while I had to endure their unsolicited advice.)

'Considering what a Hannah-fan you are,' observed Chris, 'I bet you'd have a face on you that could turn milk if she walked in with Paul right now.'

I pretended to look for the champagne but could feel myself starting to flush.

'Listen, Mel,' he continued. 'I know this might sound a bit harsh and for the life of me I don't mean it that way but seeing as we're about to begin a new year, why don't you do yourself a massive favour and just move on? Hanging on to Paul is doing you no good at all.'

I could feel tears pricking at the back of my eyes before Chris had even finished.

'If it was that easy, don't you think that I'd have done it by now?'

'Of course it is,' replied Chris oblivious of the look of disbelief on Cooper's face. 'You just have to want it badly enough, that's all. All I'm saying is that you and Paul are mates, and that's great, but I think that now he's finally moved on, maybe you should too.'

Chris:

I have no idea who had died and made me Minister of Home Truths, but whoever it was I really wished they hadn't bothered. Melissa looked absolutely crushed when I finished delivering my big piece of advice and all I could think was, why didn't I just keep my big mouth shut?

'Maybe you're right, maybe I am wasting my time here with Paul. Maybe I should just go home right now.'

I could tell that Melissa was absolutely serious about leaving and could already picture the scene Vicky would make when she found out it was my fault that her best friend was spending New Year's Eve on her own.

'You can't go, Mel. First off it's just wrong, second, you shouldn't listen to anything I've got to say because what do I know? And finally, if you go home early and Vicky finds out that it's because of me she will go insane.'

'She would, wouldn't she?' said Melissa, with the beginnings of a smile on her face. 'She'd make your life a misery for days.'

'Days? Try weeks.'

'Look, Chris, I know you mean well and that you're probably right about me and Paul, it's just . . . well, you know . . . some things are easier said than done. You can't really think I want to be like this. You can't think even for a minute that I enjoy waking up on my own only to end the day in bed alone, too. You have no idea how lucky you are having Vicky and William. No idea at all.'

'Look,' I replied. 'I really am sorry, mate. You just do what you've got to do and from now on I'll keep my mouth shut.'

'Okay, you're forgiven, but if you start with any of that "Melissa's a flaky Southern layabout stuff" again I will grass you up in a second.' She picked up her plastic cup of wine. 'Right boys, I'm off to find some proper people to talk to, okay?'

'No hard feelings, mate?'

'Of course not. We're fine. I'll see you later?'

'Yeah. Later.'

I watched Melissa leave the kitchen then turned to Cooper and sighed: 'It's not like it takes a genius to work out that Melissa doesn't want to hear the truth about her and Paul.'

'Certainly not tonight, of all nights,' replied Cooper. 'New Year's Eve always puts people in a weird frame of mind.'

I raised an eyebrow, relieved at the opportunity to talk about something else. 'Like you? What was all that stuff going on with your face when Mel was talking about you and Laura getting hitched? For a second I thought that you might be—'

'I am,' he replied.

'You are what?'

'Going to ask her. Not tonight. But this year, definitely.'

'You're joking?'

'No, I'm absolutely serious. I was thinking of asking her on her birthday in April. That way it'll give me enough time to save up for the ring without raiding our savings.'

'You do know you can't just get any old rubbish and

hope that she'll be so flattered that she won't notice it's gold-plated?'

Cooper grinned. 'That's why I'm planning to give it to her over a candlelit dinner.'

I picked up Melissa's bottle of champagne and took a swig. 'Well best of luck to you, bruv. I hope it all goes well when you do the deed.'

'Cheers,' replied Cooper taking the bottle from me. He took a swig and winced. 'Nope,' he said resignedly, 'still can't stand this stuff.'

Melissa:

Determined to think about something other than Paul, I ended up circulating the party on my own for about an hour, dipping in and out of conversations here and there. Most of the people I spoke to were friends I only met up with at the occasional party or summer barbecue. Most of them were settled now, coupled up with kids or tethered down by massive mortgages but there was a small yet resilient battalion who were still fighting the good fight like the last ten years hadn't happened. It was these in particular that I was always pleased to see. It was great to hear that Cathy and Brendan were still in bands, that Dean and Lewis were still actively pursuing their dream of becoming full-time artists and even that Alistair and Baxter were still running the same city centre indie club nights that they had been involved with when I'd first got to know them as a nineteen-year-old student. It felt good knowing that they were all getting on with their lives. It made me feel like I was part of something larger than myself.

In the middle of a conversation with Carl and Louisa, whose big news was that Louisa was pregnant, I realised that I needed another drink to keep me going. I made my excuses and tried to make my way out of the room but every few steps someone emerged from the wings with an air kiss and a desperate need to catch up. Manjeet and Aaron were moving down to London, Joel and Rowena had just bought a house over in Withington and Tina (formerly of Tina and Alan and currently of Tina and Susan) had left teaching and was now trying to write a novel. Beginning to feel like I was suffering from information overload, I managed to reach the door to the hallway but before I could complete my exit there was a tap on my shoulder. Standing in front of me was a tall young-looking guy wearing a pinstriped jacket with a green T-shirt with yellow writing on it. I didn't recognise him, but the way he was looking at me, convinced me that I must have met him before at some long forgotten party. I was about to kiss him on the cheek and ask him how he was doing before politely making my excuses when he did something really odd. Raising his foot in the air so that I could see that he was wearing brick red baseball boots just like my own, he said: 'Snap.'

Billy:
It had taken me over two hours, three cans of Carlsberg, and all the courage I possessed in order to approach the girl in the red Converse.

I'd spotted her the moment she entered the living room sometime after nine. I'd been bored out of my mind making small talk with my sister's mates when boom, there she was. I thought she was amazing pretty much straight away, different from the other women at the party. Prettier. More thoughtful. Older than me but without making me feel like it would require a huge leap of the imagination to picture us together. That, along with the style of her hair, the cardigan, her frayed jeans and the fact that she seemed the total opposite of Freya, made me think that if I was going to pull at this party then this girl would be it.

Normally I would never have dreamed of trying to chat up a girl like that in a million years, especially with a line that boiled down to "Wow, look at us, we're wearing the same footwear." And what made it worse of course was the fact that it was so obviously just a cheesy chat-up line. I might have been better off just saying: "Do you think that at some point this evening you might be drunk enough to consider getting off with me, a complete stranger?" At least then I might have gained a few points for sheer brazenness.

Still, since the girl in the Converse was unknown to my sister and her friends (I'd already checked out that avenue) I knew that if I was ever going to have a hope of talking to her I had no choice but to try something on my own. So looking over at the three remaining cans of Carlsberg I'd brought with me and placed on the mantel, I decided that if Dutch courage was what I needed to make this work then Dutch courage it would be. I pulled one can out of its plastic carrier, opened it and gave myself the deadline of eleven o'clock to make my move.

Melissa:

You can imagine how weird this was. There I was, trying to escape the room, when this guy just appears from nowhere, taps me on the shoulder and says: 'Snap.'

I was confused to say the least.

I decided to humour him. 'Great minds, eh?'

'I was thinking the same thing,' he replied.

I played for time and gestured to his chest with my empty plastic cup. 'What does your T-shirt say?'

He pulled his jacket open so I could read the words of his t-shirt—a cryptic fake film review that said: 'An athlete, a criminal, a brain, a princess and a basketcase bond in detention at a Chicago High School (1985).'

'*The Breakfast Club*,' I said, grinning. 'I love that film.'

'Me too,' he replied. 'What's your favourite bit?'

'I haven't seen it in ages. How about you?'

'The bit when they're all dancing—and pretty much any scene with Ally Sheedy in it.'

'So you're a Sheedy man?'

'All the way.'

I remembered how at school you could always divide boys into the ones who considered themselves to be tortured poets (and therefore fancied Ally Sheedy) and the boys who were just boys (and therefore fancied Molly Ringwald). I had to smile at the thought that this guy in front of me fancied himself as a tortured poet.

'This is really awful of me,' I said after a few moments, 'but I seem to have completely forgotten your name.'

'That's because we've never met before,' he said looking slightly uncomfortable. 'Can I be straight with you? I only came over because . . . well . . . you seem nice and it's New Year's Eve . . . and we'll all be singing 'Auld Lang Syne' in a bit . . . so I just thought I'd come over and say hello.' He offered me his hand and was about to tell me his name when he stopped and looked over my shoulder. Instinctively I turned around too and there, standing right behind me, was Paul. And Hannah was nowhere to be seen.

Billy:

Even without knowing anything about either of them I could tell straight away that these two had history. The second Melissa saw Paul she lit up like a switch had been flipped. Freya was the only person who could make me feel the way this girl was feeling.

'We all thought you weren't coming,' said Melissa.

'I'm just a bit late, that's all,' he replied.

Melissa bit her lip. 'No Hannah?'

'No, she . . . er . . . she couldn't make it.'

Melissa looked concerned. 'Nothing wrong is there?'

'No, nothing's wrong,' replied Paul. 'She's fine.' He paused. 'So what have I missed?'

'Nothing much really, Helena wants to go travelling and Cooper wants to save up for a deposit for a house and it's all going to end in disasters; and Chris and Vicky are well, you know . . . *Chris and Vicky* and I . . . I . . .'

I could tell that Melissa had just recalled the fact that prior to Paul's arrival she had actually been in the middle of a conversation with me and now I was just dangling, like some kind of spare part, wishing one of them would put me out of my misery.

Melissa looked at me apologetically.

'Paul this is . . .'

'Billy,' I replied. 'My name's Billy.'

'That's it, Billy,' said Melissa. 'This is Billy. And Billy, this is Paul. He and I are old friends.'

'Very old friends,' added Paul. 'How long has it been? Ten or eleven years?'

'Twelve,' replied Melissa. 'Twelve long years.'

Melissa:
Half past midnight. Thirty minutes into a brand new year. And Paul and I—having shouted, cheered and done the 'Auld Lang Syne' thing with everyone else at midnight—were in Ed and Sharon's back garden sitting on their damp patio furniture with a freshly purloined bottle of wine, watching a series of fireworks explode in the night sky. I could feel the damp of the table soaking right through my jeans to my underwear but I didn't care. There was something different about Paul tonight. I could sense it.

'Genius idea of yours,' I said, as yet another firework popped and sparkled in the sky. 'Leave the comfort of a nice warm house and sit outside in the rain.'

Paul shrugged. 'You could've said no.'

'And miss out on all this? Never.'

Paul took a sip of wine and handed the bottle to me. I put it to my lips, took a long, deep swig and swallowed. It felt good to drink wine like this. An instant reminder of the days when finer graces genuinely didn't matter.

'I haven't drunk straight from the bottle since the year we all went to Glastonbury. And for some reason I've done it twice tonight.'

'I remember that year at Glastonbury,' he said raising a small nostalgic smile. 'That was the year we bought those bottles of home-made wine from that hippie guy near the main stage and Cooper refused to drink it in case it was laced with weed killer. Do you remember? Like a hippie hasn't got better things to do than poison a bunch of middle-class layabouts.'

'I remember the hippie . . . and I sort of remember handing him the cash but other than pushing the cork into the bottle with my keys, I don't remember much about that night at all.' I paused. 'Still, somehow I just get a sense that it might well have been one of the best nights of my life.'

'Easily up there in the top ten.'

I took another swig and glanced at Paul. He looked thoughtful and pensive.

'So, are you going to tell me what's going on?'

'What do you want to know?'

'Well, where's Hannah for starters?'

'I'm guessing she's at home. I don't know for sure. We split up just before Christmas.'

There it was. Paul and Hannah had split up. It didn't seem to make any sense, given how happy they had been last time I had seen them together—all loved up and fawning over each other.

'How did she take it?' I asked carefully.

'How do you know it was me?'

'Come on, Paul,' 'this is me you're talking to.'

'She'll be fine,' he said obliquely. 'It wasn't like I was the love of her life.'

'And you'd know that how?'

'You think I was?'

I shook my head. 'I doubt you'll ever be the love of anyone's life. It would be tantamount to making a public admission that you didn't really have much of a life to begin with. I have to admit I'm surprised though. I would've put money on you and Hannah going the distance.'

'Even though she was so young?'

'She was twenty-three. That's not so young.'

'Do you think?'

I sighed. 'It looks like it was more your problem than hers.'

Paul pulled at the label on the wine, eventually tearing off a small strip. 'I wasn't right for her. And I think she knew it.'

'Ah, so it was Hannah's fault you split up?' I replied. 'You were actually doing her dirty work for her? Come on, surely not even you believe that?'

Paul didn't reply and I didn't say anything to ease the tension.

Paul proceeded to tap his left foot in time to some imaginary soundtrack in his head, which made me want to sit as still as I could just to be awkward. It was only when Ed and Sharon's back door opened, spilling light and music into the garden, that we both jolted back to life and only relaxed when we saw that it was Vicky.

'Everything okay?' she called out.

'Yeah we're all good,' replied Paul.

'I'm just letting you know that Chris and I will probably be getting off in a minute.'

'We'll be in soon,' I replied. 'Don't go without saying goodbye, okay?'

Neither of us spoke as Vicky closed the door, plunging us both back into the darkness and silence. Paul coughed nervously. 'Do you know Chris and Vicky will have been married ten years this coming year? A kid. A proper home. A proper life. All in ten years.'

'Does that make you feel a bit weird?'

'Not really. I suppose it's just got me thinking—you know—about wasted time.'

I put on a rubbish American accent in the hope of lightening the mood and said: 'You're preaching to the choir.'

Paul smiled and I went to take another swig of the wine but misjudged the manoeuvre, missed my mouth altogether and spilled some down my chin. I wiped my face with the sleeve of my cardigan and looked over at Paul to see if he'd seen. He was watching me with an odd look in his eyes.

'Have I still got wine on my face?' I asked, wiping around my mouth.

Paul shook his head.

'Then what?'

'You wouldn't believe me if I told you.'

'Try me.'

He stood up, turned to face me and held my hands. 'You think you don't want what other people want,' he began. 'You think that all you want is to be alone. But it's not true. The day will come when you'll be so sick of being alone that you won't know what to do. And when it happens, come and find me and we'll pick up right where we left off.'

'Do you think that's funny?' Pulled my hands away from him. 'Is that what you think? That I'm some kind of pathetic joke?'

'Of course not Mel,' he said urgently. 'If you would just listen to me for a second I'm trying to tell you that you were right.' He grabbed hold of my hands again. 'You asked me earlier why I'd split up with Hannah and here's your answer: I split up with Hannah because of you. I did feel for Hannah, it's true. I liked her a lot. But the thing I couldn't escape was that she wasn't you.'

'I don't understand,' I replied. 'I don't understand what you're saying.'

'Well understand this,' he said kissing me as a firework roared up into the sky and exploded, filling the air with a rainbow of tiny stars. 'Understand that right here and now I'm asking you to pick up right where we left off.'